THE List

THE List

a novel

Finding Love Was the Last Thing on Her List

Melanie Jacobson

Covenant Communications, Inc.

Cover image: *Beach Vacation* © arekmalang, courtesy of iStockphoto.com.

Cover design copyright © 2011 by Covenant Communications, Inc.

Published by Covenant Communications, Inc.
American Fork, Utah

Printed in the United States of America
First Printing: March 2011

17 16 15 14 13 12   10 9 8 7 6 5 4 3

ISBN-13: 978-1-60861-051-8

For Kenny,
My dream come true

ACKNOWLEDGMENTS

WRITING, LIKE READING, IS NO fun without companions to share the journey that every book takes you on. I found myself in the best company on this journey as friends and loved ones cheered me on. My husband, Kenny, was again the biggest fan of nightly story time, revelling in the plot twists that each day brought. He also proved to be a fabulous surfing consultant. Amy Lou Bennett and Jen Schumann were honest and insightful critics. Becca Wilhite and Susan Auten were generous with their time and praise in reading my manuscript through, and once again, I found the opinions and feedback of my critique partners Aubrey Mace and Sue Marchant to be invaluable. I owe a special thank you to Josi Kilpack, who spent far more time and effort than she needed to in the midst of her own deadlines to offer suggestions and counsel that strengthened not only my plot points but me as a writer.

I also owe a thank you to the family, both immediate and extended, who have supported me and encouraged me, and to my children, who let me carve out a little time each day to visit my imagination.

Chapter 1

I NEEDED MATT GIBSON IN a bad way.

He stood before me in sun-bleached surfer glory, the solution to all my problems. Too bad he was at the center of the singles ward linger longer hive, surrounded by a half dozen girls vying for queen bee status. Stifling a sigh, I began calculating the odds of enlisting Matt as my personal surf coach this summer. Rumor had it he had taken on his five-student limit already.

Everyone wanted lessons from Matt Gibson, either for themselves or their kids, and they paid a premium to get him. I hoped to get some instruction for the bargain price of my company and offbeat sense of humor. If I didn't learn to surf this summer I might never get the chance again, not to mention that The List would be all screwed up.

My cousin Celia was watching him too. "Um, Ashley? What are you going to do if you can't talk him into it?" she asked.

"I'll convince him," I said.

"Right. But if you don't . . ."

"I will. It's on The List," I reminded her.

Celia didn't roll her eyes, although I could tell she wanted to. I'd probably even let her get away with outright mockery since she was cool enough to share her bedroom with me for the summer while I crossed "learn to surf" off my list of twenty-five things to do before I got married—or died, if it took too long.

The late August start date for my grad program at BYU loomed in front of me, a dark vacuum of a deadline sucking up all my future fun. I needed to knock out the next five items on The List fast before I drowned in the book stacks of the campus library, drained dry by research and devoid of the will to live, much less finish off a list of adventures. That's why Matt Gibson was so essential to item thirteen: learn to surf. Two weeks in Huntington Beach and I still couldn't stand on my board without falling. And that's when it was on the sand.

Okay, that's an overstatement. But not by much. My current teacher, Celia's older brother Dave, just returned from a mission to Bulgaria, and he had two years of his own surfing to catch up on. If the waves were good, he headed out without me—his hopeless surfing neophyte of a cousin—in tow. If the waves were mushy, he'd try to squeeze my lessons in around his schedule at the Beach Sport Warehouse, but bad waves aren't any better for beginners than they are for veterans.

I needed the sensei of surf, the Obi-wan Kenobi of boards, the . . . oh, whatever. I needed Matt Gibson.

The question was how to get him.

I studied the situation with a critical eye. Matt topped the Beachside singles ward hierarchy with the guys because he could shred on the waves, and with the girls because . . . well, he's hot. Even by Beachside standards. My three Sundays in the ward had been long enough to determine a few key facts: people in Orange County, California, are largely blond, tan, and even more attractive than the glut of TV shows based here make them out to be. The very best-looking of them litter the halls of LDS chapels like life-size Abercrombie & Fitch posters. Except with more clothes on.

The three girls in Matt's immediate orbit were no exception. Dressed in cute cotton summer dresses, they stood with their perfectly manicured toes peeking out of trendy sandals and their bright hair shining even in the unflattering fluorescent light of the cultural hall. A polite smile flashed over Matt's face, revealing his even white teeth as he listened to their chatter.

"He's so hot," Celia sighed.

"Not the point," I reminded her, waving a hand in front of her face to snap her out of her mini-trance. "Focus."

I surveyed the linger-longer ebb and flow for another moment. The activities committee had set out popsicles for everyone to snack on while flirting—er, visiting. The tropical flavors came in neon hues that turned more than a few tongues green or orange. Matt passed on the popsicles, standing instead with his hands in his pockets and rocking comfortably back on his heels as he listened to his entourage of fresh-scrubbed femme fatales.

They were no doubt cute, but growing up in Utah, the land of countless Scandinavian descendants, had prepared me well for competing with blondes. While I admired their pale, shiny locks, I learned long ago to embrace my sister Leila's beauty advice: "We look stupid as blondes, so don't bother. Sun-In is not your friend. Work with what you've got. And by that, I mean *work* it." Which is how I'd learned to see my loose chestnut curls as an asset and to realize brown eyes are only boring if they're the wrong shade of brown. My sisters and I all have a shade that's gold-flecked. Artfully wielded mascara and plum eyeliner does wonders to make them pop. And Barrett girls learned early on to bat their lashes with the best of them.

However, I needed a different tactic here. Matt already had a flock of conquests lash-batting like mad. Even with my darker, curly mane to differentiate me, I was going to need a little something extra. I looked past him to the refreshments and back again, a plan blossoming in my mind.

"I need to get a popsicle," I said to Celia.

"You said you weren't hungry."

"I don't need to eat it. I just need to get it." My small head nod clued her into the fact that a trip to the table would take us directly through Matt's path.

Understanding dawned. "Oh, I get it. You'll walk past Ma—"

An elbow in the ribs silenced her.

"This will work if I time it right," I said. I watched Derek, a scruffy but cute beach-bum type, head to the table. I had figured out during last week's ice cream sandwich linger longer that Matt usually hid behind Derek when he got tired of girls. They would devolve into highly technical surf conversations that discouraged all but the most hard-core surfers from joining in.

I wandered over to where Derek stood pawing through the open cardboard box looking for the right flavor. When he noticed me waiting, he offered a sheepish grin.

"Sorry," he said. "I was trying to find a lime one." He offered me the box so I could take a turn.

"I'm not in a rush," I smiled. "Can you snag a red one if you see it in there?"

"Sure," he said, staring for a second longer than he needed to before redirecting his attention to his flavor hunt. A moment later, he waved a popsicle at me.

"It's red!" he announced, which kind of went without saying, but I accepted it with another smile. If I was going to dye my tongue with artificial food coloring in the service of The List, I was at least angling for a color that might occur in nature. I eyed the bright red popsicle. Maybe.

"You're new, right?" Derek asked, pulling a green one out and wrangling the plastic wrapper off.

"Yeah. I was here last Sunday too," I said.

"So are you from around here or just visiting?"

It was a common question in a ward that regularly quadrupled in the summer.

"Both, I guess. I'll be in HB all summer, but then I go back to school," I answered. As we talked, I angled my body to keep Matt in my peripheral vision. I listened to Derek's chitchat about a barbecue later in the afternoon and felt a small sense of satisfaction when I saw Matt break away from his entourage with a smile and head to Derek. And me, by default.

He nodded at me with a slight air of distraction before turning to Derek, who offered him a fist bump.

"Maxed out on chicks, yeah?" Derek asked with a smirk.

Matt flushed slightly but dipped his head to indicate that Derek had nailed it. I fought a smile at his obvious relief over escaping his admirers, which caught his attention.

"Sorry," Matt said. "Nothing personal."

"No worries," I answered. "Besides, how could it be? You don't even know me."

"Oh yeah," Derek interjected. "I didn't get your name. It's . . ."

"Ashley," I said.

"Ashley, nice to meet you." Derek turned to Matt again and explained, "We were just talking about how she's in town for the summer and I thought I ought to do the neighborly thing and invite her over for our shindig later."

"Sure," Matt shrugged, looking around the room. His enthusiasm was overwhelming.

"You up for it?" Derek asked, turning back to me.

I offered a shrug of my own. "I don't think so. Thanks, though."

Matt's left eyebrow crept up slightly and he exchanged a look with Derek. Now I had his attention.

"You a vegetarian or something?" Derek asked. "We got veggie burgers too—you know, for the misguided people who don't get that we're at the top of the food chain."

I laughed. "It's not that. It's just . . . I'm guessing there will be lots of people there?"

"Yeah. We do this all the time in the summer. We get a pretty good Sunday dinner crowd," Derek said.

"Well, there's the problem. It sounds like I'd have to socialize."

"You're antisocial?" Matt finally spoke again, a slight trace of amusement in his tone. "This linger longer must be downright painful for you, then."

"I'm here because my cousin Celia said I had to be. She really wanted a popsicle and she's my ride, so I get a popsicle whether I want one or not," I said. I gave the unwrapped popsicle in my hand a little shake to illustrate.

"Okay, so you hate popsicles and socializing. What do you like?" he asked.

"I don't hate popsicles. I'm just not confident enough to pull off a neon tongue," I said. Derek stuck out his tongue and crossed his eyes in an attempt to stare at it, apparently checking to see if it was green. It was.

"What if I found you a banana-flavored popsicle?" Matt asked. He took a quick inventory of me, not in a sketchy way, but in a curious analysis. Instead of the bright summer dresses that most of the girls around me wore, I had on a white pencil skirt and a killer pair of yellow suede heels that I couldn't resist last week at the Steve Madden clearance sale. I topped it off with a yellow button-down blouse. The sleeves had tiny little gathers at the shoulder for a soft, feminine look, and clever tailoring in the bodice darts. As long as I didn't turn around, he'd never see the Star Wars bandage on my calf covering the fading bruise I'd picked up from a stingray on my second day in the water. Note to self: buy normal-colored bandages.

"Banana could work." His theorizing snagged my attention again. "Maybe people would just assume you were making a fashion statement by matching your tongue color to your outfit. Like those watches with the bands you can swap out."

"Are you comparing me to a plastic Swatch?" I asked.

"That's high-quality Swiss engineering," Derek interrupted, trying to help his buddy out. "Like a BMW."

"BMWs are German," I said.

"Yeah, but the Swiss speak German," he said.

"Okay, but I don't think they eat as much sausage, so it's really not the same thing," I said.

"Yeah, I guess . . ." Derek trailed off, looking confused. I bet he wore that expression a lot.

Celia wandered up right then, brimming with nervous energy but trying to play it cool.

"Are you ready to go?" I asked.

"Not so fast," Derek protested. "Is this your cousin?"

"Boys, this is Celia. Celia, meet Derek and . . ." I turned to Matt with an apologetic shrug. "I'm sorry, I didn't catch your name."

Celia's eyes widened at this little falsehood, but she didn't say anything.

"It's Matt," he answered. "It's nice to meet you, Ashley," and he held out his hand for a shake. I always think it's kind of awkward when people my age do this, but I took his hand. He surprised me by squeezing mine lightly instead of shaking it, then letting it go. "Hi, Celia," he continued, including my awestruck cousin in the introduction.

She blushed and squeaked out a mangled "hi" in return.

"So now that we're old friends, you're coming to the cookout, right?" Derek wanted to know.

"I don't think so, but seriously, thanks for the invite." I turned to Matt. "And I don't hate socializing," I said, smiling. "I just have a lot of stuff to do."

He looked intrigued but was too polite to ask what else I had planned. Celia, unfortunately, was not so polite.

"What stuff?" she demanded.

"Boring stuff that no one wants to hear about," I said, cutting off her next protest with a warning glare. I felt Matt's gaze following the whole exchange with interest.

"I'm out of here, I guess," I said, addressing our two onlookers. "See you around sometime." I threw the last remark over my shoulder, having already turned to head for the exit with Celia reluctantly in tow.

"Definitely," Matt said. "Nice Band-Aid."

As soon as the doors clicked closed behind us, Celia whirled on me, bristling with irritation.

"Why aren't we going to the barbecue?" she almost wailed. "Do you know how hard it is to get an invite?"

"No, I don't. It sounds like they have a ton of people over every time."

"People *your* age," she said. "They don't notice anyone under twenty-one. My friends would kill for an invitation to their place."

"Then your friends don't have enough going on," I said.

"I don't get it," she complained. "You want Matt Gibson to teach you to surf, but you just rejected his invitation to hang out."

"I turned down Derek's invitation," I corrected her. "When Matt Gibson invites me, I'll say yes."

"But you don't know if he'll do that," she said. "Especially since you already said no."

"Oh, he'll invite me again," I said. "He has to. Because Matt Gibson just became number seventeen on The List."

Chapter 2

1. Climb a mountain
2. See a show on Broadway
3. Sing karaoke
4. Read all the standard works
5. Get a master's degree
6. Study abroad
7. Serve a mission
8. Learn to make sushi
9. Own a pair of Louboutins
10. Complete a triathlon
11. Snowboard on a black diamond trail
12. Read a Russian classic
13. Learn to surf
14. Visit Europe
15. Do a humanitarian project
16. Get a sports car
17. Have a summer fling
18. Take a cruise
19. Skydive
20. Learn a foreign language
21. Publish a poem
22. Learn to play guitar
23. Be a movie extra
24. Try Internet dating
25. Learn to tango

CELIA DROPPED ME OFF AND headed to a friend's house. I climbed on my bed and dug The List out of my beat-up scripture tote. It was yellowing a little at the edges, and the purple gel pen I wrote it in was fading, but wear and tear aside, the content looked exactly like it did the night I made it. The List was born six years ago as an act of rebellion on my eighteenth birthday.

When the last candle flickered out on the cake that night, my older sister Leila had joked, "Good for you, Smashley. Now you're officially old enough to get married without needing Mom or Dad to sign the license."

That had gotten a good laugh from the rest of my family. As the third of four kids with my only brother after me, I'd watched both of my sisters marry and start popping out kids by the time they were twenty. Everyone assumed I would follow the Barrett family tradition of settling down young. My mom had done it, encouraged both of my sisters to do it, and now their sights were set on me. Too bad I had other plans.

"Good one, Leila," I said. "But I'm not getting married."

My mother's smile had died a quick death.

"I mean I'm not getting married right away," I had clarified. "I'm going to graduate from college and have some life experiences first." I didn't add that Leila's epic battles with her husband for the past three years and Juliana dropping out of college at twenty when her twins were born had helped fuel my determination. That night, I sat eating the excess frosting off the cake board and brainstorming my list.

Some of the items I blame on a sugar-induced stupor (Learn to tango? Really?), but I've never changed or altered it, checking each item off one by one. It's not a deep list, but there's a strange, convoluted logic to it. If it sounded fun and I thought it would be impossible to do with a family to worry about, it went on The List. Funny how a half-hour brainstorm has dictated the last six years of my life.

Celia nagged me into letting her see it after I took over half her room. She had all kinds of questions. "Read a Russian classic?" she asked in puzzlement. "First, why would you want to? And second, why can't you do that after you're married? Are you not allowed to read anymore?" But I know the idea of finding time for a little Dostoevsky would make my sisters laugh hard enough to shoot the chocolate milk they filch from their kids out of their noses. Celia's lack of understanding was exactly why almost no one saw The List.

Anyway, there's stuff that you just can't logistically do with a kid, like a service project in a developing nation. How was I supposed to dig freshwater wells with a toddler clinging to my legs? And hello, the sports car thing? It's not like the backseats are made for baby carriers. Not to mention the things I wanted to try that would be stupid to risk once I have kids, like snowboarding on a black diamond trail. Chasing after babies in a full body cast seems like an awful lot of trouble. And then there's all the stuff that falls under the vague category of overcoming my fears, like skydiving or learning to surf. Or singing karaoke. My pathological aversion to singing in public made wading through *The Brothers Karamazov* seem easy by comparison.

In hindsight, I did put some stupid things down. I might have also read too many chick lit novels as a teenager with their ideas about what cool girls should do, be, and have. Own a pair of Louboutins? I worked two or even three jobs all summer long, every summer, so I could pay for school. I would never blow a whole semester's tuition on a pair of shoes, but patience and crafty bidding scored me a killer pair of red stilettos on eBay. Saving like a maniac and compulsive bargain hunting took care of some of my other high-ticket items too, like the sports car. I bought a Miata at a police auction. (The List didn't specify that it had to be a *cool* sports car.) The police had seized the car in a drug case, and I got it for a song. But I sold it after a year for two reasons: First, a Miata is a very bad idea in a Utah blizzard, and second, I had a recurring nightmare that one day I'd get pulled over and the officer would let Killer, the drug-sniffing police dog, check out my car. It ended with me busted for a cache of drugs undiscovered in a wheel well before the car went to the auction. I ended up switching the Miata for a Jeep Wrangler with a few miles on it and no obvious history of drug dealer ownership. I still got to cross it off, though. Bye-bye, number sixteen.

Some of the items on my list I thought would be impossible, but they turned into easy cross-offs with creative planning. I worked three jobs the summer before my junior year of college, waiting tables at a fancy mountain resort at night, doing an early morning call center shift for an appliance store, and working as a part-time manager at a bookstore during the day so I could afford a semester abroad in the winter. The hard work led to three fabulous months in Spain where I polished my beginning Spanish skills and studied the Moorish influence in their country for my senior project paper. I traveled with other university students for short trips to the surrounding countries, too, and got to see other parts of Europe. Study abroad, travel Europe, and learn a foreign language . . . Done!

The basic Spanish I learned was enough to get me sent on a mission to Ecuador—number seven. When I got home, my stake president asked me to chaperone and translate on a youth conference trip doing a home-building project for a poor village in Mexico. That took care of number fifteen. When that ended, I pretty much hit the ground running. I finished my bachelor's in liberal studies and called my aunt and uncle for a place to stay. Now I had a whole summer in Huntington Beach to tackle surfing. Oh, and Matt Gibson.

This was the summer to focus on list items still undone before the stress of grad school put a cramp in my style. Which of course meant it was time to bust out my Bible. Number four was taking too long and I blamed the Old Testament.

* * *

A light flicked on and woke me up. I lifted my head from the crinkled page in Numbers that had defeated me. I think Numbers was so named because of the countless times I had tried and failed to make it through. I blinked my eyes, trying to clear my vision. The blob in front of me materialized into my cousin Dave sporting the Huntington Beach Sabbath uniform of white shirt, chinos, and flip-flops. Celia's bedside clock revealed I'd been asleep for at least an hour.

"You've got a little drool on your chin," he said.

"It's a natural moisturizer," I retorted but wiped it away.

"I don't have to work tomorrow. You want to hit the waves in the morning?"

"You mean, like when they're actually good?" I asked.

"Yeah. Maybe you'll stand up this time," he said.

"I'm in. What time?"

"Seven-ish. I'm not coming to wake you up so if you're not ready when I leave, I'm going on my own."

"I'll be ready," I promised.

"Cool." He turned to leave.

"Dave?" I waited until he turned around. Mustering my most syrupy voice, I cooed, "Thanks for making my dreams come true."

He snorted and flipped the switch off again as he left. After fumbling my way over to the switch and flipping it back on, I pulled out my iPhone and clicked on my calendar. I had thirteen weeks of summer to figure out. I am a compulsive planner, as if The List weren't proof enough. Celia got me a job at Hannigan's, the steak house where she's a hostess, and based on my table tips for the last two weeks, if I worked about twenty-five hours a week I could earn enough to cover my summer expenses and my fall tuition. I already had a teaching assistant job lined up for the school year as a glorified paper grader in the Intro to Art History class, so I wouldn't need to worry about my monthly expenses when the semester started.

If I budgeted my time creatively, my work schedule still left me plenty of play time. List time. Time to figure out how to pull off something like skydiving. Or sushi classes. I didn't even know if there was such a thing as sushi classes, so I did what any college graduate with a research-driven degree would do: I pulled out my laptop and fired up Google.

Prior research had already netted me the names of some local casting agencies so I could investigate the movie-extra thing. Another hour and a few detours on time-sucker Google Earth later, I discovered which local joints had karaoke nights and where to get skydiving lessons. I also stumbled onto a couple of LDS dating sites. I might already have my summer fling victim identified, but I figured I should start lining up a handsome and sympathetic Prince Charming for the fall when I needed the occasional distraction from my textbooks. I had to finish number twenty-four,, anyway.

So far, the most promising site was called LDS Lookup. It reminded me less of cruising the cultural hall at a dance for fresh meat and more of hanging out in the halls at church and striking up a conversation with a stranger. Low threat, laid-back vibe. I took the free site tour, checking out profiles of different people, making sure they were normal and would be allowed to hang out at my house. Still, I hesitated to set up a profile. I might have thought Internet dating sounded good at eighteen, but . . .

How was I supposed to fit this in on top of everything else? I glanced at The List again. The whole point of this summer was to get stuff out of the way since I expected grad school to be crazy busy.

With a sigh, I filled out the profile prompts on my preferences, favorites, and criteria for a match. Now anyone who cared to look could find out that I have a chocolate addiction, listen to alternative rock, compulsively watch *Gilmore Girls* reruns, and squeeze in the occasional snowboarding, plus a dozen other pieces of random information. Nosy things, these dating profile questionnaires.

With that done, I tucked The List back inside my scripture tote and turned with a sigh to the Old Testament. Yanking it toward me, I found my place in Numbers again and began reading for the twelfth time.

Chapter 3

Seven o'clock rolled around extra early on Monday morning, but I didn't want to miss my chance for some tutelage on the *good* waves. Dragging myself out of bed, I pulled on a cute blue-striped tankini, a cotton knit cover-up, and located my beat-up Reef flip-flops wrapped inside a damp beach towel underneath the bed, all in the dark. I only heard the tiniest moan from Celia. I snagged my wetsuit from the chair by the door, proud of myself for having the foresight to leave it there the night before so I didn't have to grope for that in the dark too.

I was halfway through a bowl of peanut butter Cap'n Crunch goodness when Dave rolled in, looking disheveled and still half asleep. He grunted at my breakfast choice, grabbed a banana, and downed it before he was alert enough to comment, "Your cereal is gross."

I scooped up the last three nuggets floating in my milk and heaved a blissful sigh. "No matter how nicely you ask, you still can't have any," I told him.

He rolled his eyes and headed for the door, which opened onto the driveway. Three seconds later, he was back.

"Keys," he said.

"Why mine?" I objected. "We can take your truck. More room for the boards."

"My dad needs it to haul our old dryer somewhere. And you're not driving if I'm in the car, so give me the keys."

"I keep telling you, I've never had an accident."

"Probably because it wasn't on The List," he muttered, barely audible.

"What did you say?"

"I said that's just luck, you maniac."

"Wimp."

"Surfing by myself . . ." he threatened.

"Not unless you walk," I said.

"Fine, Ashley. You're a great driver who never, ever goes too fast. I just golly-gee-whillikers would sure like to drive your fancy Jeep."

"You had me until the fancy part." My Jeep is utilitarian at best, although I did try to liven it up with beach-friendly, hibiscus-print seat covers, fuzzy dice on the rearview mirror, and a yellow smiley-face ball on the antenna. My sister Juliana dubbed it the Cliché Cab, which meant she got the joke. When I got a free moment, I planned to find a couple of lame bumper stickers and an engraved license plate frame to finish off the look. I'm leaning toward the classic, IF YOU DON'T LIKE MY DRIVING, STAY OFF THE SIDEWALK, flanked by a BYU sticker and some kind of CTR decal.

Deciding that a real surf lesson was worth giving up the driver's seat, I followed Dave out and around back to the shed so he could grab the new board he'd just bought with his first post-mission paycheck and I could snag the one Celia gave me, one of her old ones. We loaded them into the back of my topless Wrangler, and Dave pointed us toward Pacific Coast Highway. Barely ten minutes later, we were parking on Ninth Street to surf Taco Reef. Dave usually took me farther north to Bolsa Chica State Beach where the waves are gentler. Noting my surprise, he explained, "I'll have a shot of catching a decent ride here too." I shrugged and jumped down from my seat. We had prime parking next to the abandoned Taco Bell that gave the surf spot its name, so we didn't even have to do the ritual of hunting underneath the seats for quarters to feed the meter on PCH.

I grabbed my board and my gear, followed him down to the sand, and after dropping the whole load, I yanked off my cover-up and started the undignified little dance required for getting into my wetsuit. Squeezing into the black neoprene looks like a spastic hokey-pokey, except way less cool. After completing the little contortion to pull up the back zipper, I strapped the leash around my ankle and stood up, ready to go. Well, equipped to go, anyway. In case of a wipeout, a leash tethers a surfer to her board via an ankle strap. The idea is that the board stays with the surfer and doesn't get lost or bang someone else in the head. So far, mine made sure that my board stuck around to bang *me* in the head. Regularly.

It was almost eight o'clock by now, and the waves were dotted with guys enjoying a morning ride on the rhythmic swells. I did see the occasional female paddling out and even a few little kids, which Dave told me to call "groms." That's short for grommets, which for reasons he couldn't explain, is slang for kids who surf.

I took a deep breath before hitting the water. Since there's no way to brace for the cold slap of the Pacific, I charged in and yelped, but I kept going until it reached the top of my thighs.

"Do the stingray shuffle!" Dave yelled.

I waved to show I heard him, dragging my feet along the sandy bottom to avoid stepping on one. Dave told me on our first day at the beach that I should worry way more about stingrays than the puny sand sharks that hung out in Huntington. He showed me how to avoid startling the rays by shuffling along the sandy bottom to let them know I was coming. A stingray had zapped me on the back of my calf the week before when I forgot, and I wasn't about to make that mistake again. My aunt had laughed after making sure I was okay when I limped in that day.

"Your uncle Joe has lived here his whole life, and I've been here for twenty-five years, and no one in this family has ever been stung. Leave it to you to do it inside of a week."

I pushed farther out into the ocean, stingray-free. When the water crept to my waist, I hopped on my surfboard, lay on my stomach, and began to use my arms as paddles on either side, propelling myself out far enough to catch a wave.

This part, I had down. I could wax my board like a pro, strap on a leash like I'd done it for years, and even had enough endurance built up to paddle out without giving away my novice status by wheezing and puffing. In fact, I had the whole surfing thing down perfectly until the part where I had to actually stand up and ride a wave. For the first few lessons, Dave would follow me out without his board so he could hold mine for me. It reminded me of being six and trying my bike without training wheels. When the white foam of a wave formed behind us, Dave would push me off. That was my cue to look for the right moment to get to my knees, then move to a standing position. So far, in eight outings, I had failed dozens and dozens of times. It felt like the second I stood, my feet propelled the board in front of me at light speed but sent me the other direction. And then: whack! A nice little crack on the noggin when I surfaced, spluttering, and my board reinforced its dominance in our relationship. As if I needed the reminder.

Today, I felt a little niggle of optimism. The waves were about four feet high, perfect for a beginner, but consistent enough not to be boring for an experienced surfer like Dave. I could even see a couple of groms hopping up like pros. I stopped for a moment to watch, studying how different people pulled it off. Dave made me spend one entire lesson last week practicing that move over and over again on the sand, but it didn't translate in the water.

"Ashley!" Dave's shout caught my attention. He was about ten yards ahead of me, and I waved to show I heard him.

He gestured for me to hurry up, so I paddled faster. When I pulled even with him, I mimicked his stance by pointing the nose of my board toward the shore and then straddling it.

"Here's the deal," he said. "We don't leave until you get up by yourself today. So I'm only taking one wave for every two of yours. That way, we can focus on you standing."

I nodded, trying not to show a lack of faith in myself. It might be a very long day.

"Remember, grip the sides, wait for your moment, and then hop up. When you're secure, stand. It's easy. You'll get it," he said.

"Except for the part where I keep picking the wrong moment," I answered.

"I'll help you," he promised. "Just do what I say when I say it, and you'll be fine."

"You're bossy," I said.

"Uh-huh. And that's an incentive to help you . . . how?"

"What I meant to say was, yes sir, Dave. I'll do whatever you say."

He pushed a damp lock of hair from his forehead. "I thought that's what I heard. Just wait for the board to plane."

"This will go better if you don't use physics-type words," I grumbled.

"Or if you weren't such a smart aleck."

"How smart can I be if I don't understand your surf vocabulary? Explain it another way, please." I clasped my hands in front of me and begged.

He sighed. "Okay, you know how when you're driving in the snow back home and you hit a patch of black ice and the car skids because it doesn't have any traction?"

"Yeah. That's bad, right? Because that's when you wreck, and I'm looking for the opposite here."

"Stop talking, Ashley. Just listen."

I decided that was probably a good idea. "Okay."

"So that's bad when it's on ice, but that same feeling is exactly what you want when you're trying to catch a wave."

"Okay . . ." I said again, this time with some uncertainty. A heaping gob of uncertainty, because I didn't follow his logic. I couldn't quite get the black ice analogy to jibe.

"Give it a shot," he said. "There's a nice set rolling in."

I lay flat on my board and watched behind me, trying not to tense as the water swelled to form a mound that hurtled toward me way too fast. Still, when Dave gave my board a slap and hollered, "Go!" I paddled like crazy, helped along by the momentum of the wave building beneath me. I concentrated hard on feeling for the "plane" that Dave described, even though I didn't have the faintest idea what he was talking about. Taking a guess, I braced myself in push-up position on my knees, ready to clamber to my feet, and then watched with a strange detachment as the nose of my surfboard plowed into the water in front of me despite my manic splashing. Steeled for a face full of water, I entered what experienced surfers call a classic pearl dive. I'd seen enough other beginners do it to know what they were doing wrong when I saw it happen, but somehow I couldn't figure out how to avoid the same mistake myself.

With a sense of resignation, I felt myself slip off the front end of my board and into the frothy surf. I prayed as I scrabbled up through the brown water that maybe this time my board wouldn't be waiting to deliver a well-deserved head thump for being so pitiful. I broke the surface and drew in a frustrated breath, grabbing my board in time to prevent a whacking. Standing, I pointed it toward Dave and began the trudge out to him again. "What did I do wrong?" I asked when I reached him.

"You fell off," he said, smirking.

"Thanks for pinning that down for me."

"That's why you're paying me the big bucks."

"No, I'm paying you to tell me something that makes more sense than blah blah black ice blah blah."

"What are you paying me with? I forgot."

"Back talk and a bad attitude?" I offered with a hopeful grin.

"How about I pay *you* back?" he asked.

"Um, I don't really like paybacks."

"That's what I thought." He splashed some water at me. "Shut up and get ready. There's a good wave coming." I did as ordered, lying down and paddling with the wave's momentum.

I've heard that the definition of insanity is doing the same thing over and over again and expecting a different result. After my next wipeout, I picked some seaweed out of my hair, wrangled my surfboard, and decided that I was crazy. I turned to look for Dave and saw him perched on his surfboard, shaking his head. Even thirty yards out, I could feel his amusement.

"Hit the sand!" he called through cupped hands.

I nodded, tired, and waded back to the shore, still pulling on the seaweed tangled in my curls. I can't believe that people pay money to get wrapped with the slimy stuff in spas, but it's a good bet those people didn't spend much time around real seaweed. Five minutes at the beach and you'd get all the free seaweed wraps you wanted. Just maybe not where you wanted them.

I rolled the top half of my wetsuit down to my waist and collapsed on the sand, letting my muscles recoup some of the energy spent paddling against the waves for yards at a time, trying to soak up some warmth while Dave waited for his wave to come in. The sun had already broken through the stubborn marine layer that often shrouded the coast until lunchtime. I felt my gooseflesh smooth out as the rays lazily did their job, and kept an arm crooked over my face so I could enjoy the heat without the glare.

I must have been lying there for over ten minutes when I felt a shadow block the beams. "Move it," I grumbled to Dave. "I'm still cold. You can't make me go out again."

"Are you sure you're not antisocial?" a voice about an octave deeper than Dave's asked. A rich, mellow voice that brought the gooseflesh back.

I turned my arm from a sun block into a backrest and pushed up on an elbow to see Matt Gibson standing there. He looked amused, his deep green eyes crinkling at the corners. Again. Which would be fine if I was *trying* to make him laugh. His dark blond hair was still dripping, so I could tell he was fresh out of the water, but I didn't see his board anywhere. Surfboards are at low risk for theft once they're on the sand. Code of the surf or something, I'm sure, but most people didn't leave their boards unattended, just in case. That led me to wonder who was watching his.

"Are you surfing with Derek?" I asked, looking around for his friend.

"No," he said. He inclined his head toward two kids, boys about nine and eleven, who sat hunched in the sand several yards off with an extra surfboard between them. "I'm doing a lesson for President Pearson's grandsons, but they needed a break."

I sat all the way up and wrapped my arms around my knees. "I sympathize," I said.

He sank down beside me in one fluid move. Flicking his glance toward my secondhand surfboard, he asked, "So you're in Huntington to surf for the summer?"

"To learn," I answered.

"How's that going?"

"You mean after two weeks of constant practice and a cranky stingray?" I asked and then shrugged. "It's not."

"A stingray? Ouch. Is that what the Band-Aid was for?"

I nodded.

"Bummer. Have you gotten up?" he asked.

"No. But I've got a killer pearl dive technique."

The corner of his mouth crept up, threatening a grin. He straightened it out, but not before I saw the flash of a small dimple I hadn't noticed before. Nice.

"Practice is the right thing," he said. "It'll come to you."

"I guess," I said, then climbed to my feet and tried to make the struggle to get back into my wetsuit look cooler than it had the first time. Matt stood, too, and looked at me questioningly.

"Leaving so soon? Was it something I said?"

"Yeah," I replied. "You said to practice. Break's over, so I better go."

He nodded and reached down to hand me my board. "Good luck."

I offered him a tiny smile and took the board with a thank you, then headed for the waves. Once again, I could tell I had surprised him by leaving.

Well, good. It would keep him guessing long enough to take the bait. He didn't need to know embarrassment over my less-than-awesome seaweed hair was really driving me back to the waves.

I braced for the sting of the cold water and plowed in. Matt was a catch, and I had every intention of hooking him.

Chapter 4

I SHRUGGED INTO MY WHITE button-down shirt and black pants and slid on a pair of serviceable black shoes to complete my work uniform. The Monday dinner crowd at Hannigan's, the steak house where I waited tables, demanded a lot of energy and patience but tipped well. Since Monday nights were sacrosanct at my house growing up, it surprised me how many people ditched their kitchens in favor of a restaurant meal after their weekends. It meant skipping the ward Family Home Evening activity every week so I could work, but I didn't miss those anymore than I did the ones from my childhood. As much as I love my family, those lessons were little more than a weekly giggle fest where my siblings and I squirmed impatiently through my dad's teaching efforts and waited for the activity portion of the evening: a cutthroat game of UNO followed by dessert. Singles ward FHEs were the same; everyone put up with the lesson so they could get down to the real business of eating refreshments and flirting with one another. I'd rather make some extra money.

I figured a night of, "How would you like your steak prepared?" beat the FHE grind if it meant two hundred bucks in tips. Besides, the food was way better at Hannigan's. I had yet to run across a stale Little Debbie brownie or second-rate chips and salsa.

The night ended up even busier than I expected. I ran from the time I got in the door and started refilling salt shakers until my last customer left and I tipped out the busboys. As soon as I was on my bed and recording my haul in my little budget book ($175, thank you very much, table full of rich businessmen at eight o'clock), Celia walked in and plopped down on her bed across from me. Settling against the wall, she yawned and said, "You missed out tonight."

I waved a fistful of cash at her. "I don't think so."

"Seriously. Matt was at FHE. He asked about you."

I glanced up. "You have my attention now."

"He wanted to know where you were," she said.

"Did he ask in a way that suggested he was wrecked because I wasn't there?"

"Uh, no. He said, 'Hey, Celia. You here with Ashley again?' and I said that you had to work at Hannigan's."

"And that was it?"

"Then he said he liked my shirt and went to get food."

Her shirt was a fitted tee with the logo for The Board Shack, a local surf shop, scrawled across the front. "Maybe I should borrow that shirt some time, then." I eyed it with a speculative gleam.

"Go get your own. He owns the shop. Maybe you could bump into him while you're buying it."

"He *owns* it? But he's . . . young." It surprised me that I hadn't heard this tidbit before.

She shrugged. "It's not very big, but it seems to do all right. It's right off Main. You should go check it out. If he asked about you, he obviously wants to see you."

"He *kind of* asked about me. I want him begging to know where I am."

"I didn't realize you were such a game player," Celia said.

"It's unavoidable," I responded. "It doesn't do me any good to tell him that he really wants to get to know me. He's got to figure it out for himself, and I have to help him by giving him opportunities to realize it."

"It wasn't a criticism," she said. "I'm not any better. I just stalk a guy until he asks me out because I've worn him down."

I rolled my eyes, knowing better. I'd witnessed Celia go on dates with two different guys already since I'd been here. "That's all I'm doing. I just keep a really low profile about it so he never figures out he's being stalked." I started sorting my tips by denomination, my little pile of ones growing the fastest. "Right now he's trying to figure out why I keep walking away from him instead of wondering why I'm always around."

"And this will work because . . . ?"

I grinned. "Eventually, he'll be the one coming around trying to figure me out."

"That's a little bit genius," she said. "Did your sisters teach you that?"

"No. That's pretty much the technique that always gets my attention because I'm vain and shallow."

She shook her head. "No, you're not. You're just pretty and not lame enough to be all fake modest about it. Being pretty is something you should be proud of, anyway."

"I don't think so."

Celia looked surprised by my opinion.

"Well, I don't," I continued. "Taking credit for being pretty is like congratulating yourself for being tall. We're just made a certain way, and it doesn't make any sense to feel all superior because you won the DNA sweepstakes. I'd rather have someone compliment me on something I can control, like a sense of humor or good fashion sense."

"Uh-huh. So if Matt tells you you're pretty are you going to kick him in the shins and make him take it back?"

"Yes. Then I'll steal his lunch money."

She shook her head. "Do you know you're crazy?"

I smiled and went back to sorting my money. I love money. Not the purchasing power or the status. Just the actual green bills. When I was a little kid, I had a makeshift piggy bank that had been a cheap heart-shaped Valentine box in another life. I liked the shiny pink polyester satin ribbon on it, so I kept my cash inside. About once a week, I would set up the ironing board and steam and iron my dollar bills so they were nice and flat. My sisters mocked me, but they were always first in line for a loan. I made them repay me with ironed dollar bills.

Constant cash flow was another perk of waiting tables. It would be the perfect job if it weren't for the customers. People got cranky if the kitchen was slow and their food wasn't on time. Oh, and my hair always smelled like grilled onions when I got home. I didn't like the backbreaking labor either, which explained why I was getting a master's degree in something besides waiting tables. I tucked my money inside my backpack, ready to deposit in the morning.

"Want to go to the beach tomorrow?" Celia asked.

I made a face that suggested a root canal might be more welcome.

"Not to surf," she clarified. "Just to lay out."

"I can do that," I said. I needed a break from my board.

"Matt likes to surf by the pier," she said. "Want to go there?"

"The idea is *stealth* stalking, Celia. So maybe not by the pier."

"Yeah, but the volleyball nets are all by the pier and that's good for hottie observation."

"Fine, but we're going in the afternoon when Matt's less likely to be surfing."

"Deal."

* * *

"Once again, I have to ask if you're crazy," Celia griped from the sidelines of one of the sand courts the next day.

"What?" I said, distracted by the game in front of me.

Celia waved a hand in front of my face. "You're really considering playing?"

"Well, yeah. Why not?"

"Well, let's see, we don't have any more Star Wars bandages for when you get hurt, and you *will* get hurt."

I waved off her concern. "No, I won't."

"Because all your sports-related broken bones, sprains, and stitches were a coincidence?" she demanded.

"Of course not. They were flukes."

"You got stung by a stingray your second day in the water. We've lived here my whole life and no one in my family has ever been stung. You attract freak accidents. Do. Not. Play," she said before wandering toward the waves.

Unfortunately, the lure of the volleyball courts proved irresistible, and instead of relaxing on a towel, I found myself in a hard-core sand battle with a group of very good girl players. I had made our city all-star volleyball team in high school but didn't have time for both work and sports in college. For the last five years, I'd only played for fun. Turned out being able to hold my own in the pick-up games at the college gym was nothing like playing on the HB sand courts. Surely some people must show up and play just for giggles, but I gave it everything I had and still managed only to stop a hair shy of embarrassing myself. It wasn't until one of my teammates congratulated me on hanging in the game that I found out half the girls playing were on a nearby university squad.

Oh.

I hung in through a second match and would have played through a third, but after I jumped up to block a hit, a sharp pain in my foot when I landed stopped me cold. After limping to the sidelines, I discovered a small piece of broken beer bottle stuck in my sole. Disgusted, I hobbled over to Celia, who delivered an I-told-you-so lecture while flagging down a lifeguard. He cleaned it and pronounced the cut too shallow for stitches but recommended a tetanus shot. I declined.

"You're going to die of lockjaw," Celia said. "You shouldn't have played."

"I got all my shots before my mission," I said. "I won't die of lockjaw."

"Well, stupidity is going to kill you eventually."

I ceded the field and followed her to the car.

At home, I limped in after Celia to change. Despite the dull throb of my cut, I decided I felt good. Even if I wasn't tall enough to deliver kills over the net, I made some pretty good saves, and I had fun.

Now I had to wash the sunscreen and sand off so I could head to Institute that night. Old Testament, of course. I refused to let the *begats* defeat me.

The sting of the shower spray invigorated my tired muscles. By the time I combed my favorite Aveda conditioner through my hair, I felt my energy reserves fill up again. I blew my hair dry and played up the curls, letting them run a little wild. I gave up taming them long ago. I dug through my drawer in Celia's dresser and found my favorite jeans: a pair of Luckys I've had since high school, which translates to being perfectly broken in. A quick riffle through the closet produced a cute green button-down shirt. I slid into my Roxy ballet flats to complete the look. Some people might not like plaid canvas tennis shoes, but it's like Leila always says, you just have to know how to work it.

When I walked into Institute, it was nearly empty, except for one notable exception. Matt sat sprawled on the edge of the middle row, his scriptures sitting on top of his chair desk. There were still five minutes before class started and only a handful of other students milling about, so when he patted the seat next to him and smiled at me, I didn't have a good excuse not to take the seat. I guess I didn't have to run away *every* time he tried to talk to me in order to pique his interest.

"How's it going, Ashley?" he asked.

I don't know why, but I really like it when people use my name. Maybe I'm an egomaniac, but I think it's more because it makes what someone says to me feel more personal. I noticed that Matt used my name pretty often, earning him another brownie point. I meant what I said to Celia about good looks not being that big of a deal. My parents gave birth to four obnoxiously attractive children. Being pretty opened some doors, but it slammed others shut. Like in dating. I've always gotten lots of dates, but the handful of guys who were interested in me as something besides arm candy was pitifully small. I could sense Matt looking past my exterior, trying to figure out what made me tick. Major brownie points. Big, gooey Ghirardelli Double Chocolate Brownie points.

"It's going," I said belatedly. "How are you?"

"Tired. I caught a late set."

"And you still came here after surfing?"

He shrugged. "I like Sister Powers's class. She's rad."

"Even though it's Old Testament?"

"Especially since it's Old Testament. There's some crazy stuff in there."

"I've heard. I never seem to make it much further than the Creation."

"So that's why you're here?" he guessed.

I nodded. "I'm hoping it'll help me get past Numbers. I want to finish reading the whole thing."

A few more people filed in, including a pair of perky blondes who looked disappointed to find that Matt had a seatmate already and there was no desk on his other side. One of them, the shorter one, shot me a dirty look on the way to the chairs directly behind us. Then she leaned over to coo, "Hi, Matt. Looking forward to class?"

"Sure," he smiled.

"I love Sister Powers. She's such a good teacher, and I always feel the Spirit so strong, you know? I just love that feeling so much."

Since she didn't address me when she sat down, I kept my back to her and felt free to let one of my eyebrows creep up at this assertion.

"Oh, uh . . ." Matt seemed nonplussed for a moment. "Well, that's good."

The blonde beamed at him and then began to rustle around. Twisting slightly to take in the action, I watched her lining up several perfectly sharpened colored pencils and a stack of brightly colored sticky notes. Her friend sat quietly with her scriptures on her desk. The chatty blonde looked entirely too pleased with herself. *Don't judge,* I scolded myself, and resolved to play nice.

Turning for a better view of her, I smiled. "Hi, I'm Ashley."

"I'm Megan," she answered coolly.

I tried again. "I like your pencils." Hey, it was the best I could do since she wasn't making it easy.

She didn't unbend at all. "Thanks," she said in a frost-bitten mumble.

Sister Powers strode in while I was debating making one final effort and welcomed everyone. The quiet blonde behind me stood to play the opening hymn, and by *play* I mean she hit the key on the electric piano that had a prerecorded version of "How Firm a Foundation." Some people don't like this automated way of handling the accompaniments, but after eighteen months of painfully limping through the hymns with either no piano or a badly played one in the little branches where I served, I was a big fan of the good ole electric piano.

When the hymn was over, a petite girl on the front row offered an opening prayer and then we were off and running in our lesson. I had missed the first two classes in the bustle of settling in, so this was my first exposure to Sister Powers's teaching. I could understand why Matt enjoyed her lessons. Her balance of humor and insight kept the pace moving. After a few more stragglers wandered in, the class was nearly full, a cool trick for an Old Testament class.

After the closing prayer, I gathered my scriptures up and started to rise.

"Are you in a hurry a lot?" Matt asked.

I paused in surprise. "No. Why?"

"I don't know. You always rush off as soon as stuff is over. Linger longer, Institute . . ."

"That's because it's *over*. That means it's time to go. Just because I realize that doesn't mean I'm in a rush."

"Where are you from, anyway?" he asked.

"Salt Lake."

"Okay, maybe that explains it. You're probably used to sharing a building with fifty-seven other wards and running around trying not to get in each other's way. Around here when something at church is over, it means it's time to hang out. You should try it."

I blew about a thousand words out in one breath. "Why do you keep saying to relax? I'm totally relaxed. If I get any more relaxed, I'll pass out and have to be carried out to my Jeep and driven around until the wind resuscitates me with its relentless . . . windiness. But I'll be all freaked out about being in my Jeep without knowing how I got there, and then I'll get all wound up and so tense that I'll have a stroke or something, so you really shouldn't tell me to relax anymore." I kept a straight face and gave it my best woman-on-the-edge delivery.

Matt scrunched his forehead in a moment of excessively cute confusion and then asked, "Relentless windiness? Really? That sounds like kind of a personal problem, but I'm glad you feel comfortable sharing."

I grinned and sat back down. "You flinched. You bought that for a second. You really think I'm too wound up, don't you?"

"Nah. I'm still more worried about your antisocial tendencies."

I leaned forward with a flirtatious smile and employed the same coo Megan had used when she sat down. "Oh, Mattie, you're such a sweet-talker."

"It's a gift," he agreed without missing a beat.

The cooing must have summoned Megan because she leaned in, forcing him to turn so he could acknowledge her. Well played, Megan.

"Didn't you just love the lesson?" she said—and not to harp on it again, but she cooed. Maybe cooing and spitting icicles at me were her only two settings.

"Sure," he answered. "It was as good as usual, I guess."

"I love how she makes the scriptures come to life," she continued, determined to demonstrate her extreme spirituality. I personally prefer it when someone has an invisible halo I can sense versus one they shine and buff themselves while I watch. But maybe Matt liked that kind of approach. I settled back to watch him.

"Right, yeah. She's good at that," he answered, smiling. I saw him make a tiny shift with his shoulders, like he was about to turn back to me, but Megan caught it too and rushed in with another gambit before he could disengage.

"President Pearson is my uncle," she said, name-dropping the stake president. "My cousins love taking those lessons from you. Well, I guess they're not really my cousins because they're his grandkids. Or maybe they are cousins but the removed kind, like twice removed? Or maybe they're just my second cousins. I get so confused with that."

She continued on with some story about cousin removal and placement, determined to hold Matt in his seat with sheer word power. I decided it was a good time to slip out and surrender the playing field to the wordier player.

Matt turned when I stood and I waved good-bye, trying not to laugh at his longsuffering expression as Megan prattled on. When he saw my smothered smile, he shot me a grimace but then turned again to listen to her detailed family genealogy.

I headed out to my Jeep, letting my smile blossom into a full-blown grin. Unless I was mistaken, Matt Gibson was bummed to see me go, and it had only a little to do with being stranded with Megan.

He had taken the bait. Now I had to step it up and reel him in.

Chapter 5

"HOW'S THE CONQUEST GOING?" Dave asked the next morning over breakfast. I had moved on to Lucky Charms. There's nothing like the marshmallow-dyed milk that's left after the last piece of cereal makes its way to my mouth.

"The surfboard? You've been at all my surf lessons. You should know."

"No, your other conquest. Aren't you stalking Matt Gibson?"

I narrowed my eyes. "You aren't supposed to know that."

"Whatever," he shrugged. "I don't think Matt knows he's being stalked."

"Sure he knows he's being stalked," Celia said, diverting her attention from her yogurt for a moment. "It's just hard to tell which girl is doing the stalking at any given moment, is all."

"No kidding," Dave said. "I know he's a good-looking dude, but how does he pull so many hot chicks?"

"Probably by not referring to them as chicks," I retorted.

"Are you a feminist or something?" Dave asked.

"I just have a little self-respect."

"But I don't care if you call me a dude. Why do you care if someone calls you a chick?"

"*Dude* isn't insulting. What if I referred to you as a puppy or something? They're all cute and cuddly and stuff. Wouldn't you like that?"

"No, but that's because puppies aren't manly."

"And chicks are fluffy and useless."

He shook his head. "I think college is ruining you. That's the problem with chicks and higher education."

I was about to go after him again when a balled-up napkin bounced off the side of his head. "Quit messing with her, Dave," Celia ordered.

He grinned at me. "I'm kidding," he said. "I respect women. But you can't deny that it's mostly the chick variety who go after Matt. They don't get it."

"Get what?" I asked.

"They think he's just a surf bum and they like that he's all buff, but the guy has a lot going on upstairs."

"You know him well?" I asked.

"A group of us surfed together before my mission and we would talk. Matt's pretty smart, actually. He's got some good ideas."

"Ideas about what?"

He shrugged. "They're his ideas. You should ask him."

"Oh, she can't," Celia said. "Ashley stalks by not talking to him or being anywhere in his vicinity."

"Not true," I defended myself. "I just make him come to my vicinity. That's all."

"That's a pretty good plan, cuz," Dave said. "Is it working? Because there's a cute girl I saw at FHE that I might try ignoring completely if this works out for you."

"It won't work if everyone does it, so you'll just have to go back to lurking and hope she notices you," I teased him.

"Dave's not a lurker," Celia said.

"Thanks, sis."

"Yeah, he's more of a skulker," she added.

He rolled his eyes and scooped up the last of his Grape Nuts. "I'm done with this estrogen fest," he said. He took his bowl to the sink and then headed for the back door. "The Taco Reef Express leaves in one minute if any chicks in here are trying to get some surfing in."

He barely ducked to avoid Celia's yogurt container as it bounced off the door frame behind him, leaving a small splatter of pink gunk in its wake.

"You got one minute, Barrett!" he called to me over his shoulder. "I hear the pearl beds are hopping today."

Knowing I needed the practice, I dumped my marshmallow milk out with a sigh and hustled after him. It looked like I'd be washing down my Lucky Charms with mouthfuls of sand and seawater instead. Yum.

I secured my board in the back of Dave's pickup and hopped in. He pulled out, and as the wind whipped through the rolled-down window, I scooped a fistful of hair out of my face and turned to face Dave. "How come you didn't mention you know Matt?"

"How come you didn't mention you were trying to replace me with *him* as your surf coach?" he responded.

"I don't know. I guess I figured you didn't like teaching me and you'd be happy to get rid of me. He seems like a good bet."

"And I guess I thought you were looking around for someone better." He kept his tone even, but I could sense a slight trace of hurt.

"No way! I just feel bad that I keep carving out chunks of your surf time when you already have to squeeze it in. I'm sorry, Dave. I didn't mean to hurt your feelings."

He was quiet for a minute. Then he shrugged. "Well, in that case, maybe I'll help you get lessons from Matt Gibson. He pretty much *is* the best guy around."

"You can do that? He's already full for the summer, I heard."

"Yeah, but he speaks dude. I'll make it work."

"That would be awesome!" I was excited for almost ten seconds, and then I frowned. "Wait, are you just trying to get rid of me so you don't have to teach me anymore?"

"Yep."

"Then *my* feelings are hurt now."

"But you get Matt Gibson as a consolation prize."

"Oh yeah. Good trade." I thought for another minute. "Can you do this in a way that doesn't blow my covert stalker status?"

"Trust me."

"I don't really have a choice."

He snorted and cranked up the radio. "That's the best thing about you, Ashley. That great attitude."

I grinned and spent the last few minutes of the drive watching the houses downtown roll by. Old original beach bungalows nestled between small apartment units and large McMansions with tiny front yards. The crazy hodgepodge of architecture always entertained me. If I lived here, I'd probably hole up in one of the little cottages with their wooden porches and low roofs. They reminded me of my favorite old-school neighborhood, the Avenues, back home in Salt Lake.

Dave turned down Ninth and situated us next to the Taco Bell again. We jumped out, wiggled into our wetsuits, grabbed our boards, and then waited at the light with a few other surfers and some dog walkers on their way to Dog Beach. After two weeks, standing in front of the Pacific and watching it stretch endlessly before me still gave me a flutter in my stomach. The waves were about waist high again, and when we hit the water, I stayed right behind Dave. He watched the waves roll in, checking for a rideable one.

"The first one that comes in and looks good is yours. Be ready to go when I tell you, okay?"

I nodded and stayed focused on the swells. I saw one forming up that looked right.

"This one's yours," he nodded toward it. "Let's go."

We turned our boards toward the shore and I took off, paddling fast to match the momentum of the wave. A strange, weightless feeling stole over me for a moment, almost like the texture of the wave had smoothed out beneath me.

I was about to tell Dave that I thought I finally got "the plane" he described when he asked, "Do you trust me?"

I turned around in confusion. "What?"

"You have to trust me. Stand up!"

I did as ordered, feeling for the first time ever that I was on the shoulder, the prime spot for taking a wave in. A giddy bubble of adrenaline welled up inside me, and then suddenly, a sharp tug on my ankle sent me headfirst over the nose of my surfboard. When I broke through the surface of the water, Dave was almost on me, looking angry.

"How many times do I have to explain this to you, Ashley?" he demanded, irritation furrowing his brow. "It's standing up. Just stand up!"

Too confused to speak because I knew Dave was the one who had yanked my leash, I treated him to a cold shoulder and paddled toward the sand when I heard Matt say, "Hey, Dave," his voice mellow.

"Hey," my cousin spat back. Whoa.

"What's going on?" Matt asked.

"I've been trying to teach Ash here to surf for two weeks. I'm over it."

"Have you stood yet?" Matt asked me.

I shook my head. "Only in the white water."

"She doesn't get the timing, and I'm running out of ways to explain it to her," Dave said. "You know what, Ashley? I quit. I'm going to go catch some of my own waves. Stay here if you want a ride back home." Then he stomped off to grab his own board and headed for the water.

I think my mouth was slightly open, unhinged with shock at this little display. I snapped it shut and managed a joke. "I hope he doesn't come back and kick sand at me."

Matt smiled. "I'll help you brush it off if he does."

When I looked at him funny, he added, "Uh, that was an accidental double meaning. I just meant I'd help you."

"Yeah, that's what I need. Help. Like remedial surf tutoring." I didn't know if I was more embarrassed over how wrecked I must look from the wave bashing or the fact that he'd seen my pitiful attempts to stand up. It was a humiliating toss up.

"Surfing is a little easier if you're relaxed," he said.

I mustered a weak smile. "Again with the suggestion that I'm uptight. I'm not uptight. I just lose all sense of coordination in the water. I'm pretty athletic everywhere else, so I don't even have an excuse." I plopped down on the sand, deciding that dejected loser status could only work in my favor. "It's bad when even family quits on you."

My patheticness was a black hole that sucked him down on the sand next to me. "I could help," he offered. He stretched out his sand-dusted legs, which extended from black board shorts.

Nibble, fishy, nibble.

"How? Are you going to yell 'Relax!' from the sidelines every time I fall off my board?"

"No, I just mean I could teach you."

"You heard Dave. I'm hopeless." I held my breath, hoping I was throwing out just enough line.

"I've watched you on the waves a few times. It's possible Dave might not have explained a couple of things to you that would help."

Almost there, almost there . . .

"Really?" I asked, allowing curiosity to color my voice. "Like what?"

"Like you need to change the angle of your surfboard when you're paddling to catch a wave. You always point straight toward the shore. Starting diagonal would help you."

"That sounds so easy. How come he never told me that?"

Matt shrugged. "I don't know. Sometimes people who are really good at something don't know how to explain it. It's just what they do. That's what my sister says about math, so maybe it's true about surfing."

"So you'd still teach me even though I stink after two weeks of lessons?"

"Yeah. I'm out here most mornings, anyway."

Tugging on the line . . . !

"I'm pretty broke, so I can't pay you."

"Just make me dinner and we'll call it even. I'm tired of Derek's burgers."

"What if I'm a bad cook?"

A slight grin twisted his lips. "You can't cook worse than you surf. I'm sure I'll live."

"Hey!"

"I'm just kidding." His grin widened. "*Can* you cook?"

"Yes, as a matter of fact." My mom had insisted that all of her daughters learn to make some fierce meals as part of our Early-Marriage Prep training. Goat cheese stuffed chicken breasts? Unbelievably rich beef stroganoff? I'm your girl.

"Okay, then. How about we trade? A surf lesson for a meal."

I heaved an overly dramatic sigh. "And I so hoped you would do it just for the chance to hang out with me."

"Who says I'm not finding a way to do that twice?"

Hooked.

He climbed to his feet, and I looked up, way up, to see his face.

"I think my client is rested enough for me to finish his lesson right now and I have another one after that, so I need to go, but what are you doing in an hour?"

I shrugged. "I don't know. I'm stuck here waiting for a ride with Dave whenever he decides he wants to leave."

"If you're still here and the waves are still right, I'll take you out."

"To tell you the truth, Matt, chances are I'm going to lose my balance and my board is going to take *you* out."

He grinned and pointed to an older gentleman in a comically small wetsuit sitting several lengths down the beach. "That guy was standing halfway through our first lesson. You'll be fine."

"If I get bored working on my tan and you only find an Ashley-shaped indentation in the sand where I used to be, I'm probably at the volleyball nets."

"See you in an hour."

"Sure," I agreed, and watched him saunter off. He had a world-class saunter. I leaned back, enjoying the steady heat from the sun until a spray of cold droplets rained down on my face. I gasped and jerked upright to discover Dave standing over me, dripping, with a crafty smile on his face.

"Why did you yank my leash?" I demanded.

"Come on, cuz. You're the queen of strategy around here. You know why I did it."

"Because you were trying to make Matt feel sorry for me so he'd offer to teach me instead?" I guessed.

"Yep."

"You little schemer. I'm so proud." I slapped him a high five.

"I knew you would be."

"But I totally owe you for knocking me off my board. I was going to catch that wave, for once."

"You caught Matt instead. You're a very demanding female to want it both ways."

"Haven't you heard, Dave? The new generation of chicks wants it all."

He sighed and began toweling his hair dry. "As dudes, do we have any say in that?"

"Nah. Total world domination."

"Okay, but I want to be kept alive as a breeder when the revolution comes."

"That's disturbing."

"I try. You ready to go?" He held out a hand to help me up.

"I'm waiting for Matt to give me a surf lesson."

"Good work," he grinned. "I need to try some of your reverse voodoo on my FHE girl."

"Or you could talk to her and ask her out."

He stared at me, one eyebrow arched. "Did you just give me advice on being straightforward in a dating situation?"

"Yeah." I paused. "It felt weird."

He laughed. "If you're sure you're okay, I'm outta here."

"I'm cool. You can go."

He headed off in the direction of his truck, and I stood to test my injured foot. The cut from the glass throbbed but not too badly. It would do. I shucked my wetsuit off so I could play volleyball. Maybe I should add "Become an Olympic medalist in beach volleyball" to my list . . .

* * *

An hour drags by like days when you're getting your pride handed to you on a sand court, but right as I missed another dig, I heard Matt call, "Ashley," to get my attention from the sideline. Ah, the sound of my name on his lips. It was a gentle reminder that my ego was about to endure even greater abuse from the waves.

I swapped out with another girl watching from the sidelines and jogged over to my new surf guru who looked tanned and relaxed.

"Are you going to have the energy for this?" he asked.

I nodded. "My energy's fine. It's my self-esteem that's been sucked dry."

"Why? I saw you make some great returns."

"Did you happen to notice all the ones I missed?"

He laughed, the rich sound sending a shiver down my back. "Ashley, do you know who you were playing against?"

"I didn't memorize all their names or anything."

He pointed to a girl in a bright yellow bikini with sporty stripes. "She's on the AVP tour. And that one," he said, indicating a girl in a swimsuit underneath a tank top, "is trying to qualify for it this year. They're not exactly amateurs."

The AVP is the pro beach volleyball organization that sponsors stars like Misty May-Treanor and Kerri Walsh. I felt a little less dismal about my performance.

"I thought they were bionic or Amazons or something. I feel better now," I said.

"See? You're not as bad as you thought at volleyball *or* at surfing. Where's your board?"

I pointed it out, and once I was back in my wetsuit we made our way toward the waves.

"I want to watch you a couple of times in the white water first, then we'll go from there," he said.

The volleyball courts are right by the pier, which is where more experienced surfers hang out. They get a little impatient with beginners cluttering up their waves, so we moved a few hundred yards down the beach. I paddled out to the right break point and when the first wave rolled in, I hopped up straight and rode the froth until my board scraped sand. I'd been doing that since the first day. It wasn't real surfing, but it's how everyone had to start. Since I had that trick down pat, I scooped my board up and waited for Matt's assessment without too much concern.

"Not bad, Ashley," he said. "You look comfortable in the water, and you're steady on your feet. Let me see you do it a couple of more times so I can check out your form."

I lifted an eyebrow, and he shook his head. "That's exactly why I don't teach girls over the age of about six."

I grinned and plowed back through the water, standing the next two times successfully as well. Matt came out to meet me after the last attempt. "Ready to try something bigger?" he asked.

I shrugged. "Sure," but my stomach was in knots. Now that the goal of getting him to coach me was a reality, I realized I had overlooked the details. Stuff like how I was going to look like a total idiot when I ate it on wave after wave. And details like how that would adversely affect him falling madly in love with me for the summer.

"Let's walk back to Taco Reef and try there so we're not in anyone's way," he said.

Neither of us said much on the short walk down the sand. I tried to decide if the silence felt uncomfortable or companionable. Putting my stress aside, it was nice to hang out without saying much. I looked over at Matt and smiled.

"What?" he asked.

"Nothing," I said. "I just realized that this is the first time I've seen you without a herd of girls."

His eyes crinkled at the corners as his mouth turned up in a sheepish smile. "It's kind of ridiculous, I guess, but I don't know how to make them go away. I don't want to be rude."

"Poor baby."

"Maybe I should copy you and not talk to any of them," he teased.

"I talk to people."

"Not really," he said. "You talk to your cousins. You talk to people if they talk to you first, like Derek. You don't socialize, though."

"How do you know? We just met on Sunday."

"And yet it's taken me more than one Sunday to figure that out," he said.

Wait. Did that mean he'd been watching me more than one Sunday? Props to him if that was true, because I hadn't noticed, and I'd been watching *him* for three weeks.

Huh.

I didn't want to explain the dynamics of being a pretty face in a new ward. The girls view newcomers as a threat and are mean until they know you, and the guys treat you like fresh meat. I find it easier to keep a low profile and meet people gradually until I make a few friends and prove to the girls that I'm not there staking out anyone else's territory. To Matt, I said only, "Guess I'm just shy."

He grinned. "Yeah, right."

We reached the spot where he found me earlier and dread formed a fist in my gut as I tried not to think about the number of sand sandwiches I was about to eat in front of him.

"Paddle out," he said. "I'll be right behind you."

I turned to the water and followed directions, eventually lying on my board to paddle as the water got deep enough. Matt stayed even with my shoulder a short distance away.

Finally, Matt stopped and straddled his board. "You ready?" he asked.

"Yeah."

"Okay, I'm going to watch you again and see what I can figure out."

"Are you going to tell me which wave to catch?"

"Yeah. But I want to see what you know about riding it once I pick it, okay?"

I nodded, gauging the waves to see which one he would choose. A few rolled by that he told me to skip, explaining why each wouldn't work. I tried to let his mellow voice soothe my nerves, but I still felt like I was wound tighter than a Joan Rivers face-lift. He finally picked one, and I turned to paddle, my sense of impending disaster in full force.

My arms picked up speed, but whatever instinct I had almost tapped on my last run with Dave deserted me. Making my best guess, I jumped up on my board and stood for about three seconds before the nose began to sink and I knew I wasn't going to be riding this one in. I jumped to the side, desperate to avoid a more painful wipeout.

When I did my cool break-through-the-surface-and-sputter routine again, I found Matt already waiting for me, the water at his waist, his hand calmly keeping his board in place as a maverick wave rolled in and tried to buck against it. "What's the diagnosis, doctor?" I joked. Lame.

"I think you're mainly going to need to work on timing because you have good body mechanics. If you just put them together at the right point on the wave, you'll get it down fast."

"Well, that's better than the coordination transplant I thought you were going to suggest."

"Surfing doesn't require a lot of athleticism, Ashley. If it did you'd still be fine. I saw you on the volleyball court. Even without it, if you can learn patience and flow, you'll get it."

"Patience and flow?"

"Yeah," he said. "This is where we sing 'Kumbaya' and light incense."

I laughed, feeling a measure of tension dribble away.

"Okay, I'm going to give you a couple of things to feel for on the next wave. It should help."

"Yes, sir," I saluted. "Hey, do you have an official title? Like coach? Or sensei or something?"

"I prefer Supreme Boardrider and Wave Master. But usually I forget that's my title so I might not answer if you call me that. Let's stick to Matt."

"You're a funny guy, Matt."

"Thanks. Are you done avoiding the next wave?"

"No?" I said, without any real hope that I could stall.

He shook his head. "I'm going to have to do a power of positive thinking lecture and I really hate those, so just smile and paddle back out, please."

"Fine."

"This is what I want you to think about," Matt said as we watched the next set roll in. "You don't have to finish every wave you start. If it's not working for you, wrap your legs around your board and pull on the rails until the wave passes. Less wrecks that way."

"But why would you tell me to take a wave that isn't good?"

"You can't always tell by looking whether it's going to wall up. Sometimes you're ready to take off on the wave when it starts closing off on both sides, and it's time to pull back and wait for the next one."

That speech actually made sense to me, thanks to Dave's penchant for surf lingo. "Okay," I nodded. "Don't finish every wave. What else?"

"This is something you may not have thought about before. Have you noticed when you're paddling to catch a wave that there's a point where your arms don't do you any good anymore because the wave takes over?"

"Not really," I admitted.

"Watch for it," he said. "It'll be really obvious once you're looking for it."

"And if I notice it?"

"That's a good time to hop up."

When he spotted a wave that looked right, he said, "Go get it."

I turned my board and paddled toward shore diagonally and then I felt it—a split second where I realized the wave was doing the work and my arms were doing little more than splashing. Without thinking too much harder, I jumped up. Again, I had a three-second window where I felt a little thrill of victory, and then my board shot forward like I was a clown on a banana peel, and I braced for my next dunking.

This time, I scrambled up and found Matt looking pleased.

"That was really good," he said.

"And yet I'm in the same place as I was after the last wave," I retorted.

"Because you were too far back on your board. But you stood at exactly the right moment, and I think it might have been on purpose."

I stared at him. "It was." That took me aback for a moment. "Whoa."

"Feels good, huh?"

"Really good."

"Let's go home, then."

"What? I'm just getting started!" I protested.

"Yeah, you are. So now's a good time to savor the victory. I'm going to take you home so you can think about what you're making me for dinner on Friday."

"I can't Friday. I have to work." I couldn't trade away a lucrative shift like that, even if it meant hanging out with Matt.

"Great. I'll come over for lunch, then."

"I'm not a lunch chef. I top out at sandwiches."

"Perfect. Sandwiches are always better when someone else makes them."

"Yeah, and spaghetti."

"To tell the truth," he said, "I'm not much of a cook so pretty much anything tastes better if someone else makes it."

"Reeeeally?" I drawled. I felt the bite of an idea coming on. "Then we're going fishing."

"We are?" he asked in confusion.

"Yeah. Come over on Friday at noon. We'll go fishing then."

Curiosity mixed with the confusion on his face.

"Let's get you home, then," he said. "I have to drop you off so I know where this fishing expedition starts on Friday."

Hook. Line. And Friday I'd make sure he swallowed the sinker too.

Chapter 6

WEDNESDAY NIGHT I STUMBLED THROUGH the door and wound my way back to my bed, then collapsed in a pile of throbbing muscles and strained arches. I knew popping an Advil and counting my tips would prove amazingly restorative, but for the moment, I wanted to give my aching joints a moment to do nothing. Due to some tragic understaffing, Hannigan's had looked more like a zoo than a fine-dining steak house. The night manager had expected a normal, slow Wednesday and didn't schedule a full wait staff for the evening, but we experienced one of those unfathomable slams that defy prediction. The handful of servers working had hustled like mad to keep up with our persnickety customers. The downside to wealthy diners and their expectation of perfection from food to service was far outweighed by their generous tips when they got what they wanted.

I sat up on the bed and pulled out the wad of tips from my purse. Peeling off the crisp fives and tens soothed me like a baby with a binky. With a sigh of satisfaction, I dropped my last bill on top and sat back, content that one night's work had just taken care of my monthly car insurance payment.

I put the money away and pulled out my laptop so I could work on The List with a little help from Google. I didn't get past my home page because a small stack of messages in my inbox all bore the subject line, "You have a message at LDS Lookup." I'd halfway forgotten about my online dating project. I hadn't heard anything since posting my profile the previous week, but I guess my picture must have finally been approved. Being free to look was part of the online dating appeal, and I get that, but it seemed kind of shallow that my personality profile alone couldn't elicit at least a few responses.

I logged into my Lookup account with my screen name, TwinkieSmash. I earned that nickname during a childhood incident when a neighbor boy refused to give back a Twinkie he stole after I asked nicely. Instead of telling my mom so she could referee, I snatched it from him and squished it in his hair. I blame exhaustion for the screen name pick, but I decided to embrace it and move on.

The first message was from "Excalibur" who requested "my fair hand" as his Guinevere in a Dungeons and Dragons-esque role-playing game adventure so he could "destroy the taunting legions by having the hottest princess." There was no picture, but I'm pretty sure even killer good looks wouldn't tip the balance in his favor. I deleted the message.

The next message, from "LonelySearcher19" led me to wonder first, how many lonely searchers there were, and second, why the fifty-year-old in the picture was contacting women half his age. Delete.

"MooseMan" in the next message included a picture of himself in a football jersey for his favorite NFL team, posing in front of a wall covered in color-coordinated sports memorabilia. I'd like to say that I was simply turned off by the way his team's colors clashed, but I admit I was worried about the unusual size of his head and accepted that this made me a bad person.

Option four looked fine at first. The solid screen name "Scott93" accompanied a picture that indicated the 93 was *not* his age, and his occupation of "law school" didn't raise any red flags. Then I realized that he apparently didn't believe in using capital letters or any kind of punctuation. That was the end of our thirty-second romance.

Not an auspicious start to the Internet dating project, but I had a whole summer to sift through my options. Browsing through the site before I joined had reassured me that normal guys hung out in places like LDS Lookup too. Maybe it took a little time for them to find the normal girls like me.

* * *

Thursday passed in a blur of clattering dishes on a double shift. It was a good tip night. I even cajoled one of my regulars, crabby Mr.

Waite, out of a bad mood and into leaving a tip. It was his second time in my section that week, and it made me smile to see him sitting there, even though he growled his orders. I have a soft spot for curmudgeons.

The busy day made Friday come faster, and now I had only one table set for two in my kitchen. My uncle and Celia were at work, Aunt Trudy was fabric shopping, and Dave was surfing. I studied the supplies laid out on the counter with a critical eye. While I would be serving up lunch for Matt, I would not be cooking it. Matt would. He just didn't know it yet. He said he would drop by at noon, leaving me only a few minutes to wait. I suspected I had a very entertaining afternoon in store.

The doorbell rang right on time, and I took a deep breath before answering it.

"Hi," Matt said, standing on the porch looking super yummy. He wore gray board shorts with a cool black graphic scribble all over them and a vintage black surf tee shirt stretched over his well-defined chest. I stood back and waved him in with a smile, noticing that his shirt made his return smile look even whiter. Noticing the flip-flops lined up inside the front door, he slid his off and nudged them neatly into the row, an informal and widespread beach town tradition.

"I wasn't sure how to dress for fishing, so I hope this is okay."

"You're fine."

He grinned, and I rolled my eyes. "I thought female adoration embarrassed you," I said.

"You don't adore me, Ashley. You tolerate me, so I take my compliments where I can get them."

"I admit you're pretty tolerable. Come on back and we'll start your fishing lesson."

Confusion puckered his brow. "Are we fishing in the tub? Or do you have fish from the market in the sink or something?"

"Patience, Mattie-boy."

"Only people older than me are allowed to call me Mattie. Or my sister. She isn't technically allowed to either, but she hasn't listened to me since she was twelve."

"How old are you now?" I asked. I assumed he was my age.

"Twenty-six. There's no way you're older than me."

"You're right, I'm not. Matthew."

He grimaced, and I laughed. By now we were in the kitchen, and as he surveyed the counter covered in food, I announced, "This is where we're fishing."

He shook his head. "I don't think I've ever seen the fishermen out on the pier use any of this stuff."

"Yeah, but they catch literal fish," I explained. "We're going after figurative fish."

"Okay . . ." he drawled, looking interested.

"You know the old saying about giving a man a fish and he eats for a day?"

"But teach a man to fish and he eats for a lifetime?" He sighed. "I'm making my own lunch today, aren't I?"

"Yep. This way you can fend for yourself when Derek leaves you for one of the perky blondes you've rejected."

"I had no idea he was such a schemer," Matt said, amused.

"Oh, he's not," I reassured him. "He's just going to seize his moment *and* one of your leftover blondes one of these days."

"Is that antiblonde bitterness I detect?"

"Totally. I resent the fact that I can't pull it off myself."

He lightly brushed one of my curls with his fingertip and then self-consciously pulled back his hand. "Dark is good," he said.

"Yeah, that's the Barrett girl motto—Come over to the Dark Side," I joked, trying to smooth over the little flutter that his touch had provoked. It was a curl, for pity's sake. No reason to flutter.

Matt didn't notice that I was all atwitter. He walked to the counter and looked over the supplies. "I had no idea this many cheeses came presliced," he said.

"Find the deli counter of your local grocery store, and then learn it, know it, love it," I said. I watched as he fingered a pile of fresh basil.

"What's this?" he asked.

I tore off a leaf and gave it to him. "Taste it," I ordered.

He chewed it willingly and that impressed me. Plenty of guys would have made a big production over trying something new. "What do you think?" I asked.

"It's good. Kind of tangy, I guess. What are we using it for?"

"Grilled cheese sandwiches."

That brought the first skeptical eyebrow of the afternoon to a peak. "I'm pretty sure I've never had this on a grilled cheese sandwich."

I pointed to the fresh loaf of sourdough bread and a red onion. "You've probably never had those on one either," I said. "But that's because you've never had my ultimate grilled cheese sandwich."

He eyed all the other ingredients laid out and waiting. "I know I'm a kitchen rookie, but I don't think all of this fits in one sandwich."

"It doesn't," I agreed. "I'm making a salad while you work on the sandwiches."

"Oh," he said with a touch of relief. "That would explain the pecans and strawberries."

"They're not so good on the grilled cheese part," I reassured him. "You ready to get this lunch started?"

"Let's do this."

By the time he had slathered the bakery bread with cream cheese and layered it with cheddar, pepper jack, onion, and basil, I knew he'd never go back to Kraft singles on white.

While he added each new ingredient to the sandwiches, I chopped spinach and sliced strawberries for a tangy summer salad. He announced that he was ready for the skillet, and once I determined that his two sloppily compiled sandwiches were on their way to a golden crust, I had him start measuring out the ingredients for my mom's killer poppy seed dressing recipe.

"I can't believe you make your own salad dressing from scratch," he said. "I should introduce you to my friends Wishbone and Paul Newman."

"It's not the same," I said firmly. "You'll see."

He shrugged but gamely added each ingredient I asked for and shook the container vigorously when ordered.

By the time he had flipped his sandwiches, the salad was ready, and I waved him into a seat at the table. "You did the cooking," I said, "so I'll do the serving."

"You did way more work," he protested. "Let me help."

"Just consider it my warm-up for work tonight."

I watched Matt as I chewed my own little bite of bliss, enjoying the mellow way that the basil combined with the melted cheeses and played over my taste buds. Matt took a hearty first bite and chewed a few times before stopping as a strange look crossed over his face. Then he chewed with renewed vigor, his eyes half closing. When he finished, he looked at me with respect. "I had no idea what I was missing. I think I'm breaking up with Wonder Bread."

Guys have proposed marriage on the strength of my ultimate grilled cheese sandwich. Matt was so low-key that I guessed his decision to abandon Wonder Bread grilled cheese equaled high praise for him.

"That's not the only thing I'm about to ruin for you. You haven't tried the dressing yet. Eat some salad," I urged him.

"No way. I'm not putting this sandwich down until it's done."

When he finally took a bite of his salad, he shook his head again. "Yeah, it's going to be hard to hang out in Hidden Valley after this," he said.

"Thanks?" I said, unsure how to respond to his not-quite compliment.

"No. Thank *you*. Best lunch ever."

"Oh. You're welcome."

His salad disappeared with impressive speed, and I jumped up to clear the table, but Matt stood and intercepted me en route to the sink.

"Uh-uh," he said. "That's my contribution. I'll do the dishes. Take it easy, Ashley," and he nodded toward my empty seat.

"I feel stupid sitting here watching you clean up after me," I objected.

"Then you can entertain me while I work," he said. "Tell me more about you."

"Like what? You want my GPA? My deepest, darkest secret? What kind of entertainment are you looking for?" I joked, uncomfortable with the idea of blabbing about myself.

"How about you start with why you're in HB this summer?"

"That's easy. I'm learning to surf."

"Okay. Why?"

I hesitated. I learned a long time ago that most guys have an odd reaction to The List. Some viewed it at as a red-flag challenge. Others branded me as a raging feminist for my anti–early marriage stance.

The rest of them just thought it was weird. I didn't really know where Matt would fall but none of the options suited me, so I gave a truthful—if slightly incomplete—answer instead.

"I'm starting grad school in the fall, and I thought I better squeeze in some adventures before things get too crazy," I said.

"Grad school?" he asked. "In what?"

"Art history."

"Any particular era?"

"Uh, twentieth-century European stuff," I said, feeling awkward. Most people didn't ask that follow-up question, and the answer left me with my nerd slip showing beneath my cool-girl façade. I tried a change of subject. "So what got you into surfing?"

"Wait, I want to know more about grad school," he said.

"I could give you the oral summary of my senior project," I joked.

"That might be kind of interesting," he said, "but I meant more like, where are you going to school? And what do you do with a degree in something like that? Are you going to be a college professor?"

I shrugged. "I'm at BYU. And I was thinking more of being a museum curator." Yeah, my nerd slip was hanging all the way out.

"That would be kind of cool, except only if things really came alive at night like in the movie," he said.

I stared at him blankly, wondering if I needed to adjust my gauge of his intelligence. Then I caught his sly grin as he turned back from the sink.

"Good one," I said.

"Admit it, that would be pretty cool."

"Except I'd have to be the night guard to see any of it, and I wouldn't need a master's for that."

"Yeah, waste of time if you only want to hang out with the stuff at night. Maybe you have time to back out. When does school start?"

"The first week of September."

"So cancel the tuition check and start applying for night jobs at the museums around here."

"Good idea, except the exhibits don't tip and that's what pays the bills right now," I said.

"Yeah, that could be a problem."

"Only if I want to eat."

"Speaking of which, I'm taking care of dessert. You ready to go?" He stuck his hand in his shorts pocket to give his keys a quick jingle.

"Sure. Where?"

"I thought we'd go downtown to Jamba Juice, then maybe watch the surfers from the pier. I could point out some more techniques."

I didn't hear anything after "Jamba." I smiled. "Fruit smoothies make me happy."

"Let's go, then."

We shoved the lunch fixings back into the fridge, and I followed him out to his car. It was a late-model FJ Cruiser with shiny black paint, silver trim, and the ubiquitous HB surf rack sitting on the white painted top. His surf shop must be doing all right, indeed.

As usual, the Huntington Beach pier boasted a summer swell of crowds. Locals fished and jogged along its concrete length, and tourists lined the rails with cameras aimed toward Catalina Island, a distant blur of land on the horizon. Concrete benches dotted the sides of the pier, and Matt gestured toward one that an elderly couple had just vacated. We were halfway between the shore and the fifties-themed diner that sat at the pier's end. Below us surfers sat on their boards and scanned the horizon, waiting for the right wave to come in.

"This is a good spot to check out when and why these guys are taking their waves," he explained. "Watch for what they catch, what they let pass, and when they try standing."

I nodded and sipped on my raspberry and peach calorie bomb, finding the rhythmic crash of the waves and warm sun hypnotic. We watched one guy catch a wave and ride it all the way in, maintaining a classic surfer stance with slightly bent knees, arms held ready to help balance himself.

When the wave faded into white water near the beach, he stepped off his board, then scooped it up and tucked it beneath his arm and jogged off toward Main Street. We stayed for another twenty minutes or so, Matt pointing out technique or lack thereof when he saw something teachable.

I tried to listen, I really did. The rise and fall of his words seemed to keep time with the waves, the rich tones lulling me into a daydream more than once. I gave myself a mental shake each time, sure if Matt caught me I would look like a zoned-out space cadet, but he didn't seem to notice.

Or I thought he didn't until I startled to find him waving a hand in front of my face, smiling when I focused on him.

I blushed. I never blush. But I felt almost as stupid as if I'd fallen asleep on his shoulder and then drooled. Almost.

"I can see you find this fascinating," he teased me.

"I do, I promise. I think I'm just so relaxed that my brain is trying to go on break too."

"That's kind of why I like surfing," he said. "I feel completely focused and totally relaxed at the same time."

"Yeah, I seem to do one or the other. What's the trick to doing both at once?"

"Practice."

"I was hoping for something where there would be less work involved, more along the lines of a magic wetsuit."

"You don't need it. If you can take the relaxation you feel right now and transfer it to when you're out on the board, you'll do better. You'll be able to feel the waves more, I guess is how to explain it."

I gave him a nod and a cheesy thumbs up, which, along with my fake smile, tipped him off that I didn't get it all.

"You're an interesting girl, Ashley," he said.

"Why do you say that?" I asked.

He shrugged. I thought my generation tried to communicate entirely too many things through shrugs, so I kept my gaze on him until he shifted and felt obligated to answer.

"You're unexpected," he said. "You look all remote and serious, but you're pretty . . ." He trailed off, searching for a word.

"Pretty what?" I prompted him. "Pretty goofy?"

"Just pretty."

"Coward," I said, giving him a light poke in the side.

"Didn't anyone teach you to accept a compliment?"

"Fine. Thanks for saying I'm pretty and not finishing the thought."

"You're welcome."

"You're pretty . . . too," I said.

"Pretty what?"

"Just pretty," I teased.

"I'll have to work on that. Maybe lose my comb or something." He reached up and tried to muss his hair. It just came out looking more beach tousled than messy.

"I don't think it would help," I mumbled beneath my breath.

"What did you say?" he asked.

"Nothing," I said, a little louder.

He leaned down until he was eye level with me and grinned. "I heard you. Thanks."

I refused to flinch. "You're welcome."

I'm not sure how long I would have stayed there, drinking in the warm brown pools of his eyes, but a shriek several yards down the pier broke the spell. Matt's head whipped around, and I could sense him tensing for action. A sunburned woman held a floppy straw hat to her head with one hand while the other hand held a camera and waved excitedly out to the water. He relaxed. I could barely make out her cry of, "Dolphins, y'all!" but it was enough to perk me right up. I looked at Matt hopefully.

"Would you like to go check them out?" he asked.

I nodded. He stood up and offered me a hand, which I accepted as I shook the last of my sun-induced lethargy off and climbed to my feet. Tempting as it was to hang on to him, I let go as soon as I stood. Hand-holding felt intimate to me at an emotional level. I didn't like the vulnerability of putting my hand in someone else's, an opinion that has earned the mockery of more than one college roommate given how freely I've been known to kiss unnamed boys in my past. All part of the Ashley Barrett charm, I guess.

We meandered down the pier a little farther near the small crowd gathered to watch the dolphins. I could see about three or four of the sleek animals arching and splashing in the water. According to Dave, surfers see dolphins quite often, but for me it felt like I had prime seats to a live showing of nature. I watched in awe as one of them leaped several feet in the air and then landed and playfully butted one of his companions. I grinned, delighted.

When they finally swam away, I turned to find Matt studying me intently again.

"What?" I asked, still smiling.

"Unexpected. Totally unexpected. You're not remote at all."

I dropped his gaze again, bothered that I couldn't hold it. I felt like I kept losing a dare. "I should get going," I said. "I need to do some stuff before work tonight."

"Sure. Let's get out of here."

He drove me home, and when he walked me to the front door, I turned and blurted, "I like that you're quiet." And then I blushed *again*. I like that you're quiet? Where did that come from?

He grinned. "See you, Ashley," he said, backing down the walkway with his hands in his pockets.

Oh yes, Matt Gibson. You better believe it.

Chapter 7

THE REST OF THE NIGHT and most of Saturday passed in a blur of demanding customers and the sound of my mental cash register as I racked up my tips. Even the Saturday lunch shift, usually a server's purgatory, delivered a nonstop rotation of diners through my section. I welcomed the distraction because it gave me less time to wonder why Matt hadn't called.

By Sunday, the hectic pace caught up with me, and for once I could appreciate the late start time of the Beachside Ward. Normally, starting church at one in the afternoon makes the whole day feel like it's been swallowed up by church, first with waiting for it to start, and then with sitting through it for three hours, not to mention lovely extensions like linger longer. But today, having time to sleep in and time after that to soak in the shower and eat a leisurely bowl of Fruity Pebbles felt like a little Sabbath gift.

I took extra care with my hair, combing through some curl fixer and wielding my diffuser with the skill perfected after years of experience. Satisfied that it had the proper bounce and sway, I turned my attention to my half of Celia's closet, mulling over what to wear. I studied and dismissed a few blouses and skirts, skipped over a couple of dresses, and then pulled out the perfect solution. My sister Leila had given me a bright green wrap dress when I got home from my mission, part of her effort to ensure that I didn't stay in what she called my "sister missionary frump fashion." The dress, in a bright shade of lime that I normally shied away from, totally worked with my deepening tan. I threw on a pair of strappy stilettos and a cool little peridot pendant from the bottom of my jewelry box.

I opted to squish into Dave's truck with Celia because the top on my Jeep was down and I didn't want to screw up my hair. We enjoyed the Beach Boys all the way to the chapel, that being Dave's version of Sunday music. I think his criteria were that it discuss nature and have no swearing. When I pressed him for an example, he cited "Surfin' Safari" as dealing with the ocean, which was made by Heavenly Father. Props to Dave for his mad rationalization skills.

We made it into the chapel as the opening hymn started and headed for the first open seats we saw on the front row of the over-flow. I'm not a big fan of the metal folding chairs; they were the main reason I was almost never late to sacrament meeting. I love me a cushioned pew.

I had three more verses of the song after sitting down to scan the chapel for Matt. I found him seated way up front, waiting to pass the sacrament. While I appreciated the fact that he was willing to serve the ward that way, I also appreciated the good things his white shirt did for his tan. But mostly I thought about the importance of passing the sacrament. Okay, maybe it was fifty-fifty. Or sixty-forty, with his tan in the lead.

I gave myself a mental head slap and refocused on the words of the hymn, determined not to be distracted. I did well until the sacrament ended and my train of thought derailed to speculate about where Matt would choose to sit after he was done passing the sacrament. One surf lesson and a date might not be enough of a lure to draw him to the seat next to me, the one I had strategically maneuvered Celia away from in case Matt felt the pressing need to sit there.

He didn't. He took a seat next to Derek near the front, never looking my way. No problem, I decided. Sitting together in sacrament meeting screamed, "We're practically engaged so don't talk to either of us," so sitting by his roommate made sense. I guess. I turned my attention to the speaker. She was about five minutes into a really interesting talk when someone slipped into Matt's rejected seat. I glanced over at my new neighbor and discovered an extremely good-looking blond guy settling in. He flashed me a bright smile, which I returned before turning back to the girl at the podium. I got caught up in her talk again, but a minute later Blond Smiley Guy leaned over and whispered, "I'm Aaron," and held out a hand.

Startled, I shook it and whispered, "I'm Ashley," then dropped his hand and turned back to the speaker, signaling that I wanted to listen. I thought. That I was signaling, I mean. Apparently not, because Blond Aaron, still leaning toward me, whispered, "Are you new in the ward?"

I turned to him with a slightly incredulous look. "I'm sorry," I answered. "I can't hear you *over the speaker.*"

Too bad my pointed hint was lost on Blond Aaron. He tried again. "I asked if you're new to the ward."

His stage whisper caused Dave to snort. I only liked to make people laugh on purpose, so that chapped my hide even more.

"Yes," I hissed, not giving him any material for a follow-up question.

He asked one, anyway. "How new?"

"I'm visiting for a while this summer so I can be with my fiancé," I hissed, and wondered if the chapel ceiling would lift off so the lightning could strike me without damaging the building. It couldn't be good to lie in church. Or ever, really, but especially not in church. But he didn't ask any more questions, so I didn't feel too bad. By the time the service ended, he took off, presumably for easier hunting. I went to stake out my claim on the back row of the Relief Society room where my Sunday School class of choice was held.

I walked in expecting to find the usual teachers, a team of a girl my age and a guy a year or two younger. Her close reading of the scriptures was a good balance to his less studied but utterly sincere zeal. Instead, I saw Matt standing there, setting up like he was going to teach. This put me in a position to feel like an inadvertent public stalker and also admire his super cool gold tie. I wavered for a moment before taking a backseat, not wanting to make things awkward by turning around to walk out for no apparent reason. Unless I counted "I kind of like you and don't want you to think that I do so I can't come to your class if you think I'm here just to see you" as a reason. Which I did not, because that would be so junior high. I like to operate on at least a sophomore level.

Actually, despite the slightly hardened shell I have after years of dating and the thick outer crust of cynicism I developed after watching multiple variations of the same tired games play out, I really think that once you get past the games and dig a little deeper, things work out. I couldn't think of any other reason for the millions of marriages taking place each year. But that was exactly why treating dating like a game worked for me. It kept things light, and as long as I was honest, no one got hurt. If a guy started getting too attached, I withdrew and left him free to find someone else who was looking for the same level of commitment.

I made the mistake of getting too comfortable in a relationship once. A couple of years before my mission, I dated a guy from my ward named Dylan. I was so into him it would have been ridiculous if he hadn't been so into me too. The problem was that inside of a month, I found myself neglecting my coursework and trading away work shifts to spend time with him. My grades and my finances suffered, and when he started talking marriage, I realized I was heading down a dangerous road. If he could distract me from my goals so quickly while we were dating, there was no chance I would stay on track if I got married. I hated hurting him, but it was better than resenting him later like Leila did with her soon-to-be ex-husband.

Matt posed an interesting challenge. I felt myself drawn to him. My play-it-cool approach had worked to pique his interest, but now that I had it, I didn't feel my usual need for a buffer, and I couldn't figure out why. In the split second I had to think about it before he headed toward me, I decided it was because leaving at the end of the summer *was* my buffer. Leaving offered me an escape hatch from any relationship, which in turn gave me the freedom to relax with him a little more, knowing anything between us would end when August did. I had no time for messy entanglements past that.

"Hey, Ashley," he said, slipping past me to the seat on my right.

"You're teaching today?"

"I'm subbing for Shelley," he said, naming the girl who normally taught.

"What about her partner?"

"Tod? He says things don't go well if he teaches by himself, so he asked me to take over for today."

"Are you nervous?" I doubted it. He never looked anything but calm, cool, and collected.

"Not really. I accept that I don't know nearly as much as half the room does about the lesson and move on."

"I doubt that's true or he wouldn't ask you to teach the lesson."

"He just asked me because I used to be Shelley's partner."

"Ah, but you folded under the pressure, and they had to replace you?" I teased him.

"Or else I travel too much in the winter, and they needed someone who's actually here every Sunday."

"Why do you travel so much during the winter?" I asked.

"The shop," he said, and I waited for more, but a wave of people spilled through the door before he could elaborate, and he smiled and headed toward the front of the room.

Once the milling had about settled down, Matt invited a guy on the front row to say an opening prayer, and then he dove into the lesson involving some chapters in Alma. I noticed that he avoided interjecting his opinion, instead guiding the discussion from one person to the next and using their own comments to connect ideas by paraphrasing. I could see a pleased face here and there when someone felt like he or she had made a point that was validated by Matt, rather than overtaken and engulfed in his own point. Much like the first part of sacrament meeting, I paid less attention to the lesson than I should have, focusing instead on watching Matt work and the room respond to him.

I noticed my new BFF, Megan from Institute, sitting on the second row, eager to shoot her hand up and answer every question, whether her point made sense or not. I even paid close enough attention to figure out that Matt called on her every fourth time she raised her hand. I gave him credit for keeping the class on track in spite of her observations. At one point, the discussion turned to the Savior's parable of faith as a mustard seed, and Megan threw in her bizarre two cents. "I grew a mustard plant once. I started it from a seed, and then when it produced, I dehydrated the mustard pods and decided to try a mustard jelly instead of an actual mustard because I believe in kitchen creativity."

Matt didn't even crack a smile. The guy was a rock.

When the lesson ended, a throng of females immediately surrounded him. I waited for him to look up before I waved, then headed for the drinking fountain and a little liquid refreshment while I waited for the Relief Society room to clear. I was standing in the hallway perusing the bulletin board (which had clearly been done by a sister with a surplus of Stampin' Up tools) when Blond Aaron sidled up to me. I don't like sidling. Matt and his excellent saunter were a totally different thing than Blond Aaron's oozy sidle.

"Hey, there," he said. "Ashley, right?"

He acted like retaining that information in the hour since sacrament meeting constituted a major accomplishment. "No, I'm Barb," I said, just to mess with him.

"You are?"

"No, I'm Ashley. And you're . . . ?" I knew it would not be a good idea to let on that I remembered his name even for an hour.

"Aaron," he prompted me.

"That's right. I had a dog named Aaron, but it was bad and ran away a lot and got hit by a car."

"Oh. Sorry to hear that," he said. I might have felt bad for killing off an imaginary dog if Aaron looked like he genuinely sympathized. But no. Instead, he used my fake dog's death as an opening.

"I hope you're not still too bummed about that," he said. I felt an almost physical urge to wrinkle my nose at his manufactured charm, but I refrained.

"I was two, and I didn't really like the dog. Did I mention it was bad? Bad, bad Aaron," I said, shaking my head in sorrowful emphasis.

"I'm glad you've had time to get over it, but I could offer you a shoulder to cry on if you really needed it," he said, unsubtly flexing to draw attention to his muscles. Unfortunately for him, it also drew my attention to the fact that he had less neck than I preferred on guys, and that sealed his fate. His player vibe didn't help him, either.

I was about to extricate myself from the conversation via another imaginary issue. "Gotta scoot. I have cramps," works well in these situations, but he suddenly straightened and took a slight step back. Before I could look over my shoulder to follow his gaze, Matt slid an arm around me.

"How's it going, Aaron?" he asked.

"Hey, Matt," Aaron said, backing up even farther. "Sorry. I didn't realize you were engaged. I'd talk, but I'm late for priesthood," and he ducked around the corner to the gym before I could open my mouth to refute his misconception.

"Ashley," Matt said seriously, removing his arm. "We need to talk." He moved so we were face-to-face and then took both of my hands in his. "You make really good poppy seed dressing, but that doesn't mean I'm ready to marry you."

Without missing a beat, I squeezed his hands and stared into his eyes. "But what about the grilled cheese, Matt? *What about the grilled cheese?*"

"I made that," he whispered gently. "If *you* had made it, maybe things would be different right now."

A laugh bubbled out before I could stop it. "In that case, I guess I'll quit telling everyone we're getting married."

"What was that all about, anyway?" he asked, still smiling.

"He wouldn't stop talking to me in sacrament meeting, so I invented a fiancé, and when you walked up, I guess he thought I meant you. Sorry about that," I said.

"No problem," he shrugged it off. "But seriously, he's bad news. Staying away from him is a smart move."

"Why was he was so desperate to get away from you?" I asked. "I think that was fear in his beady eyes."

"There might have been an episode while he was dating my sister when I invited him to never come around again and told him ignoring me might pose a serious threat to his health."

"Wow, remind me not to cross you. Do you have to beat up guys for her regularly?" Best to get any undisclosed rage issues out now.

"No. I've never been in a fight, but I'd be happy to take a swing at Aaron if I ever had a reason," he admitted.

"Okay, I promise not to change my mind about him."

"You made it up so quickly?"

"Yeah. I think I settled on narcissistic and ego-driven game player who seeks out fresh meat because the locals are on to his tricks."

"Then you're a great judge of character." He cocked his head and asked, "What have you decided about me?"

"Hmm, Matt Gibson . . ." I pretended to mull. "You are—" but I was saved from an answer when a cute redhead appeared at his elbow and batted her lashes.

"Hey, Matt. Are you barbecuing today?"

I grinned when a slightly exasperated expression flickered across his face before he restored his polite mask.

"I'm not. Sorry," he said.

"Oh," she said with a little pout. "That's a bummer. Your thighs were so good last week. Maybe next time." I think I missed her exit because my eyes nearly crossed in an effort to control my inappropriate giggles.

"She's talking about the chicken I made last week," he muttered, obviously embarrassed.

"Of course she was," I said.

"Are you coming over tonight?"

"I thought you just said you weren't barbecuing."

"I'm not. Derek is. She didn't ask about Derek," he said with a smile.

"Well, thanks for the invite, but I don't think I can make it," I said.

"Is this the antisocial thing again?" he asked.

"No, this is the getting-ready-for-the-week thing," I retorted. "Trust me, you'll never even miss me in the crowd." I took a step backward, toward the Relief Society room. "Maybe I'll see you at Institute or something." Then I gave him another small wave and made my way to class.

* * *

I cursed myself for being a bonehead later that night. Rejecting the barbecue invitation left me with the alternative of spending the evening with some scary LDS Lookup options. Like TwinofAdonis, who had a profile picture of himself shirtless and flexing. Um . . . no. I also took a pass on LonelyLeland, who looked pleasant enough in his profile picture, but included a preoccupation with building model trains and railroads in his list of interests. In fact, his description of his hobby-turned-passion verged on essay length and did a fair job of providing a subtext for the "lonely" part of his screen name. WolfMan didn't include a photo, maybe because his profile was new to the site, but I knew I wouldn't be waiting around to see it after reading that he was "looking for a cool girl that wasn't crazy like my first two ex-wives."

I set my laptop aside and lay back on my bed to stare at the ceiling. I could be enjoying over-grilled hamburgers and generic potato chips right now if I had accepted Matt's invitation. But no, I had to go be all cool and mysterious and let him think about why I wasn't there.

I picked up my cell phone, toying with it for a minute, but yelped when it vibrated with an incoming text. *It's Matt*, I read. *Can you really pass up carne asada?*

I texted back. *How did you get my number?*

Dave narced it out. Kill him later, eat carne asada now.

Now how was I supposed to say no to steak? *No frozen bulk burgers and store brand cheese curls?*

Living the high life. Come over.

I need the address, I typed, and jumped up to raid the dresser for something to wear.

By the time my phone chimed to let me know that his address was waiting, I already had my head halfway through a cute turquoise long-sleeved shirt, sleeves being essential on a cool summer night near the beach. With a pair of denim capris and some white flip-flops trimmed in silver beads, I felt ready to meet Matt on his turf.

Celia took off for a friend's house earlier in the evening or I would have invited her too, but for the moment, I was flying solo. Matt's place turned out to be a run-down little house on Seventeenth Street, just a couple of blocks from the water. In Huntington Beach, any twenty-something guy with a surfboard would gladly trade nicer digs for a shack if it meant having the proximity to the beach that Matt and Derek enjoyed. In between cars whizzing by on the nearby coast highway, I could hear the crash of waves against the sand.

I could have found the house easily with only a street name and no house number, because tiki torches on the lawn illuminated people spilling past the yard's white fence and onto the sidewalk. I recognized several faces from around the ward, and I scanned them in search of Matt's. I found it as he picked his way through the crowd.

"Hi, Ashley," he said, hands shoved into the pockets of some tattered cargo shorts. The faded insignia on the front of his worn sweatshirt was indiscernible in the half light of dusk. Glad I had settled on a tee shirt instead of trying to get dolled up, I mentally thanked Celia for her insistence that no one dresses up for anything in HB during the summer except church.

"Hi," I said back. "You mentioned carne asada?"

"Coming right up," he said. "Let me show you where the grub is."

I followed him through the gate. Instead of leading me up the front porch steps, we wound around to the back of the house where the smell of grill smoke mingled pleasantly with the salty air. It was nearly eight o'clock and the sun had set, but traces of daylight hung on long enough to mute the flames from the barbecue as they licked at the meat sizzling on the racks above them. Derek manned the grill and waved at us absentmindedly. A table flanking the sliding doors at the back of the house offered up chips, salsa, and . . .

"Guacamole," I breathed happily, heading for the table. I grabbed a paper plate and served myself a healthy heap of the squishy green goodness, tortilla chips, and a couple of chewy Chips Ahoy that hadn't been gobbled up yet. I was debating the wisdom of adding carrots and ranch (more for the ranch than the carrots) when Matt started laughing.

"I feel like I'm rescuing you from starvation," he said, gesturing to my full plate.

"I like to eat," I said. "You thought I came here for the company?"

"I hoped." He grinned.

"I might have," I conceded. "It depends."

His eyebrow crept up. "On what?"

"Do you know any good jokes?"

He took a seat on the shabby sofa opposite the grill and patted the cushion next to him, which I claimed.

"Uh, okay. Two surfers are getting ready to paddle out. The first guy says, 'Hey, guess what! I got a new long board for my wife!' and his friend answers, 'Great trade!'"

It was my turn to lift an eyebrow at him, then I twisted around and pretended to huddle over my food and eat it while ignoring him.

He groaned. "All right, I've got another one. How do you get your dishwasher to start working?"

I waited.

"You slap him?" he offered hopefully.

I faced him again. "Better," I pronounced.

"Yeah, well, as long as we stay in the sexist joke genre, I should be pretty safe," he said.

"Why is that?" I asked.

"Because I learned a bunch of them when I was a teenager to drive my sisters nuts. And since I forget the punch line halfway through most jokes I've heard since, I'm stuck with those from way back then as a punishment, I guess."

"At least you made the dishwasher a guy. My brother-in-law always tells it the other way to rile my sister."

"I'm guessing it works?"

"I've seen her throw food at him before," I answered. "But that's only if he's able to time it so she's in the worst possible mood."

"Uh-huh. And is throwing stuff a normal response to anger in your family?"

Rather than explain Leila's brink-of-divorce drama of the last two years, I spread my hand underneath my plate and pretended to test its weight. "Sure," I said. "But it's not a big deal if you duck fast."

"How about if I don't make you mad, and then we never have to find out who's faster?"

"Good plan."

"Hey, D," he called to his roommate. "Dibs on the next batch of carne, yeah?"

"Yeah, bro," Derek called back, still focused on the meat.

"He's in the zone," I whispered, entertained by his roommate's total concentration on the grill.

"Don't mock. He's a barbecue guru."

"Then I'm going to eat my way through this guacamole so I have room on my plate," I said.

"I could just get you another plate," he offered.

"What, and make me look like a pig?" I waved my hand over my laden plate. "If I eat fast, no one will ever know how much I started with."

He leaned forward and narrowed his eyes. "Great strategy, except I'm a witness. How will you buy my silence?"

I thought for a moment. "Can I bribe you with homemade fudge?"

He looked offended. "Hey, I have standards. You'd have to throw in ice cream for me to even think about it."

"Done," I said, liking how easily the conversation flowed between us.

"Yeah, me too," Derek interrupted. "Meat's ready."

Matt grinned. "Looks like you're getting two plates, anyway." He climbed to his feet and grabbed another plate, returning it to me piled with a healthy portion of fragrant steak. I immediately set the guacamole aside.

"Why aren't you eating?" I asked, before taking my first bite.

"I think I already put away a pound of that stuff before you got here," he answered. "If I thought there was a snowball's chance in Texas that you'd show up after I texted you, I would have waited for you."

"I said I'd be here," I reminded him around a delicious mouthful.

"Yeah, but you don't do a lot of things that I expect."

I stopped chewing for a minute and studied him. "You have expectations, plural? For me? How long is this list?"

He fidgeted. "I meant that . . . you, uh . . ." He stopped, trying to regroup. It was fun to discomfit him for once.

Derek wandered over again with another spatula heaped in meat. "He means that you don't do like the other chicks do and fall all over him, so he can't figure you out," he said. Then he dropped the meat on my plate and returned to the grill.

"Thanks, Derek," Matt called, and although it was hard to tell in the fading light, I'm pretty sure he was red.

Derek didn't turn around, just kept his gaze trained on the food and waved his spatula behind him. "Yeah, bro."

I grinned. "You were telling me about your expectations?"

He cleared his throat. "You're different, is all."

"Be still my heart."

That elicited a full-blown sigh, colored with exasperation. "I just mean that it's interesting to see what you're going to do next."

Which wasn't really an answer, but I let him off the hook. "I'll drop it for now because you're feeding me."

"Aren't we supposed to be talking about you bribing me for my silence, anyway?" he asked.

"No. We settled that. I'm making you fudge and ice cream."

"Oh yeah. Then we should move on to how you're going to pay me for your lessons."

"You mean an amazing grilled cheese sandwich and my undying gratitude isn't enough?"

"Definitely not. I get that all the time."

I rolled my eyes and his crooked grin reappeared.

"Then what can I offer you?" I asked.

"You have to take me on a real date," he said. "One where I can do my hair and wear my new heels."

I snorted before I could help myself and then tried to cover it with a cough, but I could tell by the twinkle in his eye that it didn't fool Matt. "Uh . . . you're kidding, right?"

"Only about the heels. They hurt my arches."

"I have a weird schedule," I warned him, unsure of how I felt about this "real date" business. "I end up working most weekends, so it could mean staying out late on a weeknight."

"Good. Live dangerously."

"Okay, so . . . a real date. Making sandwiches and eating them at my kitchen table doesn't count?" I stalled, trying to get a sense of exactly what Matt was suggesting.

"Nope. That's hanging out. Derek and I hang out. But Derek doesn't take me anywhere nice, so now I'm depending on you."

"Does renting a movie and graduating to the living room count as somewhere nice?"

He crossed his arms. "Is that all I'm worth as your surf sensei? Maybe I better reconsider this whole lesson thing."

"Relax. I was just asking. *Of course* I meant that we're going to do something super exciting. As in, beyond fantastic." I just had no idea what. Small glitch. "Here," I said, thrusting one of my plates at him. "I got you some carne asada as a thank-you gift for your help so far."

He laughed. "You only ate half of it. I thought you were hungry."

"Yeah, well, my eyes were bigger than my stomach." I didn't mention that my appetite had shrunk when the "real date" contingency kicked in.

A sudden crest of giggles preceded a small wave of girls as they rounded the corner to the backyard. Matt looked wary, while Derek straightened his spine and puffed his chest out.

"Ooh, looks like my cue to get more guacamole," I said.

"Don't do it," he said. "I saved you from Aaron."

"Yes, but you weren't in any danger. One of these girls might hurt me if I don't give up my spot."

He opened his mouth to argue, but the first, "Hi, Matt!" trilled forth from a petite cutie on the vanguard of the wave. I hopped up with a grin and headed for the snack table. No way did I have room for any more food, but it removed me from the line of fire and gave me a great view of the action.

The tiny blonde had settled right into the space I vacated.

"Hey . . ." Matt trailed off, struggling to come up with a name.

"Kelsey." She giggled.

"Right, sorry. Hey, Kelsey."

She giggled again, I guess finding it funny that Matt forgot her name.

"Great party," she said, and the band of gigglers with her nodded and murmured their agreement.

"Thanks," he said. "Did you guys get enough to eat?"

"Oh, I don't have much of an appetite," Kelsey said. "It's a curse."

"I'm sorry to hear that," Matt replied. "Derek does a great job with the grilling."

Kelsey bounced a little in her seat. "You guys have such a great place here," she said, all shiny enthusiasm. She kind of reminded me of this plastic whistle I used to have when I was a kid. It was bird shaped, and when I filled it with water and blew it, it emitted the same strangely unbalanced warble that kept bursting out of Kelsey.

"Thanks," Matt said. Despite having nothing to work with conversationally, Kelsey charged ahead.

"I mean, it's a little on the shabby side, but it won't take much to make it shabby chic. If I lived here—"

Oh, no she didn't! Did she? Did she really admit out loud that she foresaw herself comfortably ensconced in Chez Matt some day? Way to send him slinking in the opposite direction, Kelsey. I settled against the table to enjoy the show. It was getting good.

"If I lived here, I'd slap some blue paint on the walls, trim everything with a nice, bright white, rustle up some nice slip covers for the sofa, and find some cute little pillows to toss everywhere."

Matt didn't strike me as a cute little pillows kind of guy.

"And I'm a great seamstress," she continued. "I can make slipcovers for way cheaper than you can buy them. I learned how to sew when I was little. My mom thought it would be a good skill for me to have when I'm a mother. You know, so I can save money by making my kids' clothes."

Matt nodded, looking uncomfortable with the miniature beauty queen sizing up his furniture for renovation. The kid talk injected his expression with a touch of panic, to boot. I decided he needed to twist a little longer so he could *really* appreciate my rescue.

"Homemaking is a lost art," Kelsey said, earnestness furrowing her smooth brow. "I mean, we live in such a disposable society, you know?" Matt nodded again, although he seemed unsure of where she was headed.

"Tell Matt about your business idea," a member of her entourage chimed in.

"Oh, he doesn't want to hear about that," she said, fishing.

Matt smiled and neither confirmed nor denied, but her friends egged her on.

"It's such a good idea!"

"Yeah, you should tell him!"

"Don't be so modest!"

The chorus of encouragement overrode Matt's lack of cues and Kelsey said, "Well, I haven't worked out all the details yet, but I'm thinking . . . surfboard covers!"

Matt looked interested at that. "Really? What kind? Mine are always wearing out."

"I'm thinking something designer," Kelsey said. "All the ones out right now are so practical, you know? Just boring colors and materials. I thought I could sew up some nice fabric ones with all kinds of bright colors and prints, give them a little pizzazz and all."

Matt's expression shifted to doubtful. Surf culture is not really about pizzazz, but Kelsey didn't notice. She barreled along, outlining her ideas for bright floral prints that guys would actually like, and when she prattled into piping and trim territory, Matt began sending me pleas for help with his eyes.

Those yummy eyes . . .

I sighed. "Derek?" I murmured, low enough not to interrupt Kelsey's plans for masculine lace because, as she assured Matt with a tinkling laugh, there really was such a thing.

"Yeah?" he grunted, a little annoyed that none of the feminine wiles were being cast his way.

"I really liked your carne asada."

He turned to look at me. "Thanks," he said, looking somewhat vindicated.

"So forgive me for what I'm about to do."

"Huh?"

But I was already headed for Matt and rescue duty.

Chapter 8

"MATT, I'M SO SORRY TO INTERRUPT," I mewed pitifully and then slumped onto the arm of the sofa next to him. I pressed my hand against my forehead and squeezed my eyes closed, then barely audibly I whispered, "I don't feel good."

Kelsey looked nonplussed by my arrival and her minions stirred, confused by my interruption. Deciding they still weren't getting it, I pressed my hands to my stomach and hunched over with a whimper. "I feel sick," I croaked.

The girl directly in front of me scampered back, presumably to avoid any unpleasantness that my guts might have in store for her. Matt leaped to his feet and bent over me. "Is this for real?" he whispered in my ear.

I moaned softly and shook my head no. To our rapt audience, it appeared that my misery was increasing.

"Let's get you inside," he said at normal volume. He helped me up and then kept an arm around my shoulders, gently urging me toward the door leading inside. As we passed Kelsey, I caught her shooting a squinty-eyed dagger glare my way. I emitted another theatrical groan, causing her mouth to narrow in irritation.

Matt squeezed my shoulder and murmured, "Watch it. You're going to sprain your drama if you're not careful."

I nodded, hunched over a little farther, and shuffled alongside him into the house. As soon as the door shut behind me, I straightened up and grinned. "You're welcome," I said.

"No kidding," he said. "That's good for at least two more surf lessons."

"Whew. I guess I'm off the hook for a date, then," I joked.

"You are if you want to be," he answered.

I held his gaze for several seconds and then confessed, "I don't."

"Good."

"So, what do I do with you now?" I asked. "Do I throw you back to the . . . uh . . ." I faltered, not willing to characterize the group of girls outside as sharks out loud.

Matt smiled like he knew what I wasn't saying. "I don't deserve that. I rescued you, remember?"

"Oh, right. From my imaginary illness."

"What pretend sickness did you catch, anyway?"

I rubbed my stomach. "I'm going with spontaneous food poisoning from the carne asada."

He winced. "Derek will be crushed. It's his specialty."

"I told him I was sorry in advance."

He smiled in admiration. "Man, you really think on your feet."

"No, I don't. Thinking and my feet don't work together at all. That's why you have to help with the surf thing."

"Right. Lucky me."

And before I could wonder if he was being serious or sarcastic, he scuffed his flip-flop lightly against mine and said, "Thanks, Ashley's feet."

The door squeaked open again and Kelsey's head appeared around the side, approximately level with the door knob. Well, maybe not *that* low, but she was short. Just saying.

She eyed me, obviously suspicious, and asked, "Are you feeling any better?"

Matt threw his arm around my shoulder again and I leaned against him like he was the only thing holding me up.

"I feel okay," I mumbled. Matt squeezed my shoulder. "I mean, except for being really, really sick," and then I groaned again. This time I got a pat.

"Oh, that's too bad." And I knew Kelsey only meant that it was too bad because my "spell" was keeping me glued to Matt's side.

"Yeah, I think I'm going to make sure Ashley gets home okay."

Her face fell. "You're leaving?"

"Yeah. I feel responsible for her getting sick at my house. Stay and enjoy the party, though," Matt offered.

"Sure," Kelsey said, but it was kind of pouty.

Since I didn't know how far Matt planned to take this, I kept my mouth shut and followed his lead. He slid his hand from my shoulder, down my arm, and slipped it around my hand. With a soft tug, he led me back toward the front of the house, skillfully navigating the clusters of people hanging out in islands of conversation all the way to the front door. Even traveling the relatively short distance took quite a while as friends stopped Matt to greet him or offer him the casual surfer "What's goin' on?" It gave me time to observe his house. It was a typical bachelor pad with worn furniture and scuffed wooden floors. Very few personal touches showed besides the snapshots stuck to the fridge and some surf posters on the wall. The only exception was a large framed photograph in the living room of him and another guy posing with huge smiles in front of a store under a sign reading THE BOARD SHACK.

Holding my hand seemed to ward off other girls, and he didn't let go, so when we made it through the front yard and onto the street, I was growing used to his warm grip. I wondered as we drew even with my Jeep if he would let it go and kind of hoped not.

Instead, he held his other hand out for my keys and said, "I better drive since you're sick."

"What? Are you ditching out on your own party?"

He shrugged. "Our barbecues are an excuse for people to hang out. They wouldn't notice if Derek and I left unless we took the food with us."

"All right, I'm in. Where are we going?"

He smiled and said nothing.

"You're not going to tell me," I guessed.

"Nope. But don't take it personally. It's just because I don't know where we're going yet, either."

"That's one of my favorite places."

"Yeah, mine too, on a Sunday." He looked up at the night sky. "What do you think? Is a coast drive still worth it even without the daylight?"

I dug my keys out of my pocket and plopped them in his hand. "Definitely."

Chapter 9

Twenty minutes later, we were cruising down Pacific Coast Highway, or PCH. We'd already headed through the coastal towns of Newport Beach and Corona del Mar without stopping. An approaching sign showed that Laguna Beach was up next.

"How about there?" Matt asked.

"Sure," I shrugged. It seemed like nearly every person under the age of twenty-five who had ever lived there had a spin-off show on MTV. *Laguna Beach, The Hills,* and probably a half dozen more I'd never heard of. Might as well check out the ruckus.

Matt followed the highway until it slowed down to wind through a bustling downtown area. He parked on the first side street he could find and hopped out to open my door. By the time he came around to my side of the Jeep, I had already grabbed a hoodie from the back and jumped down. He looked at me in surprise. "I would have gotten the door for you," he said as I shut it.

I shrugged. "I know, and I appreciate it, but it's more efficient to let myself out. I don't mind if you hold it open when we get back in, though."

"All right, but don't tell my mom. She'd kill me." He nodded in the direction of the main sidewalk. "You ready?"

"Sure."

We walked side-by-side toward the noise and laughter spilling out from café tables and open doors. Matt stayed close, but he didn't try to take my hand again.

"Have you been here before?" he asked.

"No. I just know Laguna Beach from that MTV show."

He laughed. "It's a little different from how it looks on TV," he said. "A ton of artists live around here, and there are all kinds of galleries and studios and stuff everywhere you look."

"Sounds like my kind of place."

"Yeah. You'd probably like the Pageant of the Masters here too. They make exact replicas of famous masterpieces using real people. It's pretty trippy."

"You mean they're all life-sized with people in costumes and everything?"

He nodded. "You have to see it to believe it."

We rounded the corner to join the sidewalk winding along PCH. People strolled by, peering into shop windows or calling to friends. On the other side of the highway, couples meandered down the narrow wooden boardwalk winding along the beach. My hand itched, missing Matt's. Almost like he read my mind, he reached over to take it, and I felt content again. I decided not to analyze why I didn't flinch like I would have with anyone else.

We made it to the next block, commenting occasionally on different window displays or the live music pouring from a corner coffee shop. Halfway down the sidewalk, a soft light floated from the window of a small art gallery. Matt stopped to check out the pieces on display. There were two sculptures, one made from polished wood and the other from smooth stone. They were sinuous and twisty with no real form, more the hint of a feeling.

"That wood piece reminds me of how I feel when I wake up from a nap," Matt said.

I looked at him, impressed. "I didn't know you were an art connoisseur."

He snorted. "Ha. I'm not. I'm just saying, it looks like a big, long stretch."

I studied the piece again. "Huh. I can totally see that." I pointed to an abstract painting hung on the display wall behind the statue. "What's that mean?"

He looked at the picture, full of sharp angles in different shades of blue and red. He tilted his head and thought for a minute. "Oh yeah, it's speaking to me," he murmured.

I stifled a laugh, and he squeezed my hand.

"I've got it," he said. "That's a commentary on partisan politics in America."

"No," I said.

"No?"

"I can't believe you don't see it. The artist is clearly imagining what it would look like if Superman got smooshed."

"No way," he said. "Smooshing would be swirly. That's pointy."

"Well, it's definitely not about politics."

"You're right." He narrowed his eyes and stared at the picture again. "Okay, I just had to use all of my awesome art interpretation skills, but I figured it out."

"Lay it on me," I said.

"That is a rendering of the struggle for primacy between red and blue crayons."

"Primacy? That's a two-dollar word."

He looked sheepish.

"Hey." I tugged on his hand and caught his eye. "I love two-dollar words."

"Oh, really?" he drawled.

"Really."

"How much?"

I tugged on his hand again, but this time I kept the pressure consistent, drawing him down toward me. When he was close enough, I leaned up and kissed him just to the left of his mouth. "That much," I said.

He stared at me for a long moment.

"Antidisestablishmentarianism," he said.

I gave him another peck.

"That's the longest word I know," he objected. "It's only worth as much as *primacy?*"

"No, but we haven't even had a first date. I can't be giving you the wrong impression." My insides went all squishy knowing that he was fishing for a juicier kiss.

"And whose fault is it that we haven't been on a date?" he asked. "Seems like one of us is responsible for putting that together, and it isn't me."

"How'd that happen, again?"

"I'm your awesome surf coach."

"Oh yeah. Well, I'm not a slacker. I pick Wednesday for our date. Be there or be square."

"Be there or be square?" he teased me. "1985 called, and they want their catchphrase back."

"It's not fair, you know."

"What's not fair?" he asked, moving closer to me to allow another couple room to pass us on the sidewalk.

"It's not fair that I can't tease you back," I murmured, distracted by his scent. He smelled faintly spicy.

"Why can't you?"

"You're holding my surf lessons hostage. I have to be nice or I won't get any," I sighed.

"Oh, that's a bummer," he said.

He tugged me back into the sidewalk traffic and continued down the strand of shop fronts. Four stores down, he stopped again. We were in front of a dimly lit window showcasing antique tobacco pipes.

"I have a solution," he announced.

"To what?"

"To the surf lesson hostage crisis."

"I'm listening."

He turned to face me and took my other hand, then peered down at me intently. "Turns out I kind of like giving you lessons. So I'm going to do it just because. No barter or trade."

"But—"

He shook his head. "You can't change my mind. This way, if we hang out, it's because you want to, not because you have to so that you can get a surfing session."

"Oh."

He released one of my hands and turned to walk again. I nestled beside him, liking how he made sure to stay between me and the road, and how our hands didn't seem to sweat even though they'd been connected for a while now.

"Hey, Matt?" I said after a couple of easy minutes passed.

"Yeah?"

"You want to go on a date with me Wednesday night?"

"Yeah."

Just then my cell phone chirped with a text message. I dug it out of my back pocket and tapped the display. It was from Celia.

Where are you?

Ah, a dilemma. I wanted to see her face when I told her how I spent the evening. "It's Celia," I said to Matt. "Do you care if I text her back really quick? I don't want her to worry."

"No problem," he said.

I looked at him expectantly, but nothing happened. Finally I shook our joined hands gently. "I need mine back," I said.

"Another bummer," he answered, but he let go.

I tapped out a quick answer to Celia. *Been captured by pirates. Don't wait up.*

I slipped my hand back into Matt's and returned the phone to my pocket where it immediately chirped again. He loosened his grip once more, but I held on. "Don't worry about it," I said. "She can wait."

"You sure?"

I nodded.

"Let's hit the beach."

We crossed the next intersection right as the time was expiring on the walk box. The sand had little traffic now that the sun had set, but a few people dotted the benches along the boardwalk, quietly taking in the lap of ocean waves. A playground perched near the side of the boardwalk, empty of children. I pointed. "Can we?"

Matt smiled. "Definitely."

I scampered over to the swings and then slipped off my flip-flops, enjoying the feeling of the cool sand sliding over my bare feet.

"Need a push?" Matt asked.

"Nope. Grab a swing," I invited him.

He settled onto the one next to me and began a lazy sway back and forth. I swung higher and dropped my head back, trying to pierce the evening clouds and see the night sky.

"So far, the only thing I like better about Utah is summer nights," I murmured.

"Why's that?" Matt asked.

"Stars," I said.

"I've heard of them," he said. "We don't see those here with the marine layer."

"That's too bad. They're pretty spectacular."

He waved toward the ocean. "That's our consolation prize. Lots of sun and ocean breezes."

I took a deep breath of the salt air. "You guys aren't doing too badly for yourselves down here."

He laughed. "Thanks for noticing."

Despite the darkness enfolding the playground, I could still see the flash of his teeth when he smiled. I liked that smile. Its brightness owed everything to the contrast against his tan and not whiteners, I suspected. Feeling foolish for mooning over it, I dug my feet in and stopped my swing. I flicked a foot toward him, showering his shins with sand.

"Did you just kick sand at me on purpose?" he asked.

"It's the playground," I said. "It brings out the kid in me."

"And what's your favorite part of the playground?"

I thought about it. "Swings are pretty awesome, but it's hard to beat a good twisty slide."

He nodded toward the dark shape of a jungle gym several yards away. "You up for it?"

"If there's a twisty slide, I'm totally in," I said.

He helped me out of the swing and we trudged toward the hulking shape, parapets and a rope bridge melting out of the darkness as we approached the playground castle. The tallest parapet covered the top of a spiral slide.

"Is it calling to you?" Matt asked.

I grabbed the rung of one of the ladders hanging off the side and climbed. "Totally," I said.

Matt followed behind me. The parapet enclosed a cozy space. I sat with my knees beneath my chin, my arms wrapped around my legs, and Matt pressed against my side as he scrunched himself up so we could both fit. With a little effort, we arranged elbows and feet in a way that kept us both from getting poked.

"I don't even want to go down the slide. I like it right here," Matt said.

"It's kind of cool," I agreed. "Do you hear how everything sounds different in here?"

He listened for a minute, noticing like I did the way the metal captured and amplified sound from outside. "It's like being in a seashell."

I dropped my head back against the wall. "I love the sound of waves."

We sat there for several long, quiet moments when I heard a new sound in the background. Someone was shuffling through the sand on the playground, gradually getting closer. Matt straightened, obviously hearing it too. The footsteps stopped, placing whoever it was very near our turret.

"Should we say something?" I whispered to Matt. He hesitated for a moment and then shook his head.

"Let's just wait for them to leave."

I had no sooner nodded than a giggle floated up toward us.

"Is this where you wanted to take me?" asked a female voice.

"Yeah. It's private here." The second voice was male and sounded adolescent.

"So . . . you wanted to tell me something?" prompted the girl.

"Um, yeah. I mean, yes." The boy sounded nervous. He cleared his throat. "I wrote you a poem."

I clapped a hand over my mouth to stifle the laugh I felt bubbling up.

"Oh, Chase, I can't believe you did that for me! I want to hear it!" the girl exclaimed.

Chase obliged her, and I heard the sound of a paper unfolding. He cleared his throat once more and began.

"Jennifer, you are so dope, I hope you like this poem I wrote. Your hair is fly, your curves are kickin'. I'd choose you over Mom's fried chicken."

I felt Matt begin to shake next to me, his laughter obviously getting the better of him. I pressed my lips together, determined not to start. But it was hard.

The high school Romeo beneath us wasn't done yet, though.

"Some girls think that they're so hot because they're rich, but really they're not. They just got money but not the looks, you may be poor but you're off the hook."

Matt shook harder, and although Chase was a terrible poet, I figured he didn't need the added humiliation of having two strangers listening in. As he started the third stanza, I scrambled for a way to give him an out. I eased my hand toward the pocket of Matt's shorts where I'd seen my keys disappear. Chase continued, unaware that I was trying to save him from public disgrace.

"You're so fine, you blow my mind. In the rain or sun, you're the one. You put me in a whirl, will you be my girl?"

I could tell Matt was on the verge of losing it completely. I snatched my keys from his pocket, startling him, and then dropped them on the metal beneath us, startling Chase and Jennifer, who gave a feminine shriek. At least, I think it was Jennifer.

"Who's there?" Chase called, manfully controlling a quaver in his voice.

Rather than answer, I scuffed my flip-flops all over the place, letting the noise telegraph our presence to the couple.

"What is that?" Jennifer whispered.

"I don't know," Chase answered. Matt got in on the action, thudding his head against the turret walls a couple of times and producing an ominous boom. I glared at him, trying to communicate that he shouldn't overdo it, but he couldn't see me in the dark.

I heard the shuffle of feet moving quickly in the opposite direction and Chase's voice floating back to us as he reassured his new girlfriend. "I don't know what that is. I'd check it out if I was by myself, but I don't want to put you in any danger."

Jennifer's reply came back even more faintly as they sped farther away. "You're so awesome, Chase."

Matt and I waited for a few beats, and then he broke, laughing so hard he had to gasp for breath. "I guess she liked the poem," he managed when he calmed down a little.

I crawled over him onto the slide. "You're mean." I sniffed and slid down.

"What?" he called down to me. "I felt you laughing."

I crossed my arms and glared up at him.

"'I'd choose you over Mom's fried chicken?'" he repeated. "That's funny. Admit it."

I fought a smile.

"'You may be poor but you're off the hook'?" he said. "How can you not laugh at that?"

It was getting harder not to. He took the slide down and landed in front of me.

"'In the rain or sun, you're the one,'" he reminded me.

That did it. Laughing, I held up my hands to fend off any more terrible poetry. "Okay, it was bad, but you have to give him credit for trying," I said.

"No, I don't. He should have said it with flowers because his rhymes stink."

"Flowers? Is that your strategy of choice?"

"Strategy for what?" he asked.

"You know. Getting a girl. Maybe he's too poor for flowers."

"First of all," Matt said, "I'm not a big believer in strategy. And secondly, he's probably just too cheap for flowers. Five bucks would get him some kind of flower at any grocery store."

"I think the poetry was sweet. It was from the heart."

"'Your hair is fly and your curves are kickin','" Matt mused. "Yeah, from the heart, all right."

"Jennifer liked it. That's what counts."

"You're right." He took my hand and we headed back toward the boardwalk. "Is it true that all girls like being swept off their feet?"

"You mean by doing stuff like whisking a girl away for a drive down the coast and wandering through a beach town holding hands?" I squeezed his hand. "Maybe."

"Maybe I believe a *little* bit in strategy." He grinned. "It worked on me, after all."

I narrowed my eyes at him. "What are you talking about?"

"Oh, I don't know. Always being where I am, at the beach, at Institute, in Sunday School class."

"Whoa, buddy. If you're going to accuse me of using strategy on you, at least accuse me of the right one."

"Which is?"

I shut my mouth almost as soon as I opened it to answer. That was a neat little trap, but I sidestepped it. "To be hot and funny and irresistible."

"You're awesome at that strategy."

I laughed. "Uh-huh, well, it requires massive amounts of beauty sleep, so I probably need to take you home."

"That's supposed to be my line, I think."

"It would be if we weren't in my Jeep," I said, giving the keys a slight shake.

"Good point. You forgot being smart in your strategy list."

"I kind of am, aren't I?" I pretended to preen.

"And modest."

"I rock at being modest."

"You totally do. Wow, Ashley, is there anything you aren't great at?"

I sighed. "Surfing."

"Right," he nodded. "Good point."

"But that's all your fault, so it shouldn't count against me."

"How do you figure it's my fault?" he asked, surprised.

"I've had one whole lesson with you and I'm not a pro yet. That doesn't seem right."

"I guess you need another lesson," he said.

"I'm just saying."

"How about Wednesday morning?"

"We have a date that night," I reminded him. "Are you going to get sick of me?" I asked casually but surprised myself with how much the answer mattered.

He pulled me closer to his side. "I'll risk it."

"Fine. But proceed with caution."

This time he stopped. "No."

"No?"

"No. No caution." He crossed his arms across his chest and stared down at me. "You're only here for a couple of months, right? I'm going to make it count."

My stomach flipped. In a good way, I think.

"Does that make you nervous?" he asked. "I'm trying a new strategy called being up-front. What do you think?"

"I've never heard of such a thing," I joked. I wasn't sure what to say, but Matt just waited me out.

"Up-front, huh?"

He nodded.

"Okay, then being up-front, I should tell you that I'm not looking for anything serious this summer. Just hanging out, having fun. I don't want any attachments when I leave for school," I said.

He shot me a sharp glance. "A girl who doesn't want commitment?" he asked.

"Yep."

"Where have you been all my life?"

I laughed. "So you're okay with that?"

"Yeah," he said. "Sure."

Relieved that I had spelled out my terms, I hid a small smile. Number seventeen?

Check.

Chapter 10

TUESDAY NIGHT, I DRESSED CAREFULLY for Institute. I hadn't talked to Matt since I dropped him back at his house after our Laguna escapade, but he texted me three times on my shift Monday night. The first time he wanted to know what went on the ultimate grilled cheese sandwich. I sent him the list. The next message read, *It works a lot better when you make it,* which didn't exactly inspire hope that he'd remembered our lesson. The final text . . . well, that one I saved.

I pulled it up and read it again. *Does Wednesday seem kind of far off all of a sudden?*

Granted, Matt didn't profess his undying love, and I didn't want him to, but it felt good to know he was looking forward to our surf lesson as much as I was. Not that surfing sounded great at the moment, considering my long, unsnapped wipeout streak. But hanging out with Matt again in any circumstance held some major appeal. I grabbed my scripture tote and headed for Old Testament class.

Since I was a bit early, I had my pick of seats. I chose a desk in the middle and flipped open my scriptures so I could review the assigned sections for tonight's class. Not two minutes later, I felt a slight jostling as someone took the seat next to me. I looked up to find my good friend Megan settling in, beginning the tedious process of lining up her colored pencils. Two seconds later, her quiet friend slipped into the seat on my other side with an apologetic smile. Megan was employing a little strategy of her own, it seemed, ensuring that no matter where Matt sat, it wouldn't be next to me. Nice one.

"How are you, Mary?" I asked.

"It's Megan," she corrected me. Brrr, the chill was back.

I turned to her friend. "I don't think I ever caught your name," I said.

Before she could answer, Megan interrupted. "That's Laurel," she said, and her tone implied I was stupid for asking.

"Hi, Laurel," I said, and offered my hand for a shake.

She smiled wanly and took it but didn't add anything else.

Deciding that was a dead end, I stifled a sigh and turned back to my scriptures. Maybe I should skip the review and read scriptures about loving my neighbors instead, and then work *really* hard to liken the verses to myself before I accidentally knocked Megan out of her desk.

Another minute passed while I ignored the *scritch* of Megan sharpening every one of her pencils with a CTR-shaped sharpener. Where did she even find such a thing? I felt my nerves winding tighter with every turn of the sharpener, but I kept my eyes on my begats and showed no reaction. I turned a page, crackling the paper as loudly as possible. Megan's scritching picked up speed. I dug in my purse for a pack of cherry passion Tic Tacs and shook one out, satisfied with the distracting rattle of the candies as they bounced around in the container.

I turned to Laurel. "Would you like one?"

She shook her head and shrank a little, possibly trying to become invisible. I turned back to my Bible and noticed out of the corner of my eye that Megan had just picked up her last pencil. The tension leaked from my shoulders now that the end was in sight. Refocusing on my reading, I found my place and got about a third of the way down the page when a distinct snicking sound froze me. She couldn't possibly be . . .

I turned slightly. *She is!* Megan was sitting right there, clipping her fingernails not eight inches away from me. I hate that sound. I stared, appalled, as a sliver of nail sailed over to land on my desk. My involuntary whimper caught her attention, and she followed my gaze to the offending fingernail now garnishing chapter four of Leviticus.

"Sorry about that," she shrugged. And then left it there.

She left it there!

Unsure how to handle this enemy encroachment, I gingerly picked my scriptures up, climbed over a reddening Laurel, and headed for the garbage can, where I disposed of Megan's nail clipping. Then I blew on the page, although I'm not sure why. Can you blow cooties off something?

I marched back to my seat and examined it for more stray fingernails before I sat down. This time I turned to the Ten Commandments and read number six over and over. "Thou shalt not kill, thou shalt not kill." *Snick.* Aargh! I concentrated on not flinching. *Snick.* Don't flinch. *Snick.* Don't flinch. *Snick.* Don't flinch.

Just when I could almost hear the sound of my last nerve snapping, Sister Powers walked in and Megan put her clippers away. I breathed out, long and deep, but as quietly as possible. I didn't want to give her the satisfaction of a huff. As soon as Sister Powers arranged her materials on the podium, she welcomed everyone and beckoned Laurel up to "play" the piano. This time Laurel hit the button and the opening bars of "The Spirit of God" tinkled out. I kept one eye on the hymn book and one eye on the door, looking for Matt. I'd given up by the time the hymn drew to a close and we bowed our heads for prayer, so I nearly jumped out of my skin when we all murmured amen and a voice from over my shoulder whispered, "Boo."

I whipped around to find Matt seated behind me. He grinned at my surprise and that little tickle burbled in my chest somewhere, that Matt Gibson phenomenon I couldn't seem to stifle.

Megan gave Matt an enthusiastic wave, which he returned with a cool nod. My smile for him grew wider. I turned back around to focus on the teacher, who directed us to the first scripture of the night. Even with Megan's "help," by the time Sister Powers was done connecting all the dots, I had a slightly better attitude toward the Old Testament. I guess I'd been looking for a better way to relate it to my life, and Sister Powers's lesson offered a good strategy.

As soon as the volunteer for the closing prayer said amen, people were out of their seats and mingling. I stayed put, waiting for Matt to find his way over. Megan hopped up and pushed her desk out of the way so she could walk straight back to him instead of talking to him over the back of the chair. It gained her about twelve inches of proximity, but in her rush (and I was totally giving her the benefit of the doubt here), she accidentally shoved her desk into mine and knocked my scriptures and purse to the floor.

"Sorry," she said. "Do you want me to help with that?"

No scenario existed where I would *ever* ask Megan for help, so I waved her off and crouched on the floor to pick up the scattered mess. "I've got it," I said.

Matt stepped forward through the gap in the desks to help instead, squatting down and fumbling with the loose papers that had flown everywhere. Megan was stewing over our shoulders, foiled in her attempt to snag Matt's attention. Deciding to make her own opportunity since none presented itself, she leaned over and tugged on Matt's shirt sleeve. "Hey, Matt, I'm thinking of buying my neighbor's surfboard. Can you come check it out for me and tell me if it's a good deal or not?"

"Now?" he asked, surprised.

"Yeah, I tied it to my car out in the parking lot."

Wow. Give the girl some credit. She dragged a surfboard all the way to Institute to create an excuse for getting Matt alone. Well played.

He looked at me apologetically, but I smiled to let him know it was okay. When he stood, Megan took his arm and asked him questions as she led him out of the room. I turned back to my mess, not at all annoyed. Megan could talk used surfboards all she wanted to with Matt, but he was taking me out surfing in the morning and that's all that mattered. I reached for another stray program, and without a word, Laurel slipped to the floor and began picking up odds and ends to help me. There was still a lot to pick up even though Matt had thrown away a decent pile for me on his way out. I smiled my gratitude, and when she handed me a small stack of miscellany, I shoved everything back into my scriptures and climbed to my feet.

"Thanks," I said.

She nodded and smiled in return but didn't say anything, just slipped from the room. I stared after her for a minute. Interesting girl. She had such a pretty face, but being so quiet, she kind of blended into the background as Megan's faithful shadow. A shame, considering I got the distinct impression she didn't always enjoy Megan's antics, either.

I passed Megan and Matt on the way to my Jeep, grinning at Matt's look of longsuffering patience as Megan gesticulated toward her beat-up surfboard. He caught my grin and scowled, but I didn't feel at all repentant and smiled even wider as I cranked the ignition and drove away.

A minute later, a text dinged on my phone. I checked it at the next stoplight and laughed out loud at Matt's message. *You are so going to pay for that tomorrow morning. Be ready at 8.*

I couldn't wait.

Chapter 11

"ARE YOU SURE ABOUT THIS?" I asked, eyeing the high swell of the wave rolling in. "That's bigger than I'm used to." The waves broke about chest high, and while I'm not tall, it was an awful lot of water to tame with eight feet of fiberglass.

"You'll be fine," Matt answered. "You've got all the skills. You just lack the confidence. Believe you can achieve."

I turned to gape at this piece of hackneyed wisdom and caught his impish grin. "Oh, I get it, this is where you make me pay for leaving you with Megan." I smacked the water to splash him. "Getting me killed doesn't really fit the crime, does it?"

"Relax, Ashley. Nothing's going to happen to you. And yes, I think it's funny that the waves are high today, but you've got nothing to worry about. Today's your day, I can feel it."

I sighed. "Let's do this, then."

Twenty minutes later, I trudged the last several yards to the sand, flopping down in frustration. Matt was about a minute behind me and took a seat next to me, bumping me with his shoulder. I stayed put, my arms on my bent knees, my face hidden in their cradle. I didn't want to face him after yet another ugly wipeout.

"You hurt?" he asked.

"Just my pride. You know, the usual."

"That was pretty good," he said.

"What, the show I just put on? I aim to please."

He shook his head. "No, I mean you picked the right wave, you got up right. That was good. You did a lot of things right."

"And yet I still ate it," I grumbled. "This is hopeless."

He was quiet for a long moment. My nerves stretched with the silence, and I snuck a peek at him. He was watching me.

"Give it to me straight," I joked. "How bad is my surf mojo broken?"

He shook his head. "I keep telling you, your surf mojo is fine. It's your confidence that's busted." He studied me for another minute. "Why did you decide to do this? Learn to surf?"

I hesitated, then shrugged. No way was I telling him that I was removing another one of my obstacles to marriage and crossing it off my list. I wasn't telling him about The List at all. Some people thought it was nuts, and I couldn't care less, but it would bother me if Matt thought so. I pieced together an explanation that held as much truth as possible. "I guess it just seemed like a great adventure," I said. "Something exciting and different from boring old Utah. I've wanted to try it ever since I used to visit Dave and Celia on vacation. I watched them out on the waves with their dad while I got stuck playing in the sand because I didn't know how to surf."

He leaned back on his hands and tilted his face toward the sun. "Okay," he said after a while. "How much does it matter to you to say that you did this, to pull this off?"

I thought about it. My list said, "Learn to surf," not "Try surfing a few times and quit." I'd been true to every item on there since the day I wrote it six years ago, and I had no intention of letting this challenge defeat me.

"It's important," I answered.

"Then maybe you should use that." He opened his eyes and looked at me again. "You have this in you, Ashley. Focus on your determination, but don't let it stress you out. Stay loose out there. You are *so* close."

I pondered that.

"Okay," I said.

"Okay?" he echoed.

"Yeah. If you say I've got what it takes, then I figure you ought to know. So I'm going to do it."

"Right now?" he prodded.

"Yes. Right now." I stood then pulled him to his feet too.

"Let's go," he said, and I followed him into the water once more, determined. I hadn't failed at one thing on that list yet, and it would take more than the Pacific to get in my way.

I watched the waves roll toward me, letting a couple of good ones go in favor of waiting for the *perfect* one. And then I saw it. It moved at the right speed and height. "I'll take that one," I told Matt.

"Good call," he said. He turned his surfboard in sync with mine, offering encouragement the whole time. "You've got this, Ash. You've got the form down, you've got the right wave coming in, and you're in control. Just take it easy and feel for the pocket."

I paddled, picking up speed with the wave but refusing to let anxiety force me up before it was time. I felt the acceleration and braced myself, and suddenly there it was: a split second where I felt my board being pushed and pulled simultaneously. I jumped up, settled into soft knees and a slight lean forward, and then relaxed. I could sense the motion of the ocean telling me which way it was going next and then . . . I was surfing. I had the wave, and I knew it. It felt incredible—fast and smooth and huge. I rode it with single-minded focus, loving the knife-point balance that divided exhilaration from frustration, success from failure.

The wave petered out as it drove toward the beach, and I heard Matt slightly behind me. "Oh yeah, Ash! You did it, you did it!" he was yelling.

Laughing, I jumped from my board and whooped with joy. Arms in the air, I hooted in delight at finally doing it, finally riding a wave all the way in, and danced in the wavelets around my ankles. Suddenly, Matt was there, tossing his board aside and grabbing me to whirl me around, laughing with me. He set me down after a dizzying spin, and I squeezed his shoulders to steady myself, then realized what I was doing and stepped back, self-conscious.

"You did it," he said, grinning.

"I did it," I nodded. "Thank you." Feeling that the occasion called for something more, I held up my hand for an awkward high five. Instead of slapping it, Matt reached over and pulled me into another hug.

I grinned and tightened the hug, savoring the moment a little longer. I mean, I was standing in the Pacific with Matt Gibson's arms wrapped around me, him smelling like sea salt and fresh air. It wasn't the kind of thing you cut short. I might have stood there indefinitely except that an extra-pushy wave chose that moment to break against

Matt hard enough that some of its spray caught me full in the face, and I broke away from him again, sputtering and laughing, wiggly with surf triumph.

"I did it!" I hollered and accompanied the reminder with a stomp in the water that sent droplets splashing toward my coach.

"I know!" he said, splashing back.

He watched as I cranked my leg back to return a splatter salvo and held up his hands.

"Wait, you're just going to cruise on automatic after one wave?" he asked.

I halted my splash kick. "No. Of course not. Why would you think that?"

"No reason," he said, lowering his arms. "I just wanted to make sure you weren't trying to avoid your next ride with a water fight."

"No way!" I said. "Let's go again!" And with a grin, I snatched my surfboard out of the water where it bobbed on my ankle tether and waded right back in toward the deep. "Last one out buys Jamba," I hollered over my shoulder.

I heard Matt's laugh and kicked up my speed, paddling out for the next wave, hearing him right behind me.

The next hour passed in a blur of laughter, waves, two more wipeouts, and three more successes. I was three rides closer to saying that I really could surf and that I liked it. *Really* liked it. I maybe even understood Matt's explanation of being totally focused and completely relaxed in the same moment, and it felt . . . like freedom. For once I was glad that I had a whole summer to keep it up instead of dreading all things surf-related. Getting it right felt pretty good.

When at last exhaustion anchored me to the sand, I watched Matt take another wave in. He looked so sure on his board, his adjustments so fluid as he followed the motion of the swell. It was strange to think of guys as graceful, but there was no other way to describe the way he moved on his surfboard. Power and grace. It was intoxicating to watch. In the shallows, he paused for a moment, looking. He spotted me and a slow smile crept over his face. I felt an echoing smile turning up the corner of my mouth.

I knew I should worry that it took so little from him to make me giddy as a school girl, but right at that second, I didn't care. I had the beach every day and a good-looking guy to hang out with all summer, and I didn't need anything else out of life for the next three months except a steady stream of tips at the restaurant. What more could I want?

Chapter 12

My feet and shoulders ached in protest as I hefted my last tray for the afternoon. I'm sure that given a little time, surfing all morning and busing food trays all day would come easier, but right now, my muscles screamed from overuse. I had one last table to serve and clear out before I could soak my aching body in a bath and wash the smell of grilled onions from my hair. Then I could replace the fifty thousand food orders cluttering up my brain with nothing more taxing than outfit choices for my date with Matt tonight.

I managed to place the right steak in front of the right tourist, then scuttled back to the kitchen to finish off my side work, filling empty bottles of ketchup and topping off salt and pepper shakers. It took me a second to realize that the gentle shaking I felt was coming from my cell phone vibrating in my pocket and not my exhausted fingers. Fumbling it out, I smiled when I saw a text from Matt come in. I read it and my stomach sank. *Something came up. Have to cancel. So sorry. Rain check? Please?*

I slumped against the counter behind me with a sigh. I'd been looking forward to our date, but it wasn't like my plans wouldn't keep. I thought it would be fun to go check out the Pageant of the Masters that Matt had mentioned on our Sunday excursion, but it ran all summer. Plenty of time to do it another night. Anyway, it wasn't smart to spend all my free time with Matt. It might send the wrong message. He was my summer good-time guy, which is exactly what I wanted when I wrote "summer fling" on The List. I *might* have been heavily influenced by the sweet summer romance between John Travolta and Olivia Newton-John in *Grease*, a DVD in heavy rotation at my house my senior year of high school, but whatever. Going away for the summer and meeting a cute guy sounded fun when I was eighteen, and now at twenty-four, with Matt Gibson in the picture, it sounded even better. I had the added bonus of the utter surety that there wouldn't be any sticky entanglements when school started in the fall. I couldn't suddenly run into him like Sandy did when her parents moved to the same town.

I sent Matt a quick answer. *No problem. Call me later.* It wasn't until an hour later when I sat soaking up the last of the bath water's warmth, my muscles unknotted and the smell of fried food rinsed away in jasmine salts, that it occurred to me to wonder why Matt canceled. All he said was, "Something came up." That could mean anything from being called in to help negotiate peace in the Middle East to getting a flat tire.

Or another date.

Huh. I sat up a bit. What if that was it? Maybe he figured since he already saw me this morning that he ought to spread the love to some of the other girls who kept him in high demand. I turned that possibility over a few times and then sank until the water rose to my chin again. Whatever. Matt was a great guy, but a good-time guy nonetheless, and he was welcome to his free time too.

When the water cooled too much to be comfortable, I shrugged into my rattiest, comfiest old bathrobe, a survivor of both college and my mission, and wandered down the hall to my shared room with Celia. My aunt and uncle had four bedrooms, but the fourth housed Aunt Trudy's sewing supplies, and I'd much rather inconvenience Celia than my aunt, so we doubled up. My cousin looked up when I walked into our room.

"Feel better?" she asked.

"Way better."

"You definitely smell better," she said after a cautious sniff.

I made a face and collapsed on my narrow twin bed, plucking at the quilt tie beneath me. One of Aunt Trudy's sewing projects, probably. She was a quilting maniac, turning out three for Relief Society projects and one for a baby shower since I'd been here.

"Celia . . ." I began, knowing I sounded hesitant.

That caught her attention since it's a rare condition for me.

"Yeah?"

I paused before spitting my question out, not wanting to sound obvious, but deciding the more I dithered, the worse I would make it. "Do you know if Matt's dating anyone else right now?"

She looked at me strangely. "No. I told you that when you hatched your grand plan to get him to teach you."

"I asked if he had a girlfriend. I guess I'm asking about casual dating now."

She thought about it, then shrugged. "Yeah, he goes out but not usually with the same girl more than a few times. Why? You want to size up the competition?"

"Not really. I'm just trying to figure out why he's still single. It seems like there are plenty of girls ready to fill the significant-other position."

"It's probably hard for him to keep a girlfriend because of his winter schedule."

"What about it?"

"He works super long hours."

"Is the winter surfboard business that demanding?" I wrinkled my forehead in confusion.

Celia shrugged. "I don't know. I know he travels a lot, but I'm not sure why. Maybe he's following the waves. A lot of guys here go down to Mexico or Costa Rica to surf in the winter. Or maybe he goes on buying trips at surf fashion shows during the off season." She grinned at the picture she'd painted.

I was intrigued. My conversations with Matt centered around surfing or the occasional goofy analysis of abstract art. Thinking about it, I realized he was very good at extracting information from me and somehow never leaving an opening for me to return the questions in kind. It was a little odd.

"You should ask him about that stuff when you guys go out tonight," she said.

"We're not going out anymore," I answered. "He said something came up and asked for a rain check."

She studied me for a few seconds. "That doesn't bother you, does it?"

"Nope," I said, and it was true. Mostly.

"Why not?"

"He's not my boyfriend, Celia. He's just number seventeen on The List, and he can do whatever he wants. I don't want him to get all attached to me and stuff."

She stared and then burst out laughing. "You're a piece of work, Ashley. Every other girl in the Beachside Ward would sign away their future firstborn to get a date with him, and you're worried that he's going to get too attached?"

"It happens to me a lot," I said. "Guys think I'm playing hard to get, and then they chase me even harder, and it turns into clinginess somewhere along the line. I want to keep my summer low-key."

"But you *are* playing hard to get," she pointed out.

"No, Celia. I *am* hard to get if someone's looking for more than a few fun times. I've got too much going on to get sucked into a relationship right now."

"Either way, Matt's either too busy or too bored by his current options to date anyone seriously, I think. I haven't seen him go out with anyone more than a few times since I've been in the ward, and that's almost two years now. I'm sure he's not looking to settle down with you or anyone else."

I leaned back against the wall, mollified. "Good," I said. "Time to work on number twenty-four."

"The List again?" she asked.

"Oh yeah. I've got the wonderful world of Internet dating to explore."

"Why are you bothering with the online thing when you've already got Matt to hang out with?" she asked.

"I'm setting things up for the fall. If I'm lucky, I might have something all ready to go by the time the semester starts."

"But you don't want a relationship."

"No, I don't. But I do want someone to hang out with from time to time."

"But you'll be at BYU. Won't you have tons of guys in your ward or apartment complex or whatever to date?"

"Maybe," I shrugged. "But if I meet someone online, I can skip all the time wasted trying to get to know someone and then finding out that you're a bad fit, anyway."

Celia shot me a doubtful look but said nothing and buried her nose in her book as I hauled out my laptop. When I logged on to my LDS Lookup page, I found eleven messages waiting for me. Eight were from the same guy. Using the screen name ChickMagnet, he had sent me the first message two days ago saying, "Hey. Wassup?" Even if I had logged in anytime in the last two days to check my account, which I hadn't, his moniker and greeting left a lot to be desired. Six hours after his first message, a second one came in reading, "Cat got your tongue? I'm good with shy chicks."

Charming. They improved steadily from there, if by *improved* you mean "grew increasingly demanding and intrusive." The second-to-last one screamed, "WHY WON'T YOU TALK TO ME?" followed by a surly good-bye promising, "I hate stuck-up chicks. I'm not e-mailing you anymore." Well, I could only hope. I deleted the stream of his craziness from my inbox and moved to the next messages.

A guy named PaulOnion sent a "wave," a preformatted icon provided by the LDS Lookup site that was used to say hello. I couldn't decide if this was shy or lazy. His picture showed a sweet but faintly dorky looking guy in an ill-fitting Western-cut plaid shirt. Deciding PaulOnion and I were probably not predestined soul mates, I sighed and deleted his wave too. Discouragement crept in as I scrolled through to my last two messages, deepening when I opened the next one. HandsomeDan, who, based on his profile picture, was overstating the case somewhat, had sent me a message to let me know that he thought I was hot. That was it. "I think ur hot."

Exasperated, I sent him to the recycle bin along with all of my other rejected admirers. How was I supposed to try Internet dating if I couldn't even find anyone I wanted to e-mail back, much less meet for a date? I clicked around the site for a while to reassure myself that there were cool people I might actually want to meet and found a few intriguing possibilities. One guy calling himself BoardRyder had a really cool profile. His picture didn't show much, just him in some snowboard gear taking a mogul, but he liked some awesome bands and movies. His info said he was in Salt Lake. Why couldn't a guy like that e-mail me?

A tap sounded on the bedroom door, then it flew open to admit Dave. He staggered two steps in and threw himself on the floor, muttering something like "I hate girls," into the carpet.

I raised an eyebrow at Celia, who closed her book with a sigh. "I guess we're going to have to explain the female species to him," she said.

"Again?" I asked. "Can't he just watch Dr. Phil or something?"

Dave moaned.

"What's wrong?" Celia asked.

"Don't act like you care," he mumbled into the carpet. "I've been lying here forever."

"Forever minus all but thirty seconds, maybe. Spill it."

"I already did," he said. "I hate girls."

Celia blew out an irritated breath that sounded suspiciously close to a raspberry. "Sit up like a man and say that to my face," she said.

Dave hauled himself to a sitting position, discouragement radiating from every line of his hunched over body. "I don't understand girls at all," he complained. "How am I ever supposed to figure you out if you never talk to me?"

"Uh, we *are* talking to you, cuz," I pointed out.

"Not *you*, specifically. I mean girls in general."

"Yeah, I don't know how you missed that," Celia chimed in. "He was clear as mud."

He slumped a little lower. "It's no use," he said.

"What isn't?" asked his sister.

"I don't know."

"Okay, well, thanks for clearing that up," she said.

I listened to the exchange in amusement and decided to intervene before it turned into a flame war.

"Dave, did something happen at Institute tonight?" I asked. He attended Sister Powers's Book of Mormon lectures every week.

"Yeah," he said. "I saw that girl again."

"What girl?" I prompted. Drama seemed to limit Dave's communication to short-syllabled sulking.

"The girl from FHE."

I racked my brains and came up empty. "Uh, Dave? There are lots of girls at FHE. Could you give us some details here?"

"Wow, you guys don't hear anything I say, do you? If her name was Matt Gibson would it help you listen better?"

I threw a pillow at him but he ducked it. Luckily, Celia's flip-flop caught him in the chest a millisecond after he deflected my shot.

"Remember we were all sitting around the table while you guys ate gross cereal and talked about how Ashley is the biggest stalker in the world?"

"I remember that part of the conversation . . ." Celia said, and I glared at her.

"What about it?" I asked.

"Remember I was saying I might try ignoring this cute chick at FHE to see if it would work for me too?"

"I do, actually. And I remember telling you to leave that tactic to the pros," I said.

"No kidding. It didn't work."

"Maybe you better break it down for us," Celia said. "What happened?"

"Well, I was sitting at Institute waiting for class to start, joking around with Blake Thomas about some stuff when that girl walked in. She sat down a couple of rows ahead of me, and so I was all like, 'Hey! You should come sit here,' and she ignored me."

"Ignored you how?" Celia asked. "Maybe she just didn't hear you."

"I wish. She heard me, all right. She turned around when I said hey and then just whipped back the other way and squished down in her chair. Then Blake laughed at me, and I had to punch him in the arm."

"It's good you know how to handle negative emotions," I said.

"Says the girl who just threw a pillow at me."

"Good point. What else happened? Did you try to talk to her again?"

"No. Because I decided to do the ignoring thing. Then the teacher walked in and the girl got up to play the piano, and I took off after class so I couldn't get publicly burned again."

"You're lucky you have someone who actually plays the piano in your class," I said. "We just have someone who pushes the button in ours."

"That's what I meant," he said. "She didn't actually play."

I perked up at that. "What does this girl look like?"

"She's cute."

"Oh, *her,*" Celia joked.

"Details, Dave. I need details," I said.

He thought for a minute, then shrugged. "She's pretty, you know? Blonde hair, nice skin, medium height."

Celia rolled her eyes at his version of "details," but I pressed him a little further.

"Have you ever heard her talk?"

"To me? No."

"No, I mean have you heard her talk *ever*? Has she ever answered a question in class or said a prayer or anything?"

He thought for a minute. "I've only seen her a few times, but I don't think so. She's kind of quiet, you know?"

"I do know," I said. "One more question. Does she hang out with a girl named Megan?"

"You mean that one that's *never* quiet? Yeah."

"Well, your mystery woman is named Laurel, and I don't think she was ignoring you." I delivered my revelation with a small degree of satisfaction.

"You know her?" Celia asked.

"Sort of. She's always with Megan who, like Dave pointed out, never shuts up. Maybe she uses up their word allowance when they're together, and Laurel doesn't get to say anything."

"Meow," Dave said.

"Megan bugs," I said.

"You don't hang out with her so why do you care?" Celia asked, then giggled. "Wait, don't answer that. I know. It's because she's always hanging around Matt Gibson."

"Not like it does her any good," I said. "And I *don't* care."

"Of course not," Celia said and then exchanged looks with her brother.

"I saw that."

"Megan's harmless," Dave said. "She's always glomming onto some dude or another. She'll be on to someone new next week."

"Maybe not," Celia contradicted him. "She's been stuck on Matt for longer than usual. Not that Ashley cares."

I sniffed. "I don't. And this is not about me or Megan. This is about Dave and his deep love for Laurel."

"I think she's cute. I'm not going to propose yet. Early marriage is a Barrett thing, not our side of the family."

Celia snickered, and I shot her an evil look.

"So," he prodded me. "What's up with Laurel? Why doesn't she talk to me? I'm a good-looking guy."

"You're not supposed to say that out loud," Celia said. "You're supposed to act like you don't know that you're good-looking."

"I've only seen her twice," I said, "but I think she's kind of shy. Maybe she just doesn't know what to say."

"But I made it easy for her. I invited her to sit with me and everything. Even a shy girl can say yes to taking a seat."

Celia chimed in again. "Did you say you were sitting with Blake already?"

"Yeah. So?"

"Maybe the idea of taking you and Blake on together is overwhelming," she explained. "You guys are super rowdy, you know."

"I think that's about right," I said.

"Then what do I do now?" he asked. "You guys are supposed to be helping me."

"Obviously, you need to talk to her without a wingman."

"I agree," I said. "I have no idea how shy people think, but I'm guessing one-to-one odds are going to scare her a little less. Maybe I can go with you to talk to her on Sunday, and she'll be more comfortable with another girl there."

He shook his head. "I see where you're going with that, but I haven't seen her at church. Just activities and Institute and stuff."

"Interesting," I mused. "Okay, next plan. When will you see her again?"

"Probably Monday night for FHE. That's where I saw her the first time."

"That'll be perfect," Celia said. "It's more relaxed than church, anyway. Now you have to pick an outfit."

"Why? That's like, five days from now. I don't even know what will be clean by then."

"Oh, man, Dave. It's really good you came to us. I had no idea we were going to have to go into remedial dating strategies," I joked.

"Are you saying I don't have game? I got game," he said. "I've got lots of game."

"People who have game never use the phrase 'I've got game,'" his sister argued. "And besides, if you pick out something now and put it aside, you can be sure it'll be clean by Monday, and you can look halfway decent."

"I have nice stuff," he said. "I wear all the name brands."

"You wear all the surf name brands," I said. "It's a little different. It's good for a girl to know that a guy owns more than just a closet full of Quicksilver tee shirts."

"Hey! They're cool shirts."

"I know. But I think we can compromise. How about you can wear a Quicksilver shirt but it has to have a collar?" I said.

He hedged for a minute. "Can I still wear shorts?"

"Yes."

"Okay, then I'll wear a collared shirt."

"Good."

He still looked grumpy. "So far your advice is to dress different from my normal self and don't hang out with my friends. Aren't you supposed to tell me to be myself and relax and she'll totally dig me?"

"As your smartest cousin, Dave, I feel like I need to break this to you gently. How should I put this? It's not that you need to dress fancy. It's that a girl needs to look at you and know that if you got married, she's not going to have to spend the first six months making your wardrobe over."

"Married!" he almost yelped. "We haven't even gone on a date. You Barretts really are nuts."

"It's not a Barrett thing," I said. "It's a girl thing. Sometime on your first date, she's going to be deciding how well your personalities will fit if you get married and how much work she's going to have to do to fix you."

"You're not this crazy, are you?" he asked his sister.

"It's not crazy. It's just what most girls do. Ashley didn't say we're always trying to decide on a first date if we're going to marry a guy. She just said we think about what needs to be tweaked *if* we married someone."

"That's still crazy," he said.

"Take it from two girls who haven't run out and married the first guys we've dated or kissed. We think about it. I can tell within fifteen minutes of talking to someone whether I could marry them or not, and even when the answer is yes, I still probably won't go on a third date."

"Reeeeally?" he drawled. "Now we're getting somewhere."

I eyed him, wondering at his impish tone.

"Matt's had way more than his fifteen minutes of fame with you," he continued. "Could you marry him?"

"I refuse to answer that on the grounds that no matter what I say, I am totally positive my answer will come back to haunt me soon."

"Back to the subject," Celia interrupted. "I want to read, and you're distracting me. You're going to wear a nice shirt with a collar, shorts without any holes, and you're going to go up to Laurel without Blake or any of your other buddies around, and you're going to talk to her. Got it?"

"Got it. Uh, what am I going to say?"

"Depends on the moment," I said. "But probably a question would be good, something where she can't just shake her head yes or no. Maybe ask for her opinion about the activity and then follow that up with a question about her idea of a cool FHE activity."

"That's lame," he said.

"Yeah, it is," I agreed. "But it's real. It's a conversation that makes sense at the moment, it's low threat, it tells her you want to talk to her, and opens the door to talking about other things."

"Okay," he said. "I can do that. But what if she still won't talk to me?"

"Compliments," Celia said. "Pay her lots and lots of compliments."

"Oh, and if you can, try really hard to catch her when Megan's not around," I said. "Neither of you will get a word in edgewise."

"Bitter much?" Celia asked.

"Not bitter! Realistic. I'm not talking to either of you two anymore," I said. "I have really important work to do." I grabbed my laptop and hauled it back on my lap.

"What's so important at this time of night?"

"I've got serious research," I murmured. By the time Dave slunk back upstairs to contemplate his wardrobe, I had descended deep into the depths of Google and a search for karaoke nights in Huntington.

Chapter 13

THE NEXT WEEK FLEW BY, swallowed up in work. Thank goodness our restaurant didn't serve breakfast or I might have broken down and started living in my uniform. I surfed with Matt twice early in the morning, feeling more confident and in control of my board every time we headed out. We flirted at church and texted back and forth a few times, but the scheduling trolls at Hannigan's had tied up my weekend with double shifts on both Friday and Saturday. It meant plenty of extra cash, so I didn't complain. Much. But I felt bad I hadn't been able to redeem Matt's rain-check request.

By Tuesday night, I was more than ready to see him at Institute. I escaped the restaurant without much of a fight because Tuesdays are notoriously slow all over the dining out industry, and they could handle business with a skeleton staff. I was standing in front of my half of the closet. Actually, my quarter of the closet. I didn't have nearly as many clothes as Celia did, just what fit into two giant suitcases when I drove down for the summer. She was sweet to give up even part of her overworked closet space for me to shove a few things in.

Bored with my choices, I decided to make sure it would be worth the effort to dress nice.

Are you going to OT tonight? I texted Matt.

Who is this?

Ashley!

Who?

I snorted. *I'm the brunette with a great sense of humor. We surf together sometimes.*

Oh yeah. You.

Yep. Are you going to OT?

Why? You going to ditch?

No. But if you're going, I might actually drag a brush through my hair or something.

You'd brush your hair for me? Cool. I think you like me.

I laughed. I usually did when we were going back and forth about something. *I think you're all right,* I texted back.

You're making me blush.

Good. Are you going or ditching?

I'll go if you promise to sit by me.

Done. I have to go brush my hair now.

Want to ride over with me?

A knock on the bedroom door distracted me.

"Ash?" Dave called. "Can I come in?"

"Sure."

He poked his head in. "Can I go to Institute with you?"

I wrinkled my nose. "You want to take another religion class? Do you miss your mission that much?"

"Funny. No, I'm hoping Laurel will be there. She wasn't at FHE last night."

"Hold on. Let me ask."

Can Dave come? I tapped out to Matt.

No problem.

OK. Come and get us.

"You can come, but I'm catching a ride with Matt," I reported to Dave.

"Cool."

He ducked back out again, and I returned to my outfit search with purpose now. I settled on a white cotton skirt and snagged a cute pink hoodie from Celia's side of the closet. We had an informal trade working where she could raid my makeup box anytime she wanted to and I got to borrow from her to expand my wardrobe. I rustled my flip-flops from under the bed and dug out my brush. When my curls refused to cooperate, I gave up and braided two long pigtails. Checking out my full-length reflection on the closet door, I convinced myself that my look could pass for bohemian chic and not a girl who lost a fight with her hair.

I had barely slicked on my favorite strawberry Lip Smacker when a knock sounded on the front door, right on time. Dave beat me to it, but I enjoyed the extra moment I had to admire Matt when the door swung open. Man, he was hot. He had some cool Von Zipper sunglasses tucked into the neck of his light green shirt, and it hardly seemed fair that he had to do so little to look so good.

Dave turned to glare at me. "How come I have to wear a collar? Matt doesn't have one." Dave had taken our advice about making a little effort with his appearance for Laurel and wore a short-sleeved button-down shirt with some cool snaps on the front.

"You're wearing shorts, so you have to counteract that with a collar. Matt is wearing jeans, so he doesn't need a collar," I answered.

Matt looked perplexed. "Is that true?" he whispered as I walked out the door.

"I have no idea. It sounded good."

"You had me convinced. I thought maybe I'd been a fashion don't for years, and nobody told me."

"You're fine. Dave has to wear a collar because he's trying to impress a girl, and he needs to compensate for his age deficiency."

"Age deficiency? Isn't he twenty-one?"

"Yeah, but that's human years. In guy years, he's barely fifteen."

"What the heck is a guy year?"

I shrugged. "By middle school, pretty much every girl has figured out that we mature twice as fast as guys. In human years, we might be the same age as you but in guy years, you're emotionally only half as developed. But don't worry, it all evens out around twenty-five."

"I see. So, I'm pretty much grown up now that I'm twenty-six?"

"Yeah." He'd grown up quite nicely from where I stood.

"Good to know. You've put a lot of thought into this."

"No, I haven't. Girls just know this stuff."

He shook his head. "But you don't tell *us* and then wonder why we can't figure you out."

"We do tell you, though. That's what we mean every time one of us tells a guy to grow up."

He shot me a glance full of mock concern. "You're not going to get your chick card revoked for revealing girl trade secrets, are you?"

"I told you, you're old enough to know now."

He helped me into the car while Dave scrambled into the back, and we headed out for Institute. Megan and Laurel were already seated when we got to class, third row center, as usual. Dave threw me a slightly panicked look. "What do I do about Megan?" he asked out of the side of his mouth.

"You're the one that said she's harmless," I reminded him.

"Fine, she's the devil incarnate. Now will you tell me what to do?"

I thought about it for a minute. "Maybe I can draw Laurel off. She seems to like me okay." I mean, it was hard to tell from our non-verbal communication, but she did help pick all my stuff up the week before. "I'll give it a shot," I said. "I'll get her talking, and then you can come join the conversation and I'll introduce you."

"Who are we talking about here?" Matt asked.

Dave nodded his head in Laurel's direction. Since our vantage point was behind the girls, they wouldn't catch us ogling and conspiring unless they turned around. "The blonde next to Megan."

Matt smiled. "Good choice."

"Thanks, man."

I set out for the pair, intent on my mission. Sliding into the seat next to Laurel, I said, "Hi. If I promise not to let Megan knock over any more of my stuff and make you clean it up, can I sit next to you?"

She looked confused and before she could answer, Megan jumped in.

"That was an accident. It didn't look like such a big deal that you would need help." She sniffed.

I raised an eyebrow at her. "If I asked you for the time of day, would you give it to me?"

"I'd probably fudge it by fifteen minutes."

That startled a laugh out of me, and I felt an unwelcome twinge of respect for her.

"Good strategy," I said. "I'd probably only have lied by ten."

A reluctant smile tugged at her mouth. Laurel's head swiveled back and forth between us, her expression growing confused.

Matt chose that moment to wander up. "Hey, Megan," he said. "Did you get that surfboard?"

She nodded. "Thanks for the advice," she said.

"You should probably get a surf rack for your car," he said. "I can check it out really quick for you before Sister Powers gets here, maybe help you figure out which one would work best."

Way to take one for the team, Matt. I knew he didn't relish Megan cornering him in the parking lot again, but it was a great way to get her out of Dave's way. Megan touched Laurel's shoulder and said, "I'll be back."

Laurel nodded and Megan shot me a small, satisfied smile before following Matt out of the classroom.

"So, you're Laurel, right?" I said.

She looked uncertain.

"Isn't that your name? Laurel?"

She nodded.

"Do you like coming to Sister Powers's class?"

Another nod.

"Have you taken any other classes from her?"

A head shake.

I began to feel a little frustrated. This girl was beyond shy. I'd never had such a challenge in pulling actual words out of anyone before.

Changing tactics, I groped for an open-ended question.

"What did you think of the assigned reading for today?"

She hesitated, forced to choose between breaking down and talking to me or being outright rude and not answering. I waited her out. She swallowed, licked her lips nervously, and then said softly, "It was hard to follow."

Her voice sounded strange, a little hollow even, and I wondered if she was hoarse or something, but I felt encouraged that she answered so I pressed on.

"Yeah, I thought so too. I mean, the pieces are starting to come together for me, but there's a lot of really arcane stuff, and I get a little lost sometimes, you know?"

She looked confused and then trapped. "I'm sorry," she said. "I have a hearing loss. Could you repeat that?"

And then it hit me. The quality to her voice that I couldn't quite place . . . it sounded like I do inside of my own head when I'm talking and my ears need to pop but they won't. Perfectly clear but kind of far away.

"You're deaf?" I asked.

She nodded, shy again.

"Wow, that's great!" At her look of surprise, I hurried to add, "I mean, it's not great that you're deaf unless you think it's great that you're deaf. I mean it's great that you weren't ignoring my cousin Dave the other night."

"You talk really fast," she said.

"Sorry! You need to read my lips, right?"

"Right," she smiled. "And they move really fast."

"I'll slow down," I promised. "Have you always been deaf?"

She nodded. "I was born deaf."

"So are your parents deaf too?"

"No, hereditary deafness is kind of rare. The doctors aren't really sure what caused my hearing loss."

"You read lips really well," I said.

"Thanks."

From the corner of my eye, I could see Dave approaching.

"Hey, do you care if I introduce you to my cousin? He thinks you're cute."

A flustered look crossed her face. "The deaf thing kind of bothers most guys," she said.

I grinned. "Dave is not most guys. Come on, let me introduce him."

She sighed but nodded.

I waved my cousin over, and he stuck his hands in his pockets and strolled toward us, trying really hard to appear casual.

He stopped a little behind us, and I pulled him around so Laurel could see his face more easily.

"Dave, I'd like to introduce you to my friend Laurel. Laurel, this is my cousin Dave."

"Hi," he said.

"Hi," Laurel answered quietly.

I sat back, deciding to let them carry on the conversation since my introduction was done. A long, awkward pause ensued.

At last, Dave mumbled something that sounded like, "So you mblf nnngr mmmml class?"

Laurel looked at me, anxious and unsure about what Dave had said since he spoke to the floor.

"Dave? Laurel needs to see your lips when you talk."

His head shot up, confusion creasing his forehead.

"I'm deaf," Laurel said.

Dave brightened. "That's cool," he said.

I stifled a laugh, and he hurried to clarify, "I mean, it's not cool, exactly. Not that it's *not* cool, but I didn't mean that—" He interrupted himself and started over. "I think it's interesting that you're deaf," he said. "My best friend on my block when I was a kid was deaf. I learned some sign language from him. I forgot most of it, but it was a great experience."

He made sure to speak clearly enough that Laurel could keep up, and she answered, "I was raised orally, so I didn't learn to sign until a few years ago, but now I love it."

Dave slid into the seat on her other side and began peppering her with questions. Satisfied that they were off to a good start, I moved back a couple of rows, leaving another empty seat by Laurel so that Megan could sit there and not by oh, say, Matt.

When he and Megan returned a couple of minutes later, he made a beeline for me, and Megan threw me a glare before reclaiming her seat next to Laurel.

"How was it?" I asked quietly enough to avoid having Megan eavesdrop.

"Oh, you know," Matt said.

"Don't be stingy with the details. I want to hear all about your fantastic parking lot field trip."

He rolled his eyes. "This is what I get for trying to help."

"No, it's not. *That* is," I said, nodding toward Laurel and Dave, who were still engrossed in conversation. "The satisfaction of knowing you did your part."

Laurel headed for the piano to "play" the opening hymn by pushing the preset button, which also made a lot more sense now. After the song and prayer, Sister Powers began by saying, "Time for fun with ancient scripture."

When the lesson ended despite Megan's best efforts to extend it with multiple off-topic responses, Matt twisted in his chair to confront me head on.

"Do you have some sort of bias against weekends I should know about?"

"No. Why?" I asked, caught off guard by the slight impatience in his tone.

"I think you're trying to duck out of our date."

"I am not!" I protested. "You're the one who canceled last Wednesday."

"No, that was a postponement, and you won't let me cash in my rain check. What's up with that?" He crossed his arms and waited for my answer.

"I have this thing about making a living," I said. "Weekend shifts pay the bills."

"Fine. No weekends. How about tomorrow night?"

"For your rain check? Yeah, sure," I said, suddenly stumped as to how to come up with a good date idea quickly.

"You sound way excited," he teased me.

"I am," I said. "I want to hang out with you. I'm just going to have to think of something to do for our date."

"How about if we go to the ward activity?" he said. "I know that sounds kind of lame, but my sister is the activities chair and I told her I'd go. It would be way better if you were there."

"Okay," I said. "I can do that."

"Good," he smiled, and I felt a little curl of attraction unfurl somewhere in my chest. He had an amazing smile.

When I saw it stretch a little wider, I realized I was staring and gave myself a mental shake.

"Don't be getting all attached to me and stuff," Matt joked.

"I wasn't. You have something in your teeth and I can't look away."

He snapped his lips closed and began poking around with his tongue.

"Is it gone?" he asked, baring his teeth once more.

"Yep," I said, feeling slightly guilty that there wasn't anything there in the first place.

"Anyway, the activity tomorrow is sushi. Are you down with that?"

"Sure. I love sushi. Are we meeting at Tuna Town?" I asked, naming a popular downtown spot.

"No, at the church. I guess we're going to be learning how to make California rolls or something."

Score! That meant I could potentially cross off number eight: learn to make sushi.

Noticing my happy grin, Matt asked, "You really like sushi, huh?"

"Yum," I said and left it at that. Dave walked up looking pleased.

"How'd it go, dude?" Matt asked.

Dude is a favorite HB word. Everyone gets called dude. If you see a girl in a cute outfit on Sunday, it's totally acceptable to call out, "Dude, cute skirt," and no one thinks twice about it. People use it for everything from saying to their buddy, "Dude! That's a sweet wave!" to saying, "Dude, nice doilies!" to their grandmother. I hadn't adjusted to this, even after a month, but hearing it out of Matt's mouth, it sounded pretty good. Mellow. Full of surferness.

"That chick is cool," Dave said. I winced. "Just messing with you," he said. "That's a cool *girl*."

I smiled at him. "She seemed super nice."

"Totally," he agreed. "She said I could call her sometime, so it's all good."

"Call her?" I asked in confusion. "How are you supposed to call her?"

Now Matt looked confused. "I'm guessing with a phone? That's how it's usually done, right?"

"She's deaf," Dave explained.

"Oh." Matt looked even more confused. "How *are* you going to call her?"

Dave shrugged. "She said there's this thing called a video relay or something. But I guess I just call her, and someone interprets for her."

"Whoa, that's cool," Matt said. "I wonder how it works."

"Maybe like Skype?" I suggested.

"It sounds a little bit like Skype except she's the only one with a screen to look at," Dave said.

Making sure that Laurel wasn't looking, I slapped him a five. "Good work, cousin. I'm proud of you."

"Thanks, Ash. From the Strategy Queen, that means something. I think I have a tear."

"Strategy Queen, huh?" said Matt. "Tell me more."

"Ha ha, silly Dave," I said. "Uh, I need to check with you about something out in the hall. We'll be right back, Matt."

He nodded, a skeptical eyebrow raised.

In the hallway, Dave eyed me. "What is wrong with you?"

"With *me*? What's wrong with *you*, making that crack about the Strategy Queen?"

"What are you freaking out about, Smashley? He has no idea what I'm talking about. Until you lost your mind and yanked me out here, he probably thought I was talking about the advice you gave me. Now he's going to wonder what else is going on."

I unhinged my jaw to light into him but snapped it shut again when I realized he was right.

"That's what I thought," he said. "Seriously, why did you just freak out?"

I had no idea, except that Matt and I were in a good rhythm where everything felt organic. I almost forgot that I had engineered the whole thing. I worried that if he knew how hard I worked to make sure we "fell" into hanging out, he would see our relationship as being far less casual than I wanted him to. If he thought I had put tons of effort into attracting his attention, versus it being a happy accident, well . . . he might not believe that I really meant no attachments. This could cause him to either back away or hold on tighter. And since I very much liked things with Matt the way they were, the overwhelming urge to wipe out Dave's comment had temporarily hijacked my brain function.

Deciding that it was too complicated to explain to a cousin who hadn't yet graduated from Remedial Dating, I offered a different explanation. "It's possible I have a chemical imbalance caused by too much Cap'n Crunch and my brain went temporarily soggy. That's normal, right?"

"For you? Probably."

"So I guess I made an idiot of myself. What do I do now?" I muttered, more to myself.

"I think I can fix this," Dave said. "Do you trust me?"

"Last time you asked me that you shoved me off my surfboard."

"So that's a yes?" he grinned.

"I have to, since I have no good ideas of my own."

"Cool. Let's go back in."

I followed after him, trying not to show any anxiety over what he might say or do next.

"Get yourselves all figured out?" Matt asked when we walked up.

"Yeah. Ashley's been coaching me on how to talk to Laurel because we thought she was shy, not deaf, and my cuz had some ideas on how to work around the shy thing. Anyway," he continued, "Smash gave me some great advice on how to get Laurel to talk to me, but she's afraid you're going to think she's all like, manipulative and stuff just because she gave me good ideas for getting Laurel's attention. She was telling me that it was bad manners to point out her part in it."

I bit the inside of my cheek to prevent another outburst and forced a smile instead. Sounding like a complete nag probably wouldn't help my image either, but interrupting and clarifying would only make me look like a control freak. I kept smiling and said nothing.

Matt laughed. "Considering you just laid out the whole guy-years-versus-girl-years thing for me and pulled back the curtain on that big mystery, I don't think manipulative ever crossed my mind. I'm leaning more toward blunt." When I winced, he hurried to add, "But I'll think of a word that sounds nicer. Like forthright?"

I shook my head.

"Frank?" he tried again.

Another shake.

He paused and thought for a minute. "How about direct?"

I nodded. "Yeah, I'll take that one. Direct."

I could see Dave fighting back a smart remark about my "direct-ness" and decided to remove the temptation. "Hey, look, ping-pong," I said, pointing him in the right direction. "Why don't you go show them your sick paddle skills and flex extra hard if Laurel's looking?"

I barely finished before he was trotting off to wait his turn. The boy never could resist a round of table tennis.

"Do you play?" Matt asked.

"No. I always hit too hard. Darn ping pong ball is lighter than it seems," I said.

"What about the real deal?" he asked. "Do you ever play regular tennis?"

"In like, middle school PE, I think? By high school I had enough going on with swim team and volleyball to keep me too busy for other sports."

"Well, it seems like it's a summer of new stuff for you. You want to try tennis too?"

"Sure." I had no idea how I'd fit that in around work and the fifty thousand other things I wanted to do for The List, but I nodded, anyway.

"Cool. I haven't gotten to play much since my parents left on their mission. It used to be a thing with me and my dad."

I laughed. "I don't think I'm going to give you the same challenge," I said.

"Oh, I don't know," he shrugged. "They've been gone six months and I haven't played much. I'm pretty rusty, and you're pretty athletic. It might all balance out. You don't work on Saturday morning, right?"

"No, not a huge demand for filet mignon at eight a.m."

"Then how about sushi tomorrow night and tennis on Saturday?"

"Sounds good. Except for the part where I want to surf too. Can we do that this week?"

"Yeah, any day. Name it."

"I pick Thursday." I only had a night shift and didn't have to worry about exhausting myself before lunch.

"I have three students that morning, but if you don't mind heading out around eleven, then that'll work."

We finalized our plans and I realized that Matt had managed to carve out a slice of nearly every one of my days for the week. Or maybe I had managed to carve out slices of his. It was hard to say. But one thing I knew for sure was that doing anything with Matt Gibson was a great way to start the day, and ending it with him was even better. Between morning tennis and evening sushi lessons, I could feel the rest of the week shaping up just right.

Chapter 14

AFTER MATT DROPPED US OFF, I shut the door behind him and leaned against it with a happy sigh. Dave walked past me and confined himself to an eye roll, but I didn't care. Every time he busted my chops, he gave me that much more ammo for when he finally started dating someone. Just one more reason to pull for him and Laurel.

I headed for bed and my laptop to check my messages for any LDS Lookup activity. A handful of interesting guys with psycho-free vibes had sent me messages, which was cool. Somehow, though, I couldn't muster the enthusiasm to answer back. I snuck another peek at BoardRyder, but none of the other profiles did anything for me. I skipped an analysis of Matt's influence on that decision and wandered onto my sisters' blogs.

Leila, my oldest sister, had posted a new family picture. The candid shot showed her buried under her four kids with the youngest one, a little redheaded imp named Justin, sitting practically on her head. Her soon-to-be ex-husband Mark was nowhere to be seen.

It was no surprise. She got married the youngest, six months after graduating high school, to the missionary she'd been waiting for since she was sixteen. They had struggled from day one. She stayed home with the kids from the time Jack was a baby, and the pressure of working and finishing school made Mark short-tempered and impatient. Leila, by far the most high-strung Barrett girl, grappled with depression over failed expectations and financial stress. There never seemed to be a break, and a couple of a times a year she showed up back at my parents' house with the kids in tow, swearing the marriage was over.

Ironically, Leila rode me the hardest about marriage. It was why we didn't talk much anymore. I think she wanted to live through me, to experience vicariously the romance and marriage that she meant to have instead of the one she settled for.

I closed my laptop. I didn't want to think about it anymore.

* * *

I figured making sushi at the church called for casual clothing, so when Matt swung by on Wednesday night, I had on denim capris again, a black tee shirt, and a cool chunky silver necklace I picked up at the Orange County swap meet after some haggling. A quick swipe of lip gloss and mascara finished the job. The great thing about a summer tan is how much makeup it eliminates. Bye-bye blush, hello sun-kissed cheeks.

Matt smiled when I opened the door for him. "You look great," he said.

"Thanks," I responded, pleased at the compliment. "You too."

He had a polo shirt on, but it had a funky retro stripe of brown and green running through it, saving it from being too preppy. It fit his vibe—and his shoulders—perfectly.

I caught him up on my rare whole day off and told him about my run-in with some peevish ducks while I explored Central Park.

"Central Park is pretty cool," Matt said. "Did you do any disc golfing?"

I stopped on the sidewalk leading up to the church's double doors and stared at him. "Disc golfing? Is that like snipe hunting or watching the submarine races?" I asked.

"I didn't make it up, I promise," he said. "The other side of the street across from the library is all part of Central Park, too, and it's got a really well-known disc golf course."

"Okay. What's disc golf?"

"If you don't know, I'll just have to show you."

"In between making sushi, tennis lessons, and surfing?" I joked.

"Yeah."

"Hey, are you trying to monopolize all my free time?" I half hoped he was.

"That depends," he hedged. "If I say yes, are you going to freak out because you think I'm getting too attached?"

"*Are* you getting too attached?" I asked.

"*Too* attached? No. You're fun to hang out with."

"That's true," I agreed. "I am."

He laughed.

"Answer the question, though," I prodded. "Is this a monopoly?"

"On the condition that you don't freak out, yes. It's a monopoly."

I heard someone on the sidewalk behind us and we headed toward the door. Matt held it open for me, and, taking his hand, I dragged him down the hall to the stage steps, then tugged him down to sit beside me.

"I'm okay with that," I said. "But what would happen if I went on a date with someone else?"

He gave me a long, thoughtful stare. "Do you have someone in mind?"

"Not exactly," I answered. "I guess this is more for clarification."

"Geez, Ashley," he joked. "I take you out surfing a few times and you repay me with a 'define the relationship' talk? Worst payback ever."

I rolled my eyes. "Matt, I really like you. But I'm leaving at the end of the summer to dive into a really intense research program, and it's not fair to either of us to be heartbroken about that fact. I won't have the time to give to a relationship when school starts again, and I'm just trying to be honest about that."

"Relax, Ash," he said. He leaned forward and tucked a strand of hair behind my ear without thinking about it. "You are exactly what I need right now. I'm aware of your time limits, I'm aware of your commitment restrictions, and you are crystal clear about your boundaries. I'm fine with all of that," he said.

Deciding to test that, I asked, "Does that mean you don't care if I date other guys?"

"Nope. Doesn't bother me," he said.

I tried not to scowl. Instead, I said, "You keep dating whoever you want to date, too, then."

"I'll do that," he said. I stifled another scowl. "Can I ask one favor?" he continued.

"You can ask. My answer depends on the favor."

He smiled. "If you're going to go out with other guys, just don't do any kissing."

I raised an eyebrow. "You want me to spend the whole summer not kissing anyone?"

"That's not what I said. I asked you not to kiss anyone else. Just me."

My stomach flipped. "I haven't kissed you."

"Yet," he said, and I could hear a soft promise in his voice.

Oh, boy.

I felt the sudden impulse to throw myself across him and blubber, "Anything you want, Matt Gibson!" but a tall, gorgeous girl about my age walked up and saved me from myself.

"Hey, Matt," she said, but she was giving me the laser eye.

"Hey, Lou," he answered back lazily.

"You have to go do sushi," she said.

Kinda bossy, dark blonde hair, and a clear, green-eyed gaze. Hmm. "You must be Matt's sister," I said. "I'm Ashley."

"I know who you are," she answered. Her tone didn't suggest whether that was a good or a bad thing.

"Allow me to introduce my sister. This is Lou," Matt said.

She scowled. "It's Louisa, *Mattie.*"

"Right. I forget."

I grinned. It sounded like me with my sisters. Or Dave. Seeing the grin, Louisa unbent just a little.

"It's nice to meet you, Ashley. Are you ready to learn how to make sushi?"

"Yeah. I've been wanting to do this for a while," I said.

"Really?" she responded. "This is convenient, then."

"Louisa's the one who put this activity together," he said. "She's in charge of the activities committee, which is how I end up at half of these things."

"Ignore him," Louisa said. "I make him come to *all* of them. He's trying to act like he's too cool to show up, but he never crosses me."

"Actually," Matt interrupted again, "the truth is that for some crazy reason, I kind of like Louisa, so I hang around."

This time Louisa grinned. "As brothers go, he's a keeper. Mostly," she amended.

"Making sushi is such a creative idea, but how on earth did you get the bishop to pay for it?" I asked.

"I didn't. It's free. There's a new sushi place opening up over on Brookhurst, maybe a mile away, and they agreed that doing a demo for their target demographic made good advertising sense."

"Louisa majored in marketing," Matt said, and I could hear pride coloring his voice.

"The demo was your idea?" I asked, feeling a measure of respect for her.

"Yeah. Wednesday is the perfect night for something like this because—"

"—it's really slow for them," I finished. "Great thinking."

She cocked her head at me and said, "Thanks." I got the impression she was reevaluating me.

Matt climbed to his feet and pulled me to mine, not letting go of my hand once I was standing.

I squeezed his back. "Who else is going to ask me out if you're always holding my hand and stuff?" I asked.

"Are you saying I'm cramping your style?"

"Maybe."

"Bummer. Good luck figuring that out." And he hauled me down the hall to the kitchen. I was glad he couldn't see the cheesy grin on my face. Granted, I truly did not want any attachments, but it felt good to be wanted.

There were already about fifteen people mingling in the kitchen, including an Asian guy in a chef's smock.

"Bet you a Jamba that guy's the sushi man," Matt said.

"That's a sucker's bet. I'll buy you a Jamba, anyway."

"Matt!" Louisa called from the other side of the kitchen. "I need you to set up chairs."

The crowd in the kitchen trickled out to take seats in the extra-wide hall space on the other side of the counter, and more people drifted in through the back doors. Before long, a crowd of roughly thirty people sat chatting and waiting for the sushi show to get going. Louisa called for quiet, picked a guy to say the opening prayer, and introduced the sushi man. His name was Kisho Nobu, he told us in a nervous voice, and his family had just opened their own sushi restaurant.

He began by explaining a little about the history of sushi and how it fit culturally in his native country of Japan. When he explained that

sushi originally meant fermenting the fish in vinegared rice to pre-
serve it, several noses wrinkled in response, mine included. Mr. Nobu
smiled and continued his brief history. As he picked up steam, his
nerves faded and he began to joke and smile with the curious onlookers squished together in the chairs in front of him. He demonstrated
each of his tools, his hands moving deftly, his quick, sure movements
following a rhythm. I slipped into a pleasant daze as I watched until
the sensation of my own hand being thrust into the air startled me.

"You, pretty lady, come here," Mr. Nobu called.

I looked around.

"Black shirt, come here," he called again.

"I just volunteered you to make a California roll," Matt whispered.

I narrowed my eyes at his high-handedness but then shrugged. It
was on The List, after all.

I rounded the kitchen door to take my place next to Mr. Nobu
and waited for direction. When I saw him looking for another victim, I tugged on his smock and whispered in his ear. He smiled, then
straightened.

"This pretty lady says Matt Gibson loves to cook too," Mr. Nobu
said. "He will also demonstrate California rolls."

There were hoots from a couple of guys in the audience, the loud-
est coming from Derek, sitting in the back row. Matt shuffled around
the doorway to take his place.

"Okay, now you watch," Mr. Nobu ordered, and he began to
assemble his California roll, scooping the rice onto the bamboo mat,
shaping it into a long thin strip, and placing his remaining ingredients at one end of the rice. Then he took one side of the mat and with
sure fingers, rolled toward the other end, causing the California roll to
emerge with the crab and avocado perfectly placed in the center of his
rice roll when he sliced it.

"Easy," Mr. Nobu said. "You do it."

Matt lifted an eyebrow, like maybe he thought "easy" was an exag-
geration, but he reached for the steamer and plopped some rice down
on his own mat. When he began poking at it, I started on mine. I
concentrated hard to get the rice just like I had seen Mr. Nobu do it.
I could hear him clucking at Matt's attempts to shape things properly.
When I thought I had it right, I picked out some juicy crab and some

pretty green slices of avocado and laid them at one end of my newly formed rice strip.

"Mr. Nobu," I interrupted him, trying to save Matt from the rather hilarious berating Mr. Nobu was dishing out. "Is this right?"

He checked my work and his furrowed brow cleared. "Ah, pretty lady makes pretty sushi!" he exclaimed. Then turning to Matt he scolded, "No cooking. Find something else that's better for you. Like the pretty lady," he said and shooed Matt in my direction.

Matt strode over and stood behind me, resting his hands on my shoulders and nestling my head under his. I saw Derek's eyebrows shoot up all the way on the back row, and several other girls exchanged glances in the audience. I pretended not to notice and focused on rolling my sushi the way Mr. Nobu did.

"You heard the man," Matt drawled. The vibrations from his chin tickled my scalp. "You're better than sushi, straight from the mouth of a sushi expert."

"Smooth, Gibson," one guy called from the middle row. I reddened. Mr. Nobu grinned, so I asked, "Is my California roll done?"

"Yes. Slice and eat," he said.

I scooped up a section and then whirling quickly, popped it in Matt's mouth just as he was opening it to protest me moving, forcing him to chew instead of speak.

"No more talking," I murmured with my back to the audience. Then in a slightly louder voice I asked, "Is it good?"

Mr. Nobu hurried over and nodded Matt's head for him like he was a puppet. "It's very good," Mr. Nobu proclaimed in a voice two octaves deeper than his own. While the audience laughed, he ordered, "Everyone clap for the pretty lady and this guy."

The audience obeyed and we took our seats again. After whipping out over thirty California rolls in an eye-poppingly short span of time, Mr. Nobu ended the demonstration and we enjoyed the samples. Several people in the group planned to head over to Mr. Nobu's restaurant to keep the feast going, but when Matt asked me if I wanted to join them, I shook my head.

"I love sushi," I said, "but more for lunch than dinner."

"Then I can take you out for dinner somewhere else."

We decided on a Chicago-style pizzeria downtown on Main Street, not far from Hannigan's. One barbecue-chicken pizza later, we rolled ourselves out of our cozy corner booth and walked another block down to PCH, then crossed it and wandered down the pier. It was a pretty night, a nearly full moon clearly visible even beneath the usual evening cloud cover. Standing out at the end of the pier with nothing but a rail in front of us, we watched the moon's reflection gleaming and rippling on the dark water beneath us, stretching and re-forming in rhythm with the waves slapping the concrete support pylons.

Another comfortable silence descended between Matt and me. I savored it, appreciating how we could spend an hour over dinner cracking nonstop jokes and then slip into these quiet moments. Matt leaned next to me, his forearms resting on the rail as he stared out at the ocean. Shifting slightly, he angled his body to face me instead of the water, his head cocked, watching. I let him, not minding. When a small gust of wind snagged a long tendril of hair and blew it across my face, he reached out and replaced it with a tuck behind my ear, much like he had on the stairs at church.

"You never said whether we have a deal or not," he murmured.

"What?" The question came out sounding sleepy, the waves having lulled me into a gentle trance.

"Kissing," he said, capturing my complete attention.

"I'm a big fan of it," I assured him.

He chuckled. "Yeah, me too. But how does that fit with your attachment issues?"

"What do you mean?"

"I mean, if I kiss you, I'm kissing only you, no matter who else I might go out with," he said, causing me to feel an alarming twinge somewhere near my liver. "Are you okay with kissing only me right now?"

"You're saying it doesn't matter who I date as long as I'm only kissing you?" I asked.

"Yeah."

"And you'll only kiss me if I agree to that?"

"Well . . . yeah."

I pretended to think about it, although there wasn't any argument from me. I'd always been a kissing monogamist no matter how many guys I'd dated at any given moment. And for the record, that number was only three, and it was a summer many, many moons ago when it sounded like a good idea. It wasn't.

"Then I agree."

He leaned forward, his lips scant inches from mine.

"Ashley?"

"Yes?" I managed to strangle out in a hoarse, tense syllable.

"Is that your way of saying you want me to kiss you?"

"No. This is," I whispered and narrowed the distance between us to almost nothing. Almost. I wanted him to close the gap.

And he did.

Chapter 15

I DON'T KNOW HOW LONG the kiss lasted because I think time stopped when my breath did, but the sound of a rowdy group of kids rounding the restaurant behind us broke the kiss up. For a split second, I decided I fervently hated teenagers, but their cheerful laughs and jokes with each other overcame my aggravation. In fact, I appreciated the distraction because it gave me a moment to recover from an unexpected weakness in my knees. Matt smiled at me and turned back toward the water but kept his arm touching mine on the rail. Despite the moon's brightness and the steady beat of the waves, the spell was broken. I took the hand he offered, and we headed back toward the shore and his car.

"We need to do that again some time," he said.

"Kiss? Sure."

"Wow, Ashley. I meant eat pizza and take a walk, but I'll make out with you if you really want me to."

I socked him, and he pulled me to his side.

"I'm kidding," he said into my hair. "And just so you know, I'm totally not attached."

"Good," I said.

"But I think I should test that pretty often with more kissing."

"If you think it will help," I sighed, sounding put upon.

"I do."

"Then I guess I'm there for you, buddy," I said.

"Thanks, pal."

I gave him a soft hip bump to let him know I was teasing and snuggled even closer to his side.

"I'm not attached, either," I said. "Just so you know."

"I never doubted it," he said.

* * *

By the time my surf date with Matt rolled around the next morning, I had lectured myself at least three separate times over the ridiculousness of being nervous to see him. Even though we had kissed. Several times. And it was amazing. And . . . . Yeah, there went another tingle.

Scowling at my traitorous nerves, I wrangled my surfboard into the back of the Jeep and got in to head to Taco Reef, our surf spot.

"You surfing with Matt?" Dave called from the back doorstep.

"Yeah."

"Where are you going?"

"Our usual spot off Taco Reef."

"You guys have a spot? Wow!" he teased.

"I didn't mean that as in *our* spot, our spot. I meant it like that's just where we usually go." I wanted to kick myself for taking Dave's bait.

"Sure, Smash. Whatever you say."

My scowl deepened and I backed out of the driveway faster than necessary, decapitating my aunt's mailbox when I whipped the Jeep onto the street. Stifling a sigh, I parked at the curb and rushed back into the house carrying the mailbox. My aunt had painted a nest with a mother bird hatching a brood of pastel-colored envelopes, and the sad mama bird's head now sported a disturbing dent.

"Aunt Trudy!" I called.

"Yes, dear?" I heard her reply faintly from the direction of her sewing room.

"I decapitated your mailbox, and something bad happened to Mama Bird."

"That's fine, dear. You can help your uncle fix it later. Have a good time!"

"Thanks!" I hollered back and hustled back to the Jeep. I decided not to read too much into my compulsive need to hurry to see Matt.

A creative interpretation of the speed limit got me to the beach on time, and Matt was there waiting for me. After a big hug, he nodded toward the ocean. "Ready to tame the beast?"

An hour later, I limped out of the water, exhausted but satisfied after managing to catch a few good rides, and collapsed on the sand. The marine layer had disappeared earlier than usual, leaving the warm welcome rays of the sun to beat down on the beachgoers. Matt dropped down next to me, digging out a comfortable groove in the sand and then settling into it.

"You're really improving, you know," he said. "You look way more confident out there than you did even a week ago."

"That's because I know a wipeout isn't going to kill me and also because I'm the boss, not my board." I gave it a friendly pat.

"Ah, the two main principles of surfing."

"I thought those were relaxing and focusing."

"That too," he said, smiling.

We lapsed into silence, letting the sun work its magic.

Matt stirred himself after several minutes to ask, "Now that you've mastered surfing, what else are you going to tackle this summer?"

"I haven't mastered surfing," I protested. "I've mastered wiping out less."

"You'll be pro soon at this rate," he teased me. "Are you still going to talk to me when you're rich and famous?"

"Oh, are there a lot of rich and famous women surfers out there?"

"Uh, maybe not rich." He thought for a minute. "That one girl that got her arm bitten off by a shark while surfing is pretty famous, though."

I blanched.

"You didn't hear about that?" he asked.

I shook my head.

"It was a few years back," he said.

"Tell me it happened in Australia or something."

He paused. "It happened in Australia. Or something."

"Great." I regarded the ocean with a suddenly suspicious eye.

"Don't worry. The sharks around here are all sand sharks. They can barely gobble bait. Your toes are safe." He leaned on one elbow and stared down at me. "Are you going to answer my question now?"

I lost my train of thought as I watched the muscles flexing in his shoulders while trying to pretend I wasn't staring. "What question?"

"What other adventures do you have planned?"

He'd handed me the perfect opening to tell him about The List, but I hesitated to take it. I didn't want to open a potential can of worms about how he was on there as a summer fling and make him feel like our friendship meant less to me than it did. *Not to say that it means more than a friendship either*, I scolded myself. Then I sighed and abandoned the argument in favor of hashing it out with myself another time. I answered Matt with a version of the truth.

"I think it'd be kind of fun to try skydiving."

"Really? I've been before." He leaned back on both elbows again, away from me, and I stifled a sigh.

"Did you love it?" I asked.

"The final seconds before you fling yourself out of the plane are kind of brutal, but the fall is totally worth it. Why skydiving?"

"I don't know. Why did you do it?"

He shrugged. "I'm kind of an adrenaline junkie, but I'm trying to be more mature," he said. "I guess breaking a couple of bones and making it hard on yourself to get around for a few months will do that."

"That happened to you?" I winced just thinking about it.

"Yeah. Two winters ago I busted my ankle and a wrist after an idiotic BASE jumping attempt. Lesson learned."

"What's BASE jumping? I think I've heard of it, but remind me."

"It's when you jump off tall stuff like buildings or bridges with a parachute or this wingsuit thing," he explained.

I laughed. "Don't worry. BASE jumping is definitely not on The List."

"What list?" he asked.

"Oh, uh, my bucket list. Everyone has one, right?"

"A bucket list? I guess," he said and closed his eyes, turning his face to the sun.

Somehow an awkward silence had sprung up between us. I didn't like it nearly as well as the comfortable ones that we enjoyed. Groping for a way to restore our usual good vibe, I asked, "If I went skydiving, would you go with me?"

"Are you seriously up for it?" he asked.

"Yeah, I really am."

"I still have the contact info for the place I went when I did it. You want me to set something up?"

"That would be great." I felt an increased measure of respect for Matt. He disproved time and again the stereotype I had of surfers as flaky space cadets. He had a laid-back vibe, but the alertness he surfed with translated into everything else he did too. It was attractive. It worried me that I hadn't found one off-putting thing about him yet.

"I should probably get going," he said.

"Already?" We usually lazed around on the sand and chatted for a while before taking off after surfing.

"Yeah. Today's a busy day for work," he explained.

"Teaching?" I asked, because that's what he usually did in the mornings.

"Nah. The shop."

"I'm totally embarrassed to admit this, but I have no idea what you do there," I said. I felt a twinge of sheepishness that he knew so much about the details of my life when I knew so little about the details of his.

He shrugged. "I probably haven't mentioned it because a lot of it's kind of boring," he said. "Don't worry about it."

"Yeah, well, just so I don't feel like a total narcissist, will you tell me about the store? Celia said you own it, right?"

"Don't be too impressed. I co-own it with my buddy. And it's mostly menial labor, like today."

"What's today?"

"I have to spend the rest of the day loading trucks in a warehouse in Santa Ana," he said, naming a city farther inland. "It's going to be super hot. Feel free to make a 'you are where you work' joke there."

I rolled my eyes and waited for more details but none came. "That's it?" I pressed. "That's all there is to tell?"

He grinned. "I told you it was boring. Are you working tonight?" he asked in a sudden change of subject.

I resolved to get more information out of him later. "I have the later dinner shift," I answered him. "I think I'm going to see if I can get some volleyball in."

"Cool. I'll walk you over."

We split up at the edge of the sand courts after a long hug. One girl on the sideline caught my eye and nodded at Matt's retreating form. "Nice," she mouthed. I grinned.

Surfing, a date with Matt on Saturday, and sand volleyball. I liked this town.

* * *

"I hate this thing!" I announced two hours later, menacing Aunt Trudy's mailbox with a hammer. "I can't get the dent out!"

Aunt Trudy eyed me over her glasses, unperturbed. "You're doing fine," she said.

"No, I'm not." I stared in discouragement at Mama Bird's head. It now bulged in the opposite direction, the result of trying to hammer the dent out from the inside with too much force. "She looks like her head's going to explode from bird flu or something."

Celia wandered over. "She's right, Mom. I guess Ashley can fix mailboxes about as well as she can surf," she joked.

"Hey! I'm learning," I protested.

"You'll learn with the mailbox too, dear," Aunt Trudy reassured me, then turned her attention back to her needlepoint. It looked like a cross-stitch sampler of two surfboards flanking the word *Mahalo*.

I sat back and glared at the mailbox. "Can I just get you a new one?" I asked.

"I like mine decorated," Aunt Trudy said. "I don't have time to paint another one right now."

"I'll do it," I said.

"That's even more work than fixing it," she pointed out.

"Painting has to be easier than trying to get this dent flat," I said. "I'd rather try that."

"If you're sure, Ashley," she said. "I don't want to put you to any extra trouble."

"It's no trouble, I promise. I want you to have a happy mailbox, and I don't think I can make it happen for little birdie here," I said, with a sad tap of the hammer on Mama Bird's head bulge.

"All right, then. Sooner is better than later," Aunt Trudy said. "Mr. Jimenez doesn't mind running our mail up to the door, I'm sure, but I hate to make him do it longer than necessary."

"I'll have it done by Saturday," I said.

"How are you going to do that?" Celia demanded.

"You're going to help me," I said. "What do you know about

mailboxes?"

She sighed. "I know you can probably get one at the hardware store on Adams and Magnolia."

"Let's go. I've got three hours until work."

As it turned out, the neighborhood hardware store didn't keep a huge standard stock of mailboxes, so we chose the one that looked easiest to paint and I paid for it, then jammed it into the back of the Jeep and headed home.

I undid the cardboard and set the box on the table. It suddenly looked like a huge canvas, considering my limited art skills.

"What are you going to do with it?" Celia asked.

"I had this vague idea of finding some stencils and making something happen, but . . ."

"Are you any good at crafts and stuff?" she asked.

"Not really. You didn't happen to inherit any of your mom's skills, did you?" I wheedled.

"Uh, yeah. But I don't have time for a project like this. I work as much as you do, you know."

I did know, since it was her connections as a hostess at Hannigan's that got me my job there in the first place.

"Okay. I'll figure this out. I'd better let your mom know that I haven't abandoned it, and then I need to get ready for work. You want a ride?" I asked.

"No, thanks. I'm off before you, and I don't want to hang around waiting."

"Fair enough."

I popped my head into Aunt Trudy's craft room to let her know that I'd put the mailbox project on temporary hiatus and then went to my room to scrounge around for my work clothes. While I dressed, I thought about how to solve my Mama Bird problem. I grabbed my phone and punched out a text message to Matt.

Have to take a rain check on Saturday tennis.

He answered by the time I finished brushing my hair.

Why? I swear I'm not getting too attached.

Ha, ha, I sent back. *I have to do a project instead.*

What kind of project?

I have to paint a mailbox.

Why?

I sighed before responding, not wanting to admit to poor driving. *I may have accidentally run over the old one.*

Crazy girl. Whose mailbox?

My aunt's.

Ouch.

Yeah. Anyway, I'm not good at painting, so I need the time on Saturday.

I think I can help you. Does it have to be repainted with birds or whatever?

No, just something nice.

Tell your aunt I'll stop by to pick up the mailbox after work. And plan on tennis Saturday, OK?

K.

I gave Aunt Trudy the message then headed out, curious about Matt's plan. Work pretty much crowded the curiosity out of my head, though. I ran nonstop to deal with a huge dinner party but earned a small fortune on the tip. By the time I closed out the last of my tables, tipped out the busboys, and limped home, I only had the energy to notice that the new mailbox no longer perched on top of the dining room table. Thankful that it was no longer my problem for the moment, I texted Matt a quick thank you.

I washed away the lovely meat smell clinging to my curls with a quick shower and my favorite jasmine vanilla shampoo, then crawled into my pajamas and pulled my laptop to me. Maybe tonight I'd have an LDS Lookup message from someone cool like BoardRyder. I sure didn't want any of the other ones I'd been getting.

Chapter 16

EVEN THOUGH MY FRIDAY SHIFT ran later than usual because Hannigan's stayed open until eleven on the weekends, I woke up early Saturday morning, eager to play some tennis.

Okay, in the interest of honesty, I couldn't care less about tennis. But I wanted to see Matt. I'd gotten a couple of mysterious texts yesterday with questions like *Does your aunt like surfboards?* And *Does she have strong feelings about hibiscus?* I'm pretty sure the text reading, *Country kitchen–style geese, yes or no?* was a joke. I hope.

When Matt knocked a few minutes after eight, I'd been flipping through the cable channels for twenty minutes already. I opened the door to find him holding the coolest mailbox ever. The plain silver box I had bought now sported a painted row of brightly colored surfboards stuck in straight, clean lines in the sand, with the ocean in the distance. When he turned it around, I could see small intertwining purple hibiscus flowers forming a border around my aunt's house number.

"Whoa!" I said and reached out to touch it in disbelief. "How did you do this?"

"I helped the guy who paints our boards do it," he grinned. "Do you like it?"

"I love it!" I assured him. "Aunt Trudy's going to flip! Do I have time to show her right now?"

"Sure, of course," he said.

I fetched her from her craft cave and drew her into the living room where Matt still stood cradling her new mailbox. Her eyes lit up when she saw it.

"That's mine?" she asked.

"If you want it," he said.

"I do, I do! Oh, it's beautiful, Matt. Did you do this?"

He nodded, his cheeks suddenly pink. I grinned at him, and the pink deepened.

"This is wonderful. I'm making Joe put it up right now. Go get your young man some breakfast, Ashley," she added before taking the mailbox and heading off in search of my uncle.

It was my turn to blush at her calling Matt "my" young man, but I did as ordered and headed toward the kitchen.

"How hungry are you?" I called over my shoulder.

"I'm at about a six on a scale of ten."

"That's breakfast smoothie hungry," I said.

"Sounds good. What's in it?" he asked.

"Lots of protein to start your day. Raw eggs, tuna, mayo to thicken it, a little celery for roughage."

"Oh," he said. "I meant I was only like, a two, on that scale."

"I'm just kidding, Matt," I said. "How about a banana and strawberry version?"

"And just like that, I'm back to six. It's amazing."

He sat, and I threw together enough fruit to make two smoothies, then plopped his down in front of him and took my seat.

"Where are we going to play tennis?" I asked after enjoying a few swallows.

"Um, about that . . ." he started.

I eyed him.

"I kind of can't go this morning," he said.

"So you came here to stand me up in person?" I asked.

He smiled. "No. I have to go out of town for a while and I'm taking off today."

"Sounds mysterious. Are you on the lam from the law?"

"No, but I owe my business partner a big favor, and we have some stuff out of town, so I'm stuck."

I sat back, nonplussed. Unsure what to think, I managed to ask, "How long are you going to be gone?"

"Four weeks," he sighed. "I'm not happy about it but it has to be done."

"Wow. Where are you going?"

"I kind of have to travel all over the place. It's going to be a long, boring trip."

I struggled to maintain a neutral expression and Matt could tell.

"Are you mad at me?" he asked.

"Of course not! Work is work," I shrugged.

"You look kind of bummed," he said. "Ashley, are you getting *attached?*"

"No," I said, trying to keep the sulk out of my voice.

He grinned. "Just checking."

"So what are you doing on this trip?" I asked, attempting to dig for details again.

"Oh, I don't know. I'll be checking out new retail space, scouting locations, stuff like that."

"That doesn't sound too bad."

"It is if you have to live out of a duffel bag and eat cardboard-tasting drive-thru food," he said.

"Those might not be my favorite parts, either," I admitted. "I feel for you."

"Maybe it's good timing," he said, which I found ironic since I'd been thinking what incredibly bad timing it was.

"How so?" I asked.

He hesitated but held my gaze. Dave picked that moment to wander in, bedhead in full effect. He nodded at us and started digging through the fridge.

"Can we step outside for a minute?" Matt asked.

"Sure," I said. I led him to the backyard and the Adirondack chairs my aunt and uncle had set on the deck for barbecuing and visiting. We settled in and I waited for him to speak, my stomach suddenly clenching with nerves.

"Here's the thing," he began, rubbing his hands down the sides of his shorts. I wondered if they were clammy. "I hear you loud and clear when you say you don't want any attachments. So now is a good time for me to take a break in order to avoid that."

I mulled that over for a minute.

"Did you just dump me?" I asked.

"No. We can't break up if we're not together, right?" he asked.

"Right," I parroted back at him, but I felt bewildered.

"I just think you're super into me, and I want to give you a chance to carve out a little space for yourself," he said.

I stared at him, my jaw dropping a half inch until I saw his sly grin. I grabbed a chair cushion and flung it at him.

"Very funny!" I said.

"Come on, that was totally funny," he argued.

I sniffed. "It was a *little* bit funny."

"Seriously," he said. "I promise I'm not attached, but could you try not to date like crazy while I'm gone? You know, leave a little room on your schedule for me when I get back?"

"That smells vaguely like commitment," I hedged. I didn't want to tell him that nobody else I'd seen around interested me even remotely compared to the pull I felt toward him, so I didn't. Instead I said, "I guess I'll have to beat off all the guys chasing after me with a stick. Oh, wait. There aren't any."

"That's only because they've seen me hanging around," he said. "When I take off, you'll see a feeding frenzy unlike any other happen around you. Just watch."

"I'm flattered that you think so, but I don't really have time for much dating, anyway. You know, unless someone else is willing to hang out with me at eight in the morning," I said with a smile.

"So you'll pencil me in for when I come back?" he asked.

"Sure," I said. "But it's not like I won't talk to you before then, anyway. Unless your dialing finger is broken."

"I'll be in touch," he said. "But I'll be taking care of business at some crazy hours so I'm not sure when that'll be."

"Whatever," I said. "We'll talk when you have time, no big deal."

"Cool."

"So does this mean I don't have to go play tennis?" I asked.

"Have to? I figured you'd pick it up fast since you're so good at sports."

"It's just . . . you've seen my track record," I said. "I'm athletic but ridiculously accident prone. Maybe I'm dodging a bullet by avoiding the tennis court." I pointed to my calf, the pink stingray scar on it still visible.

"You're off the hook," he said. "I've got my stuff in the Cruiser and I'm hitting the road as soon as I leave here."

I nodded, not sure what to say. Matt didn't say anything either, and one of our rare awkward silences crept in, subtle as the morning fog that hadn't yet burned off. Eager to dispel it before it grew thicker, I blurted, "So what about kissing?"

"What?" he asked, a startled laugh escaping.

I squirmed. "I mean, if I'm not kissing you, does that mean I can kiss one of these imaginary Romeos you say is going to show up?"

"Sure," he shrugged. My stomach sank a bit, and it annoyed me to discover that I wanted him to protest. "Can I put a condition on that, though?" he asked.

"Depends on the condition."

"I'm going to kiss you good-bye and do my best to make it good enough to last for a month. If I do, no kissing anyone else. You got a problem with that?"

I grinned. "Not at all."

His return smile spread slowly, starting with the flash of a shallow dimple in one cheek and stretching to reveal his even, white teeth. He climbed to his feet, in no hurry, and I felt my nerves begin to stretch, tension mounting, making my toes curl. He reached down and gave my hands a gentle tug, pulling me up to join him. When I gained my feet, he wound my arms around his neck and then settled his hands around my waist. He dipped his head to whisper near my ear. "Are you ready?"

"No," I whispered back, because I couldn't find my voice.

"Good."

And he kissed me.

I thought our first few kisses were good. No, great.

This kiss? This was something else. When Matt finally broke away after several dizzy, breathless moments, I felt marked. The kiss practically shouted that Matt had staked his claim. I tried not to look shaken while my insides rioted. He backed away, a small smile lingering around his lips.

"Bye, Ashley."

I mustered the energy for a small wave. "Bye . . ." And stood a bit shell-shocked as he let himself out.

* * *

Work passed by in a blur and so did a few of my customers' orders. I found myself serving people the wrong steaks and salads, distracted by the memory of Matt's good-bye kiss on the backyard deck. I collapsed at home, exhausted at the end of the night, glad my screwups made only a minor dent in my tips. Shoving the wad of cash from my double shift into my drawer without counting it, I lay back and gave myself a good scolding.

What is wrong with you, Ashley? It was a kiss. Get over it. You've had lots of kisses. An embarrassing number, in fact. This one wasn't that special.

Except that it was. Even thinking about it made my stomach flip.

Great. I shared a really amazing kiss with Matt, but it didn't mean anything.

Only it did.

In spite of Matt's prediction that guys would start lining up to date me once they realized he wasn't around, the idea, which should have sounded fun, held no appeal at all. I sat up, annoyed that I felt bummed. I needed a shower to clear my head, and then I'd be able to see this all more clearly. I'd put Matt in his proper place: a neat little box labeled "Summer good-time guy."

A half hour later, feeling refreshed and far more alert than I expected to at nearly midnight, I returned to my room with a solution. To keep Matt in his place, I needed to remind myself that he wasn't the only game in town. Or, to put it more accurately, that he might be the only game in *this* town to catch my interest, but I had a whole other town to consider. My online dating project practically begged for a reboot, so in the dual interests of weakening Matt's pull on me and crossing off another number on The List, I opened my Lookup account and reviewed the e-mails with renewed determination to find a Utah connection for the fall.

Despite my best efforts, nothing really jumped out at me from my unread messages. Discouragement lurked as I discarded one message after the next. Until I reached the last one in my inbox.

It was from BoardRyder, the only guy I'd looked at more than once on the site. Opening his e-mail, I read, "Did you really read *Don*

Quixote? Great book." I paused in surprise. His question referenced my profile, where I had listed the Cervantes novel among my favorites. Although I had read it for an assignment during study abroad in Spain, I fell in love with it immediately, all thousand-plus pages, and it impressed me that he had read it too.

Curious, I pulled up his profile to refresh my memory. His picture showed a guy wearing snowboard gear in midair over a mogul. I couldn't tell much about his face with the goggles on other than that he had a strong jaw. I glanced over his profile again. He lived in Salt Lake, had an MBA, and showed a huge range in his interests. Besides snowboarding, he claimed to enjoy travel, reading, outdoor sports, movies, cooking, and underwater basket weaving. I liked his gentle poke at the standard questions in the site's questionnaire. He listed several favorite books besides the usual Clancy and Koontz guy titles, even including a couple of classics. Right in the middle, he included *Don Quixote*. Nice. I remembered liking his taste in music, which included several of my favorite bands. Nothing raised any red flags.

Clicking reply, I typed, "I read *Don Quixote* for school, and I thought it was great." I sent it off and then, feeling encouraged, navigated to the home page so I could do a search for other interesting possibilities. I checked out a couple of decent profiles but decided to let them hunt me down rather than pinging them first. I was in the middle of a fantastic lesson on "Internet Dating Don'ts" in the form of HereForTheLadies and his train wreck of a profile, when an IM alert from Lookup popped up on my screen. HereForTheLadies listed his pet peeves as "Girls who think back hair is gross" and "Freaking idiots in freaking foreign cars," and although I drove an American-made vehicle, I didn't feel I could negotiate on the back hair. I closed his profile and opened the IM request. It was from BoardRyder. He worked quickly.

BoardRyder: So . . . Cervantes, huh?
TwinkieSmash: Yup. Like I said, school. What's your excuse?
BoardRyder: Hard-core nerd tendencies.
TwinkieSmash: You're speaking my language.
BoardRyder: My favorite uncle loved that book, so I gave it a shot one summer.

TwinkieSmash: Ambitious.
BoardRyder: It's been said.
TwinkieSmash: So you read a lot?
BoardRyder: When I have time. Busy with work. You?
TwinkieSmash: Busy? Yeah.
BoardRyder: And reading?
TwinkieSmash: Not as much as I want to.
BoardRyder: Let's pretend I didn't read your profile.
TwinkieSmash: Okay . . .
BoardRyder: And then I can ask you what else you like to do for fun.
BoardRyder: You know, like I don't already know.
TwinkieSmash: Right.
TwinkieSmash: Huh.
TwinkieSmash: Can I go read my own profile real quick to jog my memory?
BoardRyder: Ha, ha. Been too long since you had fun?
TwinkieSmash: No, I have lots of fun, but most of it's been surfing lately.

The screen stayed idle for a minute, and then BoardRyder was back.

BoardRyder: You're here in Salt Lake? I've seen that lake. It's not that much like the ocean.
TwinkieSmash: Funny. I'm not in SLC right now.
BoardRyder: Oh, sorry. I just snuck over and got that from your profile.
TwinkieSmash: No prob. I'm from there, I'll be there again soon, but I'm just not there now.
BoardRyder: Now you're somewhere surfing?
TwinkieSmash: Yep.
BoardRyder: How mysterious.
BoardRyder: Let me guess . . .
BoardRyder: It's summer, you're Mormon, you're single, you're surfing . . .
BoardRyder: You're in HB, right?
TwinkieSmash: Bingo.
BoardRyder: Impressed?
TwinkieSmash: No. Half the people down here are summer transplants from Utah.

BoardRyder: So true.
TwinkieSmash: You've been here?
BoardRyder: A few times.
TwinkieSmash: Did you like it?
BoardRyder: Yeah, I'd say so.
TwinkieSmash: But you're a Utah boy at heart?
BoardRyder: No. Just here for business.
TwinkieSmash: Which is . . . ?
BoardRyder: The fascinating world of sporting goods.
TwinkieSmash: Cool.
BoardRyder: Sometimes.
BoardRyder: What do you do?
TwinkieSmash: School.
BoardRyder: Down there?
TwinkieSmash: No, up there. That's why I'll be back.
BoardRyder: The U?
TwinkieSmash: The Y.
BoardRyder: Why?
TwinkieSmash: Why ask Y?
BoardRyder: Funny.
TwinkieSmash: It's been said.
TwinkieSmash: Oops. I just yawned. I think that means bedtime.
BoardRyder: Catch you another time?
TwinkieSmash: Sure. See you around . . . Board?
BoardRyder: You can call me Ryder.
BoardRyder: What should I call you?
TwinkieSmash: Twinkie.
BoardRyder: As you wish . . .
TwinkieSmash: Or Ashley. That's fine too.
BoardRyder: Bye, Ashley. Nice chatting with you.

I closed my laptop, said my evening prayer, and climbed into bed. *Don't you go thinking about Matt's kiss,* I scolded myself as I drifted to sleep. But I didn't listen.

Chapter 17

AFTER CHURCH THE NEXT DAY, I admitted to myself that Matt might have known what he was talking about when he predicted my dating prospects. Within minutes of walking into the linger longer with Celia after Relief Society, a near-constant stream of guys rotated through our orbit. After she fielded a returned missionary I felt was far too old to date, she whispered to me, "Don't ever, ever move away." She stifled a giggle when the fifth guy in less than twenty minutes wandered toward us with an ice cream sandwich, today's refreshment. "Do they all think bringing you a treat so you'll talk to them is an original idea?"

"Yes," I grumbled. I wanted to leave, bored and a little irritated by the attention. Not wanting to disappoint Celia, I stayed and tried to think of a new, polite way of turning down the approaching guy's sandwich. Louisa saved me the trouble, calling my name and waving me over, leaving the guy to veer toward Celia instead.

"Matt's right," she said, when I reached her where she leaned against the stage. "He should have made a bet with you."

"About what?"

"How quickly the guys would move in when he left," she said.

I sighed. "Don't get me wrong, they all seem like nice guys, but this is kind of excessive. What on earth is going on?"

She grinned. "You're a status symbol now."

"A *what?*"

"A status symbol," she laughed. "Matt's way too humble to tell you himself, but a lot of the guys around here rush in to date anyone he's dated because they think it elevates their social standing."

"That's ridiculous," I said.

"Maybe, maybe not," she shrugged. "It totally embarrasses Matt, but it happens every time he breaks up with someone."

"They only want to hang out with me because I went out with Matt a few times? I felt a little stupid over all the attention before," I said. "Now I feel really stupid."

"Enjoy it," she said. "Most girls would."

"Not me," I shook my head. "I don't have time to figure out how to sort through all of these guys and figure out which ones aren't total wastes of time."

"Poor you," Louisa joked.

I sighed. "I know I sound either totally stuck up or completely ungrateful for the attention, but the truth is, I suddenly feel like a juicy bone in a yard full of dopey Golden Retrievers," I said, eyeing the plethora of blond guys loitering in the cultural hall. "This is silly."

Louisa nodded. "I understand, actually. They all just want you as arm candy right now, right?"

"I guess," I said. "It's lame."

"So no one caught your interest yet?" she asked, and I wondered if it was for her own information or if my answer would get back to her brother.

"Not really," I said.

"I know Matt hogged a lot of your time," she said. "You don't see anyone here that can plug the holes in your schedule?"

"Honestly? No," I said. "I think I'm just going to have to get used to having some free time."

Louisa studied me, looking amused. "Matt's dated a lot of girls that I didn't really like," she said. "But you're all right. I'm going to do myself a favor and make sure you stick around so he doesn't have to go date someone else obnoxious when he gets back from his trip."

"I'm scared."

"Don't be. But I'm going to start nagging you about attending all of the ward activities when you're not at work so that I keep you too busy to date anyone else," she said.

"I don't know, Louisa. I don't usually go to activities and stuff like that much," I said.

"Don't say no yet," she ordered me. "You don't even know what we have planned."

"You're bossy," I said. "Matt didn't exaggerate that."

"I'm totally bossy, but I get away with it because I'm usually right."

"Okay, I'll bite," I said. "What's next up?"

"We're doing Beachside Idol this Wednesday."

I cringed. "A talent show? Ugh. Not my thing," I said. It was that whole fear of singing in public. Leila and Juliana got all the voice talent in our family, leaving me completely self-conscious about being nearly tone deaf.

"Oh no," she corrected. "This is more like an anti-talent show. Have you ever done karaoke?"

"No," I said, my stomach sinking. If I had a shot at a List item, I might have to take it.

"We're hosting our first annual Beachside Idol karaoke competition. Bishop Danvers and his wife will judge, and we're going to give out awards for stuff like 'Best Cruise Ship Performance' and being 'Soooo Karaoke,'" she said. "The worse you are, the better."

"I stink."

"Perfect," she said. "You'll be here Wednesday, then?"

"I don't know," I hedged.

"Don't know what?" Celia asked, choosing that moment to join us.

"I'm trying to convince her to come to the activity on Wednesday," Louisa explained.

"The karaoke one?" Celia raised her eyebrows at me. "The *karaoke* activity?"

I could tell her emphasis was intended to remind me of The List. "You kind of have to go," she said.

I guess I kind of did.

* * *

Wednesday dragged its feet before arriving and it still came too soon. Normally, I had Tuesday night's Institute class with Matt to look forward to, but without him there, only the mild entertainment of watching Dave flirt with Laurel made the evening worthwhile. I couldn't focus on Sister Powers's lesson, wondering what Matt was up to and when he would call. I'd had a couple of texts from him, but nothing with any meat to it.

Ironic. The guy I didn't want a relationship with refused to call and it bugged me.

I yanked my wandering thoughts away from Matt every two minutes at work and focused instead on choosing a song for my Beachside Idol disaster. I mean, debut. By that night, I had selected and discarded over a dozen possibilities before settling on one. In rare instances I landed on key; it was in a narrow range. My voice isn't interesting or even very strong, so I needed to choose a song that fit my limited abilities. Dave and Celia insisted on coming to cheer me on, so we squished into Dave's truck and headed to the church.

In the gym, Louisa and her committee had set up the chairs and stage already. A deejay stood to the side of the stage, fiddling with his equipment, large binders stacked on the table in front of him. Another table, slightly elevated on a riser directly in front of the stage, boasted hand-lettered signs for STEVEN, J-LO, and RANDY. We grabbed seats somewhere in the middle of the audience. The second we sat down, Dave started craning his neck around, looking for someone.

"Is Laurel supposed to be here?" Celia asked.

"I'm not sure," he said. "She usually comes to activities."

"So, do I get to meet her?"

He shrugged. "No."

"What! Why? Ashley got to meet her and she's only your cousin," Celia protested.

"That's kind of the point," he said. "I don't want to make it some big deal like I'm introducing her to my sister and it means something. Besides, Ashley met her before I did, so you can't hold that against me."

I tuned out the rest of the argument when I saw Louisa heading my way.

"Hi," she said. "You're singing, right?"

"I guess." Sweat beaded under my tee shirt.

"Then go sign up before the slots are gone and you miss your chance."

"Thanks," I said.

"Sure," she nodded and then hustled off to go boss one of her committee minions.

I made my way to the deejay booth and put my name on the sheet. There were only about four slots left after my name, and I wished I had dragged my feet a little longer so that they were all taken. Scanning the list, I didn't see anyone else that had picked my song, and after checking the large binders to make sure that the deejay had it, I wrote the title down and headed back to my seat.

"Are you nervous?" Celia asked.

"No," I said. My toes felt numb.

"But you said you can't sing."

"Not very well," I agreed. Now I was losing sensation in my fingertips.

"Then why aren't you nervous? Aren't you afraid you're going to make a fool of yourself?"

"I'm not nervous because I'm terrified. There's a reason it's taken me six years to get to this item. This is Juliana's fault," I muttered, wiggling all my digits to make sure they still worked.

"How's that?" Celia asked.

"She was always looking all sassy up on stage when she did pageant performances and stuff, and she tricked me into thinking it would be fun to try too."

"But you can't sing."

"I know!" I glared. "I think I put karaoke on the list because I thought it would be easier than trying to do a talent show like she used to, but it's not."

Dave sighed. "I don't know why you're stressing out about this so much. Just bag it. It's *your* list."

"I can't," I said. "Once it's on The List, I have to do it, no exceptions."

Celia laughed. "I'm going to start penciling in stuff just for the fun of it," she said. "Audition for the Miss Hawaiian Tropics contest, lead the Fourth of July parade, enter the U.S. Open surf competition, and you'll be stuck doing it because it's on The List."

"I'm pretty sure I'd notice those additions," I answered. "Especially since I capped it at twenty-five when I made it."

The deejay did a mic check, signifying that the evening was about to get under way. Satisfied that the sound worked just fine, he handed it off to one of Louisa's helpers, a tall blond guy with an amiable face. He said the opening prayer, but it was much too mild for the divine intervention it would take to get me through the night with my pride intact. The deejay got the mike back and began to hype up the audience.

"Welcome to Beachside Idol!" he shouted. This produced a moderate wave of applause. Trying again, he yelled even louder, "Are you ready to see the worst of the worst, the performances so bad that they wouldn't make the *American Idol* reject reel?!"

This time, the applause sounded more enthusiastic with some whistles thrown in for good measure.

"Then let's get started!" he hollered. More whoops from the audience.

"We need Anne Gedson to the stage, please," he announced, and a moment later a cute little blonde giggled her way up the steps. He asked her a few getting-to-know-you questions and then handed her the microphone. Stepping behind his table, he fiddled with his laptop and within moments, the opening strains of Natasha Bedingfield's hit from a few years before, "Unwritten," wafted out. Anne stood beaming, not looking the least bit nervous, and when she opened her mouth, I understood why. The girl could *sing*. In fact, she sang the heck out of the song, and by the time the last few notes closed out, the audience was on its feet, roaring approval.

I turned, mouth agape, to face my cousins. "I thought everyone was supposed to be bad," I managed.

Celia winced. "I guess she didn't get the memo."

"Don't worry," Dave added. "I'm sure a few of them will be terrible."

He was sort of right. Out of the next ten performances, only two were truly awful, each singer playing to his weaknesses and performing as badly as possible. The rest of them ranged from pretty good to amazing. With every new performer driving me closer to the brink of despair, my lungs were laboring to breathe properly and the beads of sweat that had formed between my shoulder blades were now a deluge. When I heard the guy who signed up just before me get called up, I begged whoever oversees things like impending train wrecks and lost causes that he would be one of the "bad" singers. He only had to sing three notes before my hopes disintegrated. Between his perfect pitch and playing to the crowd, I realized I would be following one of the strongest acts of the night.

I leaned over to my cousins. "I'm next," I said. "I feel sick. I don't think I can do this."

"Sure you can," Celia said, but she looked nervous. "If you're as bad as you say you are, just go out of your way to make it even worse and you'll get people laughing."

"Yeah, that's the way to do it," Dave said. "Don't try to make it good. It was advertised as a night for awful performances. Go be the truth in advertising, or something . . ." he trailed off lamely.

As the guy onstage wound down his rousing performance and people jumped to their feet to cheer, my stomach clenched and I wondered how obvious it would be if I ran and hid in the restroom until the night was over.

Interpreting my expression, Celia shook her head. "Don't do it, Ashley. Don't bail. It'll be fine. Just get this item crossed off The List and it'll be totally worth it. You won't have it hanging over your head anymore."

I took a deep breath and nodded. I even remembered to exhale. Until the deejay said, "Next up, we've got Ashley Barrett singing 'The Shoop Shoop Song.' Let's welcome her to the stage." Then I stopped breathing again. I think maybe I suffered a ministroke and lost the ability to move for a moment. My feet stayed put and the polite applause from the audience began to dwindle when no one moved to take the stage.

"Can we get Ashley Barrett up here?" the deejay tried again.

"Go, Ashley," Celia hissed. "That's you. Go!"

Dave reached around his sister to give me a rough nudge. "Move it, you big chicken."

A few more heads turned in our direction, scenting some drama unfolding. That more than anything unfroze my feet. They pointed themselves toward the stage and I slowly followed as the applause increased again, now that a victim had identified herself. The deejay offered a grin and asked, "So Ashley, a little nervous, are you?"

"Yes—" I croaked, and then winced. I cleared my throat and tried again. "Yes, a little."

"So is this your first time doing karaoke?" he asked.

"Um, yes," I said, my panic rising. I knew I was supposed to be bantering with him to increase the entertainment value, but with my mind a complete blank, all I could handle was one syllable at a time.

"This will be fun for everyone, then. Any reason for trying it tonight?" he asked.

"Yes," I said.

He waited for me to elaborate. That didn't happen. After an awkward silence, he shrugged and said, "Okay . . . I guess we'll turn Ashley loose to do her thing."

I thought he sounded a little doubtful at this point, but I couldn't spare the extra brain cells to analyze his tone. He crossed to his table and in the shortest ten seconds ever known to humanity, I saw the screen in front of me flicker to life while the cheerful notes opening the song began to blare out.

The words lighting up threw me and I scrambled to find my place, dropping into the middle of the lyric and mumbling my way through the next part.

If I thought I had a prayer of playing it off like I meant to be that bad, I might have stayed up there. If I could have relaxed enough to keep my spot in the lyrics, I might have stayed up there too. Instead, I lost my place again as soon as I risked a glance at my cousins to gauge how big this disaster was. Judging by their expressions, it was awful. When I couldn't for the life of me find my spot again on the monitor, I stood, mouth agape, while my worst nightmare swallowed me completely.

The chorus swelled, but even though I wore out the Cher movie *Mermaids* watching it with my sisters when I was a kid, and even though we had reenacted "The Shoop Shoop Song" scene every time, the words fell right out of my head. A world of difference separated the experience of singing into a hairbrush with my sisters backing me from standing on stage with a microphone in my hand in front of an audience that was starting to fidget in discomfort.

By the time the second verse started, I knew number three on The List would stay uncrossed. I wondered if I could fake a hamstring injury and limp off the stage. Anyone who knew my accident-prone history would totally buy that. Halfway through the second verse, I gathered my wits, jerked the microphone awkwardly toward my face and said, "Sorry!" way too loudly, and then I set it down on the ground and fled from the stage in the opposite direction from the deejay.

When I exited the stage stairs, I realized the ladies' room was just around the corner, so I ducked into it. I had no desire to listen to Celia tell me that it wasn't that bad, so instead of locking myself into a stall, I slipped into the mother's lounge. Collapsing onto the little love seat tucked just inside the door, I dropped my burning face into my hands and tried to keep my mind blank. It worked for about two seconds at a time until a flashback would intrude and my cheeks heated with embarrassment again.

The bathroom door opened.

"Ash? Are you in here?" It was Celia. I kept quiet, preferring to nurse my humiliation alone.

"Ashley? I know you're not in the Jeep because I checked." I heard one of the stall doors bang open. "Are you standing on a toilet so I can't see your feet?"

Ha. I'm no amateur.

I waited for her to give up and leave, but the door to the mother's lounge flew open and there she stood, hands on hips, annoyance scrawled all over her face.

"Why are you hiding?"

"Did you miss the part where I made a total idiot of myself?"

"No. But I'm afraid I'm going to miss the part where you bounce back and laugh this off. You need to get back in there."

I peeked at her through my fingers. "You're crazy."

"No, I'm not. You have to shake this off and go back," she insisted.

"I'm not climbing back on that stage," I said.

"You don't have to. But you should get back in there with a smile on your face and prove you're not a loser."

"Did you just call me a loser?"

"No. And you shouldn't give anyone else the chance to, either. Look, it's a forgiving bunch out there. Give them a reason to cheer for you and go back out."

I groaned. "I don't know if I can, Celia. I've never made such a big idiot of myself before."

"I don't think anyone thinks you're an idiot. I bet you have a lot of people's sympathy. But if you don't show your face again, you're going to be a sad, sad footnote to the night."

I dropped my hands and stared at her, wavering. I so did not want to leave the comfort of my hidey-hole.

"Staying in here is making this a bigger deal than it is," Celia said.

That clenched it. If going back out to show my face would help the talk die down, then I'd do it.

"Okay," I mumbled. "But I'm not getting on stage again."

"You don't have to," Celia said. "Just slip into your chair and smile like you think the whole thing is kind of funny."

"It's hilarious," I said.

"Smile when you lie about that," Celia ordered.

I stretched my lips into a grin.

"Uh . . . that looks kind of feral," Celia said. "Maybe borrow one of your sister's pageant smiles."

I adjusted my mouth and she studied the results.

"Completely plastic but definitely an improvement. Let's go."

I trailed her out of the restroom. The final few yards of carpet in front of the cultural hall doors exerted extra gravity on me, slowing my steps to a near crawl.

"No backing out," Celia said. "You're a cool girl. You can totally play this off." She held the door open for me.

I slipped past her and then took a nonchalant stroll toward my seat, moseying like I didn't have the weight of crushing humiliation pressing down on my shoulders. I slid into my seat next to Dave, who smiled.

"You're all right, Smash," he said with a nod. That made me feel a little better.

With the exception of the people in the seats around us, no one seemed to notice my return. Most of the crowd were on their feet, grooving to the raucous honky-tonk anthem the contestant on stage sang.

"I didn't know this crowd was so into country music," I muttered to Dave. "Maybe that was my mistake."

"No, I think your screwup was the not singing anything part," he said, but he gave me a light punch in the arm to let me know he was teasing.

When Garth Brooks Jr. finished his number, the deejay let the applause die down and then announced, "It's time for the last performance of the night, folks. Let's bring up Megan Lowry singing 'I Will Always Love You.'"

I cringed when I realized it was *that* Megan. How delightful to know she'd witnessed my karaoke disaster.

She met the deejay at center stage for her obligatory interview questions, but before he could ask anything, she whispered something in his ear. Looking surprised, he informed the audience, "Megan has requested a change in song. Give me just a minute to check if I have it."

After a quick trip to his table and some tapping on his keyboard, he nodded to Megan. She smiled and lifted the microphone, waiting for the music to start.

When the first few bars drifted out, I wrinkled my forehead. The tune sounded familiar but I couldn't quite place it. And then the words started, something about not liking some guy's girlfriend. Megan snarled the lyrics with relish, bouncing all over the place and giving a rocking performance I didn't expect out of her. By the time the song hit the chorus about how he could do better, I leaned over to Celia.

"I realize I'm extra self-conscious right now, but is she shouting this song at me?"

"That's not your imagination. She's definitely singing this for you."

Dave grinned. "She isn't exactly subtle, is she?"

"I can't believe this," I said, shaking my head. "This girl is a piece of work."

At the end of the song, Celia turned to me. "Well?" she asked.

I shrugged. "I don't know if I want to laugh or kill her."

"Not that she's my favorite or anything," Dave said, "but I'm trying to date her friend, so maybe just laugh?"

I grinned. "Way to make this about you, Dave."

He shrugged. "Dude, Laurel's cool."

When the applause ended for Megan's performance, the deejay announced that there would be a short intermission before the judges announced the winners. People began to stir, leaving their seats to chat with friends while the judges conferred. I stayed put.

"See?" Celia said. "No one's acting weird to you."

"No one's talking to me at all. That's kind of weird." Not that I minded, but not even the people around us seemed to know what to say, wandering off to find other friends.

"That's because it wasn't a big deal," Celia said.

"Maybe," I shrugged, but I felt a lick of hope. Maybe she was right.

Derek chose that moment to wander up. "Dude, why did you bail?" he asked when he saw me.

"Uh . . ."

"I mean, don't get me wrong. I wouldn't go up there," he said. "But why did you run off like that?"

Louisa saved me from an answer, appearing in time to deliver a light smack to the back of Derek's head. He rubbed his head and stared at her in consternation.

"What was that for?" he demanded.

"Quit being nosy," she said.

"I was just wondering, is all."

"No, you're being nosy. Stop. Go somewhere else."

He looked hurt but then caught sight of a group of girls who were watching him and giggling. He headed their way for a little flirtation and ego massage.

Louisa turned her attention on me. "How do you feel?"

"Like an idiot."

She nodded. "Derek kind of had a point—"

"That I'm a runaway loser?" I interrupted.

"I was *going* to say that he wouldn't have gotten up there, and neither would I and neither would most of the people in this room right now. And that means that we all understand."

"You're saying you would have run out too?" I challenged her.

She shook her head. "I'm saying I never would have gotten that far, and you get points for trying."

I absorbed that for a moment and let it sink in. "Thanks," I said.

"No problem," she said. "I promise that whatever activity I bully you into next will not put you on the hot seat."

"Deal," I said. I wanted to stay on Louisa's good side because she was Matt's sister, but I also found myself liking her more each time we spoke.

"Have you heard from Matt lately?" I asked. I tried to sound casual but I didn't fool her.

"Yeah. He's working like crazy right now, trying to get leases ironed out and all of that. He hasn't called you yet?"

"He's texted me a few times. He warned me he'd be pretty busy. So where is he this week again?" I was fishing, but Louisa wasn't taking the bait.

"Oh, you know. Here, there, and everywhere, just like last week. He really should slow down, but he doesn't listen to me."

I nodded like I knew what she was talking about. I couldn't believe how hungry I was for any crumb of information she dropped.

Bishop Danvers turned around to beckon her over.

"Guess I better go see what's up," she said. "I'll see you around."

"Yeah, see you," I said.

Megan sashayed over next. She literally did this little skippy dance move on her way to my seat, probably delirious with glee at my public shaming.

"Sorry you had such a rough time up there," she said. Insincerity dripped like venom from her invisible fangs.

I decided not to let her get to me. "Thanks," I said. "It's such a personal song to me that sometimes it's hard to get through."

"'The Shoop Shoop Song' goes that deep for you, huh?" she asked, and her eyebrows crept toward the ceiling in disbelief.

I flushed but refused to back down. "Yeah, uh, 'If you want to know if he loves you so, it's in his kiss.' That always makes me think, you know?"

Her face darkened. I realized she had taken that as a hint that I'd kissed Matt. I didn't mean it that way, but since it was true and it bothered her, I let it stand and felt a little bit better.

"Your song was . . . interesting," I said.

"Did you like it?" she almost purred.

I shrugged. "I hope you didn't make too many girls in the audience nervous with those lyrics. Some of the insecure girls might decide to stonewall you for something like that."

"But I was talking about—" She cut herself off. "It'll be fine," she said. "They know *their* guys are safe." For Megan, that was subtle.

I barely refrained from an eye roll and might have done it, anyway except the deejay announced that the awards were ready. Megan favored me with a gnarly glare before heading back to her chair.

"That girl is unbelievable," Celia said.

"All right, ladies and gentleman, it's time to announce our

winners!" the deejay shouted. It confused me when deejays and emcees did that. I mean, they had a microphone in their hands. Hello? Was shouting really necessary? From the stack of certificates in his hand I could tell this would be one of those situations where everyone got an award. The first one he called out was for best dance moves, which went to a girl who had sung a Britney Spears song. Her choreography had stopped just shy of calling lightning down on all of us. Mr. Honky-Tonk anthem picked up something called "The Next Generation Cowboy" award and Megan picked up the angriest rocker chick prize. That seemed apropos. Several more awards for best costume, best ballad, and the best soundalike performance went out too. Even though I knew I had one coming, I still flinched when I heard the deejay say, "Ashley Barrett won the award for . . . Most Dramatic Exit!"

I scrunched down in my chair, but Dave said, "No way. You have to go accept it." Before I could climb to my feet (and I would have!), he stood and hoisted me over his shoulder like it was nothing and strode toward the stage. I cursed his summers as a junior lifeguard and as the laughter from the audience followed us up the stage steps, I grabbed the closest part of his back I could get to and pinched him *hard.* He kept going, probably because he was skinny and there was nothing to pinch.

When he set me on my feet and walked off the stage again, I looked out at the audience in some trepidation. How many times can a girl embarrass herself in one night and still get the sympathy vote? I wondered. But almost every face smiled back at me in genuine encouragement. Celia and Louisa were right—it was a sympathetic crowd. Well, except for Megan. She sat third row center with a sneer. Such a bad look for her.

It snapped me out of my daze, though. When the deejay handed me my certificate, I clutched it to my chest, stared at the audience in exaggerated fright, and fled the same direction I had before. This time I stopped in the wings, and when I heard the applause and laughter, I poked my head back out and waved, glad to be in on the joke this time. I passed Louisa on the way back to my seat and she gave me an approving smile.

When I sat back down, Celia leaned over to examine my prize.

"What are you going to do with? Frame it?" she asked.

"No way," I said. "I'm going to watch this sucker burn."

The last few awards went out and the perky blonde who opened the show squealed when the deejay awarded her the prize for best overall performance. It was a giant ham. I watched her exclaim over it, pretty sure she didn't get the joke.

While Dave stuffed his face at the cookie buffet Louisa's committee had set out, several people congratulated me for going up on stage again. I also got several better-you-than-me comments delivered with sympathetic smiles. *Yeah, that's me, all right,* I thought to myself. *Taking the hits so the rest of you don't have to. Because you're sane. And don't have stupid lists to take care of.*

At home, Celia invited me to watch an eighties flick she found on one of the movie channels, but I passed in favor of some shut-eye. I had never been more ready for a night to end, including the time I went to prom with Nate Sperry and he puked all over my dress.

It wasn't even ten o'clock yet when I climbed into bed but it still surprised me to hear my cell phone go off. Digging around in my purse for it, I fished it out by the fifth ring and saw Matt's name on the caller ID. "Hi," I said.

"Hi, yourself." The warm sound of his voice curled my toes again. How did he do that?

"I heard you had a bit of a night," he said.

My stomach sank. "Did Louisa call you?"

"Yeah," he said. "She thought maybe you could use some cheering up. Do you?"

"I feel okay," I said. "But I wouldn't mind some conversation."

"I can do that," he said. "On the condition that you're totally fine."

"I'm not yet, but I will be by the time I sleep on it. Does that mean I get to change the subject now? And if so, I pick the subject of you."

He laughed. "Okay," he said. "Me. What about me?"

"What have you been up to? How are things going?" And as I settled in to listen to his answers, I felt my tiredness and bruised spirits flee in favor of the comfortable rhythm he and I always seemed to find. I ignored the little voice that whispered, *Back out, Ashley. You're getting too close. Danger, danger!* Matt presented no threat to me. I had earned a good conversation with a great friend.

How could Matt Gibson be dangerous?

Chapter 18

THURSDAY NIGHT I COLLAPSED ON my bed smelling like Irish Spring soap since I couldn't find my jasmine vanilla shower gel. It was still better than smelling like meat. I grabbed for my laptop, hopeful that Matt had e-mailed me. When I didn't see his name in my inbox, I decided not to stress about it. We had talked for nearly two hours the night before. Maybe he didn't feel like he had as much to say today.

Sighing, I clicked over to check on my Internet dating project. My Lookup inbox held messages from two new prospects, both of them pleasant and unobjectionable. They weren't future boyfriend material, but it was nice of them to at least say hello. I guess in the virtual realm that equated to asking someone to dance at a church function, and who didn't appreciate that? I mean, assuming whoever asked wasn't obviously a psycho or suffering severe halitosis or something.

I decided the slow but steady stream of new faces in my inbox made it worth wading through the nut jobs on the site, but it wasn't a new face I was looking for. I wanted to see Ryder's picture next to a waiting message, and it surprised me how much. We had "bumped into" each other online a few times over the week, joking back and forth for a few minutes, or chatting about random things. To my disappointment, I saw right away that he wasn't online.

I was reading my friend Amelie's blog a few minutes later when a happy chime informed me that I had an IM. It looked like Ryder had shown up after all.

BoardRyder: Good evening, Miss TwinkieSmash.
TwinkieSmash: You again?

BoardRyder: If I swear I don't spend every second of my life online, will you believe me?

TwinkieSmash: Tough one. I have no evidence to the contrary.

BoardRyder: True.

BoardRyder: Then promise not to think I'm a loser.

TwinkieSmash: I promise because otherwise it means I'm a loser too.

BoardRyder: No, you're cool. I can tell.

TwinkieSmash: Oh, really? How?

BoardRyder: I'm psychic.

TwinkieSmash: Sweet. Can I get a reading?

BoardRyder: Sure. You're totally going to win the lottery.

TwinkieSmash: Even though I don't play the lottery?

BoardRyder: Yeah, that's how good you are. It's because Venus is in Jupiter's house while the moon is rising on Saturn.

TwinkieSmash: That's astrology. I think it's different from psychic stuff.

BoardRyder: I do both.

TwinkieSmash: A Renaissance man. Impressive.

BoardRyder: Renaissance man? I've only heard my grandmother say that.

TwinkieSmash: You calling me old?

BoardRyder: You're over the age of twenty and not married.

BoardRyder: Not to be rude or anything . . .

TwinkieSmash: Hey!

BoardRyder: Kidding! Seriously, though . . .

TwinkieSmash: Yes?

BoardRyder: Can I ask? Why you're not married?

I thought about it. We had talked often enough that there was a certain comfort level in answering his question. And as much fun as we had goofing off in our IM chats, I didn't think of him as dating material yet. Seeing no harm in explaining, I typed out a warning.

TwinkieSmash: I'll tell you but it might sound a little nuts.

BoardRyder: So shoot.

TwinkieSmash: Both of my sisters and my mom got married really young.

BoardRyder: Like how young? Child brides?

TwinkieSmash: None of them was older than 19.
BoardRyder: Yeah, okay. Kinda young.
TwinkieSmash: Anyway, I have a stubborn streak. So I made The List.
BoardRyder: What list?
TwinkieSmash: THE LIST. I made it when I was 18.
BoardRyder: You mean, aka marriage age at your house?
TwinkieSmash: Exactly.
BoardRyder: Go on.
TwinkieSmash: Both of my sisters already had kids by then, and that didn't look very fun at the time.
TwinkieSmash: So I decided to make sure I avoided that trap.
BoardRyder: You feel like kids are a trap?
TwinkieSmash: I used to.
BoardRyder: Coming from someone who's been tied up, down, and to various swing sets and yard furniture by his nephews, I feel your pain.
TwinkieSmash: Thank you. I meant a more figurative trap.
BoardRyder: I know.
TwinkieSmash: I lost my train of thought.
BoardRyder: Just scroll up.
TwinkieSmash: Oh yeah. I made a list.
BoardRyder: I heard. List of what?
TwinkieSmash: 25 things to do before I get married.
BoardRyder: Seriously?
TwinkieSmash: Yeah.
BoardRyder: Awesome. What's on it?

I liked that he didn't try to ask any deep and searching questions about it or analyze the reasons why I felt the need to make it. Following The List had become almost a force of habit now, something I committed to doing and so I did it, item by item. I wasn't into having long discussions about the underlying rationale for that, especially when it was a pretty straightforward situation. I made a list, I wanted to check items off the list, and I didn't want to get married until I took care of them all.

I told him some of the items more fit for public consumption, like about skydiving and traveling. We chatted back and forth about cool places we visited and places we wanted to go, and we hit the rhythm I had learned to identify with him, where we fell into a groove and our senses of humor synced perfectly, the laughs coming quick and often. Talking to Ryder felt totally natural.

I thought for a minute, my mind wandering from our chat. Was hanging out with Ryder online while dating Matt a problem? Should I be disclosing these facts to either of them? Unsure what to do, I ran with my constant impulse to put it out there if I was ever in doubt.

TwinkieSmash: You're fun to talk to.
BoardRyder: Ditto.
TwinkieSmash: You sweet talker, you.
BoardRyder: I'm a regular Romeo. Or else I'm super lame at that stuff. One or the other.
TwinkieSmash: No, seriously. That was uber sweet. I feel all melty inside and stuff.
BoardRyder: Melty? Is that a word?
TwinkieSmash: It is if I say it is.
BoardRyder: Yes, ma'am.
TwinkieSmash: Anyway, I was saying you're fun to talk to.
BoardRyder: Thanks.
TwinkieSmash: But just to be clear, that's all we're doing, right?
BoardRyder: What do you mean?
TwinkieSmash: I mean, I'm dating and stuff down here, and I kind of see talking to you as a fun friends thing.
BoardRyder: Duh.
TwinkieSmash: Excuse me?
BoardRyder: SLC and HB are 700 miles apart. What else would we be?
TwinkieSmash: That's what I'm saying.
BoardRyder: I think it's funny that you felt like you had to point it out.
TwinkieSmash: Now I feel dumb.
BoardRyder: Don't. It's probably smart to be all straight about stuff.
TwinkieSmash: I think so.
BoardRyder: So . . . we're friends, then?
TwinkieSmash: Yeah.

BoardRyder: Good. Then you should spill the details about this dating you're doing.

TwinkieSmash: To you?

BoardRyder: Sure.

TwinkieSmash: But you're a guy.

BoardRyder: So? I'm bored. I want to know what you look for in a guy.

TwinkieSmash: Why?

BoardRyder: I just told you. I'm bored.

TwinkieSmash: But what if I decide to date you in the fall when I get up there?

BoardRyder: We haven't even met. We may not have any chemistry at all. What if I decide to not date you?

TwinkieSmash: True. And I haven't seen your face. You may be hideously ugly and send me screaming in the other direction.

BoardRyder: That's why you can't see my face in my pic. I'm a total troll.

TwinkieSmash: Seriously, why no face shot?

BoardRyder: Meh. I put up a shot that shows me doing what I love. It's more true to me than a cheesy smile.

TwinkieSmash: Maybe you could just do a picture where you glare or stare all serious into the camera.

BoardRyder: Oh, pull a Blue Steel, right?

TwinkieSmash: Yeah, strike your best nonsmile, model pose face.

BoardRyder: I totally tried that already.

TwinkieSmash: And?

BoardRyder: I looked constipated. Let's talk about your love life.

TwinkieSmash: You're nosy.

BoardRyder: Yep.

BoardRyder: Come on, it'll be fun. I'll help you analyze things from the guy's point of view.

TwinkieSmash: Tempting.

BoardRyder: You know you want to.

BoardRyder: Is it more than one guy? That'd totally be worth my advice.

TwinkieSmash: No, there's just one guy.

BoardRyder: I thought you didn't want anything serious.

TwinkieSmash: It's not serious. I only have time for one guy.

BoardRyder: And he is . . .

TwinkieSmash: Tall.

BoardRyder: I meant, what's his name?

TwinkieSmash: Let's call him Mr. G.

BoardRyder: That's a dumb name.

TwinkieSmash: It's not his real name.

BoardRyder: Oh really? Thanks for clearing that up.

TwinkieSmash: Anyway, he's in the singles ward down here. He's, like, top dog or something.

BoardRyder: Top dog in the pound is not so great.

TwinkieSmash: Jealous much?

BoardRyder: No. Totally objective. Continue.

TwinkieSmash: Anyway, I came down here to surf, but I was awesomely bad at it.

TwinkieSmash: Mr. G is the best coach around, so . . .

BoardRyder: You figured you'd get him to teach you.

TwinkieSmash: Yeah, but I can't actually afford to pay for lessons, so I had to convince him to do it out of the goodness of his heart.

BoardRyder: Did it work?

TwinkieSmash: Yeah.

BoardRyder: For the price of a few makeouts, right?

TwinkieSmash: NO! I'm not that kind of girl.

BoardRyder: Sorry. I was kidding. Go on.

TwinkieSmash: Anyway, he's a great teacher, and now I can surf.

BoardRyder: So now you're done with him?

TwinkieSmash: No. I made him #17 on The List.

BoardRyder: Which is . . .

TwinkieSmash: Promise not to think badly of me?

BoardRyder: Promise.

TwinkieSmash: #17 is to have a summer fling.

BoardRyder: Whoa. What does that mean, exactly?

TwinkieSmash: Have a fun summer romance with a definite end in sight, enjoy the moment, leave, and then have a great memory to look back on.

BoardRyder: But explain the romance part.

TwinkieSmash: You know, it's just hanging out, flirting, spending time, being giddy.

BoardRyder: He makes you giddy?

TwinkieSmash: No comment.

BoardRyder: I see. Does he know it's just for the summer?

TwinkieSmash: Yep.

BoardRyder: So you're just a put-it-out-there kind of girl, huh?

TwinkieSmash: Yep.

BoardRyder: Does he know about The List?

TwinkieSmash: I maybe didn't put that out there.

BoardRyder: Why not?

TwinkieSmash: Guys sometimes react weird.

BoardRyder: You told ME about it.

TwinkieSmash: Yeah, but we're friends now. FRIENDS.

BoardRyder: True. Do I have a number on The List?

TwinkieSmash: Maybe.

BoardRyder: Maybe? Isn't that a yes or no question?

TwinkieSmash: Well, there's #24.

BoardRyder: Yeah?

TwinkieSmash: Try Internet dating.

BoardRyder: That isn't me?

TwinkieSmash: Not yet. I might not want to date you when we meet, remember? You're a troll.

BoardRyder: Oh yeah. I don't know if I want to date you, either.

TwinkieSmash: Why not?

BoardRyder: You're so high maintenance.

TwinkieSmash: Very funny.

BoardRyder: I try.

TwinkieSmash: That's why you're a maybe. If I decide I want to date you, then you'll be #24.

BoardRyder: But what if I don't want to date you?

TwinkieSmash: Then there's always ChickMagnet or HerefortheLadies. They send me lots of messages.

BoardRyder: Ha, ha! At least you don't have MarryMe or SweetSpirit pounding down your inbox door.

TwinkieSmash: Sorry, but unless one of them has a sad obsession with toy trains, I win.

BoardRyder: Toy trains? For real?

TwinkieSmash: Yeah.

BoardRyder: You definitely win.
TwinkieSmash: I don't want to.
BoardRyder: Too bad. I surrender the title of loser magnet. It's yours.
TwinkieSmash: Thanks. I have to go.
BoardRyder: Already?
TwinkieSmash: Yeah, I'm gonna go polish my loser-magnet crown.
BoardRyder: But you didn't finish telling me about Mr. G. I didn't give you any advice yet.
TwinkieSmash: You have advice already?
BoardRyder: Yeah. Tell him about your list.
TwinkieSmash: No.
BoardRyder: Why not?
TwinkieSmash: I'll tell you another time. I really want to get to my crown.
BoardRyder: Yeah. You're not off the hook, though. You owe me more details.
TwinkieSmash: Are you really this bored?
BoardRyder: Maybe. See you here tomorrow night?
TwinkieSmash: Maybe. It depends.
BoardRyder: On what?
TwinkieSmash: If Mr. G calls.
BoardRyder: Check in, anyway. I might be around.
TwinkieSmash: You sound like a stalker.
BoardRyder: You wish. I have a date tomorrow night too.
TwinkieSmash: Really? With who?
BoardRyder: Hot girl who's been chasing me. I let her catch me. Maybe I'll tell you about it.
TwinkieSmash: A little quid pro quo?
BoardRyder: You got it.
TwinkieSmash: So, I'm kind of impressed that you know what quid pro quo means.
BoardRyder: Don't be. I heard Robin Williams say it in Aladdin when I was a kid, and I asked what it meant. My Latin starts and ends there.
TwinkieSmash: You're funny.
BoardRyder: I've heard.
TwinkieSmash: Good night.
BoardRyder: Later.

I pushed my laptop away with a satisfied sigh. I felt good knowing that Ryder was clear on me dating other people. Now I needed to have the same conversation with Matt.

* * *

That opportunity presented itself sooner than I wanted it to. When my shift ended at ten on Friday, a voice mail from Matt was waiting for me. "Hey, Ashley. You're probably at work. I just wanted to say hi and tell you that I had a great time talking to you the other night. Why are you so cool? And why do I have to be traveling right now? Anyway, call me if you don't finish too late."

The message was about an hour old. I listened to it about ten more times before calling him back. The first five times, I felt a little thrill. The last few times, I felt a little panicked. What did he mean why did he have to be traveling? That meant he wanted to be back in HB. With me? It made me nervous. I wanted him to come back too, and that was a huge red flag. *Danger! Danger!* My instinct blared. *Attachment encroaching! Attachment encroaching!*

Of course I called him.

"Hey, you," he said after the second ring.

"Hey, yourself. Did I wake you? I'm not sure what the time difference is where you are."

"I wasn't sleeping," he reassured me but didn't address the time-zone hint. "How was work?"

"Same old, same old," I said. "A couple of cranky customers, mostly some nice ones, and enough tips to make it all worth it. How was work for you?"

"Oh, I don't know. Okay, I guess. I really want to get back home, though," he said.

"I can imagine. Tired of living out of your duffel bag?"

"Yeah. And I miss stuff."

"Like what?" I asked and then wanted to kick myself. It sounded like I was fishing. Um, because I was fishing.

"Surfing," he said. "TK Burger. Surfing. And also surfing."

Good thing I didn't want him missing me.

"Right. Can't surf where you are, huh?" I asked.

"Not so much. And there's other stuff they don't have here, either."

"Yeah?"

"Yeah."

And even though he didn't say more than that, I knew he meant me. My stomach lurched, but whether from pleasure or stress, I didn't know. The boy had me in knots. Time to run a little defense.

"Um, so I've been making some new friends," I said.

"Cool. People from the ward? Anyone I know?"

"Yeah, some from the ward. Like your sister. Oh, and, uh, I'm also keeping in touch with a guy back in Utah, but just as friends right now," I said. "Just so you know."

"Would it bother you if I was doing the same thing?" he asked.

"Keeping in touch with a guy back in Utah? No, but I might think it was a little odd," I said.

He laughed. I liked making him laugh. It warmed my commitment-phobic heart in an unfamiliar way.

"So you're okay with that?" I asked.

"Sure," he answered. "No attachments, right? I promised to follow the rules. I won't let it bother me."

What did that mean? That it bothered him but he was ignoring it? And why did it feel good to think that it might? And why was I such a basket case? One minute I didn't want him missing me, and the next minute I did. I wanted no attachment, and yet I wanted it to bother him that he might not be the only game in town. I could hear my sister Juliana's voice in my head delivering a well-deserved lecture. "How would you like it if a guy was treating you this way?"

I hated to admit it, but if the tables were turned right now, I wasn't sure I'd be so calm about Matt chatting with another girl in his free time. Bugged by my own ambivalence, I changed the subject to something safer.

"So my aunt really loves her mailbox," I said, and that was enough to steer the conversation into shallower waters. Still, the nagging sense that I didn't know what I wanted anymore clung to me, and by the time Matt hung up, I felt frustrated. I thought about Ryder's offer to advise me on my love life and felt tempted to take him up on it. I signed into my Lookup account and smiled when

I saw the little green light next to Ryder's name, telling me he was hanging out online too.

TwinkieSmash: Hey.
BoardRyder: Hey, where have you been?
TwinkieSmash: Busy. Work and stuff.
BoardRyder: Mr. G stuff?
TwinkieSmash: Maybe.
BoardRyder: Do I get details now? I can't be your love guru without them.
TwinkieSmash: Nah. I don't want to kiss and tell.
BoardRyder: Oh, REALLY? I think you just did, ha ha.
TwinkieSmash: What are you talking about?
BoardRyder: You can't tell if you didn't kiss, and you just admitted you've got something to tell.
TwinkieSmash: Oops.
BoardRyder: Does this mean we're breaking up?
TwinkieSmash: We're not dating.
BoardRyder: Oh yeah. Then does that mean we're going to tell each other secrets and braid each other's hair?
TwinkieSmash: Hard to do that since we're in two different states.
BoardRyder: Do you have to kill all my good ideas?
TwinkieSmash: Pretty sure I've only knocked down bad ones so far.
BoardRyder: All right. That's true. So we're not talking about Mr. G?
TwinkieSmash: Well . . .
BoardRyder: What's up?
TwinkieSmash: Maybe I could use a little advice.
BoardRyder: I'm the best advice giver ever.
TwinkieSmash: Wow.
BoardRyder: No, seriously. I'm awesome. Try me.
TwinkieSmash: I guess I'm kind of confused.
BoardRyder: About what? How he feels? Common problem.
TwinkieSmash: No, I think I'm more confused about how I want him to feel.
BoardRyder: Don't you want him to like you?
TwinkieSmash: Yeah. I don't know how much, though.
BoardRyder: He kissed you. That probably means something.

TwinkieSmash: Maybe. But some guys don't think kissing is such a big deal.

BoardRyder: Does he have a reputation for kissing around or something?

TwinkieSmash: No. Actually, he wanted me to agree that no matter who we dated, we'd only kiss each other.

BoardRyder: Then kissing definitely means something to him, and that must mean that you mean something to him too.

TwinkieSmash: Huh.

BoardRyder: What?

TwinkieSmash: I don't think you're using very good strategy if you're trying to date me in the fall.

BoardRyder: Are we going to have this conversation again?

TwinkieSmash: Which one?

BoardRyder: The one where I might be a troll or I might not like you.

TwinkieSmash: Oh, that conversation.

BoardRyder: Besides, if you came back here stuck on another guy, I definitely wouldn't want to date you.

TwinkieSmash: I'm not stuck on anyone.

BoardRyder: No?

And somehow, an hour later, after some surf talk that somehow morphed into a philosophical discussion and then devolved into trading stupid pirate jokes, I found myself exhausted and still reluctant to sign off. I'd have to cut back on chat time with Ryder, I decided. I couldn't spend the whole summer dancing away from any attachments to Matt only to get all caught up with Ryder. That would make no sense at all . . .

Chapter 19

IT WAS A GOOD THING I wasn't prone to introspection or meditating on my feelings because I suddenly had less time for it than ever. My boss at Hannigan's had me taking extra shifts whenever he could stick them on my schedule while I wasn't looking. He needed all hands on deck. Between Independence Day celebrations and the US Open of Surfing, July got a little nutty.

I squeezed in a few phone calls with Matt during all the madness but kept it breezy. With Ryder, I let my guard down a bit. It felt safer to tell him things since he wasn't a romantic interest. Yet. The whole situation had this weird dichotomy: every time Matt's name lit up my caller ID, my stomach fluttered and I worked hard to keep things light. Ryder's little green light on my computer screen had zero effect on my innards, but while every chat started as a snark fest, we somehow moved on to politics or heated debates about favorite bands by conversation's end. It was kind of like having the best of both worlds without committing to either.

When I got home from work on Thursday, it was only nine. My boss had let me go as soon as it slowed down because I'd worked all day. Dave slouched on the couch, not even turning his head to see who had come in. I plopped down next to him.

"What's going on, mopey?"

"Not much," he said. "Except I didn't ask Laurel out tonight."

"She wasn't at Institute?"

"No, she was." He picked at the fringe on one of throw pillows. "But Megan never went away, and I think she hates me because I'm related to you. She gave me the stink eye all night, and the last thing I wanted was her hanging around while I tried to talk to Laurel."

"So you're going to call instead?"

He winced.

"Why not just call her?" I'd overhead him on the phone with her a few times so I knew they managed to talk somehow.

"It's embarrassing," he confessed. "That's why I want to ask her in person."

"That's a little backwards," I told him. "Usually people would rather risk rejection on the phone than face-to-face."

"That's because there are no witnesses that way," he said. "It's a little different with Laurel."

"How?"

"She uses this video relay thing when we talk, and there's always someone else listening to our conversation."

"Whoa, what? How does that work?"

"I'm not totally sure because I only know my side of it," he shrugged. "I guess when I call her, the call goes through an interpreter who Laurel sees on a screen. Then the interpreter signs whatever I say to Laurel, and then Laurel talks back."

"So like, the interpreter tells you what Laurel's signing?"

He shook his head. "I think that's normally how it goes, but Laurel's speech is good so she talks directly to me."

"It doesn't sound like that big of a deal. I think you should call her tonight," I said. "Just get it over with. Then you guys can go out this weekend and you don't have to wait a whole week wondering if she's going to be at Institute on Tuesday."

"I don't know. I'm usually pretty confident about girls—"

I snorted.

"—but she's got me all twisted up somehow."

I almost said I could relate but I caught myself before it slipped out. I could barely acknowledge Matt's effect on me in the privacy of my own mind. I wasn't about to confess that weakness out loud. Instead, I punched my cousin on the shoulder.

"Call her," I said. "She'll say yes. I know she will. I'm going to go wander off to eat some fruit and pretend I'm not dying to hear the conversation."

"Thanks, Smash," he said in relief.

"You better hurry," I said. "Celia's off in about a half hour and I don't think she's going to cut you the same slack."

I left him fumbling his cell phone out of his pocket while I went foraging in the kitchen for food. There was always plenty to eat at Hannigan's, but it turned out it *is* possible to get sick of steak. I craved something lighter. After I found and peeled a banana, I enjoyed it down to the last bite, wondering how Dave's conversation was going. It was funny to see someone fall so fast for another person. He'd only had a couple of conversations with Laurel, but twitterpation already had a firm grip on him. For all of our banter and teasing, Dave was high on my list of Good Guys, and I hoped Laurel saw it too.

I started in on a pint of fresh strawberries from the stand Aunt Trudy liked to visit on Beach Boulevard. I got to savor exactly one bite before Dave charged into the kitchen doing a jerky victory dance. I watched his graceless gyrations for a few seconds before guessing, "She said yes?"

He nodded and pointed to the phone. "It's on mute, but I asked her if you could listen in to how the video relay thing works."

"Really? Cool!"

He unmuted the sound and then said, "Laurel? Ashley's listening now too."

There was a short delay where Dave whispered, "The interpreter is signing to her." Then I heard Laurel's distinctive voice say, "Hi, Ashley."

"Hi, Laurel. Thanks for letting me listen in."

Another pause followed and then a male voice came on the line. "I'm going to let the interpreter voice for me for a minute so you can see how it is for most deaf people to talk on the phone."

It sounded so funny to hear a man saying Laurel's words. "It would be really hard to whisper sweet nothings to him to pass along," I whispered to Dave. He glared at me. In a normal voice I asked, "Do you talk on the phone much?"

"Not really," said the male interpreter's voice. "Mainly if it's something that can't be done with texting or e-mail."

"So what other cool gadgets do you get to use?" I asked.

After a pause, Laurel answered the question herself. "There's a lot of stuff. For example, when my alarm goes off, a light flashes. There's no sound."

Dave spoke up again. "Um, Ashley has a gleam in her eye that I'm learning means she's going to harass you with questions until you're sick of her. I'm cutting her off now. Go away, Ashley," he ordered.

"Thanks for teaching me about the video relay thing," I said. "I never even knew there was something like that around."

"No problem," she said. "It's kind of fun to answer questions about it."

"Oh, really?" I perked up. "Because I was wondering—"

Dave clapped a hand over my mouth and shook his head. "Sorry, Laurel. I told you she had that gleam in her eye."

I heard Laurel's soft laugh a few seconds later. The delay reminded me of when I see people interviewed on the news via satellite and the slight lapse that falls between the question and their answer.

Dave left the kitchen, still talking to Laurel, and I picked up another strawberry, eavesdropping on his suggestions for their Friday-night date. I heard him throw out the idea of rock climbing before he shut the door to his bedroom. Spoilsport. Tired but not sleepy, I debated what to do next. Call Matt? Not exactly the smartest way to take advantage of a little space and distance. I could look for Ryder online. We'd been in the middle of an interesting discussion the night before when he had to sign off to take a phone call. I had no idea from whom and found that even the idea of him talking to another girl didn't bother me. It felt more like another buffer I could use to keep him at a safe distance too. I tried not to think too hard about what it meant that the idea of Matt dropping a conversation with me to talk to another girl made me want to punch someone in the face. Like him. Or the imaginary girl in my scenario. Feeling ridiculous over my mental meandering, I decided to pull The List out again and cross off sushi making.

I put the strawberries away and headed for my bedroom. I scrounged my scripture tote out from under the bed, the place where all of my things lurk in hiding whenever I need them, and thumbed through my Bible in search of my tattered paper. I couldn't find it, so I leafed through my triple combination next. No luck. Since I threw away all the extra papers that went flying when Megan knocked my things over at Institute, my scriptures were the only thing left in the tote. It's not like The List could hide. I checked both books again, but they came up empty. My stomach sank.

I could only assume that I had managed to throw The List out with all the other odds and ends I purged that night. Maybe it and a Relief Society bulletin were locked in a permanent embrace at the bottom of a landfill somewhere. How sad. I sat for a while, stumped and mourning its loss, until I heard the front door open. Knowing it was probably Celia, I listened for her footsteps down the hall and sure enough, she shuffled in, exhausted from work. And smelling like onions, of course.

"How come you look more tired than I do when I'm the one who had to run around serving tables all night?" I asked.

"Because I get the customers when they're cranky and waiting to eat, and they all snap at me and ask when their wait is up every two minutes. It's like having a car full of four-year-olds on a never-ending road trip. 'Are we there yet? Are we there yet?'" She collapsed on her bed. "At least by the time you see them, they've got free bread and water to shut them up."

"Huh. I hadn't thought of that. How do you not beat them when they whine?"

"Deep breathing and remembering my paycheck. I think I'd stop getting one if I hit someone."

"I know you're only twenty, but you're super smart," I said.

She rolled her eyes but didn't otherwise stir.

"Have you seen my list anywhere?" I asked.

She raised her head the tiniest fraction from the mattress. "What list? *The* List?"

"Yeah. It's not in my scriptures where I usually keep it. I'm hoping it fell out in here somewhere."

"No, I haven't seen it."

"Dang."

She propped herself on her elbows long enough to ask, "Dang? That's it? Shouldn't you be having a fit or something?"

I sighed. "It's kind of a bummer, but it's not like I don't have it totally memorized. I'll just rewrite it on my laptop where it can't fall out."

"I can't believe you're so calm. You've had that paper forever, haven't you?"

"Six years, I guess. I'm sure at some point I'm going to be all depressed that it's gone, but stressing out about it right now won't make it turn up."

She stared at me through narrowed eyes for a moment. "You are one cool customer, Smashley. If I hadn't watched the karaoke meltdown, I'd think you had robot parts."

"I care," I said. "And I really do hope it turns up, but if I throw myself down on my bed and cry about it, it's not really going to do anything except for make me feel dumb. I'm just going to type the stupid thing up again."

Celia lay back down. "All right. What do you get to cross off?"

I turned on my laptop and opened a new document. "Besides the ones I already did, I can cross off numbers eight, twenty-four, thirteen, and seventeen."

"Which are?"

"Make sushi, try Internet dating, learn to surf, and have a summer fling."

"I guess Matt's your summer fling, but when did you do Internet dating?"

"I joined that LDS Lookup site. You've heard of it, right?"

"Yeah, but I didn't know you were on it. Who did you go on a date with, and how come I didn't know about it?" She dragged herself off the bed and began rummaging around in the dresser for pajamas.

"I haven't gone on a date yet," I admitted. "But I've been talking to this guy back in Utah for a couple of weeks, and he's pretty cool. I'm sure we'll go out when I get back there."

She stopped rummaging and peered over her shoulder at me. "What about Matt?"

"He's a fling. Fling means short-lived. Summer fling means over when summer's over."

"Man, you really do have robot parts. It won't bother you to leave him behind when you go back to school?" she asked.

"Maybe a little," I said. "That's why we're keeping everything light, you know? I like him well enough to have a good time with him, but we keep it relaxed so we don't get too invested in each other. That way there's no drama when I have to leave."

She sat back down on her bed and locked eyes with me. "No way," she said. "I don't believe that for a second. I've seen you sit on the phone with him for two hours, laughing and having a good old time. And I've seen you get all excited when he invites you to do anything. And I know for a fact that you'll rearrange anything on your schedule if it means surfing with him."

"I'm not saying I don't like him. I do like him."

"You're also not saying how much, and the answer is, a lot. I can tell," she said.

"Can't I like him a lot and have it still be a fling?" I asked.

She shrugged. "I don't know, Ashley. I didn't grow up watching you date, so I don't know how you work. I don't know if it's normal for you to like someone a lot and drop him when something else you need to do comes up. Is it? Normal for you to do that?"

"If you mean do I jerk people around, the answer is no. Matt knows the score the same as every other guy I've ever dated has. I don't get involved with guys who can't keep a distance."

"I realize you have way more dating experience than I do, but I have to say that your whole take on this doesn't sound at all healthy," she said. "It seems to me that if you're already into him that there's no way you can leave in August and take back every part of you when you go."

A pang around my stone-cold heart told me she might be right. I didn't like that pang. "If I'm hurt, that's my problem," I said. "But it's not like I haven't told Matt exactly how things stand. If he's hurt, it's not my fault. And I'm not going to be hurt, anyway. I might be kind of bummed at first, but I already lined up a Plan B."

"Your Internet dating thing?"

"Yeah. I'll cry on Ryder's broad shoulder, and I'll forget Matt in no time."

Celia stared at me again. Finally she said, "I can't believe I'm going to say this, but I really think Dave has a much better approach to love and dating than you do."

"That hurts."

"It should. I swear, if I had to try to keep up with the crazy logic that you use to run your love life, I'd probably never date again. It's too hard," she said.

I grasped at a chance to change the uncomfortable subject. "Speaking of Dave's love life . . ."

Celia refused to be deterred. "In a minute. When you type up your list, you can't cross off number twenty-four."

"Internet dating? Why not? I just told you about Ryder."

"Yeah, but you haven't gone on an actual date with him, so it doesn't count until you do."

"Fine."

"Now, what about Dave?" she asked.

"He called Laurel tonight. I think they're going out this weekend."

"Cool," she said. "I don't even need a love life with the two of you around for entertainment," she said.

"Come to think of it," I said, "how come you aren't going out with anyone right now?" Celia was a classic California girl: tall, athletic, blonde with a fresh-scrubbed pretty face. I knew boys thought she was cute.

"Because I'm twenty, and I'm weighing my options before I pick one," she said.

"Going out with someone doesn't limit your options. Just pick someone and say yes to him," I said.

"It limits your options around here," she said. "The rumors start flying, and everyone assumes you're together, and no one else asks you out. So a good strategy is flirt like crazy with lots of boys but only say yes to the one you really like."

"And who's that?" I asked.

"I don't know yet," she shrugged. "I keep getting distracted by the flirting part."

"Nothing wrong with that," I said. "Carry on, soldier."

Chapter 20

THE SMASHING SUCCESS OF THE go-kart racing date Dave took Laurel on snowballed into a dating marathon. Every second he wasn't at work he spent with her. The first time he brought her to the house, he made sure Celia was at work. She retaliated by threatening blackmail. Who knew Dave had a deep-rooted fear of his middle-school year-book picture being exposed? Her threat worked, and Dave let Celia tag along to Institute with us one night. She declared meeting Laurel "totally worth sitting through Old Testament stuff." Pleased, Dave brought Laurel home after class and she chatted with my aunt and uncle.

I found it all fascinating. My first impression of Laurel had been of someone shy, lacking initiative, and painfully awkward in conversation. In reality, she needed only to find her comfort level with people, and then her quiet prettiness transformed into animated beauty. I'd found her chattering away to Aunt Trudy in the kitchen several times in the last week. Dave couldn't believe his good fortune, and Celia heartily endorsed his choice.

I liked Laurel's sweetness and easy laughter, but the chance to learn about her deafness was a cool bonus. I soaked up every sign that I could bug her to teach me before Dave shooed me off. Within a few days, I had a working vocabulary of twenty-five word signs. Between my short sign language tutorials with Laurel, surfing every morning, and working double shifts almost every day, I managed to fill up the time vacated by Matt.

Unfortunately, it didn't make me miss him any less, and that made me mad. I avoided talking to him, afraid it would make me miss him more. I returned most of his voice mails with witty text messages and spent time chatting online with Ryder. Made perfect sense. Ha.

Somewhere my strategy went awry, though. I think it was *The Secret*, the self-help book that had been on bestseller lists for eighteen thousand years, courtesy of an Oprah appearance. The premise was that people should self-actualize their outcome, but for me it was working in reverse. I willed myself not to miss Matt or think about him too much, and suddenly I couldn't avoid reminders of him. Either people were constantly asking me if I'd talked to him (not lately) or when he was coming back (in about a week). Every time someone asked me about him, I felt a pang in my heart parts. So annoying.

The Thursday before he was due back, I walked into the house after work to find Laurel and Dave scrambling apart on the sofa and then looking red-faced.

"Uh, did I interrupt something?" I asked.

Dave shook his head. "No."

"That didn't sound guilty at all, Dave," I said. His blush deepened.

Laurel tried to change the subject. "Is Matt coming home soon?"

Since I had just deleted another voice mail from him that made me feel all squirmy and twisty inside, I scowled. "Next week," I said.

Laurel scrunched her forehead and turned to Dave. "Did I say something wrong?" she asked him.

"Yeah. Matt's name. She barks at anyone who mentions him."

"Stop talking about me like I'm not in the room," I complained. "And I didn't bark. I just don't know why everyone thinks I'm his personal secretary. He's back when he's back."

Laurel looked wounded. "I'm sorry," she said. "I just thought you might be excited for him to come home."

Feeling guilty, I slumped down in an armchair across from the two lovebirds. "I am."

"Yeah, you look it," Dave said.

"No, I mean it. He's been gone three weeks already but it seems like way longer. I feel like I haven't talked to him in forever, so now I'm thinking it will be kind of weird when he gets home." I spoke clearly so Laurel could read my lips.

"Do you guys talk on the phone at all?" she asked.

"Sometimes. I'm busy a lot."

"Too busy to talk on the phone?" Dave pressed. "Wouldn't you be spending time with him in person if he were here? What's the big deal about talking on the phone?"

"You can only small talk for so long," I said. "Then it gets all serious and stuff."

"Serious how?" Dave asked. "You guys chitchat for a few minutes and then spend the rest of your time professing your undying love?"

"Don't be a dork. Of course not. But it's hard to keep it light for more then a few minutes on the phone. Then it gets into deep thoughts and stuff."

Dave and Laurel exchanged confused glances before he spoke again. "I guess I'm dumb because I have to say . . . so?"

"It gets in the way of the no-attachment thing." I appealed to Laurel. "The plan is to go to BYU in the fall with no regrets. I don't want to be sad when I leave. I don't want to have a messy relationship to figure out while I'm trying to start my grad program. Especially not a long-distance relationship."

Dave interrupted again. "Let me get this straight. You think you're less likely to get attached in person than you are on the phone?" He shook his head. "You're a nut."

I shot Laurel another look of silent appeal. She looked at Dave, obviously torn between wanting to help me out and standing by her new man.

"I wish I could say I understand about the phone thing," she said. "But it's not the best way for me to get to know someone. Spending time with them in person is definitely more important."

Dave slipped his hand into hers and smiled.

"Oh, and suddenly I feel queasy," I teased. "I'm going to go sit on my bed and see if I can figure myself out."

"Good luck with that," Dave said, but the gibe was halfhearted, his attention already back on Laurel.

I headed for my room and once again, I pulled out my cell phone and laptop, trying to make a decision. I could call Matt or chat with Ryder. The upside to chatting with Ryder is that I knew I would be in for laughs and some serious conversation without worrying about where it led. Then again, I could have a great conversation with Matt if I wanted to. If I dove in instead of guiding the conversation back to shallower waters every time it got too deep, then I'd have all the depth and humor I found in my online conversations with Ryder, plus those delicious butterflies mixed in.

Choosing the coward's way and knowing it, I decided to find Ryder online. Sure enough, he was there.

TwinkieSmash: You really do live here in Lookup, don't you?

BoardRyder: Yes. I never, ever leave.

TwinkieSmash: How sad.

BoardRyder: The Internet is actually pretty spacious. Lots of elbow room around here.

TwinkieSmash: You're an odd, odd guy.

BoardRyder: Talking to an odd, odd girl. How do you know I'm here all the time unless you are too?

TwinkieSmash: Let's focus on your issues and hang-ups instead of mine. Like your online obsession.

BoardRyder: I'm here probably less than you think, you know.

TwinkieSmash: Oh, really? Prove it.

BoardRyder: All you have to do is watch your laptop screen all day so you can tell when I'm connected and when I'm not. You have time for that, right?

TwinkieSmash: Totally. I can't think of anything I'd rather do.

TwinkieSmash: Less.

BoardRyder: Then you'll just have to take my word for it.

TwinkieSmash: Fine.

BoardRyder: So I know you really are pretty busy . . .

TwinkieSmash: Yeah?

BoardRyder: And yet we talk a lot . . .

TwinkieSmash: Yeah?

BoardRyder: So where do you fit in your conversations with Mr. G?

TwinkieSmash: I don't.

BoardRyder: You don't talk to him?

TwinkieSmash: Not much.

BoardRyder: Why not?

TwinkieSmash: Don't know.

BoardRyder: Imagine me shaking my finger at you right now. You're a bad girl, and I think it's time for me to play love guru again.

TwinkieSmash: How do you spell the sound of me blowing a raspberry at you?

BoardRyder: Uh . . . pbflttttttttttt?

TwinkieSmash: Pbfltttttt!!!!!

BoardRyder: Nice. Are you going to hear me out now?

TwinkieSmash: Wait. One more. Pbfltttttt!

TwinkieSmash: Okay, I'm listening.

BoardRyder: So why aren't you talking to him? Doesn't he call you?

TwinkieSmash: Hey! I thought I was supposed to be listening. Not answering a bunch of probing questions into my utterly boring personal life.

BoardRyder: We'll get to the part where you quit typing and read soon. Just answer the question.

TwinkieSmash: What was it?

BoardRyder: Do you not understand the function of the scroll up arrow?

TwinkieSmash: You have a bad attitude, Love Doctor.

BoardRyder: You're a terrible patient.

TwinkieSmash: All right, the answer is that yes, Mr. G calls.

BoardRyder: But you don't talk to him?

TwinkieSmash: Right. Because I don't answer.

BoardRyder: I assumed that. Otherwise it would mean you answer but then just sit there not saying anything. I don't think he'd keep calling if you did that.

TwinkieSmash: Ha ha. You don't know him. Maybe some people like those kind of calls.

BoardRyder: Do you not want to talk to him?

TwinkieSmash: I do. Sometimes I even answer when he calls.

BoardRyder: But not all the time?

TwinkieSmash: Not even most of the time.

BoardRyder: This is what I'm trying to figure out. Why not? Is it a play-hard-to-get thing?

TwinkieSmash: No, not really. It's more that he makes me nervous.

BoardRyder: It's not good to be uncomfortable with someone.

TwinkieSmash: I'm not uncomfortable with him. He makes me nervous. That's different.

BoardRyder: Explain.

TwinkieSmash: He's super easy to talk to. As easy as you. But you don't make my stomach knot up, and he does.

BoardRyder: That's it. I am so not going out with you when you get back up here for school.

TwinkieSmash: No, I'm not going out with you. Remember I did a preemptive dump when we first started talking? It's still in effect.

BoardRyder: Fine. So Mr. G is just as hilarious and brilliant as I am, but he makes you all goofy and I don't. This stomach issue . . . is it the kind that makes you want to throw up? Because it doesn't take a genius to figure out that that's bad too.

TwinkieSmash: No, it's not throw-up twisty. It's more top-of-the-roller-coaster twisty.

BoardRyder: Ah ha.

TwinkieSmash: You don't have to act like this is rocket science. I know what that means.

BoardRyder: Which is?

TwinkieSmash: It means that I like him.

BoardRyder: And now you get a gold star.

TwinkieSmash: Thanks. I'll stick it where the sun don't shine.

BoardRyder: Hey, hey, this is a G-rated site.

TwinkieSmash: What is wrong with you? I was talking about putting it in my journal so the sun can't fade it, and I can always remember you. What did you think I meant?

BoardRyder: Nothing. I thought you meant the journal thing.

TwinkieSmash: Well, don't renege on my star. I demand payment in full when I get back to school.

BoardRyder: See? High maintenance.

TwinkieSmash: Totally.

BoardRyder: So you like talking to him.

TwinkieSmash: No, I don't.

BoardRyder: But you said he's super easy to talk to.

TwinkieSmash: But I hate that top-of-the-roller-coaster feeling.

BoardRyder: Interesting. I would have taken you for an adrenaline junkie.

TwinkieSmash: Sure, if it's only a bone or something at risk of being broken. Not my heart.

BoardRyder: I think I feel a tear coming on. That's beautiful.

TwinkieSmash: Shut up.

BoardRyder: Why would it be the worst thing in the world to get close to the Mr. G guy?

TwinkieSmash: It just won't work in my life right now.

BoardRyder: Here's a news flash. Life is what happens when you're making other plans.

TwinkieSmash: Hm. Fortune cookie or bumper sticker?

BoardRyder: A magnet on my mom's fridge. She's a wise lady.

TwinkieSmash: Her magnets are, anyway.

BoardRyder: So why won't this work in your life? I need to know in case I want to date you in the fall.

TwinkieSmash: I'm not going to date you, remember, you troll?

BoardRyder: Right. Just answer because I'm nosy, then. Does he have some obvious flaws that need major overhauling and you can't commit the time or something?

TwinkieSmash: Nah. He's kind of perfect.

BoardRyder: Oh, brother.

TwinkieSmash: No, seriously. He's mellow but fun, smart but not a smart aleck, he's funny, he's adventurous, seems pretty solid with the Church . . .

BoardRyder: No one's that perfect. Is he ugly?

TwinkieSmash: Sorry. He's kind of hot.

BoardRyder: I think I want to beat this guy up. He's making the rest of us look bad. Could I take him in a fight?

TwinkieSmash: I doubt it. I think he might be pretty tough.

BoardRyder: I definitely hate this guy.

TwinkieSmash: Good. So you'll quit nagging me about him?

BoardRyder: Heck no. This is the best entertainment I've had in a long time.

TwinkieSmash: You don't have much going on, then.

BoardRyder: I have tons going on. Most of it's just not interesting.

TwinkieSmash: Uh-oh. He's calling.

BoardRyder: Not uh-oh. That's good. All kidding aside, and as much as I'll be lining up first if this thing falls apart, I wouldn't touch a relationship with you with a ten-foot pole unless I knew you'd really exhausted all your options with him. You know, really checked it out? You should answer the phone.

I stared at Matt's name illuminated in my phone's window. For once, I didn't want to deny myself the little thrill I got from hearing him say my name when I answered.

I tapped out a quick sign-off.

TwinkieSmash: If I fall for him more, it's your fault. TTYL.
BoardRyder: Peace out, homie.

I snatched up the phone and answered at the last second before it went to voice mail. "Hi, Matt."

"Hi, Ashley." And there they were, those predictable and delicious tummy flutters. "It's been hard to get ahold of you lately."

"I know. Sorry about that. I'm working more than I thought I would when the summer started. Trevor puts me on the schedule about twice as much as I want him to."

"Why does it always have to be you?" Matt asked.

"Hello? Because I'm awesome?"

He laughed. "I meant to say that."

"I forgive you. It's been so long since we've talked that you might have forgotten."

"Oh, but you're unforgettable, Ashley."

I suppressed a nervous giggle. "Are you trying to be smooth?" I asked.

"How am I doing?"

"Not so awesome, since I saw that line coming from a mile off."

"I thought you might have seen through it because I don't ever actually use lines, and I'm really bad at it."

"That's what I meant."

"Thanks," he said, and his dry tone called up another bubble of laughter in my throat. "So what have you been up to besides work? Getting any surfing in?"

Even as I related some of my more spectacular wipeouts, part of my mind kept time on the conversation, wondering when the small talk would run out and I would have to choose between ending the call or moving past the chitchat.

"Are you there?" he asked, startling me.

"What?"

"I just asked you if you wanted to try surfing San Onofre when I get back," he repeated patiently.

"Sorry. Um, sure. That sounds good. That's south, right?" I tried to reorient myself in the conversation.

"Yeah, maybe an hour. Great surfing, though. It sounds like you're ready for it."

"Now that you bring it up, when exactly are you due back, anyway?" As segues go, it was totally obvious.

"Uh, Thursday, I think? All my stuff should be done by Wednesday, and I won't have to come back here for a while."

"You'll have to go back?" I kept my voice neutral by reminding myself that it wouldn't matter to me past the end of the summer, anyway.

"Probably. If Jay makes me," he said.

"That's your partner, right? He's lucky you're willing to do it."

"I'm used to it, but I'll be glad to get this trip over with. Did I mention that I'm sick of living out of my duffel bag?"

"It's come up," I said.

"Trust me when I say I couldn't possibly overstate that."

"Okay, I trust you." I meant for it to sound light, but it came out more serious.

"That was beautiful," he said. He sniffled.

I cleared my throat. "I wasn't talking about—"

"Shhhh," he interrupted. "I'm enjoying the moment. You said it, I heard it, no take backs. You do trust me, right?" Even though his tone was joking, I could sense the underlying seriousness of the question.

I grimaced. This is what avoiding his phone calls had been about. Spend enough time talking to someone, even dating casually, and real stuff came up. I tried to figure out how I felt about the drift of the conversation as it moved from the shallows. I could toss off a quick comeback, yawn, and excuse myself to bed on the grounds of exhaustion. I'd said or done similar things to avoid conversations like this with other guys in the past. One part of me, the visceral part of me that chose flight over fight every time the danger of a relationship loomed, wanted nothing more than to drop the subject. But I didn't. I couldn't. Some other part of me, a part that felt suspiciously like it was *growing,* answered the question.

"Yes, Matt. I trust you." It felt like the three hardest words I'd ever uttered.

"No joke? I thought you'd make a joke," he said.

"I can think of one really quick if you want," I said.

"No! I mean, not that your jokes aren't great and all. But I want to say something kind of serious here. Can I do that without scaring you into hiding?"

I sighed. "For the next three minutes, I promise that nothing you say will scare me into hiding. Talk fast."

He laughed. "It's no big deal. I wanted to tell you that one thing I appreciate about you is your honesty. I think it's cool that you're so straight up about stuff, and you just deal with it."

"That's almost right," I said. "It depends on the situation."

"What do you mean?"

"I don't always deal with things, and that's not so honest. I mean, I definitely tell the truth, but I might not always deal with it." I sighed again. "I think I'm going around in circles here. I mean to say that I'm a huge fraidycat about some stuff, so if forced to, I might say my piece and run away."

"Tell-it-like-it-is-Ashley? Really? I can't imagine that."

"Then you still have things to learn," I said. "I remember when I was in third grade I liked this boy named Chuck."

"Chuck? Who names their kid that?"

"Old people? I don't know. Can I finish my story?"

"Please."

"So I liked this kid, and I told my friend Annie about it, which turned out to be a bad idea because she started spreading it around the class. By lunchtime I felt like everyone was talking about me and I couldn't stand it, so I walked up to Chuck to have it out with him."

"Why Chuck?" He sounded downright indignant on long-ago Chuck's behalf. "Shouldn't you have had it out with Annie? She sounds like trouble."

"I was madder at Chuck because I liked him than I was at Annie for telling him."

"You're messed up," he said.

"I've never denied it," I retorted. "Anyway, I grabbed my chocolate milk, walked over to him in front of his friends, and told him that it was true that I liked him but that I wasn't going to be his girlfriend so he better not ask. Then I said, 'I hope I didn't make you feel bad, but here's my chocolate milk just in case.' And I handed it to him and walked off."

"Wow," Matt said. "You do not mess around. Does this mean you're about to offer me your chocolate milk?"

"No." Although if I were smart, I'd shove the metaphorical milk at him and hurry away. "I'm just making my point that I try to tell the truth, but sometimes I do it hit-and-run style."

"So this commitment issue you have goes all the way back to third grade? Poor Chuck. What did he do wrong?"

"Nothing. I told you, I liked him. But I didn't want to have to hang out with him at recess, so that's why I didn't want to be his girlfriend."

He laughed. "Being his girlfriend meant you had to play with him at recess? At my school, a girlfriend in third grade meant that you said you liked each other and then you never talked to each other again."

"At my school, it meant that you had to stand around and watch your boyfriend play with his friends and show off for you. I just wanted to jump rope."

"Are we using ironic air quotes around the words boyfriend and girlfriend in this conversation?" he asked.

"Of course."

"Just making sure I wasn't the only one."

"It's not like I'd ever know the difference. I mean, can you see this?" And I held the phone in front of me while I made a grotesque face.

"That looks weird," Matt said.

"Hey!" I yelped. "You don't even know what I was doing!"

"Sure I do, and it was mean. Does this mean my three minutes are officially over?"

I couldn't help it. I cracked up. When the giggling subsided, I tried to remember the original thread of the conversation. "Thanks, by the way," I said. "For the compliment about the honesty, I mean."

"You're welcome."

"Am I supposed to think of a compliment for you now?"

"Nah. Don't let social conventions dictate your behavior. You haven't so far."

"Too bad. I'm going to think of one, anyway. Let's see . . ." I pretended to think, then snapped my fingers. "Matt Gibson, you're good at surfing."

"I tell you that I admire your honesty and straightforwardness, and I get that I'm good at surfing?"

I grinned and rolled onto my stomach. "I meant to say that you're very good at surfing."

"That's more like it."

"And next week you get to do it again, huh?"

"Yeah. I can't wait." He sounded happy.

"I'm starting to feel that way myself," I confessed. "I never thought I'd get past the 'hate' part of the love-hate relationship with my surfboard, but I think I'm there."

"You're going to have to show me your progress," he said.

"Of course, Sensei."

There was a short pause before he spoke again. "Are you going to hang out with me out of the water too?" he asked.

"Why wouldn't I?" I countered, genuinely surprised by the question.

"Just making sure. It's a pretty fair question considering how often you've ducked my phone calls."

"I haven't been ducking them! I told you what my schedule is like."

"Okay, honest girl. You're saying every time you haven't returned one of my calls, it's been work related?"

I sighed. "No."

"Then what? Did one of the guys who's always sniffing around you on Sunday finally melt your stone-cold heart?" he teased.

"Louisa is a tattletale, and no, my heart is still in deep freeze."

"Meaning you haven't gone out with anyone while I've been gone?"

"Not really," I said.

He was quiet for a minute. "I'm going to be honest here and tell you that I'm a little bummed that wasn't an unqualified 'no.'"

"I haven't been on any dates or anything," I said. "I've just been chatting with that guy online, but . . . he kind of feels more like a friend."

"I can live with that," he said. "I haven't been out with anyone either, in case you wondered."

I didn't say anything.

"Ashley?"

"I'm here. I'm torn between honesty and self-preservation." I hesitated again. "I guess I have to say that I'm glad to hear that."

"You all right?" he asked. "You didn't break anything, did you? You know, like your stone-cold heart?"

"It's maybe chipped."

"Ah, progress. Does that mean if I ask you for a third time why you've been ducking my calls, you'll finally answer?"

I pulled my pillow over my head. "I would if I knew the answer."

"Did you not want to talk to me?"

"No, I really did," I said. "That's probably why I didn't answer."

Matt let that sit for a moment. "I'm guessing it's because you wanted to keep a distance, no attachments?"

"Pretty much." There was no point in denying something I'd said many times already.

"I don't think I've ever asked you this, and maybe I should have, but why are attachments such a big deal to you? I mean, I get that you're going back to school and you want to focus on that and all, but beyond that, I'm not sure I understand."

"Isn't that enough?" I said. "I feel like I have a whole bunch of things that I want to accomplish, and I can't get them done if I'm tied down to a relationship."

"Like what? What do you want to do that you can't do with a boyfriend in tow?"

I jumped on his word choice. "See, just think about that word. *Tow.* It means having someone tied to me that I have to drag around."

"Forget the word, then. Is it really so bad to have a sidekick on some of these adventures? Name one thing that would interfere with," he challenged me.

"Uh, how about Internet dating? I want to try that, and I bet a boyfriend would vote no. That's why I'm a dictatorship of one with no one to answer to."

"Maybe if you had a boyfriend, you wouldn't want to try it anymore. Why is it a big deal to change your mind about it?"

"You're talking like I'm a regular girl, Matt. I'm not. I'm hardheaded and stubborn. I get ideas in my head and I want things to go a certain way and I have a hard time changing gears."

"But why? That's what I keep trying to understand. Why is it a big deal to change your mind?"

What might have felt like a cross-examination from anyone else didn't from Matt. I got the impression he pressed for answers not out of nosiness but a sincere desire to figure me out. Something in me shifted and softened, and I gathered myself to answer instead of run. Totally unprecedented.

"I grew up poor, Matt. My parents married really young. My dad was barely off his mission and had no schooling yet. My mom had one year of college before marrying my dad, and it wasn't enough to really learn a skill. She got pregnant with my sister Leila almost right away. They struggled. By the time Juliana came along two years later, my dad couldn't keep going to school and still support his family. So he quit and went to work selling vacuums so my mom could stay home with my sisters. Paying for childcare would have eaten up any paycheck she earned." I stopped and drew a breath. I had no idea where all this was coming from. I'd never explained it to anyone before.

"I'm sorry," I said. "This is coming out far heavier than I intended it to."

"Don't be sorry," he said, his voice soft. "Did everything eventually work out for them? Are your parents happy?"

"They are now," I said. "They'll never be rich, but eventually my dad worked his way up the ladder at a restaurant supply company and now things are good. I came along when they'd been married for six years, but I still remember it being tough when I was a kid. My younger brother does too. We lived in perpetual hand-me-downs and thrift-store clothes. That was no big deal, but we also had to rely on the Church for food to make it through some lean months, and we had a no-frills childhood. There was no money for lessons or sports teams or classes unless we earned it."

"Do you feel like you're making up for lost time now, going after all these adventures?"

"A little, I guess. But it's more than that. I've always thought that if my parents would have waited a little longer, been more qualified for the job market, things would have been different."

"Meaning more money for things?"

I shook my head even though he couldn't see me. "It's not really about the money. It's about the struggle. It's about all the stress and worry and my father's constant sense of failure that was this little black rain cloud over everything. Leila ran out and did the exact same thing. She got married way too young, and they're still struggling. I think this time she's actually going to carry out her threat to divorce my brother-in-law."

"What about your other sister?"

"Juliana?"

"You said she married young too, right? Did the same thing happen?"

"Pretty much," I said. "They started their family right away too, but Juliana handled the stress a little better than Leila. It still took her forever to finish her own teaching degree, though. She works part-time as an independent study teacher for online high school classes, and her husband finished his MBA. She's working on her master's when she gets a chance, but it's going extremely slow. They're doing all right now, I guess."

"I'm glad it went okay for at least someone," Matt said, his tone wry.

"I probably sound like a jerk, like my sole focus is on having fun and making money."

"I don't think that," he said quietly.

"I couldn't blame you if you did." I hesitated before wading into even deeper waters. "Look, I just don't want to live a life of insecurity and regret. I want to know that I can help support a family financially and that I never see my husband or kids as holding me back. I want to be happy with them, not always thinking about what might have been."

"Let's bird walk all the way back to the beginning of this conversation," he said. "I asked you why you're so afraid of attachments. I still don't see the answer."

"What do you mean? I just explained the whole thing to you!"

"Not really. You told me you want to have financial security and a lot of fun before you settle down. How does a boyfriend interfere with that? Isn't it possible to be in a relationship with someone who wants the same things you do?"

"Sure, but relationships can lead to marriage, especially when you're Mormon. I feel like I don't want to waste anyone's time with more than a few casual dates when they're probably trying to find their future wife. That's not me," I said. "Not yet. So I stick to having fun."

"Like we have," he said, but he didn't add anything else. I tried to divine his mood from the silence, another downfall of phone calls instead of face time. Nearly a minute ticked by, and I couldn't take it anymore.

"Are you mad?" I asked.

"No," he answered slowly. "Just thinking."

"About?"

"About how you go a lot deeper than I thought."

"You're saying you thought I was shallow?" I joked.

He laughed. "No. Maybe a little. Not in a bad way."

"Uh, what's the good way to be shallow?"

"I am so not explaining this right," he said.

"Try a surf analogy," I suggested.

"There has never been the remotest similarity between girls and surfing," he said.

"Oh, come on. Not even something like the sea is temperamental and so are women?"

"Nope. I'm not going there."

"I don't buy it," I said. "The ocean is a metaphor for everything. There's gotta be something."

"Fine," he said. "I think the ocean and women both demand respect."

I snorted. "Because they will chew you up and spit you out if they don't get it?"

He groaned. "See, this is why I didn't want to play."

"I'm teasing."

"No," he corrected. "You're trying to change the subject."

"From what? You being all broody and not saying anything?" I asked.

"I wasn't brooding. I was thinking about what you said. I think you make more sense to me now."

"Are you saying I'm on your mind a lot?" I kind of hoped he'd say yes.

He didn't take the bait. "It's kind of hard to avoid thinking about you when I'm on the phone with you."

"Good, because if you confessed to deep feelings I'd have to hang up or something."

"I figured," he said. "I'm going to quit while I'm ahead because I'm afraid of getting your chocolate milk."

"Don't worry about it," I said. "Recess with you is pretty fun."

"I'm blushing."

"Shut up."

He laughed. "I better go, Ashley. I'll try to call again before I get back into town, but I'm going to be pushing really hard for the next few days to get stuff done so I can leave. My schedule may get even crazier than usual. But I'll definitely call you when I get back."

"Sounds good," I said. But I lied. How ironic that just as I felt ready to let Matt in more, work would drag him away. He took my best excuse for avoiding him and flipped it on me.

I didn't like it one bit.

Chapter 21

I SAT VERY, VERY STILL. No change. I closed my eyes and tried to meditate. Still nothing. Maybe it took longer than thirty seconds to work. I closed my eyes again and tried to keep my mind blank for another minute, doing some deep breathing.

The fluttering in my stomach only accelerated, and I growled.

"Seriously, stop it," Celia complained. "I can hear you over my iPod."

"I'm trying to stop. They won't go away."

"What won't?"

"These stomach cramps."

"There's medicine for that."

"These are the medicine-proof kind." My cell phone buzzed, and I strangled a yelp.

Celia sat all the way up and yanked her earbuds out. "What is going on with you?"

I picked up my cell phone and pulled up the text that had set it buzzing, then squeaked.

Celia grabbed it from my hand and read it aloud. "'I'm back, and I'm coming to get you.' What the heck? Who is this from? No wonder you're freaked out."

I snatched the phone back and cleared my throat. "I'm not freaked out. That was actually Matt."

Celia hooted. "You better get dressed, scaredy-cat. You've got fifteen minutes, tops, before he shows up."

I sauntered toward the closet. "I'm only going to get dressed because that's what I was going to do, anyway."

"Don't act like you aren't stoked he's coming over here."

"I would, but then you and Dave will blow it all out of proportion," I said.

"I swear I won't. Who wouldn't be excited to see a *friend* who's been gone for a month? Go ahead, let it out."

Refusing to be baited, I reached into our closet and pulled out a pair of jeans and a thin yellow cardigan with a vintage flower appliqué winding around one side. I ran a brush through my hair, fluffed my curls, and applied a quick swipe of mascara and a soft peach lip gloss. Even after hunting down my white flip-flops I still had at least ten minutes before Matt showed up, assuming he left his place right after texting me.

I sat back on my bed but after another knowing smirk from Celia, I bounced up and headed for the kitchen. Finding something to eat would keep me busy.

Digging through the fridge, I stole Dave's idea and started an omelet. I had some onions caramelizing nicely in melted butter when the doorbell rang and I dropped a piece of shell in the eggs I was cracking. Scowling, I left it for the moment and headed to the door, waving away Celia, who had tried to beat me to it. I kept my hand on the knob, waiting for her to go back to our room while I collected myself.

Matt was here. After the longest month ever, he was standing on my doorstep. After countless text messages and a few phone conversations that made me feel all squishy inside, I only had to open the door to see him again. I spared an extra second for the memory of the last time I saw him and the most excellent kiss he'd laid on me, then flung the door open.

The sun backlit him and blurred his features, but the broad span of his shoulders was clear. Suddenly unsure, I moved out of the way so he could enter. He took a step forward but then leaned against the doorway watching me, and I could see his face better. A small smile turned up the corner of his mouth, and he caught my gaze for several beats before I blinked.

"Hey," he said softly.

"Hey," I answered, and he reached for my hand, drawing me near. Taking enough time to make me scream, he reached down and wrapped his arms around my waist for a hug.

"Smells good," he said, face buried in my hair.

Distracted, I muttered something about my shampoo. I felt like an idiot for not stringing a coherent sentence together, but my train of thought felt like it was chugging through jelly.

"That's not what I meant," he said and relaxed his embrace enough to sniff the air. "*That* smells good."

I shook my head. "It's onions."

"You're having onions for breakfast?"

I nodded stupidly.

"Interesting. Should I take that personally?"

I shook my head again but with a feeling of coming to my senses. "I'm having onions in my omelet. Do you want one?"

"An onion?" He grinned. "Sure. I love onions."

"Great," I said, recovering. "I'll fry you up an onion while I eat an omelet."

"Um, if I help, can I have an omelet too?"

I pretended to consider him, then sighed. "Yeah, I guess."

"Always making me work for it, huh, Ashley?"

I shot him a sharp glance, but his face showed only his usual good humor.

"It tastes better that way," I said.

"No, stuff tastes good however *you* make it. I'm doing fine if I cook something only slightly charred."

"Oh, all right. I'll make you an omelet while you sit and tell me all about your business trip."

He grinned and followed me into the kitchen, claiming a chair while I fished the delinquent eggshell out of the bowl and then pushed the onions around so they didn't burn.

"What do you want to know?" he asked. "It seems like I told you everything on the phone."

I whipped my head around to see if he was serious. "Are you kidding? You told me nothing on the phone. Not one sorry detail."

"Probably because you never answered your phone."

"You're here now. Quit whining and tell me about your trip."

He laughed. "I looked at a lot of industrial warehouse space. Then I looked at boring retail spaces. Then I looked at more warehouses. Then I ate a bunch of fast food. Then I came home. You're all caught up now."

"When did you get in?" I asked. I forced a casual note into my voice. I'd been on edge since I got a text from him last night saying he was headed back. Nerves kept me tossing and turning all night and then reached a snapping point before his text came in this morning. I wanted to sound like I didn't care how long he'd been home almost as much as I wanted to know how long he'd waited before coming to see me.

"About four this morning."

And it was just after eight. Mr. Gibson had wasted no time getting over here. I wondered how I felt about that. Funny, I decided. It made me feel funny. "Did you even sleep?" I asked.

"A couple of hours. I really want to get out on the waves."

Of course, I thought. *He got up early to surf, not to come see you, you idiot.*

"You don't have to work today, do you?" he asked.

"You want me to go with you?" I asked, surprised. "Don't you want to bond with your board or something?"

"I want to see where you're at now. I only have another month to whip you into shape, right? I can't let the Matt Gibson surf whisperer legacy end with you."

"Right," I said. The four weeks left until the new semester started seemed to shrink into a piddling collection of days and hours at his reminder of how soon the summer would end.

I slid a plate in front of him with a steaming omelet on it. "Bell pepper, onion, and lots of jack cheese. It's my specialty."

"I thought grilled cheese was your specialty."

I shrugged. "Anything with melting cheese is my specialty."

"My kind of specialist," he said and dug in. I let him eat while I cooked up my own omelet. His was gone before I even sat down with mine.

"Sorry," he said. "I haven't had home cooking in forever."

"Right. So you ate fast food, stared at empty buildings, and drove around a lot. Does that about cover your four weeks away?"

"Yeah. I'd have to lie to make it even halfway interesting." He eyed my untouched omelet, so I pushed half of it onto his plate before taking a bite of the half left on mine.

"Well, what about now that you're back?" I asked. "Are you going to have to work as much?"

He shrugged. "I'll pick back up with my surf students and go in to work if my partner throws an absolute fit. But he should be off my back for a while," he said. "He kind of owes me big, so I think I can get in all the surfing I want now."

I nodded, and he waited until I finished another bite before asking, "What about you? Are you going to have crazy hours now that the Fourth is over?"

"No," I said. "I never wanted full-time hours, anyway, so I told Trevor I'm just going to hand off any extra shifts he gives me. That should solve the problem."

He studied me while I ate. "Can I throw something out there without you running away screaming again?" he asked.

"As long as I'm chewing. I would never abandon food."

"How flexible is this no-strings-attached clause you built into us hanging out? Because strings seem pretty flexible. They're all bendy and stuff."

"Bendy?" I stalled while trying to process the question.

He waited.

"I think these strings are more like, uh . . ." I scrambled to think of a very, very rigid string. "They're more like piano wire than yarn, I guess?" I trailed off, wondering if my analogy made any sense at all.

"Okay," he said. "What if I happen to be around Utah now and then for some snowboarding in a few months? Are you open to keeping in touch?"

"Keeping in touch" sounded nonthreatening, but I knew better. I knew because of the way the idea warmed the cockles of my stone-cold heart. I didn't really know what a cockle was, but I had every intention of finding mine and Matt-proofing it when I did.

"You promised not to run away screaming," he reminded me. "Maybe you should take another bite so you don't go anywhere."

I scooped up some more omelet and chewed, staring at him. He sat unruffled while I ate, returning my stare with a slight crinkle around his eyes that suggested throwing me off track entertained him.

I swallowed and waved my fork at him. "You signed up for no strings attached."

"Relax, Ashley. It was just a thought. I figured it might not be so hectic to squeeze stuff in with you if we had more time to hang out later, but it's fine. I can see it's stressing you out. I think there's a specific HB city ordinance against stressing within two miles of the ocean, anyway. So stop."

I narrowed my eyes and took another bite of egg.

He smiled. "You're working how many days a week now?"

I swallowed and answered. "Three. Sometimes four."

"Are your days off pretty open?" he asked.

"As of right now," I said. "But I make no promises."

"No kidding," he said.

"What does that mean?"

"Nothing. Just an observation." He glanced at my plate.

"I'm done," I said. I started to get up, but he waved me down.

"I'll take care of it so you can get dressed." He collected both of our dishes and headed to the sink to rinse them.

"Hello? I *am* dressed. Did you think this outfit is what I look like naked?"

He flushed, and I felt slightly evil and totally gratified that I'd managed to throw *him* off balance for once this morning. For the first time, I felt some of the comfort of being with him creep back in.

"I meant that if you want to go surfing, maybe you should change."

"Who said I want to go surfing?"

He glanced over his shoulder and sighed. "Ashley, are you really telling me that after surfing almost daily for two months, you aren't starting to crave it a little?"

I grinned. "No, I'm not telling you that at all. Give me five minutes."

I raced down the hall to my bedroom and dug through the drawer where my swimsuits tangled with my tee shirts. One of the greatest days of my life was when Target started carrying a whole bunch of tankinis and I had something modest besides utilitarian one-pieces to choose from. I grabbed the top of a cute black one trimmed in a black and white hibiscus print and rummaged for the matching bottom. Celia watched wordlessly until I sent random pieces of clothing items flying behind me, and then she reached under the dresser and pulled out the missing bottom.

"Thanks," I grumbled. I was back in the kitchen a few minutes later with a bright blue cover-up over my suit and my hair back in a braid to keep it from wrestling the seaweed.

"Ready," I said, waving a rash guard at him. The water had warmed from brutal to bracing and I didn't need a wetsuit anymore, but the protective neoprene of the shirt kept the wax on the board from chafing me.

"Cool," he said. "Let's go, then."

He followed me out to the deck and grabbed my board for me, and I tried not to stare too openly at his rippling biceps because it was such a cliché. Once my board was strapped down next to his on top of his Toyota, it was a short trip to the beach with the radio blaring eighties rock. Even though I was too young to remember the eighties, I loved the music.

By the time I was standing next to the water with my board leashed to my ankle, I felt the first nervous twinge at surfing in front of Matt. He got a few feet out into the wavelets before he realized I hadn't followed him. Turning and letting the water lap around his knees, he called, "What's up, Ashley?"

I didn't want to admit I was nervous. I wasn't even sure why I was nervous. It's not like he hadn't seen me wipe out plenty of times already, and he knew better than anyone how long it took to be really good at surfing. Longer than a month, that was for sure. Rather than make it a bigger deal than it needed to be, I hiked up my board a little higher and splashed in after him, quickly passing him with a joking, "Slowpoke!" thrown over my shoulder.

He laughed and raced after me, his strong swim stroke pulling him ahead within seconds. When we paddled out far enough to catch the first break, we both perched on top of our boards and waited for the right set to come in. At least a dozen other surfers dotted the water around us, watching too. The quiet of so many people doing the same thing at once was one of my favorite parts of surfing. It always felt like a unity of thought, and the camaraderie that seemed to sprout organically between surfers made sense.

I felt my comfort with Matt wholly restored by the gentle bump of the ocean beneath my surfboard. The last knots of tension eased from between my shoulders and the pit of my stomach. I leaned my head back to soak up the muted sunlight filtering through the marine layer above us.

"Look," Matt said, his voice low. Following the direction of his pointing finger I saw the smooth gray back of a dolphin finishing a dive. A huge smile cracked my face as another one surfaced in a playful jump.

"I think there's a pod out there," he said. "I usually see them a few times a summer, but this is the first time this year."

We watched, and a little bubble of delight swelled in my chest. Nothing could ruin this perfect moment.

Nothing. Except—

"Hey, Matt! I heard you were back in town!"

Megan.

Chapter 22

OF ALL THE ROTTEN, ILL-TIMED LUCK. I had no idea how she managed to find us, but there she was, paddling up on Matt's other side in a hot pink rash guard on the surfboard he'd looked over for her.

I gritted my teeth and froze the corners of my smile to keep them from slipping. From Matt's startled glance, I had a feeling I must have looked more like I was snarling than smiling. I dropped the pretense and settled down to wait her out.

"Hi, Megan," Matt said politely. "What are you doing out here?"

"Oh, I surf here all the time," she said.

"Really?" I asked. "I've been here pretty much every day this summer. I'm surprised I never noticed you."

She cleared her throat. "Well, I guess I'm by the pier a lot and sometimes by the cliffs." She shrugged. I tried not to growl. If she was surfing the pier then she had *some* skills. I wouldn't dream of joining that crowd.

"Anyway, when did you get back?" she asked.

"This morning, actually," he said. "How'd you know I was back already?"

"Oh, my sister-in-law Mandy mentioned it."

He wrinkled his brow. "Mandy Jenkins?"

"Yeah," Megan said. "She's over there somewhere." She waved vaguely in the direction of the entire Pacific. "I was on the phone with her deciding where I wanted to drop in today, and she mentioned that you were here so I thought I'd say hello."

"Hello," I said, before Matt could answer. I'd seen her at Institute once a week all month, but, unlike there, we couldn't ignore each other when there were only the three of us sitting on the same patch of ocean. Not that Megan didn't give it her best effort.

"So how was your trip?" she asked Matt, not returning my greeting. I hid my eye roll with a glance toward the incoming swells. Clearly, I wasn't invited to their conversation, anyway.

"It was fine," he said.

"Oh, good!" she said, like he'd told her he won the billion-dollar jackpot while he was gone. "You're such a good businessman, Matt."

I refrained from gagging. Barely.

"Uh, thanks," he said. "Hey, look! I think that's my wave," he said, flipping his board around and paddling to take it.

I didn't grumble while he escaped, due to me being an amazing human being. Instead I looked at Megan. "We're dating," I said.

She looked startled. "So?"

"I'm just letting you know. We're dating now, we've been dating all summer, and we'll be dating until I leave for school."

"Why are you telling me this?" she asked.

"Wouldn't want you to waste your time or anything," I said.

"I don't know what you're talking about."

"Then you have less common sense than I'm giving you credit for," I snapped, done playing games with her. "You're smart enough to see that Laurel is a cool girl, so you get points for that. But I'll be tying up all Matt's free time for the rest of the month, and if you really are smart, you'll find a new project."

A dull red flush swept over her cheeks. "Laurel told me that you guys are calling it quits when you leave. You'll just be another blip on his radar, and I'll still be here." She tensed and pulled her board around to take the next wave. "Long after you're gone!" she called over her shoulder as she executed a strong front stroke to pick up speed.

In seconds she was on the face of the wave, riding it in with perfect balance.

Aargh.

Annoyed, I focused on finding my own wave. I don't know what drew Megan to Matt. Granted, he was a good-looking guy. No, a *really* good-looking guy. But she just barely graduated from high school, and he was two years older than me. Didn't she have some preemies waiting on mission calls she could harass? Whatever. It wasn't my problem. If Matt wanted to date her when I was gone, fine. But the next four weeks were mine, and I planned to make the most of them.

* * *

An hour later, I collapsed on the beach in a tired, happy heap. Lying back to soak up every last bit of sunshine, I relaxed my exhausted shoulders.

"That last ride was awesome, Ashley," Matt said, sitting on the sand beside me.

"Thanks," I said.

"I can't believe how much you've improved in just a month. You don't look like this is your first summer doing this."

I smiled. "I was out a couple of hours almost every day while you were gone. I'm probably one of the few people stubborn enough to beat my head against a brick wall until it breaks."

"Your head or the wall?"

"Whichever comes first."

He laughed. "Why do you do it?"

I pushed myself up on my elbows. "I'm not kidding when I say I'm stubborn. That's pretty much the reason."

"I can believe it," he said. "I guess I'm wondering, why surfing?"

I lay back down. "I don't know." I reveled in the warm sand and cool breeze before taking a stab at an answer. "I think maybe I hate regrets," I said. "It would bug me to come here to learn to surf, be bad at it a couple of times, quit, and then have the rest of my life to be annoyed with myself for not at least trying every day."

"Even if you never got good at it?"

"Yeah."

It was quiet while he mulled that over. Or at least stared out at the waves when I cracked an eye open to see what he was doing.

"You'll be pretty good at it," he said after a while. "Probably even great, if you kept at it every summer."

"Well, this is my one and only chance so I had to figure it out now. I won't have next summer." I felt a pang as I said the words.

"You could. Or do you have classes during the summer?"

"No, but I'm hoping for an internship."

"You mean you would take indentured servitude over a summer of surfing?" he teased.

"I'd pick surfing if it built my resume, but somehow I don't think that's going to happen."

"I guess not," he said. He slid me a sideways glance. "Does that mean this is your last great summer for adventure?"

"I hope not," I answered. "But I want to fit in as many adventures as I can, just in case."

"Sign me up," he said. "I feel like I already wasted too much of this summer on lame business stuff. Maybe I should amp up the next month to make up for it. Speaking of which . . ."

"Yeah?" I asked, mustering my last bit of energy to crack an eye open again.

"Don't you owe me some skydiving?"

"Are we going to do that for real?" I asked.

"Oh, I don't know. It depends on what you're doing on Thursday afternoon."

"Thursday as in two days from now?" I asked, suddenly alert.

"Yeah. My buddy Cujo will take us up from the Perris Airfield for a jump if we want to go."

I shot bolt upright, wide awake. "Cujo?"

"It's a Marine thing."

"Thursday?"

"Uh-huh. Unless, you know . . . you're scared," he taunted.

"Them's fighting words," I said.

"So you're going to jump?" he asked.

"It means I'm definitely not going to miss a chance to push you out of a plane."

He grinned. "I'll tell him we'll be there."

I tried not to stare at his flashing dimple, but he caught me, anyway. His gaze narrowed and he leaned toward me, but a sudden stomach flip propelled me to my feet.

"Time to go out again," I said. "I didn't think I'd be ready so soon, but I guess I don't need as much recovery time now. I must really be building up my endurance and all, which is good because that's what I wanted to do. I mean, that's why I'm out here almost every day. And to practice stuff and everything. The waves still look good, so that's—"

"Ashley?" Matt said, climbing slowly to his feet.

"Yeah?"

"You're chattering." And he swooped down for a quick kiss on the lips. "It's really cute," he said, then grabbed his board and started back toward the water. "Last one in has a really big crush on the other!" I scooped my board up and headed out at a dead run, splashing in until the waves were waist high before I turned around to grin at him.

He waded up slowly, his dimples flashing again. "Guilty," he said. "So very, very guilty."

* * *

Hanging out with Matt meant accepting that time seemed to compress and warp around him. One minute we were joking around in the ocean and the next, I was staring from the open door of a jump plane cursing myself for ten kinds of fool. I know there was a day and a half in between where we sat together in Institute one night and watched a movie at his house the next, but somewhere along the line, I blinked and Thursday afternoon appeared.

I'm not afraid of heights, but peering out into the open space below, I discovered a sudden fear of skydiving planes. And skydiving. I ran over the instructor Leon's directions in my mind for the millionth time, reviewing the sequence for jumping and landing. Especially landing. I *really* wanted to get that part right. Matt caught my expression.

"Whoa, are you okay?" he asked.

I nodded. "Just nervous."

He moved next to me and reached down to take my hand. I tried not to flinch, knowing my palms were disgustingly clammy. "It'll be fine," he said, giving my hand a squeeze. "And you don't have to do this. You can just stay in the plane and land with Cujo."

I whipped my head around to glare at him. "The only way I'm getting off this plane is if I jump," I said. "But I'm trying hard not to think about the details."

"Think about this, then. It's one of the coolest things you'll ever do, *and* you're jumping tandem with an instructor who's got a perfectly clean record, okay? Nothing bad will happen."

I nodded, distracted by the clinking of Leon's buckles and rings as he went through a final gear check.

"You ready?" he called over the wind whipping past him from his post at the gaping door.

I nodded.

"Let's do this!" He waved me over and went through a double check. Or maybe it was quintuple check. I'd gladly let him check ten more times if it meant being sure every strap held.

Once he had tethered me to him with an industrial strength clamp, he maneuvered us to the edge of the plane. I kept one hand wrapped tightly around the cargo netting right next to the door. "The more you think about it, the less likely you are to do this," he shouted over the wind. I nodded but kept my hand where it was.

I watched the other guide, Bruce, tethering to Matt. When he had cinched and locked everything to his satisfaction, Matt grinned over at me. "You scared?"

I nodded.

"Don't be!" he yelled. "Just think of it as a giant metaphor for our relationship!"

And even as I shouted, "What does that mean?" he and Bruce disappeared in a free fall from the plane.

"Ready?" Leon shouted.

Numbly, I nodded. I heard him counting down in my ear, but the reality didn't set in until at his hollered command, I flexed my knees and flung myself out into the screaming wind.

* * *

"Whoo hoo!" The adrenaline-fueled exclamation tore from my throat, and I couldn't hold it back if I wanted to. Sitting in Matt's FJ Cruiser, waiting for our turn at the drive-thru window, I felt the memory of that dive flood my bloodstream again and a full body "Whoo-hoo" was the only way to let it out.

"Was it worth it?" Matt asked.

"Totally!" I grinned and flopped my head against the seat. "That was the most amazing thing I've ever done. I totally understand adrenaline junkies now."

"Yeah, it's pretty incredible," he said.

"It makes me want to go again," I said. "And again and again and again."

"I know. That was only my second jump. I want to get enough experience so I can jump on my own, without an instructor. Wouldn't that be awesome?"

"Yeah," I said. "I'm too chicken to go by myself yet, but I totally see why you'd want to." I dropped my head back against the seat while the car inched forward in line. "I kind of want to try all this other stuff I've seen now."

"Like what?"

"I don't know. Maybe cliff diving. That sounds fun, right?"

He shook his head again. "I don't think so. I guess it depends."

"On what?"

"On whether I have a wife and kids waiting for me after the jump. There are just certain risks I wouldn't take if I had a family to worry about."

"Naturally."

He tilted his head toward me. "You say it like it's a bad thing," he said.

"No, it's just common sense—I know that. It makes my point about marriage, doesn't it?"

"Which is?" He inched the car forward in line.

"You know . . . that there's a lot of things you don't get to do any-more because you're tied down."

He mulled that over while he stared at the shrubs outside the car window. "I thought you meant it would you hold you back from a financial point of view when we talked about this before."

"That too, but then there's all the stuff that responsible adults don't do when they have families that are no big deal when they're single."

"Like cliff diving?"

"Exactly," I said, distracted as I tried to peer around him to the window in hopes of spotting our food.

He shifted slightly, letting his broad shoulders block my view. "Here's the thing," he said. "I don't think if you found a place tomor-row and said, 'It's the best cliff-diving spot in the world,' that I would do it. Our area authority gave a talk about this last year in stake priesthood session and I've never forgotten it. He said that it isn't right for us to treat our bodies like disposable playthings in the search for an adrenaline high."

I quirked an eyebrow at him and he flushed. "Sorry," he muttered. "I didn't mean to preach."

"It's not that," I said. "I just hadn't thought about that before."

He shrugged. "I think there are certain things that are fun with low risk if you know what you're doing or go with someone who does, like skydiving and surfing. And I think there are things that I can't justify. The one time I went against my own better judgment, I learned the hard way not to be an idiot."

"You mean the BASE jumping?"

"Yep. When it took me out of commission for eight weeks and I suddenly couldn't work or teach my surf students or anything, I felt kind of like a jerk for chasing a thrill instead of thinking about the consequences." He hesitated, then added, "I guess I saw it as being selfish to worry so much about having fun that I didn't really think about others, and I've tried to avoid that since."

I squirmed uncomfortably in my seat, telling myself his reprimand wasn't directed at me. I didn't have a bunch of crazy items on my list. As matter of fact, now that skydiving was out of the way, I didn't having anything remotely risky left to cross off. And yet, I felt a nagging sense that some people, like maybe Matt, might see the whole list as selfish. I thought about that while Matt paid for our dinner and reeled in the white paper bags full of fried heaven.

The List was the opposite of selfish, really. The whole point was not to become some empty shell of a married woman all riddled with resentment and regret over things I never got to do. I didn't want to be raising kids and seeing them as obstacles to my happiness. Regret over missed opportunities would lead to that. Feeling so strongly about that had led to this six-year quest to finish these items one by one.

Even the ones you outgrew? a little voice whispered to me. *You don't really care about being a movie extra, but you won't take it off The List. How does that fit your theory?* The truth was I didn't know anymore. I mean, what if ten years from now I watched some movie with my kids and I thought to myself, *How cool would that be, to be on a movie set, just as a fly on the wall?* And what if that morphed into, *I could totally do that if I didn't have kids.* And what if that planted a little seed of resentment that took root and grew with every sacrifice I had to make because I had kids? I didn't want to live with that, to be as worn down as Leila, run ragged by her kids, stressed by her finances, and bitter as she watched life pass her by. I didn't even want to be like Juliana, finishing her education as time and life allowed, always a last priority.

The List represented an insurance policy, a guarantee that I exorcised every bit of the wanderlust and thrill seeking out of my system. I'd seen too many things pass Leila and Juliana by to think it wouldn't happen to me if I wasn't careful.

"Where'd you go?" Matt asked softly, breaking into my reverie.

"Off in my head," I answered.

"Anywhere interesting?"

"Not really."

He nodded and handed me my food. I dug into the greasy paper bag and fished out the best french fries in Southern California, but even their salty goodness couldn't dispel my sudden funk. I needed a bigger distraction.

"Are you still going to Institute tonight?" I asked.

He nodded. "Are you? Or are you too tired?"

"I'm the opposite of tired. I'm kind of wound up, to tell you the truth."

"Adrenaline?" he guessed.

"Maybe. It'll be good to get out on the waves tomorrow and work some of it out. What time do you want to surf?"

"I can't in the morning," he said. "What about after lunch?"

"No, I'm working a double. Fridays are busy. Do you have lessons tomorrow morning?"

"No, I'm training."

"For what?"

He reached over to poke me lightly in the side. "Promise not to think I'm lame."

"I promise," I said, holding up my hand in my best guess at a Boy Scout pledge.

"Well, one of the other wards in the stake sponsors a triathlon every year, and I need to train more on the biking part, so I figured I'd better get started because I only have two weeks."

"Why would I think that's lame?" I asked.

"It's not a real triathlon," he said. "It's just this ward's thing, and it's become kind of a tradition, but some people think it's stupid to spend time training for it when it's not official or anything."

"Who thinks it's stupid?" I asked.

"Derek, for one."

I decided to keep my opinion about Derek's ability to judge the relative intelligence of anything to myself. "I say if you run, bike, and swim the standard distance, then it counts. Is it too late to sign up for it?"

"Nah. Like I said, it's unofficial so the rules are pretty loose. You want to do it?" he asked.

"Yeah, I've always thought that sounded fun."

"You know, if you want to hang out more, you can just say that. You don't have to do a whole triathlon for me to spend time with you," he said, his tone longsuffering.

Knowing better than to take him seriously, I gave his arm a solid thwack. "I'm serious. I want to do it."

"Cool," he said. "Do you want to train with me too?"

"Maybe not on the swimming because I think I get enough practice while surfing. But the biking and running? Sure, I wouldn't mind having a partner for that."

His forehead crinkled in worry. "I'm not taking my own life in my hands because I'm doing another sports-related activity with you, am I? I don't want to tempt fate. You're due for another freak accident, right?"

"Look at it this way. This is where you get to prove you're man enough to hang out with me."

He snorted. "You're on."

Satisfied, I scooped up another helping of french fries. Suddenly they tasted wonderful again.

Chapter 23

"IT'S REALLY UNFORTUNATE," I GRUNTED from my crouch over my bike's handlebars.

"What's that?" Matt called, several feet ahead of me, as usual.

"It's unfortunate how many times I ask myself 'Why the heck am I doing this again?' when I'm around you. Why, Matt. Why?"

"Because it's fun!" he yelled over his shoulder.

I spared a thought for my aching backside and silently begged to differ. Stifling a groan, I dug into the pedaling, convinced the last two miles on our return trip were ten times longer than normal miles. When my calf muscles screamed through the last mile, I amended my estimate. It was twenty times longer than a normal mile. I slid off my bike in front of Matt's house, where he was already waiting. My Jeep sat parked on the road, and a flutter of white paper under the windshield wiper made my heart sink.

I dismounted and twisted over to adjust my sock so I could hide my huge grimace. Then I waddled in my cute (and by that I mean padded like a ridiculous adult diaper and not at all cute) bike shorts over to pluck the offending paper from my car. Sure enough, it was a street-cleaning ticket. I stared at it, not sure I had the energy to howl in annoyance.

"Oh no," Matt said, tugging it from my hand. "It's the second Wednesday. I forgot it was street cleaning day. I'm so sorry. Let me pay this for you."

I took the paper back. "Thanks," I said. "But that sign probably should have been my first clue." I nodded my head toward the sign six feet in front of us, clearly indicating the street sweeping schedule. "It's my fault. I swear I thought I put my common sense on when I got up this morning, but this whole day has been nothing but evidence to the contrary."

"You mean because . . ."

"Because common sense should have told me to read the sign, and, more importantly, common sense should have told me not to get on a borrowed bike for a two-million-mile bike ride."

"It was eight miles."

"Two million, eight . . . same difference."

"The triathlon is going to be a fifteen-mile ride. I was trying to start you out easy."

"Ha!" I said, with an absentminded rub of my bottom. "I think you were trying to kill me."

"No way. I survived a whole summer with you. Why would I knock you off three weeks before you go home?"

"I don't know. Maybe you're trying to knock me out of the triathlon competition."

"Considering we don't compete in the same age or gender category?" He shook his head. "I don't think so."

"Maybe you should give Louisa back her bike and tell her I never want to see it or her again." I tried my best glower on him.

"Okay, I'll give her the message, but you might lose cool points with her."

"Never mind, then. I like her so I better keep my cool points. Maybe you could just take the bike out back and burn it?"

He laughed. "I have never seen you be such a drama queen."

"That's because you didn't see me my first day out surfing. It takes a week or two for the bellyaching to stop."

"Great," he said. "Something to look forward to."

I grinned. "I *am* kind of a pain," I said. "Feel free to drop me as a training partner. It won't hurt my feelings."

"Yeah, but then I'll be hanging out with you less."

"Derek will be happy. He was complaining the other day that I was cutting into his cuddle time."

That earned an even bigger laugh and a hug. "Too bad," he said. "I'm not giving up one second of that."

I hugged him back. "I'll stop whining if you promise I never have to ride a bike again."

"You never have to ride a bike again. Until the day after tomorrow when we take the same route."

"Deal."

"Do you work today?" he asked.

"No. Wednesdays are slow so I took it off."

"Then the rest of your day is open?"

"Yeah," I said. "Do you have something in mind?"

"I was thinking we could head out to one of my favorite Mexican places for dinner, but it's more inland and we'd need to leave a little early."

"Isn't there a ward activity tonight?"

He shrugged. "Yeah. So?"

"So Louisa's in charge."

"I go to most of her stuff. She'll be fine if I miss one. Besides, I think they're doing disc golf at Central Park and that's not on—" He stopped.

"On what?" I asked.

"On the schedule," he said. "Really good Mexican food is."

"I'm not passing up a burrito," I said. "I'm in."

We hammered out the details for dinner, and he helped me stow Louisa's bike in the Jeep. When I settled into the driver's seat, I shoved the parking ticket into the glove box with a little more force than necessary before driving off toward home.

* * *

"I think I hate traffic more than broccoli," I said, staring at the same bumper that had been in front of us for the last forty minutes.

"Yeah," Matt agreed. "But this is the only freeway into Riverside, and that's where dinner is."

"You'd think if this many people are going there every day, they'd build another freeway or something," I grumbled.

"The Metrolink runs through here, but I figured it made more sense to drive than try to figure out how to get to the restaurant from the train station."

"How about you entertain me while we sit here? It's not like there's anything to see." We were in a canyon that ran through green rolling hills, but not much broke up the scenery.

"Entertain you how?" Matt asked.

"Oh, I don't know. Make something up," I said, which led to another forty minutes of bad knock-knock jokes and riddles.

When we exited the freeway, Matt drove only a couple of blocks before pulling into the parking lot of a well-known restaurant chain. I knew of two locations within ten minutes of my uncle's house.

Confused, I asked, "This is where we're having dinner?"

"Yes."

"But . . . don't we have Cactus Pedro in Huntington?"

"Sure, but the enchilada sauce is better here. You'll see."

He hopped out of the car and hurried around to open my door. I shook my head and climbed down from the truck, accepting Matt's hand and hanging on to it even after I was steady on my feet. He returned the squeeze and tugged me toward the doors of the restaurant. The hostess led us toward some seats on the patio, but Matt stopped her. "Can we sit in the bar area instead?"

Now I was really surprised. "I want to watch the game," he explained. "They have TVs in there."

"What game?" I asked.

"You know. The game," he answered and turned to follow the hostess before I could press him further. Weirder and weirder. Dinner didn't clear up anything either because my chicken enchilada tasted exactly the same as the ones I ordered in Huntington. Matt seemed distracted, but not by the baseball game airing on the screen behind me. He barely paid it any mind at all since it wasn't an Angels game. Instead, he kept an eye on the steady flow of patrons gathering around the tables in the bar. By the time the busboy cleared our plates, our part of the restaurant was packed.

"Did you like your dinner?" he asked.

"Yeah," I said, not wanting to be rude and point out that it was no different than usual.

"Good, good," he murmured, clearly not paying attention as his eyes darted around the room. The tension in his posture increased as his gaze finally settled on a guy setting up sound equipment in the far corner of the bar area. After a couple of minutes, I realized he was wrangling a karaoke machine. I jerked my head around to pin Matt with a stare.

"What's going on?" I demanded. "Did you drag me here to do karaoke?"

"Only if you want to," he hurried to reassure me. "I thought—"

"Wrong. You thought wrong, whatever it is." Unbelievable.

"Hear me out—"

"No," I snapped.

"Please?"

I crossed my arms and glared at him across the table. He wanted me to sit there and listen to his reasons for trying to re-create one of the most embarrassing nights of my life? And yet, his face was so earnest that I gave in.

"Okay," I said. "Why are we anywhere near the vicinity of a karaoke machine?"

"I know that didn't go so well at church or whatever," he said, "but it doesn't seem like you to take a defeat like that lying down. I thought maybe if you tried again . . ."

"I can try as many times as I want to. I still can't sing," I said. "So, no thanks."

"I understand," he said. "But will you cheer for me if I give it a shot?"

That startled me. "I didn't know you could sing," I said.

"I can't. But we drove all the way out here where there's no way we're going to run into anyone we know, so it seems like if I'm ever going to do it, now's the time."

"Why would you want to do karaoke if you can't sing?" I asked.

"Because I hate the thought of getting up and making a fool out of myself, and I hate that it bothers me. Maybe getting up and wailing like an idiot will help me get over myself." He didn't look like he'd convinced himself anymore than he'd convinced me.

"Okay, so this is some kind of intense group therapy thing for you?" I asked.

"Yeah. That's it. I'm going to cure myself of self-consciousness with the help of these fine people," he said, sweeping his arm to encompass the bar patrons.

"Matt, if you get up there, I'll cheer louder than anyone."

"Deal," he said.

With a squeal of the mike, the deejay announced that the weekly Wednesday karaoke competition was underway and people could sign up at his table. Matt stood and I asked, "What are you going to sing?"

He shrugged. "I'm sure I'll know it when I see it."

He turned through page after page in the deejay's binders before grabbing the sign-up sheet and writing something down.

"Well?" I asked, when he came back to the table.

"You can wait along with everyone else," he said.

It turned out to be a short wait. After a good-humored performance of a Willie Nelson song from a middle-aged gentleman, and a disturbingly militant rendition of "I Will Survive" from a tiny girl who looked barely old enough to be in the bar area, the deejay called Matt's name.

He rose, a grim line hijacking the place his smile usually occupied, and headed for the front. He stood perfectly still, the microphone gripped in his hand, listening for the opening bars of his song. When they came, I thought the DJ had played the wrong song. "I Got You, Babe," by Sonny and Cher? Why would he pick a duet?

He began to sing with a monotone as flat as his expression. The first words came out like they had all been written with the same note. I couldn't believe I hadn't noticed Matt's tone deafness even though I'd sat by him several times in sacrament meeting. I winced as the monotone continued, wondering if he lip-synched during church.

The crowd obviously wasn't drunk enough yet for this performance to strike them as funny. I sensed a low rumble starting, along with some uncomfortable seat shifting. Matt stubbornly plowed into the second verse. Sort of. Droned, maybe.

The audience's restlessness escalated, and I panicked. I didn't know the standard protocol when a group turned on a karaoke singer, but I was afraid it might involve flinging their complimentary chips and salsa. Little beads of sweat rolled down the side of Matt's face, and I realized that he was fully aware things were turning ugly.

It melted my heart a little. I knew he didn't need to prove anything to himself. He was trying to make it okay for me to prove to myself that I could do this, that I could redeem myself for my ward activity night disaster if I wanted to. He'd driven through two hours of traffic so I could do my thing in front of complete strangers I would never have to face again and now stood on the stage to demonstrate that it was okay to make a fool out of myself.

No way could I leave him hanging. Before I could think too hard about it, I crossed the room, grabbed the other microphone off the deejay's table, and joined Matt in time to hit the never-ending chorus. He grinned, and we belted out the line fifty million more times without any kind of harmony but with boatloads of enthusiasm that managed to mute the acute embarrassment scorching my cheeks.

When the song ended, I didn't dare look at the audience. I looked up at him instead. His smile grew even bigger, and I returned it. "With this happy-hour crowd as my witness, I will never sing karaoke again," I vowed, then leaned up to kiss him. With a burst of applause and catcalls, the audience reasserted itself, and I pulled away to wave to them. Matt kept a firm hold on my hand as he guided me back to our table, receiving a few high fives on the way. He asked for the check, and fifteen minutes later we were back on the road toward home.

"Thanks," I said, dropping my head back against the seat and studying his profile. "You didn't have to do that."

He shrugged. "Sure I did. After Louisa told me about strong-arming you into the karaoke competition in the first place, I felt bad that I wasn't there to cheer for you. I wanted to make it up to you. I just didn't want to do it in front of anyone I might know, so driving forty miles out of town seemed like a good idea."

"It was a great idea," I said and leaned across the gearshift to plant a kiss on his cheek. "That is possibly the dumbest, sweetest thing anyone has ever done for me."

Another shrug. "You're worth it," he said.

I didn't know how to respond, so I said nothing at all, but the way his words wormed their way dangerously close to my heart spoke volumes.

Chapter 24

I HATE MOVIES THAT MESS with time. It makes my brain hurt to figure out how what got changed in the past would then affect the future which was actually the present, which was . . .

Ack.

Yet somehow my life had become victim to a time warp. It was the only way to explain how the four weeks that Matt was gone on business stretched and morphed into an endless blob, and the four weeks until school started sped up like they were being fueled by pure caffeine. I had blinked and suddenly found myself in the middle of the Old Testament at Institute, one day away from running a triathlon and less than a week away from packing up to leave for school.

Wasn't it just yesterday that I had squeezed my dresses into Celia's closet to start my summer stay? How did August sneak up so quickly? Maybe it was the "time flies when you're having fun" thing because goodness only knew how much of an afterthought my Hannigan's shifts had become to spending time with Matt. Even tonight, a Friday, was only my third shift of the week, and I had almost traded that away because the triathlon was the next morning. Then I realized I had a car insurance payment due and showed up.

It's not like Matt even tried to carve out extra time. He just called up with a suggestion for something to do and my brain said, *No. You have bills to pay and things to do, and you hung out with him yesterday and every day before that.* But what always came out was, "Yes."

Every morning, we either surfed or trained for the triathlon. Evenings, except for the few I worked, were full of movies at his house or Sister Powers's class, or one of Matt's crazy schemes. We'd painted pottery at a craft store downtown. I made a cool polka-dot switch plate for Celia's bathroom as a thanks-for-sharing gift, and Matt painted a tall mug with death-metal logos and skulls. "It'll make me look more manly when I drink fruit smoothies," he explained. On another night, he dragged me out to a demolition derby on a double date with Derek and a girl who couldn't stop giggling. Minus the giggling, it was awesome.

I'd never known anyone with a thirst for adventure as big as Matt's. Regardless of what we did, he embraced it like it was the best time he'd ever had. He found a Tuscan pottery exhibit I wanted to see as entertaining as a night at an indoor climbing gym near my aunt's house. I'd known guys in college that I called the "gee whiz" guys who were determined to wear a happy face no matter what; I found those guys pleasant and boring. Matt's genuine curiosity about everything fascinated me. Every time I thought I'd figured out which niche he fit into, he landed on something else, and I had to rethink.

I started the summer believing he was the classic, laid-back California surfer. That perception had evolved until I saw him as someone far more . . . complex? Yet that wasn't the right word either because it implied complicated. There were plenty of surprises with Matt but no secrets or contradictions. It was more a matter of finding new things with every layer that peeled back. That made him even more fun to hang out with, which surprised me, honestly. Normally, a couple of weeks with any guy drove me to boredom or claustrophobia. But Matt . . .

Didn't.

There was no rut to get stuck in, and as much as I knew I should be working more and saving money, an underlying sense of urgency drove me to squeeze in time with him while my mental clock ticked off the moments until school started and the best summer of my life ended. Matt hadn't brought up dating in the fall again, but I found it on my mind more and more. And every time I thought it wouldn't be such a bad idea, he called with an invitation to grab dessert at a downtown pizza joint or to see a band play in some dive on the outskirts of L.A. A minute later, I'd be trading off another shift, remembering why I couldn't afford a distraction like him and doing it, anyway. He was too addictive.

I was pretty sure I was hooked.

How else to explain the serious neglect *everything* in my life was experiencing at the moment? All I did was surf with Matt, train with Matt, or go on dates with Matt. All my other settings were broken. I hadn't even chatted with Ryder online in over a week.

I put away my last serving tray and tipped out the busboys. Thank goodness for weekend tips or I'd be in a financial pinch. I shoved the wad of bills in my pocket and headed for the car. Maybe that's what I needed: a chat with Ryder to clear my head. He may have given up on me coming around anymore but I decided to try him, anyway.

Even cleaning up as quickly as I could after work, I knew it was probably too late to expect Ryder to still be awake. I logged in and realized exactly how much I had neglected my whole Internet dating project when a backlog of forty-three messages greeted me. I ignored them and ran a quick search to see if Ryder was online. The slim hope of dumping out my woes for his analysis disappeared when I didn't see the little green dot telling me he was there. I tapped out an e-mail, anyway in case he checked in soon and set my computer aside to give myself a stern talking-to.

I was right in the middle of a lecture about why giving my shifts away for Matt time was weak when my laptop beeped with a message. I dropped the lecture and jerked my computer onto my lap.

BoardRyder: Who is this?
TwinkieSmash: Ashley.
BoardRyder: Who?
TwinkieSmash: Ha ha. Sorry I haven't been around.
BoardRyder: No problem. I've been crazy busy. What's up?
TwinkieSmash: The usual.
BoardRyder: Work?
TwinkieSmash: Less than usual, actually.
BoardRyder: So then what's "the usual"?
TwinkieSmash: Mr. G.
BoardRyder: I should have guessed. No, I did guess. I figured that's why you weren't around so much.
TwinkieSmash: Yeah. It's good.
BoardRyder: Good.

TwinkieSmash: Really good.

BoardRyder: Okay, how good?

TwinkieSmash: Good, like . . . maybe I might want to date him past the end of the summer.

BoardRyder: Long distance? Yikes.

TwinkieSmash: No. Kind of. I guess he's in Utah during the winter a lot. Snowboarding.

BoardRyder: And that doesn't freak you out?

TwinkieSmash: A little bit. I think it's okay, though. Maybe.

BoardRyder: I get it. You want my advice, right?

TwinkieSmash: Yeah. I'd like a guy's perspective.

BoardRyder: My perspective doesn't really matter.

TwinkieSmash: What do you mean? How come you all of a sudden don't want to give advice?

BoardRyder: Because I don't think you need it. You already know what you want to do.

TwinkieSmash: Yeah.

BoardRyder: I thought so. What does this mean for The List?

TwinkieSmash: Nothing. I was going to have to set it aside for a couple of semesters, anyway.

BoardRyder: You're giving up on it?

TwinkieSmash: No, more like putting it in storage for a while so I can work on school.

BoardRyder: Well, at least you can cross off the Internet dating one.

TwinkieSmash: No, I can't. I didn't actually go on any dates.

BoardRyder: Then let's do that.

TwinkieSmash: I don't think that's a good idea.

BoardRyder: Why not?

TwinkieSmash: Because you and I both know my attention is elsewhere. And when I do get back to town, I'm going to be up to my ears in classes and studying.

BoardRyder: I wasn't talking about meeting up here. I'm in SoCal now for business, not too far from HB. Maybe we could just say "hello, good-bye" over a meal, and you can cross that item off your list.

I sat still, taken aback at the idea of meeting Ryder in person.

BoardRyder: Uh, hello? Are you still there?

TwinkieSmash: Yes. I'm thinking.

BoardRyder: Okay. Hit *** every now and then so I know you're still there while you think.

TwinkieSmash: *

TwinkieSmash: *

TwinkieSmash: *

BoardRyder: Cute. Done thinking yet?

TwinkieSmash: Yes.

BoardRyder: And?

TwinkieSmash: And the idea of meeting someone off the Internet is suddenly incredibly scary.

BoardRyder: You're right. What if you're a total psycho?

TwinkieSmash: Busted. I totally am a psycho.

BoardRyder: I knew it.

TwinkieSmash: Yeah, I guess if we meet it should be somewhere really public where you can't kidnap me without causing a scene.

BoardRyder: Okay. Now it scares me that you even thought of that.

TwinkieSmash: Hey, a girl can't be too careful.

BoardRyder: Fair enough. And where should meet for this hello-goodbye?

TwinkieSmash: *

TwinkieSmash: *

TwinkieSmash: I think maybe the pier. You know where that is?

BoardRyder: I've surfed there before.

TwinkieSmash: There's a little grassy area right by it. Would that work?

BoardRyder: Sounds good. When?

I sat back, unnerved. Did I really just agree to meet my Internet buddy for a blind date? I must be crazy.

Then again, everything about Ryder struck me as extremely normal, especially compared to so many of the e-mails I'd gotten from guys that were clearly a little "off." I knew better than to invite Ryder to my aunt and uncle's house or anywhere that it would be to easy to trace me once we parted ways. And I knew that even if common sense said I shouldn't meet up with people I met from the Internet, I at least had enough sense to pick a place where I would be safe if anything bad crossed Ryder's mind.

Somehow, I didn't think I'd need a contingency, but it was good to have one. My only reservation about meeting him near the pier was that it seemed like the faintest betrayal of Matt to bring another guy to our stomping grounds. But the "our" was all in my mind. Thanks to my clear no-strings-attached policy, other than ask that I not kiss anyone else, Matt had steered clear of any other requests or demands. Since I had no intention of kissing Ryder, I doubt Matt would care if I passed a little time on a public lawn saying good-bye to someone I barely even knew and had no intention of seeing again. Feeling more sure, I answered Ryder's question.

> *TwinkieSmash: How about tomorrow night?*
> *BoardRyder: A Saturday? Won't you be hanging out with Mr. G?*
> *TwinkieSmash: We're competing in a triathlon all day together. I'm sure he'll be fine if I don't hang out with him tomorrow night too. He's independent like that.*
> *BoardRyder: It's a date. A first and last date, but a date.*
> *TwinkieSmash: Cool. How will I find you? I've only seen you in snow goggles.*
> *BoardRyder: Don't worry. I know what you look like. I'll find you.*
> *TwinkieSmash: That sounds all stalker-ish.*
> *BoardRyder: You're the one who put a profile picture up. Don't blame me.*
> *TwinkieSmash: Good point. Okay, tomorrow around six, then?*
> *BoardRyder: Sure.*
> *TwinkieSmash: Well . . . good night.*
> *BoardRyder: See you tomorrow.*

He would. How weird.

* * *

"I'm going to die. I know I'm going to die."

"You're not going to die. You made it! You're fine," Matt said.

I stayed in my heap on the ground. "I can't move," I mumbled into the grass beneath me.

"Sure you can. You moved your mouth. That counts."

I mustered the energy to grab a fistful of grass and throw it in his direction.

"See, there's your arm moving. That's progress."

"When did you become so relentlessly cheerful?" I complained.

"I'm not cheerful. I'm pragmatic when I say that you just proved your body can move and so you probably ought to get off the church lawn."

I thought about it for a minute, then, with a groan, pushed myself up and brushed off the grass sticking to my sweaty skin, grumbling some more.

"Aren't you supposed to have some postrace adrenaline high?" he asked. "You know, with all these happy endorphins swimming around and stuff?"

"I think I've got the 'and stuff.' Like for example, my vision is swimming. But I'm pretty sure it's not endorphin-related. In fact, I'm positive it's because there's no blood flow going to my head right now."

He pulled me into a hug. His shoulder muffled my cry of, "I'm really sweaty and gross!" It came out sounding like "Mwph rmny frum whass."

"Me too," he said, not relaxing his hold at all.

"You're not gross," I said.

"You're not gross, either," he responded and dropped a kiss on my nose.

"Is this a *Princess Bride* moment where 'you're not gross' is code for something else?"

He pulled his head back to stare down at me. "Like what?"

"Like if you say 'you're not gross,' it really means 'you're kind of hot'?"

He laughed. "Yes. That's definitely what it is." He let go of me but only to take my hand and walk me toward his car. He must have loaded the bikes while I was facedown in the grass because they were already on the rack and ready to go.

"You did awesome today, Ashley," he said as he opened my door for me.

"If by awesome you mean finished near the end, then thanks," I said.

"No, really. You only had two weeks to train for this, and you really hung in there."

I tried not to blush.

"What's more, you didn't cause or experience any bodily injury. We should celebrate."

"With what?" I said. "Ice cream? A whole lot of ice cream?"

"I don't know if that's a good idea," he said. "Maybe you won't be able to lift the ice cream cone all the way to your face. Are you recovered enough for that?"

"Ice cream cures everything. If I eat some now, then I can recover even faster."

"I should have thought of that," he said. "Waiting until after dinner is for chumps and lightweights."

"Yeah, I'm hard-core. Get me ice cream!"

In minutes we were pulling away from a popular ice cream chain and I set about demolishing two scoops of mint chocolate chip. The thirty other flavors never stood a chance. Once at least half of the minty goodness was on its way to my stomach, I slowed down and started negotiating with myself. *When you get down to the cone, let him know you can't hang out tonight.* I finished all the ice cream on top. *Just finish the cone, and then you have tell him.* I slowed down more, eating barely fast enough to stay ahead of the melting. I didn't know how to tell Matt that I would be on a date with someone else or even *if* I had to. Keeping my business to myself was supposed to be a perk of "no strings attached," but it seemed kind of cheap to hold out on Matt that way. Then again, maybe he wouldn't care or want to know. What if I said, "Hey, Matt. I can't hang out with you tonight because I have a date with someone else," and he said something like, "I didn't ask you to hang out." And I would feel dumb and never even get to the part where I explained that it was a hello, good-bye date. But it seemed only fair to let him know.

I popped the last bite of my ice cream cone into my mouth and chewed slowly. And then more slowly still. And then it was gone and I didn't have any more excuses.

I cleared my throat. I shifted in my seat. I cleared my throat again.

"Do you need some water?" Matt asked, reaching for his sport bottle in the cup holder.

"No, thanks." I cleared my throat again. He gave me a strange look and then turned his eyes back to the road.

"So you know how I don't have to work tonight?"

"Yeah. That must be nice. You always have to work on Saturday."

"Right. Yes, it's nice. But, uh, even though I don't have to work, I . . ."

"You're going in, anyway?"

"Uh, no. But I won't be able to hang out with you tonight."

He was quiet for a moment. "No problem."

No problem? *No problem?* Did he not realize I was leaving in less than a week and our time was ticking down? He must not, because otherwise me spending one of our last evenings together somewhere else should have been a very big problem for him.

I nearly opened my mouth to tell him so until I realized what a hypocrite that made me. Since I was the whole reason we wouldn't be hanging out, it wasn't really fair to jump all over him for not being more upset about it. Stuff like that was how girls earned the "psycho" label far too often. Instead I asked, "Do you want to know what I'm going to be doing?"

"Not unless you really want to tell me."

"I don't. But I kind of think I should, and that annoys me."

We turned into my aunt and uncle's tract. Matt didn't say anything until he pulled in front of their house and killed his engine.

"Look, Ashley. I trust you. I think you've been straight with me about everything from the first time we ever hung out, and I know that what you do is none of my business. I'd love to make it my business, but you were really clear on the no strings, so I'll just leave it alone." His voice was tight.

I stared, not sure what to say. He didn't sound angry, exactly, and he wasn't asking anything from me, so I had no idea where to go next. "Okay," I managed after a minute. "I just didn't want you to be mad that I can't hang out tonight even though I'm leaving soon."

"I'm not mad."

I didn't believe him. A thick silence hung between us, full of prickles and squirminess. I stared out of the window, feeling like an idiot for sitting there instead of heading for the house.

"Ashley."

I turned to face him.

"I'm sorry. It's just—" He stopped and shoved his hand through his hair, the movement jerky. "I try to give you all the room you ask for, but the truth is, I'm a strings kind of guy. This is hard."

"Oh." I didn't know what else to say. I stared at the glove compartment for a minute until I felt a smile tugging up the corner of my mouth against my will.

"You're laughing at me?" he asked. "Great."

"I'm not, I promise," I said. "I was just thinking that maybe I wanted to revisit that clause."

"What does that mean?"

I felt the squirminess coming on again and tried not to give into it. "It means that I've gotten kind of used to you. And *maybe* it would be weird to all of a sudden not see you anymore. And *maybe* it would be kind of cool to see you when you come out to snowboard."

"Maybe," he said noncommittally.

I stared at him.

"*Maybe?*" I said, an embarrassing shrillness driving my voice up an octave.

"Maybe it would be *awesome,*" he said, grinning.

I smacked his arm, and he pulled me into a big hug. The awkward space the cup holder console created evaporated in that warm embrace. When he finally let me go, I sat back in my seat and smiled. I couldn't help it. It felt good to erase one of the boundaries I had drawn at the beginning of the summer to keep Matt at a distance. Even the thought that this could be the first step toward endangering The List didn't bother me. I sat, soaking up the moment.

"So . . ." Matt finally said after a moment. "That wasn't so bad, right? You can still breathe and stuff?"

"Yes."

He tapped the dashboard clock. "I figure you've had about thirty seconds to adjust to the idea of me being around a little more often, so how about if I drop a bomb on you now?"

"What the heck am I supposed to say to that?"

"Say yes again," he ordered.

"Yes again."

He took a deep breath and let it out. "I know I made a point of not telling you where I went on business—"

"No, you made a point of *not* telling me where you went."

"Fair enough," he said and smiled. "But I'm ready to tell you now."

"No, I want to guess. You're setting up a surf shop in South Dakota?"

"No."

"How about Georgia? New Mexico? Nebraska?"

"Don't take this the wrong way, Ashley, but you might not be very good at geography."

"Fine, then tell me."

"We're setting up a board shop in Utah. Two, actually."

I wrinkled my nose. "There's a surf clientele in Utah?"

"It's not a surf shop. It's a *board* shop, specifically snowboards." He let me think about that for a minute before adding, "That means I'm going to be in Utah all winter, getting everything set up."

I soaked that in. "Are you saying a seven-hundred-mile buffer is about to evaporate?"

"That's what I'm saying."

I rubbed at my nose like it was a magic lamp and a genie would pop out and tell me what to think about all of this. When I realized what I was doing, I stopped and laid my hands in my lap and studied them instead. Matt was moving to Utah for the winter? Holy cow.

"When do you go up there?" Maybe it wouldn't be so bad if I didn't see him until the ski season started. That way I could at least get the semester underway and into a groove that I was less likely to stray from.

"Our lease occupancy starts at the beginning of September and I need to be there to oversee the remodeling in our spaces."

"That's barely two weeks away!"

He nodded. "It's going to be insanely busy for a while. I think I can promise to stay out of your hair. At first."

He touched one of my curls as he said it. Winding it around his finger, he gave it a soft tug and added, "Only at first, though."

"Why didn't you tell me about this weeks ago?"

He shrugged. "It wasn't a for-sure thing until last month. Jay and I have been thinking about this for two years but once the economy tanked, it dropped the commercial leasing prices so low that we couldn't pass it up. We can afford to grow our business slowly while everything turns around, and we decided now is the time."

"I still don't understand why I'm just hearing about it now."

"I didn't see a point in saying anything when, for all I knew, I wasn't going to see you once you went back to school. You were pretty clear about it shaking out that way. Now that you're open to dating past the end of the summer, I thought I better let you know."

"Wow. I so did not see this coming."

"Is it a bad thing?" he asked, his voice suspiciously casual.

I sighed. "No."

"You sound so happy about that," he said dryly.

"I know, right?" I stared out the window for a few more moments trying to collect thoughts that had been scattered like a dandelion wish. "It's not a bad thing," I started again. "But it's a much different thing than I planned for at the beginning of this summer when I met you. It's not like I suddenly don't want to spend time with you just because you're going to be around more. But this intensity we have right now, it isn't going to work in the fall, and that makes me really nervous."

"You feel like this is intense?" Matt asked. "Have I done anything to pressure you or make you feel that way?"

"No, of course not. But I spend every free moment I have with you and even moments that aren't free, when I should be doing something else. It's fine now, but there's no way I could keep this up when school starts, plus all the TA stuff I'll be doing. So I guess that freaks me out a little."

"Just because I'm around, it doesn't mean you have to see me," he said with no inflection.

Realizing I'd hurt him, I rushed to fix it. "Oh, Matt, that's not what I meant at all. I'm going to want to see you all the time."

He smiled. "That's more what I was hoping to hear." He wrapped me in another loose hug. "I don't want you to stress, Ash. I meant it when I said things would be crazy busy at first. I'm going to have some major supervision to do, plus lining up all of our vendors and our advertising. Louisa doesn't really have any marketing contacts up there, so I'll be working with a new agency and everything's going to be nuts. I really can stay out of your hair," he said, even as he threaded his fingers through it in a delicious scalp massage.

"Are you going to be mad if I want to study instead of go out sometimes?" I asked.

"No. Will you care if I hang out on your sofa and read a book while you study?"

"I think I can handle that."

"And will you let me give you subtle reminders when you're working too hard?"

"It sounds like you'll need them more than I will."

He laughed. "Probably. How about you watch my back and I'll watch yours?"

"All right. I can handle that."

He tightened his squeeze and then let me go completely. "I'm going to get better at it starting now. You said you have something to do tonight, so this is me reminding you to go do it. I'll walk you to the door."

On the porch, I leaned up to give him another hug. "Thanks for letting me tag along on your triathlon. And tell Louisa thanks again for letting me use her bike."

He turned and headed down the path again. "You weren't a tag-along, Ashley. You've carried you own weight in everything I've seen you do. I'll see you at church tomorrow," he called as he climbed into his truck.

I watched until he disappeared around the corner, then turned toward the house and the problem of what to wear on a hello, good-bye date.

* * *

I scraped my fingernail across the rough concrete beneath me, attempting to file down a slightly ragged edge. I looked up every now and then, scanning the crowd of people ebbing and flowing like a human wave across the nearby pier. Unless Ryder showed up in the snowboarding gear from his LDS Lookup profile picture, there was no way I'd recognize him. My perch on the edge of one of the grassy areas descending toward the beach was designed to make me easy to find, but instead of feeling smart, I felt exposed and a little silly. I'd seen more than a dozen guys that fit the right range to be my mysterious Internet friend, but none of them did more than glance in my direction.

I pulled out my phone to check the time. There were still five minutes left until our official meeting time. I shoved it back into my purse, feeling impatient. I debated heading home and e-mailing Ryder with an apology for standing him up. It didn't make much sense to meet up with someone I had no intention of dating, and I wished I had the evening to process what this sudden shift in my relationship with Matt meant. Instead, I was waiting for a virtual stranger to tap me on the shoulder and say, "Hi."

A few more minutes ticked by, and I wondered if I should have arranged with Ryder to wear a certain color or some kind of accessory so he could be sure it was me. I glanced down at my outfit. I hadn't put much thought into it, not like I did when I hung out with Matt, but the thin purple cardigan I layered over a white tee and jeans was bright enough to catch someone's eye if they were looking for me.

I fumbled my phone out and decided to give Ryder five more minutes to make an appearance before bagging the whole idea as stupid and grabbing a Jamba on my way home. I scanned the crowd once more, noticing all the couples walking hand in hand. Somehow, without me noticing, Matt and I had become one of them, wandering up and down the pier a couple of times a week, holding hands and finishing off a smoothie or watching the surfers. I thought about how easy it felt to just be with him and decided that I had lucked out in spite of myself. And The List.

Nothing I attempted to cross off The List had gone quite as planned this summer. Learning to surf was supposed to be a been-there-done-that kind of item, but being out on the waves had become the best reason to get up in the morning. I couldn't imagine not coming back again and again to face the day from my surfboard. Karaoke had swung wildly the other way toward total humiliation, although the horrible and hilarious duet with Matt had lessened the sting somewhat. Making sushi had inadvertently outed Matt and I as a couple, and skydiving had somehow become a metaphor for the relationship that was only supposed to be a fling.

Even this hello, good-bye date proved how far afield The List had strayed. I had intended to find someone to date when I went back to school. Instead, I made a new friend who had led me to see Matt more clearly. Everything kept coming back to Matt.

Although Matt hadn't asked where I was tonight, had even said he didn't want to know, I felt bad sitting there waiting for Ryder to show up. A quick glance at my phone showed that he had passed the five minutes late mark. I made a split decision and pulled up the keyboard screen on my iPhone, then composed an e-mail to Ryder. *I'm sorry I missed you. I waited a few minutes but realized that as much fun as I had talking to you, it would feel weird to be with you and not Matt. I'm going to go find him. I hope you find what you're looking for with LDS Lookup. Thanks for all the advice.* I hit SEND and started to slip my phone back in my purse when the wallpaper caught my eye. It was a picture of all my nieces and nephews squished into a cute pile in front of my parents' Christmas tree. Maybe I would be one of those drippy girls who puts up a picture of herself and her man instead. Or better yet, a picture of Matt on his surfboard. Oh, *yeah.*

Almost like I conjured him, he spoke my name. Startled, I turned to find him standing on the terrace above me, his hands shoved in his jeans pocket.

"Matt! What are you doing here?"

He took the large step down to stand beside me. "I'm here to see you."

"How did you know I was here?" I asked. I waved my phone at him. "Did you install a tracker in here?"

He sighed. "I didn't need one. I had your IM."

"What IM? What are you—" I stopped, stunned.

"What's your middle name, Ashley Barrett?" he asked quietly.

"Kaye," I answered, dazed.

"Mine's Ryder."

Chapter 25

Instead of stretching or compressing, time just . . . stopped. I didn't breathe. I didn't blink. I just stood, frozen and uncomprehending.

My heart beat a few times and then everything sped up to normal. The noise of the ocean and the people on the pier overhead filtered in and I drew my first deep breath since Matt had said the name *Ryder*.

"Ashley? Are you okay?" he asked, his eyes full of concern. That made me angry. There should be something different in his face, like guilt or misery.

"I'm fan-freaking-tastic," I snapped.

He nodded. "You're mad."

"You're a genius."

He winced. "I'm a jerk."

"Yes." And I saw the first flash of misery ripple over his face. It made me even angrier. Turned out I didn't want to see misery after all; it implied he had a right to feel bad for himself. He didn't.

I did. I didn't want him appropriating any of my emotions. "Quit looking like I kicked your puppy," I said, biting out each word.

"Can I explain?"

"I don't even know what's going on here. Except you're Ryder. And I don't know how. Or why."

"It was an accident."

I felt pressure building in my temples. "An *accident?* Falling off the pier is an accident. Wiping out on your surfboard is an accident. Assuming a fake Internet ID is deliberate and twisted."

"You make it sound like I'm some kind of sick Internet predator. I'm—"

"Not far off. You're not far off at all, because that's exactly what I think."

"Ashley," he said, reaching toward me.

"You are completely misreading me if you think I want to be touched right now, so let me spell it out for you. Do not come near me."

He dropped his hand. "Okay." He backed up a couple of steps and sat down on the edge of the terrace. "I'm going to talk. I hope you'll listen. Anything you want to know, I'll tell you. But I want to start with this." Looking up into my eyes, he said, "I never, ever played you."

I backed up a few more steps and turned so I could watch the waves, focusing on the rhythmic swells. I couldn't think straight, half-formed questions tripping to the tip of my tongue and then fading before I could ask them, replaced by more unasked questions that washed away in new tides of hurt and confusion.

"I told you stuff," I said, latching on to that thought. "Or Ryder. I told Ryder stuff that you weren't supposed to know."

"I know," he mumbled.

"Then how can you say you never played me when you had an inside track on everything I was thinking and feeling because you were *lying*?"

He leaned forward, elbows on knees. "It wasn't supposed to happen like that."

I whipped around. "Then how was it supposed to happen?" I asked. "What sick plan did you have in mind when you asked me questions about who I was dating and how I felt?"

"When I found your profile, I didn't know you very well yet, Ashley. You do a great job of keeping people at a distance. I was already pretty interested in you and I thought it might give me a chance to get to know you better than you were letting me get to know you in person."

"What are you talking about, Matt? We've hung out constantly this summer, and we've talked for hours and hours and hours. What were you trying to get to know?"

"I know we talked. It was just . . . small talk for a long time. Anytime I tried to dig a little deeper with you, you blew me off with a joke. And I didn't go out of my way to show much depth either because I didn't want to blow the image you had of me and risk you walking away."

I stared at him, stone-faced. "What image was that? The one where you seemed like an honest, straight-up guy? Yeah, that's definitely blown."

"No, the image all the summer girls get. It happens every year, Ashley. We get a new crop of faces in May when BYU lets out and everyone comes home. They don't like the small singles wards in their home stakes so they drift to Beachside for the summer. And I don't date those girls because they're not looking for anything serious. But I am, and I hang back. That somehow gets taken as a challenge, and suddenly I'm tripping over girls."

I glared at him. "Humble, much?"

He blew out an exasperated breath. "I'm not bragging. It's the truth. It's happened every year since my mission. I think I'm supposed to be some kind of summer surfer trophy they get to add to their collection, but that's not what I want. So I stay quiet. I've always stayed quiet and tried to keep a low profile. It somehow makes the attention worse."

"Poor baby," I said.

"Don't act like you don't know what I'm talking about. I've seen guys do the same thing to you. It's stupid," he said. "Not because you aren't worth it," he added when my eyebrows shot up. "But they're just hanging around you because you're hot. They don't know you. Doesn't that ever bother you?"

I ignored the question. After a beat, he went on. "I could tell right away you were different. Even though I noticed you the first week you showed up, I just figured you for one of the summertime honeys. But I watched you. You did your own thing from day one, you know? You don't dress the same or act the same as other girls. You didn't go to every single activity and sit around giggling with Celia. And you didn't flirt with every single guy around you. Then I bumped into you at that linger longer with Derek and started to get really curious. Ashley?"

I gave no indication that I heard him, but I was listening. He hesitated, then continued. "You got under my skin. Dave mentioned that he was teaching you to surf, and I started keeping an eye out for you. I thought maybe that would be my way in since you weren't into the barbecue thing."

I turned head my slightly. "You could have just asked me out."

"No, I couldn't. You would have said no. I knew I had to play it right."

"Play it?" I whipped around. "So much for not playing me."

"I didn't mean it that way," he protested. "Are you telling me that you didn't have the whole hard-to-get thing going on? That's playing too."

Since I couldn't deny it, I stared at him in silence.

"I had to think of something, Ashley. I know guys hit on you all the time. I've seen it. I needed something less obvious, something you really wanted, and so I thought maybe the surf thing could be common ground for us. Or common ocean, I guess."

"What does surfing have to do with you creating a false Internet profile?"

"It's not a fake profile," he said. "I've had it since college when I was up at Pepperdine. There's not a ton of members there so Louisa talked me into trying Lookup. I've never really done much with the account, but every now and then I check in on it. I was shocked when I saw that you'd been checking out my profile, but I figured I had lucked out."

"How's that?"

"Because, Ashley. I learned more about you and your personality and background from reading your profile for three minutes than I had in three conversations with you. I found out about your degree and your mission and where you're from, none of which you explained to me yourself."

"I wasn't keeping it a secret."

"I know. But you hold back, and I don't think you even realize you do it. I figured I needed every advantage I could get in getting to know you if you were only going to be around for a few months. I didn't think of it as spying or anything like that. It's kind of in the public record, you know?"

"I don't care that you read my profile, Matt. If I had thought about it, I probably would have checked to see if you had one too.

What I don't understand is why you didn't tell me right away who you were when you contacted me. Why did you talk to me as Ryder and not as Matt?"

"Because you talked to Ryder as all-of-you-Ashley-Barrett and for a long time you only talked to me as part-of-you-Ashley-Barrett. It felt like the only way to get the whole picture, to really know you, and I needed that or there was no way you would—" he stopped.

I turned. "I would what?"

He stared at the ground for a long time. "You would consider a relationship past the end of the summer."

My temper spiked. "What is *wrong* with you? I told you every way I knew how that the end of the summer was the end of us. You said you were fine with it. Why couldn't that be enough?"

"Blame it on bad poetry," he muttered.

"What does that even mean?"

He stood and walked to the edge of the next terrace, watching the water, his hands deep in his pockets. "I'm twenty-six. I'm done with school, I have a growing business. I've had a couple of relationships that didn't go anywhere, but I've dated enough to know what I want."

He turned to face me. "I knew that night after you came to my house for the first time, Ashley. We were sitting there on that ridiculous jungle gym and listening to that kid spout that poem to his girl, and you got all over me for laughing even though I could tell you thought it was funny too. Something about that . . . I don't know. You could have laughed or taken cheap shots to impress me, or cracked your own jokes. But you gave him his dignity or whatever. Look," he said. "I don't know how to explain it without it sounding cheesy. It impressed me. I could have predicted what a hundred other girls would have done in the same situation. Giggled, or cooed. But not you. You see people and things clearly, but you don't see yourself as above them."

"You like me because I'm *nice*?" I ground out.

"No! I mean, you are. Kind of—"

"I'm kind of nice?"

"Stop," he said with his first hint of impatience. "You're taking this the wrong way on purpose. Look, I didn't mean for it to happen this way. I kept trying to back out of the Ryder thing, and it wasn't until this last month that you gave me, Matt, a shot at all. But every truth I told you as Ryder, every truth I told you as me, is real."

"And yet the fact that you *are* Ryder makes everything a big lie."

"It doesn't, Ashley. I swear it doesn't. That was my personality, and those were my facts. So is everything you've seen about me this summer. I didn't see how you and I had a shot past the end of this summer if there wasn't something more than having a good time beneath it all. Talking to you as Ryder was supposed to—"

"What? Build a foundation on a lie?"

"No! I figured I'd come clean with you and you'd see that there was something real between us, something more than just a shallow fling. I kind of hoped that when I showed back up that Ryder would fade away and you'd focus more on me."

He had. It was true that once Matt was back, I'd neglected Ryder. "I did because *Ryder* convinced me to! We keep coming back to that! Why don't you understand how wrong that is?"

A couple holding hands gave me a wide berth as they passed us, the woman looking nervous as they hurried toward the safety of the strand.

"I do get it, Ashley! I do. You feel like I betrayed your trust by getting all this information from you as Ryder and using it on you as Matt."

"I don't *feel* like you betrayed me. You did betray me."

"I didn't, I swear. I never dug for deep confessions of your feelings about Matt. I mean me. I only advised you when you asked for it and steered the conversation away from anything deeper than that. I was trying to give you the reassurance that I wanted to be with you. All of our other conversations were just about politics or music or movies." He sounded frustrated. "I wasn't trying to find out your innermost feelings or whatever. I just wanted to get to know you, let you see me. I swear I wasn't trying to lead you on or sucker you."

"That's a good word. Sucker." I sighed. "Like sucker punched. Or being a sucker. That's what I feel like. A total idiot."

"I never thought that about you." He stepped a little closer, careful not to set me off again. "I think you're amazing." Slowly, he reached over to take my hands and lace his fingers through mine, tugging me closer. I let him. "How much does it change things, Ashley? As mad as you are, can you forgive me? I am so, so sorry."

I stared down at our hands, joined between us, the solid wall of his chest blocking any other view. He had long fingers, his tan a deep gold against the more olive tones of my skin. I felt the warmth spreading from his hands to mine, turning back the chill blowing off the waves. He *was* sorry. I believed that. At some point down the road, I was sure I would forgive him. But he had asked the right question, because this did change things. It changed everything.

I pulled my hands back, sliding them out of his. "I can't do this, Matt. I can't be on a constant roller coaster with you and still focus on school. I can't wonder what's going to come next or wait for you to destabilize me every time I start to feel sure and grounded. Because that's what this feels like. It's like right when I figure out where you fit and I make the space for you, you wreck it. You're never what I expect you to be. You're an HB surfer. No, you're a Utah businessman. No, you're a snowboarder named Ryder."

I tucked my hands pack into my jeans pockets and found them a poor substitute for his warmth.

"I'm all of those things," he said quietly.

"Maybe. Maybe not. I don't even know now. Whoever you are, I went against my own better judgment and fell for you a little."

"I fell for you a lot."

I hardened my heart against that. "Falling hurts. It was stupid. I wish you would have listened to me from the beginning and just kept it light."

"If that's what you wanted when you went back to school, I would have accepted that," he said angrily. "But I had to try to make you think about how right we are for each other. Didn't you see that? Don't you see that still?"

"No. Maybe I thought I did for a little while. But the Matt I thought was right for me was a guy who wanted to give this thing between us time to grow. You?" I laughed, hating the edge in my voice. "You were only concerned about what you wanted. Why, Matt? Why work so hard to change my mind? Did I become the trophy this summer?"

His head jerked like my words had formed a physical slap. "If you could believe that was true about me even for one second, then you really *don't* know me."

"That's the truest thing you've said tonight," I said. Confusion and hurt welled up inside me, tightening my throat, but I held on to my anger. "I'm so over this."

He shoved his hands in his pockets and took a step back. "So this afternoon you were totally ready to pursue a relationship and now you're just done?"

"No, this afternoon I was ready to consider spending more time with you after school starts. Now I'm realizing that I was making a big mistake."

"I'm still ready, Ashley," he said, a quiet challenge in his voice. "I'm ready to accept your terms and take it slow and make sacrifices if it means being with you. Does that count for anything?"

A sick feeling crowded the back of my throat. Steeling myself against the plea I saw in his eyes, I swallowed back the pain and focused on the hurt I felt. "It doesn't. The truth is, no one could really make me change my mind about this. I just sort of forgot that for a little while."

"Right," he said bitterly. "The List."

"How did you—" I stopped myself. "Ryder. Of course." I took a few steps toward the stairs and turned again. "If anyone were to have a shot at changing my mind, it definitely wouldn't be someone who built half of our friendship on a lie. Don't call me, Matt. I'm done. And tell Ryder I don't want to talk to him, either." Then I climbed the steps toward my waiting Jeep, feeling my heart break just a little more when he didn't call after me.

Chapter 26

I IGNORED THE CHIRP OF my phone and pulled my textbook closer, trying to focus on the tiny print that swam like punch-drunk tadpoles all over the page. Leave it to the biggest book to have the smallest text. I fingered the slick page of my copy of *Political Theory and Art: The Rise and Fall of Communist Rule Traced Through Print Media.* At some point, my Art and Political Theory class had sounded like a good idea. As much as it perturbed me to hear people say the same thing about other art genres, I had to admit that one week of this class had firmly established that if you've seen one Communist propaganda poster, you've seen them all. After six weeks, I was heartily sick of the grim and urgent imagery shouted in bloodred and black Cyrillic letters.

When my cell chirped again I eyeballed it, half-tempted to answer. I considered my options: another cozy hour with political propaganda or, knowing it was either my mom or my sisters calling me on a Saturday night, an hour discussing my nonexistent social life with one of them. I chose the textbook.

I willed the squiggles to take on intelligible shapes, determined to complete the assigned reading before my seminar on Monday, but my cell phone trumpeted the arrival of a text. Flipping it open, I saw that it was from Dave. *Call me immediately. Big news.* Dave was a much easier choice over my textbook. I called him right back, glad to have a break that didn't involve any nagging from my mom.

"Hey," he barked when he answered.

"Hey, yourself," I replied. "What's the big emergency?"

"No emergency," he said. "I just had something to tell you."

Even though Dave and I had spoken only twice since I'd left Huntington Beach two days early for my return trip to school, my regular phone conversations with Celia were enough to figure out his news.

"Can it wait?" I teased him. "I have to wash my hair and do my nails and stuff."

"For all those dates you don't go on?"

"Hey!"

He snorted. "Celia spills your business to me too, you know."

"I did not know," I grumbled. Note to self: tell Celia the family gossip channel was one-way. I was set to receive, not broadcast.

"So, I guess I'm engaged."

"You *guess?*" I asked at the same time he yelped.

"I'm engaged! I'm engaged! Don't hit me again!" he said to someone on his end of the line.

"Is Laurel with you?" I asked, doing some of my own guessing.

"Yeah. I think I said it wrong when I told you. I'm going to try it again." He cleared his throat. "I'm engaged. Yeehaw! Hold on," he said. He came back on a moment later. "Laurel wants me to tell you that you're the first person we told besides our immediate family. She says to tell you thank you for introducing us."

"Tell her she's very welcome. And Dave?"

"Yeah?"

"She's awesome. Congratulations—I'm really happy for you. When are you getting married?"

"Over Laurel's spring break," he said. "I think it's the last weekend in March or something like that. You can come, right?"

"I'm not sure," I said. "You're getting married in the Newport temple, right?"

"Uh, Los Angeles, actually. They're set up better for serving the deaf. Anyway, both of our parents were sealed there, so it works out kind of cool. You have to come, Ash. You're the whole reason we're even getting married."

"Hardly," I said. "You're getting married because you're both great people who deserve each other. But yes," I promised. "I'll find a way to be there even if I'm just in and out in one day."

"Cool," he said. "We have to call some more people. Love you, cuz."

"You too," I said and put down my phone.

I sat back in my chair and smiled, happy for them. They suited each other perfectly. This called for a celebration. I headed to the kitchen to forage for chocolate. The house was quiet, the living room dark as I passed through. Not so unusual for a Saturday night in a house of single girls. Even quiet Emmy went on more dates than I did. It wasn't hard to have more dates than none.

I busted out my emergency stash of Dove chocolate from behind a jar of wheat germ I had bought in an ill-advised attempt at a long-forgotten recipe. The jar provided perfect camouflage, though. Even my most PMS-afflicted roommates never checked behind the wheat germ for chocolate. I grabbed the whole bag and then wandered to the couch to enjoy my treat, flipping on a lamp for some light and fumbling in the folds of the slipcover for the remote.

Victorious, I flopped down and stretched between the sofa arms, enjoying the rare luxury of having the couch and TV all to myself. I cruised through the channels, unwrapping a second piece of chocolate and settling on one of my mom's favorite programs, *Antiques Roadshow*. I found the drama of watching people get their grandmother's ugly ceramic hen appraised only to discover it was worth enough to fund Junior's next semester at college strangely addictive.

When the program broke to do some local-color piece on the history of wooden duck decoys, I muted the sound. Smiling, I opened another chocolate and raised it in silent salute to my cousin and Laurel. I wasn't surprised to hear they were marrying, although it was kind of quick. Still, if anyone could make it work, Laurel could. It made me laugh to think that her initial shyness hid such a determined woman. A girl after my own heart. I couldn't blame Dave for falling for her fast. Besides, she was almost done with her degree in deaf education, and if they had kids soon, when Dave was studying late at the college library or working a part-time job to hold up his end of things, Laurel might really like having a little baby to keep her company.

I glanced around at my unnaturally quiet house. Maybe Laurel was on to something.

I grabbed the remote again, annoyed at my wandering thoughts. I found myself in the neighborhood of longing and regret too often lately. I flipped through channels, searching for a new distraction.

Since I'd spent every Saturday since school started doing much the same thing, I knew I probably wouldn't find anything to watch, but there was nothing else to do. For the first several weeks of the semester, my roommates had invited me to do all kinds of things, but I guess since I never accepted, they'd given up. Now, here I was, halfway through October, with no one to share in my little celebration.

I put the fourth piece of chocolate down. I didn't want it anymore. KBYU was airing an old football game and I left the station on, scowling. I hated this feeling. This year was supposed to be about total immersion in my coursework. I was supposed to be so hardcore that nothing existed except for school and work. But my classes weren't as hard as I had expected now that I understood my professors' requirements, and the papers I graded for my TA job were pretty mindless.

I watched the quarterback for the other team pull back and launch a doozy of a pass, but just when it looked bad for the Cougars, one of their linemen intercepted it and started running it back the other way. At least that guy knew which way to go. I couldn't say the same for myself.

I had never felt so much like I was spinning my wheels. No matter how much I studied or how many papers I graded, there was an emptiness that gnawed at me in a semester that should have felt full to bursting. I didn't even know who to call for advice or perspective. Every female in my life would come up with the same answer to the problem.

Matt Gibson.

Nearly two months had gone by and he'd taken me at my word; I hadn't heard from him, and that's what I wanted. And yet, there were a couple of unexplained incidents that made me wonder . . . Once, my ringing doorbell had rustled me out of bed to find a pimply teenager standing on the front porch. He wore a tee shirt from a local burger joint and held a soda cup and a greasy brown paper bag.

"This is for Ashley Barrett," he said.

When I explained that I hadn't ordered anything, he shrugged. "I got a twenty dollar tip to drop this to you after the end of my shift," he said, and shoved the food at me before climbing back into his beat-up Toyota.

Two weeks ago, after an early October cold snap, I found a small box on my porch. A sky blue cable-knit cap and matching knit scarf sat inside. My mother and sisters all denied any knowledge of it. Convincingly. In fact, my mother had suggested that maybe it was Matt's doing, and even though I gave the most withering scoff I could muster, she was adamant. I didn't argue because I'd learned very quickly to deflect conversations about him.

Unfortunately, Aunt Trudy had tattled about Matt to my mom, who then passed it on to my sisters, and I couldn't have a conversation with any of them without them singing his praises. It didn't matter that they had never met him. Apparently, Trudy had been exceptionally convincing in painting him as The Perfect Guy, with Celia backing her up in a hallelujah chorus.

I scowled again. I had expected Celia to take my side when I got home from meeting "Ryder" and gritted out the story of his betrayal through clenched teeth, all the while stripping my clothes from closet hangers and dresser drawers, desperate to pack and leave Matt far behind me. Instead of sympathizing, Celia had defended Matt.

"You're hardheaded," she said. "I don't really see how you left him a choice. I think he should get credit for working so hard to get to know you."

She thought *he* should get *credit?* My mother was worse, deeming it romantic. And the crazy family grapevine had gone into full effect with Louisa telling Celia about Matt's comings and goings, who then passed the information on to my mom, who then beat me over the head with it.

That's how I knew he'd arrived in Utah about two weeks after me and that the new Board Shack was opening in the Riverwoods shopping center near the mouth of Provo Canyon. I had no reason to go there and if it weren't for my mother's persistent updates, I'd be in blissful ignorance. Instead . . .

Instead I dealt with a plague of intrusive thoughts, whispers of ideas that crept in when I was falling asleep or when my roommates abandoned me to my studies on a Saturday night and the house was too quiet. Ideas that nudged me to drive by and see the shop, to see if maybe I could catch a glimpse of him when I did. I glanced at the time on the cable box. 7:20. Did he work this late on a Saturday? Or was he out playing?

I dropped my head back against the sofa in disgust. As much as I resisted those little rabbit trails my brain wanted to follow, I ended up thinking about Matt several times a day. Where that used to cause a giddy flutter, now I felt hollow. If I passed the Jamba Juice in the student center and Matt's preferred drink jumped easily to mind, then I squished the memory and the pang that came with it. When I walked past the Tanner building and I remembered his joke that BYU's business school was nice if you couldn't get into Pepperdine, I changed directions and took a long-cut to meet my study group. When a Jack Johnson song came on the radio and transported me back to Huntington Beach and one of our sunset surfs, I stabbed the button viciously to change the station. There would be no more Jack Johnson in my car. Ever. And that made me mad at Matt again.

It was exhausting to miss him so much.

I pointed the remote at the TV and stabbed the volume control until it was loud, verging on uncomfortable. I wasn't keeping busy enough, was all. I needed more to do.

Maybe it was time to revisit The List. The last time I had done anything on the same planet as fun was when I was working on The List. I would not let Matt suck the fun out of one more thing for me. It was time to shake him off for good.

I hopped up and raced to my room, anxious to find my scriptures. I shuffled around piles of clothes trying to remember where I'd slung my tote after my Old Testament class on Wednesday morning. After nearly two minutes of fruitless searching in my tiny room, I realized it didn't matter. I had forgotten for a moment that The List had been missing since the early summer when Megan bumped my desk and sent all my papers flying.

I sat on my bed and thought for a minute, then remembered I had rewritten it on my laptop. I found it in the living room and pulled The List up. I began working through it to cross off more stuff. On the first pass, I hit everything I had completed prior to Huntington Beach, grinning at some of the memories. Number eighteen, take a cruise, had been a comedy of errors. Juliana and Grady had paid my way on their cut-rate Mexican Riviera cruise in exchange for me watching their kids in the evening. Bad shrimp from the buffet had laid me out for the first three days, which meant that they trundled the baby crib into my room, tucked two-year-old Trent and Tyler under my arms on the bed, and made their merry way to the theater every night for the show while I groaned for three hours and my nephews patted my head sympathetically until we fell asleep.

I was reliving the thrills and spills of number eleven, my black-diamond trail snowboarding adventure, when a roar from the TV snagged my attention. The rerun game was over and BYU students were flooding the field, swamping the football players and carrying the offensive line toward the end zone in a human tidal wave of joy. I watched the happy, cheering crowd as credits scrolled across the bottom of the page.

I flipped to a music video channel and left it on a commercial there instead. Tuning out the flashing yellow letters and shouts to get my next living room set from the largest dealer West of the Mississippi, I returned to The List to cross off my newest items and decide on my next adventure. Number three, sing karaoke, was done. Pitifully attempted in the ward activity and completed as a bid to rescue Matt in a room full of strangers, it was nonetheless *finito*. Number four, read the standard works, was close. I signed up to audit the second half of an Old Testament course so I could finish what I started in Sister Powers's class. I would be done by December, when the semester ended.

Number eight, learn to make sushi. Done, with the help of Mr. Nobu and another ward activity. I crossed that one off too. Number ten, the triathlon, I'd finished with Matt and the Fountain Valley Ward. I might have been a hair shy of losing my carb-loaded breakfast on the church lawn after the 5K run, but I did it. Numbers thirteen, seventeen, and nineteen: learn to surf, have a summer fling, and sky-dive were also check, check, and check. Thanks to Matt.

I looked back over The List, my mind racing. I had started the summer with eleven items left to finish and now I only had four, including finishing the Old Testament. Of the seven items I had completed since May, Matt had been directly involved in all of them. Feeling stunned, I double checked the math. Besides finishing the standard works, I had only "get a master's degree," "learn to play the guitar," and "be an extra in a movie" still outstanding. Even more dizzying were two separate conversations I could remember having with

Matt where he had casually suggested activities or connections that would make the latter two of those things possible.

I didn't believe in these kinds of coincidences.

How had I missed the relationship between all these items getting done and Matt somehow being involved? It was deliberate on his part, I was sure. But how did he know? *How did he know what was on my list?*

I scooped up my cell phone and dialed Celia. She answered, giggling as she said hello.

"It's Ash."

"I know. Did my brother call you?"

"Yeah, great news. Hey, did you tell Matt Gibson about The List?"

"Wait, what?"

"The List, Celia. Did you tell Matt about it this summer?" I tried not to sound impatient but I felt half crazy.

"No. Of course not. Why?"

"Because he knows about it."

"He does? How do you know? Are you guys talking again?" she asked, sounding excited about the possibility.

"No! I know because there's all these—" I stopped and took a deep breath. "Never mind. You're sure you didn't tell him?"

"I said I didn't. But Ashley, what about Ryder? You told him about The List."

"Yeah, I did tell Ryder stuff, but only that there was a list, and a few of the things on it. There's stuff that Matt knew about that Ryder never did. I don't understand."

"Well, I don't have an answer for you."

I stared unseeing at the television screen, looking past another flashing advertisement as if the answer to this mystery lay buried behind it in the cathode ray tubes of my roommate's hand-me-down set. "I think only Matt is going to know the answer," Celia ventured tentatively. She'd learned to tread any ground related to him *very* carefully.

"Forget it. I don't even know how to get in touch with him," I said. "I deleted every piece of contact information I have for him."

"Maybe you could contact his Ryder profile," she suggested.

I could tell she was waiting for me to snap at her, but I just sighed. "I would, except that in a moment of total lameness, I looked it up a month ago, and he's deleted his account."

"Okay, so that should make you feel good, right?"

"It would have been good if he did it before he ever contacted me through it."

"I'm not going there with you again," Celia said. "I can get his number from Louisa if you want to ask him about it."

"No," I said. "I think I've got it figured out."

On the screen in front of me, a whiplash-quick photo montage of extreme snowboarding shots had built to some kind of digital effect where the picture exploded. It reassembled itself into an ad for the Board Shack, complete with a phone number and address and a caption blaring the grand opening the following Saturday.

Chapter 27

I GRABBED MY KEYS AND a sweatshirt, shoved my feet into my flip-flops, and yanked the door open just as my startled roommate Emmy reached for the knob.

"Oh!" she squeaked.

"Sorry," I said. "Didn't mean to scare you." I moved aside to let her pass.

"You're going out?" she asked, surprised.

"Yeah. I know, big shock, right?"

"Yes. I mean no!" She gestured at my outfit. "Um, kind of."

The sweatshirt I threw on had a red paisley design and big surf logo on the back. It looked a little conspicuous on top of my blue plaid BYU flannel drawstring pajama bottoms. I shrugged. "It's okay. I'm not trying to impress anyone."

"Okay, but your hair . . ."

I reached up to feel the wild mess that had formed after I'd shoved my fingers through it several times while I studied. I dug inside of my purse and fished out an elastic. "Thanks," I said, wrangling my hair back into a ponytail.

"No problem," she called as I closed the door behind me and stormed to the Jeep.

By the time I hit University Avenue, I was seething. Fury that Matt's double-dealing hadn't ended with the Ryder deception fueled me, and I whipped through the turn leading into the shopping center and maintained a barely contained crawl through the crowd of diners milling about and window shopping. I had no idea where the Board Shack was, but I was determined to find it and figure out how

Matt had stolen The List. Frustrated, I steered toward the back of the complex where the larger retailers were, looking for a place to turn around.

There it was. A huge, two-story building with shiny new display windows loomed in front of me, its size making its sign, The Shack, either a nice touch of irony or the biggest misnomer ever. Other than the external security lights, it looked dark and vacant. I pulled into one of the empty spots in front and stared at it, my sails slightly deflated.

I glanced at the dashboard clock. I hadn't really thought through my plan, but if I had, maybe it would have occurred to me to wonder if Matt would even be at work at eight thirty on a Saturday night. In Provo. Where there were lots of single girls. That he was free to date.

Not that I cared.

I climbed out of the Jeep, curious now that I was here. A huge banner hung over the main doors announcing, Grand Opening Soon! The window on the left showed two mannequins in snow-boarding gear. The female wore a blue knit cap and scarf identical to the ones that had shown up on my porch two weeks before.

As I passed the front doors to check out the other window, a light winked on inside, startling a jump out of me. Two figures bustled around, guys in work clothes. I tugged at the door and it glided open. Stoking my anger again, I strode in. The two guys both looked up from their clipboard to stare.

Before either of them could speak, I snapped, "Is Matt Gibson here?"

One of them nodded and pointed toward the motionless escalator in the center of the store. A pair of sneakers at the end of denim-clad legs was descending it like a set of stairs. I felt my stomach flip, knowing it was him.

"Jeff, I need the layout plan for the men's—" he called, but broke off when he saw me standing there. He stopped halfway down, and the still escalator gave the whole scene the uncanny sense of a frozen tableau.

"Ashley," he said quietly. "It's good to see you."

"Do you have my list?" I asked.

He looked wary and took the last steps down to ground level.

"What makes you think I have it?" he asked, his voice soft and even.

"Karaoke? Sushi? The triathlon? I never told Ryder about that stuff. You, I mean. Are you going to tell me it's a coincidence that you knew about them?"

He shoved his hands in his pockets. "No."

I waited. His workers looked on, fascinated.

He stepped closer and took my arm, steering me back toward the escalator. "Why are you here, Ashley?" he asked, his voice low.

"Where are you taking me?" I demanded, pulling my arm free.

"I asked first."

"No, I did. Let me remind you of the question. Do you have my list?"

"Let's take this upstairs. My guys need to work," he added, his voice raised to cue his employees. They bent their heads over their clipboard again and pretended to ignore the unfolding drama.

"Fine," I said and began marching up the escalator steps. I got to the top and made it a few yards onto the floor before I realized I didn't know where to go. It was a maze of empty fixtures and open boxes full of clothes. Matt hung back at the escalator, watching me in amusement.

"What?" I snapped.

"Nothing. It's just nice to see you haven't changed."

"It hasn't even been two months," I said. "Were you expecting a personality transplant?"

He walked over to finger a wayward curl bouncing near my cheek. "Of course not. I wasn't expecting you at all. But I love that you're still marching around, bossing people around."

"I'm not bossy." I knocked his hand away. "Stop doing that."

"No." He grinned. "Not bossy at all."

"I'm glad you find this all so stinking hilarious, Matt, but I don't. I want The List."

He held my gaze for several seconds, testing me, checking for something. I refused to look away. I don't know what he found, but with a slight nod, he broke eye contact and reached into his back pocket for his wallet. He slid out a worn piece of notebook paper, silently handing it to me.

I unfolded it to find my original list, unchanged except for the new crease marks it had earned in his wallet. I stared at it blankly.

"How did you get this?" I asked, needing the details.

"You dropped it back in June, at Institute. It was in a pile of papers you asked me to throw away. I noticed just before I was about to toss it out. I thought you might need it so I took a closer look and figured out what it was."

"You've had this since June? Why didn't you tell me? Why didn't you give it back to me?"

He sighed and wandered to the rail overlooking the first floor, resting his arms on it. "Because I'm selfish."

I was quiet for a minute, trying to figure out how I felt about Matt carrying my list around with him for almost five months, even after I told him I was done with him.

"What do you mean?" I finally asked.

"I mean when I realized what I had fished out of your garbage pile, all I could think was that it might come in handy and I needed to hold on to it."

"Come in handy how? We barely knew each other at that point. Why would a list entitled '25 Things to Do Before I Get Married' help you?"

"You didn't come here to forgive me or give me another chance, did you?" he asked, sounding sad.

"No. I came to figure out why all seven things I crossed off The List this summer were connected to you. I know how, but I don't know why. Just answer the question and I'll leave you to your work," I said gesturing at the hundreds of unopened boxes piled around us.

"It's because of the stingray," he said.

"The *stingray*?" Whatever I had expected, it wasn't that.

"I guess it would be more accurate to say it's because of the first time I saw you on that surfboard. I couldn't believe you'd just been nailed by a stingray and were out in the water, ready to give it a try again. I don't know anyone else who would do that. I was already curious about you, but that day when I watched you take fall after fall off your board and get back up . . ." He turned to face me. "I knew you were something special, Ashley. And I knew I'd do almost anything to find out more."

"But—" He held up his hand.

"Let me finish," he said. I snapped my mouth closed.

"You kept a distance right from the very first time I talked to you at the linger longer," he said. "It was always there. You had this arm's-length thing going on at all times, and it seemed like every time I dipped beneath the surface with you that first night after our barbecue, you pushed me away with a joke or something."

"I didn't—"

"Ashley, seriously, stop. I need to get this out now before I lose my nerve."

I shut up, surprised.

"I'm not going to even ask you what you think about love at first sight," he said. "I already know the answer. A few months ago, I would have said it was bogus too. I don't know if what I felt for you was love at first sight or not, but by the end of that first night in Laguna, I knew you were exactly what I've been looking for."

I didn't dare interrupt him. He walked over to a pile of boxes and dug through it, straightening when he held a familiar blue cap and scarf.

"Recognize this?"

I swallowed and nodded.

"I have never known anyone as independent as you," he said. "And for some reason, I'm overcome with this urge to take care of you, anyway, to make sure you have everything you need." He dropped the set back in the box. "You make it really hard."

He made his way back to me and brushed the same errant curl out of my face again. "I knew you were only in HB for the summer, Ashley. I figured it would be a good place to start something since I would be up here all winter to keep it going. You made it clear you wanted none of that, and there's a certain stubbornness about you that told me if I pushed, you'd push back. I figured the only shot I had was removing your obstacles quietly one by one. And then you literally put your list in my hands." He brushed it with his fingertips. I didn't jerk it away. "I thought maybe it was divine intervention or something," he said, smiling. "Now I can see how stupid that is, but in the moment, I figured fate had thrown me a lifeline."

"We don't believe in fate," I mumbled, dazed.

"Then it must have been an answer to a prayer," he said. "I'm tired of talking about this, so I'm going to give you the honesty I owed you all along. I already lost you on the beach, so I don't really have anything left to lose."

He framed my face in his hands and The List fluttered to the floor unnoticed.

"I love you, Ashley Barrett. I love every pigheaded inch of you. I love your sense of adventure, your loyalty to your family, your intelligence, your spirit, your testimony. I fell in love with you somewhere between your Star Wars Band-Aid and your defense of that kid's weak rhymes on Laguna Beach. I figured it out when it ate me up inside every time you ignored one of my phone calls this summer and chatted with Ryder for hours instead. I wanted you to want all of me, not just the nonthreatening friend side of me."

He pressed his forehead against mine and closed his eyes. "More than anything, I'm so sorry I disappointed you. I never meant to hurt or embarrass you, and I'd give anything to do it over again, to rewind the summer and pick a point to say, 'I don't agree to your terms and I'm coming after you, anyway.' I should have fought for you openly. Please know that all those activities I begged Louisa to set up for— karaoke and sushi, all those other items I knocked out on your list—"

He broke off and stepped back, replacing his hands in his pockets. "I did it because I wanted a shot with you, and it's what ended up costing me any chance at all. I thought doing those things would make you happy. I realize it was arrogant. I hope you can forgive me, Ashley, or I'll never forgive myself."

His eyes were bright with feeling and he stayed very still, like he was afraid I would skitter away if he made any sudden movements.

I didn't know what to say. Stepping hesitantly toward him, I tried to find words to explain the crazy jumble of feelings rioting inside me. *He loves me,* I thought. *He's everything I never knew I wanted, and he's putting everything on the line for me.* When only a few inches separated us, I reached up to touch his mouth, feeling the slight increase in his breath against my fingertips. The anger that fueled my drive over had evaporated when The List slipped from my fingers, and all the loneliness I'd denied feeling from the moment I left him on the beach washed away in a tide of wild, exultant joy.

He still said nothing, but his eyes darkened, the green deepening with need and hope at whatever he read in my face. The rush of emotion pushed higher and harder as he slowly lowered his mouth to mine. *This is it, Ashley. This is worth giving up the last of your goals. Two inches forward and you can have Matt forever.*

I heard the snick of metal as a door somewhere near the back of the store opened. "Matt, where's the layout for men's winter gear?" a female voice asked. I leaped back. A moment later, Louisa rounded the stack of boxes and stopped in surprise.

"Ashley! What are you doing here? Is it because of the hat? I told Matt it was a stupid idea and that he should call instead, but I guess he was right." She gave him an affectionate slug on the arm, but his lack of response wiped the smile off her face. "You fixed it, didn't you, Matt? You told her everything?"

"I'm sorry. I can't do this." I jerked back a few more steps, suddenly terrified of the whirlpool of emotions that had nearly sucked me into Matt's vortex. "I can't do this," I said to him again, pleading with him to understand something I couldn't. "I don't see you for two months, and it still only takes you two minutes to convince me to drop everything again."

He didn't say anything. Sensing I was ready to run, Louisa said, "Wait. I know this is none of my business, but Matt showed me The List so I could help him set some of the stuff up. All you have left is guitar lessons and being a movie extra. It's not that big a deal, right? And Matt would totally support you in getting a master's degree. You guys can work this out. I know you can."

"It doesn't work that way with Matt." I directed my gaze toward him, dragging my eyes to meet his despite the hurt I saw brimming there. "I know you say you respect what I want and that you're a willing sidekick, but in one summer, you had me backing down from a life plan I've followed for six years like it was nothing. I can't risk some unintentional diversion from my education that makes me resent you later."

"But Matt isn't like that!" Louisa protested and would have continued until Matt shook his head.

"I want you to be happy, Ashley," he said, looking as unhappy as I'd ever seen him.

"It's good to see you, Louisa," I said, then burst into tears and fled to the escalator, ignoring Matt's distressed call behind me.

Chapter 28

Once, when I was six, I had a really bad week. I had the chicken pox and a stomach flu, and I was an itchy, feverish, puketastic mess. Until now, that had always stood as my Worst Week Ever.

Matt's bombshell on Saturday night had set off a record-breaking week of awfulness, but all the symptoms were internal. He seemed to be inside my head and under my skin and everywhere at once. The ad blitz The Board Shack ran made him impossible to ignore. I dove into Communist art propaganda with single-minded dedication, tore through my stacks of grading so fast I offered to take some off the other teaching assistant's hands just to stay busy, and I still couldn't crowd out thoughts of Matt.

I was desperate to shake them, to quiet the echoes of his confession, to drown out the pain I saw in his eyes before I took off. Nights were the worst. My best defenses wavered in the moments before sleep, and then I would replay the whole scene in my head, struggling with fears that bled into my dreams. I woke up tired and emotionally spent before the day began.

I dragged myself out of my last class on Wednesday, exhausted from four nights of restless sleep. As I trudged down Maeser hill toward home, the crisp October breeze whipped a loose copy of the campus newspaper into my path and plastered it across my chest. I peeled it off and bit back a squeal of frustration when I saw the full-page ad on the back. The Board Shack Opens This Saturday!!! the huge bold type screamed.

That was it! I could not take one more Matt intrusion into my life. It felt like he and his store had invaded every corner of Provo.

Every time I tried to take a breath and sort through my thoughts, shore up my conviction that being with him meant losing myself, the radio would blare an invitation to the opening and I found myself thinking, *Stop fighting. Just admit how you feel, and you won't have to run away anymore.*

"No!" I said firmly, earning a startled glance from a student groundskeeper raking up leaves.

When my phone shrilled, I grabbed it, grateful for the distraction.

"Yeah?" I growled.

"Ash?" It was Juliana, sounding out of breath.

"Yeah. What's wrong?" I asked.

"Oh, nothing! I was doing my ab exercise DVD and Sadie decided to make it extra challenging by bouncing on my stomach between every crunch," she said and laughed.

"Ouch." I winced. She laughed again.

"What's up?" I asked.

"Nothing, really. I was just thinking you might need a niece and nephew fix, so I thought maybe you could swing by to see us tonight."

"At approximately dinner time?" I bargained.

"Of course."

"Sure. I'd love to see the kids."

"Good. And now that Grady's been released from the bishopric, he'll actually be home too."

"Great. I'll be there in an hour or two," I promised.

We hung up and I picked up my pace toward home. I had one incredibly dry critical theory article to annotate and then I'd be on the road to Juliana's. Since she lived in Herriman, I saw her more often than Leila, who was all the way up in Ogden. This was just what I needed. Nothing could renew my determination to avoid marriage faster than a visit with my one of my sisters and her wild brood of kids. At home, I flew through the assigned reading, then grabbed a basket of dirty clothes to wash and pointed my Jeep toward Juliana's house. It was time to grow a new backbone in the fertile soil of her crazy life.

* * *

Grady pushed away from the dining room table with a groan. "Awesome as usual, wife."

"Thanks, husband," Juliana grinned, then caught a chicken nugget flying past her head without blinking. She set it back on Sadie's high chair tray. Her daughter grinned and hefted another nugget like she was testing its aerodynamic properties.

"Oh, no you don't," Juliana chided, whisking it out of her grasp. She shoved a small bowl of green beans toward her youngest daughter and cautioned, "Eat your veggies and don't throw any more nuggets or you don't get to play with Aunt Smash when everyone else is done."

Sadie obediently popped a bean in her mouth and chewed. "I play," she said proudly, then opened her jaw to display the last traces of bean bits.

"It's a start." Grady laughed.

Juliana shook her head and stood, grabbing up her empty plate. When she reached for mine too, Grady hopped up and waved her away. "I'll get it. You girls go visit while I finish up dinner with the kids."

"Thanks," she said, then dropped a kiss on his cheek and gestured for me to follow her out to the back porch swing.

Even though there was more than a week until the fall time change, the days were getting shorter and dusk blanketed their small backyard. A brightly painted jungle gym and an assortment of plastic toys interrupted the smooth expanse of lawn. Beyond her children's belongings, the yard lacked any distinct personality. I bet if I could see through the vinyl fencing to her neighbors' yards, I would see the same cookie-cutter rectangle of fresh sod and newly poured concrete.

My sister leaned back in the swing, lazily pushing against the deck to set us in motion. "I can't wait until spring when I get to put in some flower beds," she said.

"Won't the kids tear them up?" I asked.

"Maybe. But if they do, it'll probably be because they're trying to make me a bouquet. Besides, threats against their lives work pretty well."

"And if threats don't work?"

"Then I cut them off from Nickelodeon. That's a sure bet."

I laughed. "I can't believe how big they've gotten. It's not like I don't see them all the time."

She slid a sideways glance at me. "You haven't been here since school started. That's a long time to grow at their age."

"Are you trying to make me feel guilty?"

"Yes." She nudged me. "Is it working?"

"Yes." We shared a smile and drifted some more.

"Why haven't you been around?" Juliana asked after a few quiet minutes passed.

I shrugged. "Busy with school, I guess."

"It's that bad, huh?"

"No." I dropped my head back against the swing. "I got sick of hearing about Matt. You're as bad as Leila and Mom," I grumbled.

"Fair enough," she said. "But Aunt Trudy was so upset when you took off early like that, and Celia said it was because of Matt. We thought finally someone had beaten your list. It was an exciting moment for us. I guess I know better than to think anyone can be talked in or out of love," she said.

"Who said anything about love?"

"You didn't have to," she smiled. "That's the only thing that could make you run like that."

I gaped at her, trying to figure out when I had become so transparent, when the patio door flew open and Trent and Ty tumbled out. Both of them raced for me, clamoring to be lifted up. I laughed and hauled Ty into my lap, burying my nose in his neck and inhaling his sweet, little boy smell. He patted my cheek a couple of times and then wiggled his way down, racing after his twin brother, who had changed course for the jungle gym.

"You're happy," I said.

"Right now? Sure," Juliana replied, slightly nonplussed.

"No. You're happy all the time. You have food flying across the dinner table every night, children bouncing and crawling all over you the second you quit moving, a house barely big enough to fit all of you, and you're happy."

Juliana stopped the swing. "I've always been happy. Even when we were squished into a two-bedroom apartment and I had to feed us all on sixty dollars a week. It's nice that we can afford our own home, even if it's small, but I'm not happier here than I was two years ago while we were saving up. I just don't worry about disturbing any downstairs neighbors anymore." She flashed another grin as Trent let out a Tarzan yell. "That alone is worth a mortgage."

"Leila isn't happy," I said. "She's stressed all the time."

It was Juliana's turn to shrug. "That's Leila. She takes after Mom. She's so concerned about being the perfect wife and mother that she forgets to live in the moment."

"She shouldn't have gotten married so young," I said.

"It's none of our business when she got married," Juliana said. "And I hate to judge, but I don't think she dated enough before picking a husband. To tell you the truth, though I don't think it would have mattered *when* she got married. She's a stress case, regardless of circumstance. I'm telling you, she's just like Mom."

"You're not," I said.

"Sure I am, sometimes. But I pace myself so I only get wound up for really big crises."

I thought about that, about how the chaos in each of my sisters' lives affected them so differently.

"You're more like me, you know," she said after a while. "You handle your business and move on."

"I guess."

"I *know.* And here's something else I know. If you'd gotten married when you were twenty like I did, you would have been fine too. Maybe your life would have been a little more hectic, but you would have been happy."

I didn't say anything.

"Why are you really here tonight?" she asked. "It's not for my world-famous potato and cornflake casserole."

I grimaced. "Honestly? I thought it would remind me why I don't want to get married right now."

"And? Did it?"

I glanced out at the yard where her two adorable boys gamboled and played, now pirating boats on the imaginary high seas. Children's laughter floated over the fence from another yard, and the sound of Grady singing a silly song to Sadie while he washed the dishes drifted out of the kitchen window.

I turned back to Juliana.

"No. This is really nice, and it stinks."

She laughed. "You're looking at everything with slightly new eyes, aren't you?"

I nodded.

"Matt goggles?" she guessed.

I spared another grimace, this one laced with real pain.

"What's the problem?" she prodded. "Is he demanding that you abandon The List for him?"

I shook my head. "No. In fact, he went out of his way to help me cross off as many things as he could this summer. I only just figured that out."

"He sounds as good as Aunt Trudy made him out to be. And if he loves you, then I don't need to know anything else about his judgment."

I blushed.

"Ashley?" She leaned forward to study my face. "What aren't you telling me?"

"Uh, he does. Love me. At least, he did on Saturday night. Maybe he doesn't now, though."

Her eyebrow crept up. "Why not?"

"Because he said, 'I love you,' and I sort of ran away. Again."

"Ah." She tickled the back of my hand. "Did you slap him and yell, 'I hate you!' before you took off?"

"I didn't say anything, really. Just something lame about not being able to handle it, and then I left."

"And why can't you handle it?" she asked. "I've never seen you confront anything you couldn't handle."

"This feels different," I said.

"Why?"

"Because it matters," I whispered, tearing up. "I think I screwed up, Juli. Big time."

"Do you love him?"

I swallowed and nodded. "I think it's too late, though. I've communicated to him every way I know how that stupid stuff like learning to play the guitar is more important than him, and I walked out on him when he said he loved me. How do I make up for that?" I asked, miserable.

"What about your master's?" she asked. "Is he more important than that?"

I nodded. "Yes, but it won't come to that. He'd never want me to give that up."

"What if you got married and had kids?" She cocked her head and watched me with a small smile, her foot moving the swing gently. "What happens to your master's, then?"

"You're getting yours," I said.

"Yeah, I am." She grinned.

"So that was kind of a bogus excuse, I guess."

"Good guess."

"Matt doesn't have a very big ego," I said. "But I'm pretty sure I've shredded it. And I have no idea how to make it better."

"You can start with 'I'm sorry.'"

"It doesn't seem like enough," I said. "You didn't see his face when I walked out on him. After everything I've put him through, I can't waltz back in with just a 'sorry.'"

"I think you're underestimating him. Again," she said and silenced my protest with a pointed look. "But let's say you're right. You screwed up big, you need a big gesture to fix it. What are you going to do?"

"I don't know," I said. But for the first time, I felt the absence of fear weighing me down, a weight I realized I'd been carrying since August when I walked away from Matt and towed the fear after me.

"Think big," Juliana ordered me. "I have a feeling he's worth it."

Chapter 29

I WAS ABOUT TO DECORATE the newly asphalted parking lot in front of The Board Shack with my Cap'n Crunch from breakfast. I pressed a hand against my stomach but my insides still bucked and twisted. I couldn't believe no one had stopped to demand what was wrong with me, but despite the throng surging around the portable stage in the parking lot, no one seemed to notice me standing off to the side with a death grip on my plastic water bottle.

I watched the band setting up, my nerves winding tighter and tighter with each squeal of the amplifiers from their sound check. The front doors of the store whooshed open, and Matt stepped out and over the giant red ribbon in front of him. I dove behind a tall speaker before he could see me. I peeked around the edge and saw him talking to Kenny, the lead singer of Picture This, a popular local band that Louisa had booked for the opening. I knew that because when I contacted the band after seeing their name plastered all over the grand opening fliers, Kenny told me.

". . . ready . . . check is done . . ." Kenny's words drifted back to me. My stomach flipped again. Matt nodded and gestured for Louisa, then jumped down from the stage. She bounded up wearing a fitted purple tee shirt with the store logo across the chest.

"What's up, Provo!" she called into the mike, earning appreciative catcalls from the single guys scoring free hot dogs at the nearby barbecue stand.

"Thanks for coming out on this gorgeous Saturday morning! We are so stoked to open our very first Utah location of The Board Shack! Without further ado, co-owner Matt Gibson will cut the ribbon so you can officially shop our awesome board collection!"

I peeked farther around the speaker to catch a glimpse of Matt looking pleased and a little self-conscious as he snipped the ceremonial ribbon with a pair of oversized scissors. Customers streamed through the doors while he shook hands and chatted with different people who stopped to congratulate him. Louisa replaced the microphone then nodded at Kenny, who hollered, "1-2-3-4!" and dove into a hard-driving Rolling Stones cover with the band.

I felt my chest squeezing tight, sure I was about to pass out from a lack of oxygen. My heart was pounding so hard it nearly drowned out the thumping bass of the kick drum. All too soon, the final notes of the song wound down and Kenny gestured for me to come up.

I climbed on stage, not daring to look out at the crowd, which had erupted into good-natured applause at the song's conclusion.

"You ready?" he asked, away from the mike.

I nodded.

He looked concerned. "Are you sure?"

I mustered a shaky smile and nodded again.

"Thank you, guys!" he shouted. "We love the Provo crowd!"

They sent up their own approving cheer.

"I know a lot of you have heard us play before, but we've got a little surprise for our fans today," he said. "You know we like to keep it interesting, so we've got a guest joining us for a special solo. Give it up for Ashley Barrett!"

More friendly applause greeted me as I took the microphone, and the crowd suddenly parted to admit Louisa to the front, where she stared at me, her jaw hanging down. I offered her a nervous smile, and then the music started.

"Does he love me, I want to know," I began, my voice wobbling all over the place. I saw a few people shifting uncomfortably at the front of the crowd, but I barreled through it. "How can I tell if he loves me so?" More shifting. I closed my eyes and belted out the lyrics, hoping Matt was still outside so he could hear me, or that Louisa would go get him. By the time I reached the chorus, I gave it everything I could, every ounce of my untrained, pitchy voice pouring into the lyrics. "If you want to know if he loves you so, it's in his kiss!" I sang, horribly off-key. I pried my eyes open while the band sang the backup part, their enthusiastic singing the only reason the whole crowd hadn't dispersed, I was sure. And there, next to Louisa, stood Matt, looking even more stunned than his sister.

"What are you doing?" he mouthed when he caught my eye.

I smiled weakly and started in on the next verse, gamely plowing through it with all the talent of Britney Spears without Auto-Tune, but this time I kept my eyes on him, drawing courage from the smile playing around the corner of his lips.

"If you want to know if Matt loves you so, it's in his kiss!" I hollered into the mike, and then waved to the band to stop.

A wave of muttering from the audience reflected their total confusion about why someone had just butchered two verses of a well-liked classic.

"Hi, everyone!" I shouted nervously into the microphone. "I know you're probably trying to figure out if this is for real or not"—I stopped to let a ripple of laughter pass—"but I promise this is as real as it gets. You guys don't know Matt Gibson yet, the co-owner of this board shop, but I do, and I need to tell you about him."

I risked a glance at him. His expression gave away nothing while he waited for what came next, his arms folded across his chest.

"Matt's the best guy I've ever known. He's smart and hardworking, and he knows what's real, what's important. I'm not that smart, so it's taken a while to see what he was trying to show me," I said. "Matt?"

He returned my gaze.

"I'm sorry. I've been so stubborn and I'm so afraid it's going to cost me what I want more than anything I ever wanted on The List. Do you still have it?" I asked, praying that he had rescued it after I ran out on him.

He slipped his wallet from his pocket and walked to the edge of the stage. He pulled the worn paper out and handed it to me.

"This stupid thing has been the most important thing in my life for the last six years," I said. "I've planned my entire life around it. My work, my school, everything."

I tucked the microphone under my arm and began ripping it into tiny shreds. He watched as I threw the pieces into the air and they rained down in a cheerful confetti shower. Bringing the mike to my mouth again, I took a deep breath before I blurted out my next words in a nervous rush. "I don't want The List anymore. I want you." The catcalls sounded from the hot dog cart again, and I felt my face burning.

"What I meant to say is . . . I love you, Matt Gibson. Do you forgive me?"

He stared up at me, his expression still unreadable. The catcalls died out and the audience craned their necks to see if he was about to let me fall flat on my face. He vaulted himself up onto the stage. I smiled, trying hard not to let the edges of my mouth wobble as he stopped an arm's length away. He reached over and tugged the microphone from my hands, then switched off the sound and folded his arms.

"What are you doing, Ashley?" he asked, his even voice revealing nothing.

"Trying to make things right," I said.

"By making a fool of yourself with karaoke? I heard you swear on a restaurant full of customers that you'd never do that again." I could hear a trace of amusement in his voice.

Encouraged, I took a small step toward him. "It's for a good cause," I said with a tremulous smile. "I was an idiot when I ran out on you the first time and an even bigger idiot when I did it again last week." Aware of the onlookers craning to hear the conversation, I dropped my voice. "I know I've made this all harder than it needed to be, and you deserve someone with way less hang-ups, but . . ."

"But what?" he asked, his voice quiet.

"But I fell for you. And I just keep falling. I didn't even know I was looking for you until I found you, but now that I have, I don't want to lose you. I'm so sorry for being so confused. Can you forgive me?"

A teenage girl on the front row heaved a happy sigh, but I kept my eyes glued to Matt's, searching for absolution and a reason to hope.

He studied me for several excruciating moments before pulling the mike out and flipping it on again. "What were those lyrics?" he called over his shoulder to Kenny.

"If she wants to know, it's in your kiss, dude."

A huge smile broke over his face as he grabbed me and placed his lips on mine in the most dizzying kiss he'd delivered yet.

"Well?" he asked, when he let me up for air.

"I'm not sure," I finally mumbled. "You better do that again."

And with the cheers of the crowd behind us, he did.

ABOUT THE AUTHOR

MELANIE BENNETT JACOBSON is an avid reader, amateur cook, and champion shopper. She consumes astonishing amounts of chocolate, chick flicks, and romance novels. After meeting her own husband on the Internet, she is now living happily married in Southern California with her growing family and a series of half-finished craft projects. Melanie loves to hear from readers and can be contacted at writestuff. jacobson@gmail.com or found through her home page at www. melaniejacobson.net.